A Good Death

Michael Bagley

Clink Street

London | New York

Published by Clink Street Publishing 2018

Copyright © 2018

First edition.

ISBN:
978-1-912562-90-9 - paperback
978-1-912562-91-6 - ebook

Prologue

A Sunday in May 2028 – Lincolnshire Wolds

It was time.

Bess felt it suddenly and for no apparent reason that she could think of. But, as with so many things she did these days, she decided to forget it for the moment, trusting that, when the moment came, she'd just know what to do.

She covered the salad with one of Uncle John's ubiquitous cotton cloths, hung up the pinny - the plastic one with the photograph of Shakespeare smoking dope that made her feel exulted and vaguely uncomfortable at the same time - and opened the fridge.

Entering the garden the wonderful spring sun warmed her face and made her squint slightly as she stopped and looked. He was at the bottom, under the spidery arms of the plum tree. The breeze shook some pink blossoms free and they fluttered down onto the table he was laying. The four beeches rustled with joy and, like a timely herald from Fantasia, a white butterfly whipped past her nose, proclaiming its message: "It's coming! It's coming!" What 'it' was, of course, was the real question. All she knew was that it had something to do with why she returned so many times to spend what her mother called, "the precious weekends of your youth, darling," with her uncle.

"Bring the wine?"

She beamed and held it up for inspection. She'd known where it would be, just as she'd known the weather would be glorious and the birds would sing. And surely that was part of it; the familiarity and the wonderful, splendid certainty.

"Did you know the overflow on the downstairs toilet's leaking?" asked Bess, placing the salad in its allotted spot.

"Yah. I'll fix it tomorrow."

He turned towards her and laughed loudly. They both knew his attitude towards DIY. And that laughter. The man was so bloody uninhibited!

"Were you always such an extrovert?"

He laughed again, then glanced at her in that keen way he had, eyes narrowed.

"Only with you, lass. Most of my friends think I'm introverted."

"Yeh, right."

"Truly. I was really quite shy as a boy."

In truth she'd always sensed that, through the quips and the banter, right at his core, there was a sadness about Uncle John. And she'd often wondered, on the long car journeys over the Wolds, whether it was that tragic, distant part of him that attracted her, as if, God forbid, she were some adolescent character out of Jane Austen.

"So how's my big sister?"

His voice always changed when he spoke of her.

"Same as ever. Looking her age."

He shook his head.

"Cruelty, thy name is woman."

"I thought it was 'frailty'."

"Since when did Shakespeare know everything?"

He didn't look his age, of course and she wondered why she was so perversely proud of that.

They ate and drank under the plum tree, barbecue smoke keeping away the bees. Beyond the low fence emerald wheat rose to the badger wood.

"Lass, stop trying so hard. You're beautiful, intelligent and sensitive, and we both know how rarely those three things come together." She felt herself blushing and knew he'd notice; knew he'd make a joke to rescue her. "Consider the rest of the family, for instance." There it was. 'The family'. "I, of course, have only beauty," and she laughed gratefully.

She knew she wasn't beautiful, though. "At 5 foot 11 inches in your tights," as he liked to put it, "you could only have inherited it from your grandfather." Also, with her narrow hips and little breasts she seemed even taller, especially in heels. And, with the sure clarity of late teenage, she'd begun to see her physical features as an advantage, learning to use them to emphasise movement and gestures, so that people noticed her. All in all, she was elegant, she knew. But it was only Uncle John who called her beautiful.

"And this, of course," she said, "is from the great woman expert; someone who's never been married. If your relationships last more than three months it's been a good season."

"Makes me dispassionate; an objective observer," he said with another grin.

"You're full of it, Uncle John."

But she said it with a laugh. He turned and gazed down the brightly coloured garden, apparently watching his cat, called Cat, licking its paws. "You can't give cats names." It *was* time. She felt it so strongly now that, as she'd known it would, the plan of attack just popped in there, like the marshmallow man.

"What do you mean about the rest of 'the family'?" biting her lip.

As she knew he would, he raised his head and looked at her in that piercing way again, then down at his feet.

"Oh, nothing, I guess."

"You're doing it again."

"Doing what?"

"You know perfectly well. You suggest something, then back away from it. It's bloody frustrating!"

He put on a hurt expression.

"I know. Sorry, lass. It's just that I don't want you to think I'm a stubborn, prejudiced, middle-aged man."

"I know you're a stubborn, prejudiced, middle-aged man." He was already laughing. "In fact, you're sometimes stubborn to the point of incredulity. You're intolerant of almost anyone except me and Cat, you're often authoritarian, you're more arrogant than I am and you break wind with the frequency of a ministerial cock-up."

He was roaring now, tears in his eyes.

"Lass, that's brilliant! You *must* write it down," and he laughed again.

"John! The problem is you keep deflecting and you're doing it again. Answer me! Whenever we have a family gathering you're always taking the piss out of someone."

"Is that a question?"

"John!"

He lifted his hand.

"All right, I know. But I'm serious. I have a reputation, carefully nurtured, of being a grumbly, irritable, old sod, as you've just so ably illustrated. That way I get to spend most of my days on my own. With the exception of you, of course."

She resisted the temptation to sigh. That wasn't just polite flattery. She'd known from an early age that her visits meant as much to him as they did to her. And she'd grown up with him always there, not just physically but in her mind, like a male benchmark. All the more reason why she had to know.

"You dislike most of the family, though, don't you?"

He sipped his wine and peered at her over the rim, as if thinking how to reply, or expecting her to say more. She flicked at a fly, then sat up in her chair, determined, the wine loosening inhibitions.

"Admit it. When was the last time you talked to anyone in the family, apart from me?"

He seemed to stare at the wood. When he looked back she sensed something different.

"Yes, you're the only one I like. Happy now?"

She should call it off at this point. Let him off the hook. But she couldn't. She wanted to know; had always wanted to know. The whispered conversations at weddings and funerals.

"And there are reasons for that," she continued.

He wasn't smiling and her chest tightened.

"Of course there are reasons for that."

"But you're not going to tell me."

She continued to look at him, silently willing him to answer the question, to stay on track. Inexplicably, he smiled.

"I'd rather not, lass, if you don't mind."

She should definitely leave it now, make a joke of it, claim her small victory and be gone. Instead she stayed silent and waited.

"Where's all this leading?" he asked eventually.

"I don't know."

He was staring at her, those grey eyes hurt, accusing and she forced herself to stay quiet.

"It's complicated," he said eventually, sliding away again.

"Shall I tell you what I've heard?"

He nodded uncertainly, sipping at an empty glass.

"I'm pretty sure it's got something to do with your father. Apparently, he had an affair."

His expression changed abruptly, to one she'd only seen him use on plumbers and the Welsh rugby team. Her pulse quickened further and she felt sweat break out on her chest.

"Is that what they say?"

"More or less. I overheard Mum and Aunt Margaret talk about the *other woman*."

"You've asked your mother?"

"Won't talk about it. Refuses point blank."

A further long pause while he shifted position. For some reason, she became aware of the noises of the day: the buzz of a bee competing well with a neighbour's lawnmower, a blackbird squawking her alarm near the ancient, cream house.

"Is it true, what Mum says?"

"I doubt it. My father did have an affair. Oh, he did have an affair. But, as with most things in life, it wasn't that simple."

He placed the glass down and began to lever himself up, but there was no way she was going to let it go now. Playing her last card she conjured up her most reasonable voice - gentle, demure and childlike - the one that never failed with older men.

"Tell me about it, please."

He stopped half-way up for a second or two, then sort of flopped.

"So," he said and she licked suddenly dry lips.

"John, you can't imagine how it's been. There's a family secret and it's been kept from me. All through my life people have whispered and glanced sideways to see if I can hear. Relatives have stopped talking on my approach. It's one of the great mysteries of my childhood, for God's sake! And it's always when your father's name is mentioned or when you're on the premises. It's as if I'm a pariah because I spend so much time here. If it hadn't happened so long ago I'd think it concerned me!" She felt herself losing it and let it come. "When I ask, no one will tell me. Well I'm 20 now and it's time!"

Tears were pricking her eyes.

"I'm sorry, lass. I'd no idea."

She shook her head and fought back the stupid tears.

"I know. I'm sorry, too." She paused briefly and looked him straight in the eye. "But you have to tell me."

With a gesture she'd never seen him perform before, he stretched his eyes.

"Bess, have I ever refused to answer any of your questions?"

She knew what was coming. He only used 'Bess' when he was going to say something she'd find unpleasant.

"Don't do this to me, John. I don't understand! Why won't you tell me?!"

His chest rose and fell in a long breath.

"Lots of reasons. You see the truth is not what people think. You either won't like what you hear or you won't believe it. Probably both. Because ..... because it will change our relationship. God knows why you want to spend time with me rather than whooping it up with your own age-group, but I'm grateful you do. And I don't want it to change."

She knew this, just as she knew that daffodils grew in spring and Mozart was the prince of sound. And she was constantly racked with guilt that she was glad he'd never married, or he wouldn't want to spend so much time with her. She adored the way he showed his affection for her, in a way her parents never had.

But her heart was really racing now. She could actually feel it thumping in her chest because her instincts were telling her what her mind now did. He was going to give in. It was himself he was wrestling with.

"Your life will never be the same, if I tell you."

She just nodded, not really understanding. But wasn't that what life was for? What did he say? "There are only three things in life not worth encountering, lass: suicide, anal sex and folk dancing. Everything else, grasp to your tits and live it!"

He got up slowly and strolled over to the dying barbecue, absently stirring charcoal into a cloud. Then he placed hands in pockets and moved to the wicker fence, staring out at the newly leafed wood.

"Saw two badgers last week," he said. "Farmer says they don't have TB and he'd rather have them there, keeping infected badgers out."

Still she forced herself to wait. The neighbour had finished his mowing. The only sounds left were that of bees in the tree above, feeding on the last of the plum blossom and of the same warm breeze rustling corn stalks. Then he ambled over and stopped in front of her.

"Sure?"

"Yes," she said with relief.

"All right, but there are conditions."

"What?" immediately suspicious.

"First, whatever you discover you mustn't tell anyone, including your mother, without my permission."

She could hold to that. Talking to her mother was hardly easy at the best of times.

"Agreed."

He held her eyes for a while, then just walked into the house with that lazy, confident stroll he had. She gazed over the field, trying not to feel guilty about bullying him and for using his affection to her advantage. When he returned he was carrying a large, black binder.

"The second condition is that you can't take this with you. You can only read it here."

Bess glanced at the pages of A4 stretched tight, at least four centimetres thick, then up at John, his face uncharacteristically solemn.

"Okay."

"Well, in that case, you wanted to know about your grandfather, so read."

He said it casually but she sensed the reverence with which he handed her the file. She pulled over the cover: *Cold Eating*, a novel by John Stafford. She knew all her uncle's published writings, some of them almost by heart. This was not among them.

"When did you write this?"

"About 15 years ago. First thing I ever wrote and you're only the second person I've shown it to."

"Who was the first?"

"I'll tell you later."

She realised that, from the moment he'd handed over the binder, his eyes hadn't left it and he was looking as if he wanted to snatch it back.

"I'm not sure I've done the right thing, Bess. You're not ready for it."

"Christ, John, how bad can it be?"

He lifted his gaze to her and she saw real anxiety for the first time. Involuntarily she pulled the manuscript towards her and hugged it.

"I'm not giving it back."

He continued to watch her for a while, before seeming to consciously pull his gaze away and nodding to himself.

"No," he said. "And if you're going to make a start I'll put some coffee on."

"I want to start now," and she turned the first page.

Chapter 1

Sunday 19 May 2013 – Italy

I read somewhere that experienced novelists rarely write in the first person; that it hinders flexibility and readers simply don't like it. Well, I'm certainly not a professional writer, so that advice can't possibly apply. Besides, I intend this story to be about me. That sounds conceited but the fact is this tale doesn't make sense if you don't come to it through my journey. It's also about my father, of course. Actually, it will be a lot about him because I'm on a promise.

They also say that writers find it difficult to end a book. But I know how this story ends. What I couldn't decide on is where to start? In the end I decided it had to be in that quiet, provincial town of Mogliano Véneto, in Northern Italy.

The visit began well enough because, even though I had no idea of the street name, finding Baxter's mother's house proved to be a cinch. My ears ringing with the clamour of church bells and the angry shouts of hurrying worshippers, I spotted a busy café and Brad finally braked to a halt in a cloud of dust.

"Brad, we're trying to be low-profile!"

He just beamed that Brad Pitt smile as we moved towards the outdoor seating area, everyone staring at us.

"Take it easy, Jonno. We're not going to be able to disguise the fact that we're English and that's the way we're expected to behave."

He was probably right. He was always more in tune with popular culture. '*La barbaro Inglese*', an opinion gleaned, I assumed, from past images of football hooliganism. He ordered two espressos in that seemingly fluent Italian he'd suddenly acquired.

"How'd you know all this?" I'd asked last night, when he'd ordered our meal in Italian and even knew what was in my *merluzzo alla pizzaiola*. He'd sheepishly produced an Italian phrase book.

"As soon as I knew where Baxter would be I knew you'd have to come here. I've been swatting."

I'd laughed and children from a nearby table had looked over. Brad had been embarrassed, as if he'd committed a social *faux pas* and I'd tried not to laugh again. It was so like him to try and educate himself, whilst pretending not to. "Learning is for posh boys like you, Jonno."

So now, this bright Sunday morning in Mogliano, and with his new Italian, Brad simply asked the elderly waiter for the address. There was a risk in this, we knew, since Baxter might be told two Englishmen were asking for the house. But I'd prepared a suitable package before leaving the UK, with the house and town marked clearly. We were simply delivery men, dressed in blue overalls, with the logo of a large international bank sewn into our breast pockets.

"*Per favore*," said Brad, "*Casa Bendini?*" pointing at the package.

The man squinted uncertainly at the brown-paper parcel, wispy white hair lifting in a coffee wind.

"*Sì. Giri a sinistra*," he said, waving his hand dismissively before smiling at the next table, the Inglese already forgotten. I forgave him silently; just relieved he showed no suspicion.

We turned left and, sure enough, no more than 150 yards from the café, was the House Bendini, its name plugged onto a tall and very closed wrought-iron gate. It was a large residence, starkly white and surrounded by a high, impenetrable hedge. It was also guarded by a dog the size of a horse. Black and ugly-looking, it had crashed behind the gate. Even when we approached it didn't really stir; simply wagged its tail in a desultory kind of way. I examined the other houses in the road, all painted in various pastel shades of cream and brown and green, gleaming dark shutters closed against a cloudless sky. Two boys played football in a dusty side street, their voices loud against birdsong. It was an unobtrusive area, at peace with itself, so clearly my father had not been here.

"So what now, Jonno?" asked Brad.

"We keep walking before we get noticed."

But just then the dog raised its head and a few seconds later I heard what sounded like an automatic garage door.

"Quickly," I said, "back to the car."

We walked briskly, without running, constantly glancing back to see which way the driver turned.

"You drive," I said reluctantly and we were just inside the car when an immaculate black Mercedes with blackened windows purred passed. "Wait until he turns at the junction before moving off."

He turned left, towards Venice and Brad quickly accelerated after him. Thankfully, Baxter stuck to the speed limit and we were able to keep him in sight. On the autostrade we settled down about 60 yards behind and I took out my smartphone. This was my last, desperate attempt to get my father to talk to me.

With Brad, following Baxter from Mogliano Veneto to Venice. Intend sit on tail til you arrive.

I hesitated, imagining what would go through Dad's mind when he received this message. Also, it occurred to me rather belatedly that it might not be Baxter in the car. It could be a chauffeur or his elderly mother? I took a deep breath and hit 'Send'.

Bess paused in her reading. John was cleaning up the barbecue but he sensed her look up.

"Coffee's on," he said unnecessarily.

"You haven't started this at the beginning," she said.

"That a question?"

"No, it's not a bloody question!"

He blessed her with that infuriating smile.

"How'd you spot that?"

"Are you kidding? 'This was my last, desperate attempt to get my father to talk to me'. If that's the beginning of this story we're not related."

He nodded.

"You know, now you mention it, I've often thought that nose of yours is simply not family."

She said nothing; just fixed him with the sort of glare that cowed most men, even Uncle John.

"Okay, it's not the beginning. Does that make me a bad person?"

"Why, though?"

He flicked some plum blossom off his thigh.
"The beginning of a story is not always the beginning in time."
"God, do you go out of your way to be frustrating?"
He simply grinned back and shrugged.

The next move was up to Dad, so I settled back in my comfortable seat and watched the traffic on the dual carriageway, checking that Brad overtook on the left, just like the Merc.

"You know why you're no good at poker?" he asked abruptly.

I turned to the handsome face, marred only by a small bottle scar down its right cheek.

"No but I'm sure you're going to tell me."

"Because you don't take it seriously. You're always thinking about something else."

We'd ended last night playing poker for matchsticks in a small, open-air bar which ran alongside the train station, drinking the local *birra* in the light of candles and the weird glow of street lights. At the next table a group of locals had sung nationalist songs, drinking from bottles of wine kept in a gigantic plastic bowl of ice and getting pissed. There were seven men and one woman and the woman was the most demonstrative, the way Italian women are. Every so often a dog would bark, far off, and I'd wondered why, wherever you are in the world, there's always a dog barking in the distance. So Brad was probably right; instead of focusing on what I had in my hand, I romantically dream, desperate to achieve the unachievable.

"He's parking," he said and I brought my attention back to the present.

The Mercedes came to a stop in a car park on the island of Venice, close to the train station and Baxter got out. It was definitely him. I recognised the face from the photo Brad had found. He was wearing pink shorts, what appeared to be deck shoes, a striped golf shirt and had a navy-blue sweater slung round his neck. If he was going boating he wouldn't have looked out of place. He walked slowly, almost sauntering, like a man confident in his business and his surroundings, simply taking a Sunday morning stroll. We followed carefully. One of us stayed within about 80 yards of him at all times, hurrying when he turned a corner so as not to lose sight for too long. The other would stay back and we swapped positions every three corners or so. It was my idea which Brad approved.

I'd been to Venice before – my father had brought me when I was in my late teens - so I knew it to be choked with tourists during the summer months and that would have helped us remain inconspicuous. But the full season obviously didn't start in late May. There were some holidaymakers – obvious in their calf-length shorts and searching eyes – but not enough to hide us. Also, we hadn't had time to change from working-class delivery men to dressing like tourists and I was conscious of the fact that, if Baxter looked behind, we'd stick out like mullahs in a cathedral. But he didn't turn round – not once - just gazed in the occasional shop window as part of his promenade and used his mobile a couple of times.

So, we simply paced those narrow streets and crossed the little, hump-back bridges, over truly desolate water highways, quietly pulsing in the shadows; passed Santa Maria this and Santa Joseph that, through piazza after piazza, and pigeons fluttering like wraiths from one ledge to another, as if wary of perching for too long on the crumbling palaces.

Brad stopped suddenly on the edge of a piazza and started walking back to me, his face animated.

"He's stopped at a café in a kind of square," he said.

I thought for a moment.

"Is there just the one café."

"There's a few."

"Okay, then I suggest you sit in another café and have a coffee. Don't so much as glance at him; just sit down at a table. I'll work my way around. There must be another entrance to the square, on the other side."

Five minutes later I passed through an archway onto a bright piazza, with no less than three cafés dotted around its perimeter. I spotted Baxter immediately, talking to a man with a George Michael beard, his back to me. Brad was seated amongst a cluster of chairs across the square, ordering from an attractive young cameriera with a low-cut blouse. He could always find them. I walked about 20 yards passed Baxter, to the third café and sat down on an aluminium chair, under an enormous, predictable, Cinzano umbrella. I, of course, was served by a 20 stone, heavily tattooed cameriere, who seemed to regard my Americano order as below his dignity.

A sign above the arch I'd come through said, Campo San Barnaba. Across the square, a sunlit church was advertising a Leonardo da Vinci exhibition. The whole space was surrounded by high houses and apartments, all with bottle green shutters and pink flowers in window boxes. Birdsong – ubiquitous in Italy - sounded above a gentle echo of conversation and, just like in Lincoln, sparrows flitted between tables, scavenging for crumbs. It was so peaceful I almost forgot why we were there. Across the ancient stones, I watched Brad gazing down the waitress' cleavage as she brushed an empty table.

Then my phone vibrated, indicating a text message. I tried to be casual as I reached for it and saw the letters 'Dad' written on the screen. My stomach did a flip.

Phone immediately.

The plan had worked! Ten days he'd refused to answer my calls and now *he* was actually contacting *me*. I glanced up at Brad, who was watching me as I pressed Dad's number. It rang once.

"Where are you?"

The voice was abrupt. I tried to speak normally.

"Sitting in a café in a piazza in Venice."

"Where's Baxter?"

"Dad, we've got to t ….."

"Where's Baxter?"

I sighed deliberately loudly.

"He's sitting down drinking coffee with a George Michael lookalike. Brad's across ….."

"How far away is he?"

"About 20 yards."

"Get out of there, now! Don't hurry, don't rush. You're a tourist. Take your time but move immediately. Leave enough money on the table and slowly walk out of the piazza the way you came ….."

"Dad ….."

"Get back to your car, check out of your hotel as fast as you can, then leave Italy."

"For Christ's sake, Dad, he hasn't spotted us!"

"Of course he's fucking spotted you, you fucking idiot! You have no idea what you're dealing with!"

In my whole life he'd never spoken to me like that and the certainty in his voice made my stomach do another somersault.

"What car are you driving?"

I hesitated, suddenly unsure of myself.

"John, what car are you driving?"

"Fiat Uno."

"Colour?"

"Orange."

"Jesus, fucking Christ! Has he used his mobile phone?"

My breathing was now coming more quickly and I found difficulty getting the words out.

"Couple of times."

"John, he's sitting there waiting for some of his henchmen to arrive. They'll be ex-special-forces and they'll be very, very good. Believe me, you and Brad will have no chance. Please, John, get up and leave, *now!*"

I knew he was right then. I *was* a fucking idiot. But I was also conscious of the fact that I was actually talking to my father - something I'd been wanting to do for a while - so I gathered my resolve.

"Only if you promise to see me."

"I've already promised that."

"No, you see me now."

"I'm not in the area. Look, John, we haven't time to discuss this. You've got to leave. I promise I'll phone in 20 minutes. I'll be too damned worried to leave it any longer anyway. Don't rush, you'll be too obvious. Okay?"

I made one final glance at Baxter. Only the side of his face was turned towards me but I could see a smug grin on his face as he listened to his companion.

"Okay."

"His henchman will probably follow. You'll have to lose him."

Then the phone went dead.

Chapter 2

Now the decision was taken I wanted to move quickly; to get out of there as soon as possible. But I forced myself to follow Dad's instructions, taking my time as I stood up and took out a €10 note, casually leaving it under the half-drunk coffee cup. Avoiding eye-contact with the waiter, I saw Brad was already alert to the situation, his face anxious.

"That was my father. He's sure we've been rumbled. We need to walk fast and get out of Italy."

I set off at a fair pace and Brad kept up beside me, occasionally glancing back in the direction we'd come.

"Just like that?" asked Brad.

"Yeh. Dad says there's a hit squad coming."

"Okay," he said, "but if we've been made we'll be followed."

"I know. Keep glancing back to check. I'll look forward for anyone else."

We'd crossed two bridges before Brad said:

"He's there. Do you know he's a bit like George Michael?"

I couldn't believe Brad was taking it so casually; my guts were churning.

I forced myself to think. The first thing to recognise was that it confirmed Dad's judgement so he was probably right about the rest too.

"We can't let him know our car registration because in no time they'll find out who hired the car and where we're staying. So, we'll have to lose him. I suggest we wait round a deserted corner, then surprise him as he turns it. What do you think? This is more your line than mine."

He nodded, lips set in determination.

"I'll choose when."

We went down a narrow alley, no more than 6 feet across, which junctioned at a canal and turned right. Brad looked around and stopped.

"This'll do. And we won't throw a shadow. Stay behind me. I go in first, you come behind if I don't disable him. How tall would you say he is?"

"Six, six-one?"

Brad nodded.

"I should go in first," I said.

"Just get in close to the wall, Jonno, stay behind me and shut up."

I followed instructions. Brad was already flat against the concrete, listening. Well, eight days ago I decided I wanted some excitement in my life, but this was rather more than I bargained for.

Within seconds I heard the man's heavy breathing as he hurried to reach the corner. Brad stepped out and threw his right in one fluid movement. I followed quickly but my assistance was unnecessary. Brad had connected with the man's windpipe and he was grasping his throat with both hands, uttering choking sounds. Brad hit him again, this time in the nose and blood spattered everywhere. The man hit his head when he fell and seemed to lose consciousness. I just stood there, transfixed, as Brad rifled his pockets and came away with a revolver.

"I think we'll relieve him of that," he said and felt the pulse at his neck. "He's still alive."

I grabbed his arm.

"In that case let's go, before someone comes."

We set off, hurrying along the side of the canal.

"Slow down," I said, as I saw some people in the distance. "And I think you ought to throw that gun into the canal."

He shook his head.

"No way. We might need it."

I decided this wasn't the time to argue and looked away, across the water. For some reason I focused on two pigeons on the opposite bank, washing themselves by lifting their wings to water mysteriously dripping off a roof. Right then, Dad rang.

"Did he follow?"

"Yes, but we've taken care of it. Well, Brad did."

"Good. But you're not out of the woods yet. Far from it. Are you staying in Mogliano?"

"Yes."

"Right. You'll have to check out of your hotel as soon as you get back, then leave Italy. But you can't leave from Marco Polo; they'll have the airport staked out like Agincourt. You'll have to drive west to Milan and try to pick up a flight from there. I've checked the map; it'll take you about three hours. Okay?"

I felt like a complete idiot, any desire to argue utterly gone.

"John?"

"Okay."

"Anyone else behind you?"

"No."

"Right. Keep looking at least once a minute. You'll have to go into hiding for a while when you get back to the UK."

"What?"

"Baxter already knows who you are."

"Shit! How does he know that?

"You're not thinking, John. Were you close enough for him to see your face?"

The penny dropped into my stomach like a bad pudding. The physical resemblance between myself and my father had always been an embarrassment to me and Baxter would have known him when he was my age. Jesus, how could I have been so fucking stupid?

"How close did you get when you were following by car?"

"About 60 yards."

"Okay, then it's unlikely he would have got your car registration yet. If he fails to get it then he'll simply check all the hotel registrations in the area, starting with Mogliano. Don't forget, he's only searching for one name; Stafford. It won't take him long."

I'd slowed my pace without realising it.

"Come on Jonno, move it," said Brad.

I quickened and peered ahead. We were in another narrow alley, tall buildings either side, and what looked like an open space at the end. I recognised a large church. Not far to go.

"I'm sorry, Dad. I've been an idiot."

I felt Brad turn towards me.

"It's all right. It's my fault. Where are you exactly?"

"Approaching the car park."

"Right. Stop and put the speaker on."

I grabbed Brad's arm.

"Brad can hear you now," I said.

"Good. Smile. Look like tourists. How you doing Brad?"

"I'm great, Mr Stafford. Yourself?"

He was, too, I thought. A small smile curled his lips. This was what Brad had always wanted.

"To be honest, Brad, I'm shitting myself. Now listen up, both of you, if you want to get out of there."

This was a side of my father I hadn't heard before. It brooked no argument. Brad had also silently agreed to do whatever Dad suggested. I recognised his expression.

"When you left the piazza Baxter will have phoned his hit squad to head for the car park because he knows you followed him into Venice by car. They'll be two or three guys, either waiting for you in the car park or heading for it. So I've changed my mind about the car. You'll have to abandon it and go by train. Who's got the map?"

The sudden change threw me.

"Train?"

"Yes. Who's got the map?"

Brad was looking at me to answer.

"We haven't got a map."

The long silence that followed showed how I had, yet again, disappointed my father.

"Okay, we can deal with it. Look around you. See if you can see a street sign. Brad, you keep watching for the hit squad."

We'd paused by a well-kept bridge, it's black and gold ironwork sparkling in a watery sun. In the foreground, black gondolas rocked gently, like cold assassins. Across the water, a smart, outdoor restaurant prepared for lunch, waist-coated waiters laying pink tablecloths. Through a curtain of parched trees an army of windscreens reflected the light. I turned and there was a name, plugged dimly into the brick.

"We're at a bridge on the Fondamenta Papadopoli. The car park's about 60 yards away, across the canal, through the trees."

"I have you. The station's about half a kilometre. Head north along the canal. The sun will be about four o'clock. You'll come to a foot bridge on the left. Take it. On its crest you'll be able to see the station to your right."

"Okay, Dad, we're on our way."

"Good. The trains to Mogliano Véneto leave every twenty minutes or so." He pronounced Véneto correctly, I noticed irrelevantly. "You'll pass through Mestre, which is a large junction station that feeds the airport, and the next stop is Mogliano. You'll have to keep looking around you all the time, without appearing to do so. Do you understand?"

"Yeh."

I felt chastened.

"Can Brad hear me?"

"I can hear you, Mr Stafford."

I detected a slight American accent, a continent Brad had never inhabited, even as a tourist.

"Brad, if you spot these guys, don't even think about taking them on. You both leg it and hope you're fitter than they are. Agreed?"

I nodded at Brad.

"Okay, Mr Stafford."

"We took a gun from our pursuer," I said.

A few moments of hesitation.

"Get rid of it. Do you think they won't have guns and, unlike you, they'll know how to use them."

I felt a sharp pang of resentment but Brad didn't argue. He immediately dug into his pocket, extracted the gun and threw it into the canal.

"Once you've checked out of your hotel, get back to the train station and head north for Treviso. It's about six miles north of Mogliano. Hire another car there and head west for Milan, just like we discussed earlier, John. You can pick up a flight from there back to the UK. Don't hurry because you'll attract attention, but don't hang about either."

I wasn't going to argue any more. In fact, absurdly, I felt like repenting.

"Thanks, Dad."

"Just take care, son." He paused and I didn't know what to reply. "You too, Brad."

"You got it, sir!"

He sounded like someone out of a Hollywood action movie.

"I'll have to hang up now to conserve my battery but call me soon".

The line went dead and we were alone. I imagined him biting his lip with worry and closing his eyes in silent prayer to a god in which he had no faith. Part of my brain was thinking, if he's worried about his battery he must be travelling. Then I closed my mind to him and focused on what I had to do.

The station was crowded and I felt more secure. We had a piece of luck and just caught the train, so there was no anxious wait whilst we peered at the entrance to the platform hoping to not spot three super-fit guys in their mid-30s, with chiselled faces and crew cuts. At Mogliano the only other person to get off the train was a middle-aged woman in brand new Reeboks, carrying a pug-nosed dog nestling in a basket.

Back at the hotel we packed quickly. I watched the concierge's face as Brad told him we wished to check out immediately. He showed only natural surprise and no disappointment. But then why should he? We'd paid for two days in advance and stayed less than one. This time at the station we weren't so lucky, having to wait 15 minutes for the train. No one had checked our ticket on the trip from Venice so I decided to take a chance and not purchase one this time. Instead we waited out of sight, on a pedestrian walkway below the platform.

"Aren't we taking an unnecessary risk?" asked Brad. "Supposing there's an inspector on the train."

"We play the ignorant Inglese. The train arrived just as we got to the station and we didn't have time to buy tickets. The point is, as far as the hotel concierge is concerned we still have the car and, this way, by not showing ourselves at the ticket office, no one may notice we've got the train, or that we've gone north instead of south."

"You're starting to think like your father," he said. "I like that."

I felt another surge of resentment.

"If it wasn't for my bloody father we wouldn't be in this mess."

Brad looked at me in that frustratingly considerate way he had.

"It was our decision to come here."

I took a deep breath.

"Yeh, so it was."

He flashed that glowing smile.

"No worries. Keep thinking like him, though, until we get out of here."

So we waited out of view and I thought that it was all going too well. But the train arrived without incident and I phoned Dad.

"Where are you?" he asked immediately.

"Heading for Treviso. No sign of bad guys."

"Good. Stay safe, son, and keep in touch."

He was about to hang up.

"Dad?"

"Yah."

"Where are *you*?"

The silence must have lasted more than five seconds.

"Dad?"

"Rome."

"Heading for?"

Another long pause.

"Back to the UK. I need to rethink things. Baxter's now on the alert. I may have to do a deal with him."

The voice was tired now, I noticed.

"A deal?"

"To leave you alone." Unaccountably, guilt rushed through me again. "Don't worry. When he learns you've effectively warned him of my intentions, he'll be almost grateful to you."

"Then why are we running?"

"I said almost grateful. The main problem is I don't have his phone number, nor him mine. He's set the hunt in motion and I don't know what the consequences will be if they find you. I don't know what their instructions are but he doesn't employ ex-special-forces personnel to help with the gardening. And I don't want him to use you as a lever against me."

"I'm sorry, Dad."

"It's all right. It's my fault. I should have spoken to you. I thought I could keep you out of it but I should have known your bloody-minded nature wouldn't allow you to merely sit back and wait for events. You've done well. How did you find out about Baxter?"

"It's a long story."

I imagined him nodding. I looked at Brad, who'd unexpectedly found an interest in maize plots and headless olive trees, wilting under the sun.

"He's almost certainly found out about his accomplice by now, so he knows you're running. He'll get his staff to check the hire car outlets at Marco Polo and the hotels in Mogliano, which shouldn't take long. At this moment he's probably heading for Venice Airport, hoping to catch sight of you. Are you sure no one followed you onto the train?"

"Yes."

"All right. With a bit of luck he won't think of Milan until it's too late. But you've still got to keep alert, John."

"Dad, what I've done I've done because I love you." I don't know where it came from. I just blurted it.

"I know, son. I hope you always will love me. Take care. Got to go."

And the phone went dead.

I laid my head back against the seat and images of summers gone surged through me, of my father teaching me to play cricket in the garden and my sister giving orders, like she always did. My mother was there but she wasn't part of it; she was across the garden, quietly reading a magazine by the hedge.

"We're coming into the station," said Brad, so I opened my eyes and put my head in gear.

When we got off the train we both scanned our fellow travellers. There were quite a lot actually but no one who seemed like our crude perception of 'ex-army'. I took a seat behind a concrete divider sporting a poster of a local nightclub and consulted my smartphone, while Brad watched the station. The 3G connection worked, so I used voice activation and asked for Tourist Information in Treviso. Within three seconds the number was ringing.

"*Buon giorno. Parla Inglese?*"

"Yes".

"Great. I need to hire a car. Where's the best place."

"Hire?"

"Rent."

"Ah, *si*. There are many places. Biggest is train station."

"I'm not by the station."

"Where are you?"

"Somewhere in the centre of town. There's a big church here; looks like a Cathedral."

"Does it have green domesa?"

"Green domes? Um, yes, it does."

"*Ottimo!* Cathedral Cupolas, *si*. At back of Cathedral there is piazza. There you find taxi. All drivers have answers to questions."

"*Grazie*. You are most kind."

"*Prego.*"

"What was that charade about?" asked Brad.

"We can't hire a car from here. Once Baxter finds out we've left the Uno parked in Venice and don't turn up at Marco Polo, it's not going to take him long to figure we've headed north by train. The car rental outlets at this station will be his first port of call."

Brad was nodding.

"Good thinking. So how do we get to …" he pointed at my notepad, "this place?"

"We get a taxi, of course." I watched as Brad started to frown. "Know what you're thinking, but I'm hoping there are several taxis that ply their trade from here. It might take them a while to find the right one. An extra hour or so could be important to us. The plan's not perfect, Brad, but we're in a hurry."

He was nodding again.

"Just keep thinking like your father, Jonno."

I didn't bridle this time. Instead I glanced at my watch as we made towards the entrance. 12.25. There were three taxis lined up and we took the first.

"Cathedral Cupolas, *per favore*," I said.

The journey took less than ten minutes. Traffic was scarce and I remembered it was Sunday. I was reminded again when we lugged our bags out on to the steps of the cathedral because the campanologists were hard at work. I'd noticed that in Mogliano; on Italian Sundays bells ring like there's no tomorrow.

Another taxi took us to our true destination, where I hired yet another car - the fourth in nine days, I recalled – only one of which I'd returned legitimately. Technically, though, Brad hired this one. He suggested the smokescreen of our flight to Milan might be made even murkier if the transaction was made under his name and I had to agree. My only hesitation was that it brought him more into the frame but Baxter would know he was with me, anyway, because we'd had to show both our passports when we registered at the hotel. So, Brad finally got to use his precious credit card, while I asked my phone for a route to Milan.

The programme sent us south initially, passed Mogliano Véneto and Mestre, before entering the autostrada, which would take us due west to Milan. But I didn't fancy going anywhere near where we'd come from, so I fired up my laptop and planned a cross-country route, using Google *Earth*, south-west towards Padua. I figured it would add 20 minutes or so to the journey but would be worth it to avoid being spotted. There was a further, slight delay while we stopped in Treviso, to grab a takeaway at a MacDonald's, before heading into the flat, featureless terrain of Northern Italy, our head's full of the journey ahead but with no desire to talk about it.

Bess looked around for her uncle. He'd finished his coffee and seemed to be sleeping.

"This is all true isn't it?"

He opened his eyes and she watched him pretend to think, head on one side.

"You mean, did it actually happen?"

"Yes!"

"Well, of course, everything is seen through the blinkers of the beholder, so ….."

"John, stop the conditional bullshit! It's all true, isn't it?"

He stared at her for a few moments.

"I wouldn't have written it if it wasn't"

She nodded, satisfied. At least she thought she was.

Chapter 3

The diversion took less time than I thought it would because the roads were dead straight and deserted. They were bordered by dykes and poplars and the occasional gate with no fence. Sometimes, there was a well-tended orchard but mostly it was an endless landscape of rectangular fields in numerous shades of green and brown and yellow. If there were crops on them, I knew not what they were.

The small towns and villages were the highlight. We ghosted through them like aliens in a deserted land. Only sporadically was there movement; a quick, shabby dog darting round a corner, or an equally agile old lady, scuttling through a doorway, darkly-clad. And, once, a whole congregation conspiring on the skirts of a church, malevolent eyes following as we sped past.

We joined the A4 Toll Road, as planned, at Cadoneghe and headed west for Milan.

"You all right to drive?" I asked.

Brad looked surprised.

"Sure. You want to drive?"

"Not particularly. I'm happy to navigate, unless you're tired."

"What's to get tired?" he said.

"Okay but for pity's sake stick to the speed limit. I wouldn't put it past Baxter to listen to police radio frequencies. Two *Inglese* pulled over on the autostrada to Milan is a bit of a giveaway."

"Fair play," and he slowed down.

Seeing Brad was compliant I consulted *Earth* again.

"According to Google we should stay on this road for 212 kilometres, so I'm going to put the laptop on snooze to conserve the battery. We might need it when we get close to Milan."

"You're happy to navigate, eh?" he said.

I laughed.

"That's why I offered to drive."

"Yeh, right." He showed me that winning grin. "It's all right, Jonno. You don't have to be doing something all the time. Just do the thinking when we need it."

So I tried to sort out the confused thoughts about my father. I regretted telling him I loved him because I really resented him and what he was doing. But then my feelings towards him had always been ambivalent. I blamed him for the break-up of his marriage but I had no real evidence of what actually happened; only what my mother had told me. I was about five at the time. I sent him a text.

On autostrada to destination. No sign of bad guys.

We by-passed Verona, which previously I'd known only from Shakespeare and, in less hasty times, would have enjoyed a slight diversion, in search of sweet Juliet and that famed balcony.

"Verona," I said, hoping it would chime with Brad.

He glanced at me.

"Good to know you can still read a sign, Jonno. There's hope for us yet. Good football team."

We skirted a large lake, which Google *Earth* said was Lago di Garda and, shortly after, the Alps started to take precedence on the north-west horizon, growing ever larger as we passed Brescia and then Bergamo. For the first time since I got up that morning I started to feel comfortable and my mind drifted back to Venice.

"What are you thinking?" asked Brad.

"How any city built on trade can just live off tourism."

"What?"

"Venice. It needs to move on but, in so doing – in regaining its soul, if you like – it'd destroy its own appeal and the essence of its wealth. It's trapped. It's caught between the past and the future, and the locals simply go about their business, like Stepford Wives."

"For fuck's sake, Jonno, get your mind back on what's ahead."

"Sure."

We passed the Trezzo sull'Adda turnoff and I reckoned we had no more than about 20 miles to go when Brad said:

"Large, black Merc coming up fast".

"Shit! I'll hunker down. They're expecting two blokes, not one."

After a few seconds I heard it purr passed and made to get up.

"Stay there!" urged Brad.

"What's happening?"

"It's slowed down."

My stomach did a now familiar flip and I waited about 10 seconds before my patience gave up.

"What's happening?"

"It's just staying about 40 yards in front and the bloke is using his phone."

"Jesus! Did you notice what he looked like when he went passed?"

"Bald, thick-set, big nose, about 45 maybe."

I noticed Brad seemed anxious for the first time.

"Just the one bloke?"

"Yeh".

I tried to think. Worst case scenario, it *was* one of Baxter's henchmen. If so, he was probably phoning Baxter right now. But what could he tell him? One young man driving a small blue Fiat, keeping to the speed limit. Unless, of course, he'd noticed that Brad looked a dead-ringer for Brad Pitt.

"When he passed you, did he look at you, as well?"

"Yes."

"And when we were sitting in those cafes did Baxter get a good look at you?"

"I don't think he even knew I was there."

That was probably true. But the George Michael lookalike might have done because he was gazing straight across the piazza. Besides, if Dad was right, Baxter spotted us following and might have caught a glimpse or two of Brad in shop windows. Shit! Could we afford to take the chance?

"What's he doing?"

"Just sitting there using his phone," a touch of frustration in the voice. "What do you want me to do?"

"Wait until he finishes his call and see what he does. I can't see what else we can do. We can't outrun him in this."

"He seems to have put his phone down and now he's watching his mirror all the time. Why would you do that on a motorway?"

"Is he speeding up?"

"No."

Shit!"

"In fact he's slowing down!"

That decided it. I levered myself into an upright position.

"The games up, Brad."

"But how the fuck could they know it was us?"

"I don't know. Maybe they checked on the car registration through car rental companies in Treviso. Two *Inglese*. Maybe someone got a good gander at your resemblance to Brad Pitt. They're good."

As the Mercedes was gradually slowing to well below the speed limit, Brad was slowing too.

"He wants us to pass him but don't," I said. "Let me think.

Baxter will have assumed by now that we're heading for Linaté, so he'll have men rushing there. Although he's probably not so well staffed in Milan, he probably knows someone who is and maybe he can call in some favours. I didn't think this guy was likely to want to force us off the road. Baxter will figure he can follow us, from in front or behind, so he'll wait until the airport, where they'll be support because he'll assume we'll have to return the car to the rental company. Less risky and less likely to attract attention than driving us off the road.

"On the other hand," I said, thinking aloud, "we can't be 25 minutes from the airport. Can he get people there that fast?"

"Do we have to go to the airport?"

"We have to get out of the country. You can see how easy it is for Baxter to find us."

"So what do we do?" he asked again.

Whereas he'd been the personification of coolness in Venice, Brad kept glancing at me nervously. The Mercedes driver was maintaining his position and speed now so I considered the landscape as I thought. To our left, across the central barrier and beyond the huge wagons thundering towards Trieste, there were what seemed like warehouses. To our right, mysterious concrete blocks lined the carriageway, piled high, like a block of flats. They'd been there so long that grass and weeds were growing out of them and I realised they were spare barriers used to repair the central reservation. Beyond them was open country. We were travelling so slowly that a large Panalon tanker was overtaking us.

"Well, the way I see it there are three options. First, we stop on the inside lane, hop over the barrier and leg it across the fields. If he's 45 and thick-set he probably won't be able to keep up with us. We should get away in the short term. The downside to that is we'll be on foot in a foreign country, without our luggage – my passport is in the boot with my suitcase, by the way – with a small army of special forces after us."

"Bad move then."

"Desperation stakes, only. Second, we spot a suitable turn-off, wait until the last moment and accelerate off the A4, hopefully right in front of a lorry so he can't reverse. Do you fancy a high-speed drive through Milan?"

"No I fucking don't! If we take that option you can drive."

Brad only took his test two years ago and the only car he'd driven before Italy was his banged up old Vauxhall Astra that only got through its MOT because his brother worked at the garage.

"Agreed. We can probably swap places without stopping? Trouble is he'd see us swapping in his mirror and know we were planning something. Also, even if I managed to lose him down a side road, he'd just head for the airport and wait with the rest of his buddies. If we take that option it would make sense to head for the Swiss border and that carries risks, too. When we don't show at the airport, he'll figure out what we're doing and get his buddies to man the crossings."

"Mafia?"

"Who knows? Travelling at high speed may also attract the attention of the local police. I wouldn't put it past Baxter to have connections with the polizia. He probably does in the Véneto region. A few phone calls. The Swiss option also carries risks."

I could see an overhead direction sign in the distance, which I knew would signal a major turn-off a kilometre beyond it.

"What's the third option," asked Brad, clearly not too keen on the first two.

"We keep going as we are, as quickly as possible, until we get to the airport. Then, instead of parking sedately in the Hertz car park, we speed up, dump the car outside the main entrance with the keys still in the ignition, grab the luggage from the boot and leg it to the airline counters. We play it by ear at that stage."

"Doesn't sound like much of a plan," said Brad dubiously.

"I know. What's more Bullneck in front may be informed that his mates won't get to Linaté in time and, despite what I said earlier, he might try and run us off the road anyhow. He's bound to be armed."

We were now far enough along the autostrada to see the sign and there, in white against the familiar green background, was the word 'Linaté', with a small plane beside it and an arrow pointing off to the right.

"It's decided for us anyway! It's the third option, with a touch of the second. Quick, change places!"

Brad, with the alacrity of a small boy leaving a Catholic church, scooted across underneath, whilst I grabbed the wheel and levered myself into the driver's seat. I hit the accelerator to get back up to pace but I couldn't go far because Bullneck had slowed too and he kept on slowing. We got down to 50kph, and the turn-off was approaching fast, before I realised what he was doing. Afraid we were going to make the turn, he wanted us to overtake. Not so stupid.

Suddenly he pulled left into the outside lane and braked hard, so I had no choice but to undertake. With a loud truck's horn sounding at the Merc, I changed down, swung left in front of him and accelerated past a ridiculously long N & Atrasporti wagon. With my foot on the floor the little Fiat showed a remarkable level of low-end grunt. I got passed the truck and nipped between it and another, multiple horns deafening me as I made the turn up the ramp, tyres screaming and pedal still on the floor.

"He didn't make it!" said Brad excitedly and I felt a sudden fillip of relief.

Then the Merc appeared in my mirrors, effortlessly closing and Brad swore violently.

Realising he couldn't follow through the gap, the driver must have braked heavily and went behind the truck, just making the turning. We were going to have company all the way to the airport. So, wanting to give Baxter as little time as possible to gather his troops, I followed the signs to Linaté as quickly as I could, trying to ignore the black car behind that stuck to our tail like it was attached. I overtook frequently, hoping the Merc would get left behind but it followed us through every time, forcing its way into impossible gaps, Italian drivers honking their horns with displeasure.

We paused at yet another road toll and the Mercedes stopped right against our bumper. Having locked us in, I thought the driver might get out and attempt to drag us from the car but he'd obviously decided the airport would be more appropriate, where his mates would be there to help. Brad had swivelled in his chair again and was giving the driver the big stare.

"We could take him." He suggested with enthusiasm. "You go in one door, me the other."

"For Christ's sake, Brad! You think a thug like that is not going to have a weapon to hand? There's CCTV all over the fucking place, and we'd still have to deal with his newly enraged buddies at the airport. Besides, the way he's built I think he could take on the two of us without even breaking sweat."

Brad growled his acceptance of that logic. I wanted desperately to talk to Dad, needing his confidence and his certainty. But what would be the point? He couldn't help us and he'd only worry. I thought Brad might suggest it but he never did. It was as if he realised, too, that we were on our own and what waited for us at the airport was anyone's guess.

Chapter 4

The 'Aeroporto di Milano Linate 1k' sign came up and I felt a tightening in my chest as I swung onto the three-lane approach road. I stayed behind one of the ubiquitous white taxis, considering my options, the Merc still glued to my exhaust. To my left was open parkland and to my right the flat land of an international airport, with its radio beacons and low hangers. An overhead sign gave routes to Arrivi and Partenze, the latter with a very useful English translation; Departures. Soon, the three lanes started to be designated into Partenze, Taxi-Bus and Arrivi. I took the Partenze route, which quickly narrowed into a single lane.

The airport was fast approaching now, its frontispiece dominated by several massive Kimbo Expresso Italiano hoardings, so big they would have put Atlanta Georgia to shame. And right there, almost in shadow, was a small, unprepossessing sign saying 'Partenze'. So I made a snap decision, put my foot down, overtook an old, slow-moving Fiat 500 by bumping up the curb and shot down the lane at top speed, just as the concrete partitions appeared on left and right.

"He can't get by!" shouted Brad and I remember thinking, you've said that before. But this time it was confirmed by the sounds of a deep horn as Bullneck tried to force the rusted Fiat to move over. Glancing in my mirror I saw a small, moustachioed Italian steadfastly refusing to be bullied, whilst his whole family gesticulated wildly at him, before I sped away to approach the entrance at high speed.

"Right Brad, when I stop you grab the bags and we leg it through the doors. We don't have time to pause. Anyone tries to stop us, we barge them out of the way and run. Okay?"

"Okay!"

The nerves had gone I noticed. Brad simply had to be doing something.

I screeched to a halt between a green bus and a taxi, set the handbrake, left the keys in the ignition and exited the car like it was on fire. Brad already had the boot open and we snatched the bags before setting off at a run for the entrance, *'due barbaro Inglese'*, late for their flight, of course. Glancing back I saw that Bullneck had finally passed the Fiat and was fast approaching. Too late, I thought! It's up to your mates to stop us now.

Yet opposition there was none, only a few innocuous looking passengers waiting for the automatic doors to open, which they did just as we got there. We ran through, pausing only to locate the Alitalia desk, reasoning that it would have most flights out of Italy.

"Slow down," I said and Brad complied.

I scanned the concourse as we approached Alitalia and saw no one who seemed like our completely inexperienced definition of suspicious and no one was looking at us now. Standing by a mosaic pillar, though, scanning faces, were two policemen, Beretta machine guns slung over shoulders. Behind us, I heard the Mercedes driver coming through the entrance with a bellow. So did *la polizia*. Bullneck noticed *them*, too, and slowed down, then pretended to remember something, as he changed direction, walking the other way. Perhaps he knew he was on a wanted poster somewhere.

"Thank God for the police," I said.

"What?" asked Brad, aware only of the attractive girl at the Alitalia counter.

Using his filmstar looks and halting Italian he charmed her and we were squeezed on to the six o'clock shuttle to Heathrow, not caring that we'd have to get the train to Gatwick to pick up my car.

I started to wonder where the opposition were. This was all proving too easy. Why had Bullneck not forced us off the road before the airport if he knew there was no one here to stop us? Maybe he thought there was and there'd been a communication breakdown. A good sign.

Then, as we were making our way towards Security and I was wondering incongruously why all the signs were in English, I locked eyes with a tall man in dark suit and white shirt, standing ostentatiously on a corner between an American clothes store and a perfumery. He glanced at something in the palm of his left hand, then his eyes were all over Brad and I felt my chest tighten again.

"Man, wasn't she beautiful?" said Brad. "What is it about Italian women?"

I looked around but couldn't see anyone else interested in us. The man started using his mobile and followed, so I pulled out my phone, too, and rang Dad.

"Of course," continued Brad, "they say they explode in their late-20s."

"You all right?" asked Dad

"Think so. We're on our way to Security at Linaté. Flight's in about 30 minutes. Alitalia to Heathrow. There's a guy following but he doesn't seem threatening."

Brad looked at me, stopped and turned round. I grabbed his arm and kept going.

"So," said Dad, "he's worked it out. This guy's probably a spotter but the heavies will be there soon. How far before the security checks?"

"He worked it out a long time ago, Dad. We've had a few issues which I'll tell you about later. We're almost at security. I'll phone back when we get through."

I didn't give Dad a chance to ask questions; just hung up because the driver had suddenly appeared beside the spotter and he looked even bigger close up.

"They're getting closer," said Brad. "You want me to take bullneck?"

"I think it'll take the two of us," I replied nervously, my stomach doing its now familiar somersault as I instinctively turned towards our attackers.

But right then the pretty Italian stewardess ran past our two opponents, gushing at Brad.

"You need me for security, I think. *Veloce!*" she shouted excitedly and we broke unto a run. Our chasers left behind, we were rushed through security and across the departures lounge. "*Veloce, veloce!*" she cried again, so we ran, childishly laughing at our good fortune and our escape.

I phoned Dad as we were in the queue for the plane.

"Good." I felt him breathe deeply with relief. "I need you to hole up in a country hotel for 48 hours, maybe more, while I sort things out with Baxter. I promise I'll be in touch."

As the Airbus left the ground, I settled back and really relaxed, probably for the first time since that morning. A sense of unreality and anti-climax washed over me. I'd been a fool; a total, fucking fool. I'd attempted to get my father to talk to me and I'd been successful in that. But where had it got me? I still didn't understand. Not really. I still didn't know exactly, or even roughly, what had happened between Dad and Baxter, and I didn't know what Dad's next move was going to be. Baxter was my last card and it was played. And if it hadn't been for Dad, Brad and I would probably be languishing in some cellar right now, or worse.

The plane's air-conditioning gave off a sweet smell that reminded me of my travels in the North Georgia Mountains and that time with Lizzie and Patch and, yes, Charlotte. With a shock I realised it was only four days ago. There'd been many lows on my travels but that was the high point and I saw, then, that I really was staring at the end of the journey. I'd done what I could to stop Dad settling scores and I'd failed dismally because he'd gone ahead and done it anyway. He had his timetable and I'd messed that up a bit but he was probably back on it. I'd do what he wanted now, hole up and wait for him to contact me in his own time. It's what I should have done from the beginning. I felt myself drifting into sleep and didn't resist, thinking of that intimate conversation as the train drew into Treviso. I'd told him I loved him and was glad I had, now. What did he say in reply? "I hope you always will." Why would I not? I'd been the one to let him down in the …..

A profound and convulsive fear gripped my chest. I shot up in my seat and gulped for air, vaguely aware of Brad gripping my arm.

"He's going for her!"

"What?" asked Brad.

My thoughts rushed across the years of silence for confirmation or denial. He never mentions her, to praise or criticise, but I knew. In that moment, I knew.

"Jonno, what is it?"

"He's not going to finish with Baxter."

"What do you mean?"

"My mother."

"What?"

"He's going to kill his ex-wife."

"Shit!" said Brad.

"Shit!" said Bess. "This is it! This has to be it!"

Her uncle had decided to cut the hedge, about 10 yards away, with a pair of shears but he heard her gasp and turned round.

"And I thought this was about a love affair. Jesus!"

"Where are you up to?"

"On the plane to Heathrow?"

He nodded.

"It gets more difficult now, I'm afraid."

"You think? He's going to kill my grandmother!"

He just gazed at her, saying nothing.

"Is that what 'settling scores' means, John. Is he killing people?"

He seemed to pull his lips together.

"John?"

"You need to read the journal. The answer's there."

She wasn't used to him being guarded. She counted on his complete openness and candour, like his smile and his laugh. His frankness was his main gift to her, though he didn't know it.

"John, if he's a murderer you have to tell me!"

"No."

She wasn't used to refusals either. Then he said:

"The journal is more than a simple telling of the evidence. Context, lass, context. How do you define murder, anyway?"

Actually, pretty easily she thought.

Chapter 5

London

Flight restrictions meant I had to wait until the plane had taxied to a standstill before turning my phone off flight mode and phoning Dad. It rang out to voicemail.

"Tell me you're not going to kill Mum," I said, as calmly and as quietly as I could. "Just tell me you're not going to do it."

During the flight I'd had time to think through my options and I went through them with Brad while we waited for our luggage. So far the carousel remained immobile and tired passengers waited and brooded and looked forward. To our right three middle-aged men, sporting colossal beer-bellies, wore the latest Man U kit. From their body language I could see they'd availed themselves of the in-flight bar. I'd once watched Brad attack a man in a nightclub for doing no more than being dressed in Man U garb and, even though he was now sober, I still hoped he didn't turn round and see them. But I needn't have worried because his mind was on other things.

"Taking him at his word", I said, "and he had no reason to lie at that point, he was in Rome at mid-day. It was about 12 o'clock wasn't it?"

He was staring at me, wide-eyed. An attractive blond in tight jeans and heels, swung her hips as she walked passed us and he didn't even blink.

"It was about noon when we last spoke to him, right?"

"Yeh, yeh, it was about then. Seriously, Jonno, you could be mistaken, you know."

"I could be," I admitted, "but I've thought it through and put myself in his position. The amazing thing is that I didn't think of it before. I know some of the shit but not all of it. What I do know isn't good. His life completely changed when he divorced Mum. He loathes her, I've always known that."

41

Brad's eyes were heavy with emotion.

"But the court decided, didn't they?"

He was desperately trying to shake me out of this view. To Brad, brought up with four siblings by a single mother on a grimy council estate, loving one's mum was as natural as breast milk and a religious belief in Liverpool Football Club.

"Yes, the court decided but I'm sure Dad would have something to say about that. The only thing stopping him is me; his love for me. That's why I need to see him. And he's not coming back to the UK. That was a lie."

I saw Brad's eyes come into focus on my face.

"For fuck's sake, you're not thinking of going to back to Italy."

"It crossed my mind, if we're not too late."

"Are you fucking crazy?!"

He'd raised his voice and I felt people turning toward us. Brad did, too, and he immediately lowered his tone.

"You said you'd go into hiding. You promised your dad. *I* promised your dad! Baxter could still be on our tail. You don't even know he's going to Mogliano. We could make the journey for nothing."

He was right. I knew he was right. But …..

"Let's not talk about it now. We can't do anything 'til we get out of here, anyway."

Brad's eyes were still locked on mine, trying to read them, which, of course, he could. Anyone could.

"Anyway," I said, "I was trying to examine my options. Assuming we stay in the UK and find an out-of-the-way hotel to hole up, I can do any number of things. One, phone my mother and tell her she's in danger."

"I'm surprised you haven't done that already," said Brad vehemently.

I noticed how quickly he'd shifted his allegiance. A few hours ago my father was the best thing since front-button dresses.

"I'm thinking on it, Brad, but you don't know my mother like I do. There'd be mayhem." Jesus, that was certainly true. I couldn't deal with her right now. "Second, and I think this goes together with the first, I phone Foster and tell him of my suspicions. He may give her protection. If he doesn't she can take off somewhere."

I caught Brad's eye.

"We'll have to look for watchers when we leave the terminal here. Baxter will have acquired our flight number but anyone waiting for us won't have photographs. There hasn't been time. They'll be looking for two men in their mid-twenties, travelling together, one of whom is a dead-ringer for Brad Pitt, so we'll split up and meet on the station platform for Gatwick."

Brad's eyes hadn't left me and he simply nodded. I looked up and, with relief, saw the first bag appear.

"One thing I can definitely do is threaten him that I'll ignore his suggestion we go into hiding and that we'll head for Venice, unless he speaks to me. It worked before, when we were in Italy."

Just then my phone buzzed that I had a text message.

"It's Jude," I said, "enquiring as to our welfare."

Then, immediately, I got two more texts, as if the network had suddenly given me a signal. The first was, ironically, from my mother.

I realise that I'm low on your list of priorities but do you think you could let me know what is happening in your life? Mum x

The second, just as ironically, perhaps, was from my father.

You have email. Suggest you split up at the airport, look around you at all times and meet Brad on the station platform.

Half-an-hour later I was sitting on the platform as Brad joined me. I'd been there five minutes; long enough to consult return flights to Marco Polo. Baxter would certainly not be expecting us to return.

"All clear?" I asked.

"Yeh," he answered and sat down heavily, resignedly. "What's occurring?"

I didn't answer. Brad was apparently studying a poster showing a super-model advertising underwear, but I didn't think he was seeing it. So, I stole my courage and logged onto searcher8040@yahoo.com, afraid of what it might contain. There was just the one message, of course.

Hey Son.

Glad you're safe. Don't mind admitting I was shitting a brick back there. Never wanted to be with you more in my life.

We do need to talk. I know that. I've made a promise that we will and I'll stick to it. In relation to your mother, I've written something that might help you understand. Did it some time ago actually and never sent it. But now's the time.

43

I'll do a deal with you. (Has it come to that? We need to do deals with each other?). Text the name and address and phone number of where you're staying and I'll email you the file. I need to know you're safe, John, while I sort out Baxter. You do that and I promise I won't do anything with your mother until we've talked it through, face-to-face. Deal? Bang a reply.

All my love, Dad.

PS Incidentally, I lied to you when I said I was heading for the UK. I'm actually in Italy. I know how bloody independent you are and I had to get you out of there.

All I could think of was he hadn't denied he planned on killing my mother.

I passed the phone to Brad and stared at the poster, absent-mindedly thinking it was another lie. No woman could have a body like that, unless, of course, she was a sergeant of police in North Georgia.

"What will you do?" asked Brad, passing the phone back.

"Do the deal. It solves my dilemma. I don't need to tell my mother or the police yet, if at all."

He nodded.

"Will he stick to it?"

"Yes. He may have lied about his destination but that was for my safety. He wouldn't lie about this. He knows I'd never trust him again."

***

"*Si senor. Domenica, domenica, domenica!*" The diminutive Venetian stabbed the air in time with the words, then raised both hands in a gesture of hopelessness, licking his lips nervously and running a sweaty hand through long grey hair. "Scusi senor. He change his ... habit. He wear the boat clothes, he stop in café, talk to man, then walk back to car and drive to airport." Despair and misery were written over his cracked face. "But no boat!"

Tom Stafford gazed across the darkened Grand Canal, at reflected light on wavelets stirred up by a brisk northerly that funnelled between the tall buildings of the Piazza San Marco at his back and whipped across to San Giorgio Maggiore; an expensive marina. He raised his binoculars to span the 400 metres. Baxter's yacht, a 50 foot gin palace - equipped with twin 550 horse power diesels, a flying bridge and two additional decks - was first in line, right by the exit, as befits the largest boat in the harbour. She was fatefully called *Vengeance* and every Sunday for the last five weeks Baxter had powered her into the Adriatic with a companion from an exclusive 'escort' agency. He'd moor up in the evening back at the marina, an Indian takeaway would arrive by boat and they'd spend the night on board. Very cosy.

"It's okay, Francesco. It's not your fault. I'd have been surprised if he had sailed today." The diminutive man flushed with relief, as if being given a stay of execution. "The important thing is what he does from now on. Because he's missed his weekly sex he may not wait until next Sunday to visit the boat." The presence of his mother at home probably excluded home visits. "He may even go on board tomorrow."

The Venetian avoided the tall man's eye and Stafford knew this was more from fear than evasion.

"So, you must still watch."

"Si senor."

"You have the kit I asked for."

"In the boat on Campo de la Guerra, senor. Blue bag. Locker to starboard. We agree."

"Tell me about the handguns."

He lifted a bag for Stafford to see.

"Make?"

"Make?"

Stafford cursed his lack of Italian. He should have learnt. It was far easier than French.

"Browning? Glock? Beretta?"

"Ah, si, Beretta 70, senor. Pistols."

"Silencers?"

Francesco lifted a hand to his chest in a gesture of supplication and risked looking up into Stafford's eyes.

"I sorry, but I get only one. They are ..... difficult."

Stafford suspected that getting a silencer for one old Beretta would have been hard to find, let alone two.

"How many in the magazine?"

"Six."

"Condition?"

"I service myself, senor," he said with sudden pride. "I shoot two cartridge; one from barrel and one from magazine. They work fine."

The last thing the Venetian would want was Stafford on his tail as the result of a misfiring gun. He reached into the bag and felt the silencer first, then the pistols. He lifted one. It felt solid. Still with his hands in the bag and appearing to be studying the water, he felt for the release switch, ejected the magazine and reinserted it, then he cocked and uncocked the weapon, before imprinted its weight on his brain. He zipped up the bag and took it off the Venetian.

"Good. I'll transfer €10,000 to your account tonight."

Now the little man looked up quickly.

"I know the agreement was for 20,000 but that included two silencers. You understand?"

"Of coursea."

"If you can find another silencer quickly, or find another gun with a silencer, I'll pay you the other 10,000. They'll be another 20,000 when the job is done."

The man seemed relieved and gave a small bow.

"You are most kind, senor."

Stafford handed over a card.

"I'm staying at this hotel. You'll notice I'm no longer Vladimir Potemkin. My name is now Michel Dubois. You'll also see the phone number of the hotel in case you can't reach me through my mobile."

Francesco seemed to pause slightly. Probably recognition of the hotel, thought Stafford, which was hardly salubrious. He always used cheap hotels for a job like this, as well as embedded locals for observation and materiel. Strangers always stuck out like a sore thumb. But no one noticed the tiny man scuttling up and down the canals, least of all see him as a threat. He'd taken some finding but Stafford had been planning this for years.

Trouble was, right at the last minute, his son had buggered up the original plan and Baxter was on the alert. But, with a little patience and adaptation, there were still moves to be made. Fortunately, before John's unexpected appearance, Francesco had already entered the boat and placed a bug in a lamp by the giant double bed. It was one of his three aces, although the other two had had to be arranged rather hurriedly and had cost him a small fortune in expenses. What to do with the call girl, though? That was the question. But for the moment he was tired. He'd been travelling non-stop for two days, so Baxter could go fuck himself for the minute because bed was top of the agenda.

Chapter 6

Monday 20 May 2013

Exhausted and drunk, I slept until a call of nature at 6.30am forced me to the toilet, where I noticed Brad had already preceded me and pissed over the floor. I had the hangover from hell and, by the time I'd bent down and mopped up the mess, I was wide awake. So I fired up my laptop and accessed my email. The *Word* file was there all right, along with a brief message.

Thanks, Son. Be in touch soon.

I opened the file without reading it. Dad was always so bloody wordy. I closed it quickly and completed the three Ss, then woke Brad.

"Did you go for a piss in the night you dirty bugger?"

He just groaned.

When he joined me at the breakfast table, though, he looked as fresh as the proverbial daisy. I'd already had half a carton of grapefruit juice and two cups of coffee and I still felt like shit but then Brad could always hold his drink better than me. He caught the eye of the middle-aged waitress and she immediately came to our table, like a moth to the light.

"So what's new?" he asked me, then graced the woman with his smile. "A large jug of coffee, please, a full English and, um," glancing round at the serving table, "a large orange juice."

She scampered off to take the order of a family who'd been waiting five minutes before she'd diverted to Brad. He tore open a small carton of marmalade and spread it on a piece of my toast, eyeing my coffee pot with lust. I righted his cup on its saucer and poured him some.

"*Grazie, senori. Come sta?*"

"Okay. The file's arrived."

"And?"

I shrugged my shoulders defensively.

"And nothing. I haven't read it."

He stopped chewing.

"Afraid of what it might contain."

"Something like that."

"So what's to do around here?"

"Nothing," I said. "In fact, I think we ought to check out straight after breakfast and go to a spa I know in Hampshire. You can be pampered for a day, while I read the file and wait for Dad."

His face lit up and, when the waitress brought his breakfast, the smile he gave was enough for her to live off all morning.

Four hours later, Brad was enjoying a real massage for the first time in his life, and I was sitting in the garden of a country pub, with a pint of local ale and a fully-charged laptop. Over a pink hedge, men tended half a mile of watercress beds and, beyond, a deciduous hill of ancient alder, ash and oak rose into the Hampshire blue. The garden smelled of freshly mown grass and honeysuckle. I knew Dad's file was going to be difficult and it was the kind of place I wanted to read it. But I waited for the sparrows to appear between the tables before I started.

Extract 1
3rd April 2010 - Devon

Familiar complaint. Not sure where to start. It's a torrid tale I have to tell, son, full of darkness and despair, and I fear the telling almost as much as I fear your reaction to it. I don't come out of it well. But I must tell it and I must be truthful, however painful. And I'll try to be quick. This is not a story over which you'll wish to linger.

Perhaps I should start with your sister. You know the way she is, the way she's been for most of her life. Let's just say she's difficult and very slightly crazy. But it's not really Rachel's fault. It's the way she was brought up. And I know what you're thinking; I'm her father. But this story is, in many ways about your sister. You could say she was the catalyst.

One day Rachel's daughter will ask about her grandfather, her grandmother and why they split up. And, of course, they'll be a family scandal about what will happen, which, if Bess has an enquiring mind, she'll want to know about. But Rachel won't tell her, partly because she doesn't know all the details and doesn't want to know, and partly because she's in denial, because she does know a lot of what happened, but she's buried it, as part of the way she coped with her mother and the separation of her parents.

How is Bess, by the way? She's 2 now, isn't she? I've lost track. Keep seeing her as she grows up, John. She's going to need all the help she can get.

Her grandfather had been thinking of her when she was just two!

Rachel was very young, of course - 9 and 10 - when it happened. But that trait, of simply ignoring matters if they're unpleasant, was one she internalised and took into adulthood. The only way to truly understand something, son - says he pompously (!) - is to slit it open and peer inside. Your sister cannot do that, because she's afraid of the monster she may discover. Ergo, she will not understand her daughter. And maybe I'm to blame for that.

A whole world ago, when we all lived together as a family in Hampshire, Rachel was the brightest kid in the county - creative, inquisitive, often intuitive. By the age of 4 she had the reading age of an 8 year old and she sailed through her first 4 years at school like a Devon breeze. She was playing two instruments by her 8th birthday. Oh, there were problems, of course, which'll become apparent later, but she was so bright! Did you know she used to write beautiful poetry?

Bess looked up in amazement. John was still cutting the hedge.
"My mother wrote poetry?"
He turned round and nodded solemnly.
"Dad sent it to me. I've still got it. I'll show it to you later, if you're interested."
"Yes, please."
Granddad had kept Mum's childhood poetry.

After the army I taught for 5 years in a local college, then I got promotion and we moved up to Yorkshire. Within three years your mother and I were no longer together. Rachel's schooling deteriorated. She couldn't stick at anything and her marks were very mediocre. She began to struggle with concepts she'd previously handled with ease. She gave up the flute, took up the piano and ditched it, then the clarinet and ditched that, too. She was a talented athlete at one time, running for the County but she didn't stick at it. She was captain of the school netball and hockey teams but she dropped out of those, as well, with some mysterious affliction to her limbs that no physician could fathom. As you know, she didn't make it to University and dropped out of one job after another. For most of the time she's been living off the state. But, God son, she could have changed the world! And she could have developed the sensitivity to understand her children and those around her.

As she read, images of her mother dipped into the confused pool of Bess' mind. The endless years of confrontation.

One of the reasons I've mentioned this is because if Bess, or anyone else, starts to dig, Rachel might have to recognise certain issues, confront the reality of her past for the first time in her adult life. The last thing I want to do is sound melodramatic but I'm afraid, John. Afraid that, one day, it will all come out and send her over the edge. On the other hand, perhaps it'll help her to understand herself and other people. Am I an arrogant bastard or what?

I've just stood up, reluctant to continue. I needed some Dutch courage, so I poured myself a scotch; that Chivas Regal you like, which I bought when you were down at Christmas. I don't think you're going to be drinking it now, so it's going down the old man's gullet.

Do you remember Helen? I saw her after I broke up with your mother. You were only five at the time but I'm sure you remember her. She was a mature student in one of my classes. Keep-fit teacher. She was 30 and I was 38, although she didn't know I was that old when she started to fancy me. She wasn't pretty but she had large, soulful eyes of dark brown and long, curly hair of almost the same shade. And, of course, the body of a goddess.

But the story really begins some months before Helen became involved and I started to think of her in any way other than that of an ordinary student. That was when I saw a solicitor. I can't remember the exact date but it was around early December 1991.

You know, you always expect solicitors' offices to be old and crusty mausoleums, decked out with the red-volumed veneer of respectability; legal dust dulling ancient surfaces and briefs littering the floor like the discarded detritus of pain and death. But how wrong I was. Andrew Manton's sanctuary was tidy, modern and airy, with few books and some photos of smiling, fair-haired children in school uniform. It contained nothing really interesting, nothing on which to focus, to give sanity to dark thoughts. Because my thoughts were dark, son. I was thinking of ending a marriage, of breaking a family. It was an uncertain path, with which I had no confidence and, I have to admit, it scared me. I found myself gazing out at the grandeur of St Paul's Church, which filled the window frame. Oh, St Paul's Church! How fucking ironic that later turned out to be.

Anyway, son, I ramble and I mustn't. It must be clear for you and factual, but I also want you to understand my feelings; the experience. Manton was certainly an experience.

He was tall, about my height, actually, and about my age. He had blonde, curly hair, a cream face, rimless spectacles, a dark grey hand-stitched suit and the sort of genuine Oxford brogues that my father used to wear, so I know they would have cost a small fortune. Minor to medium public school, I thought and it occurred to me that we had very similar backgrounds. He rose as I came in (that's how I noticed the shoes) and shook my hand. I remember thinking he'd probably been a bit of an athlete. No smile. He motioned me to a chair and I took my time settling, willing myself to relax and get my brain in gear.

"Been to a solicitor before?"

He held an expensive-looking fountain pen, poised above the biggest writing pad I'd ever seen.

"About this matter, yes. A couple of times over the last 5 or 6 years, when we lived down south. I never told my wife and I decided not to take it further. Since we moved up here I haven't done anything. Am I going too fast for you?"

The head didn't move from the pen

"No. I've got your name and address. Profession?"

"I'm a manager at Hunterside College, head of department, and I also do some teaching."

"Always been in education?"

"No. I was in the Army for a while."

"Officer?"

"Captain."

"Ahuh, and your wife?"

"She teaches, too, one day a week at St Paul's School."

The pen paused momentarily and I looked up at the dark green blazers and yellow/green stripy ties in the school photos. I remember thinking how incestuous it all was, yet so alien. I wanted to get some warmth into the room, some humanity.

"Wife's first name?"

"Stella."

"Children?"

"Daughter, aged 9, son, 4. Rachel and John."

"And what has happened?"

He seemed to fix his gaze on me now and I knew it was my time. But the sceptical blue eyes seemed ready to disbelieve until proven innocent. I'd thought a lot about how I was going to tell it but knew I hadn't got it right yet. "It's because it's too close to you," Kevin had said.

Who's Kevin? Kevin Orton, College Chaplain. I know what you're thinking, a heathen like me seeking help from the clergy but it wasn't like that. Kevin and I became friends before any of this business blew up and he then counselled me through it for 18 months before I saw Manton, who was his recommendation. Anyway, back to the story.

"In essence," I said, "it's about Stella's relationship with my daughter, which is destroying the whole family." The clock on St Paul's Church started to strike eleven and I looked at it while I talked. "For the past 5 years or so, she's terrorised my daughter, both mentally and physically. She's become a non-person in my wife's eyes."

Bess broke off with a start, a tightening in her throat. John looked round at the movement.

"You okay, lass?"

"Yes."

"Solicitor's office?" he asked, knowingly and she simply nodded. "Is there anything I can get you?"

She had so many questions but knew he was probably right; the journal would give the answers. That's why he'd given it to her.

"No, I'm good."

I remember rambling on.

"Rachel can't do a thing right. She's shown no affection by Stella. Every night I come in, Rachel is standing by the door in disgrace and I'm expected ....."

I trailed off and glanced at him. He lifted his head and peered at me with no expression, like an android. Basically, he didn't care. It wasn't his job to care, or to even believe. Rachel wasn't important, only success. It all felt about as natural as a bad play.

"I've got up to where your wife showed no affection towards your daughter."

I had to tell him clinically, analytically, not emotionally. It was what he wanted.

"Let me start again."

He didn't cross anything out, simply stared at me with that bland gaze. I unclenched my hands and tried to think objectively. At least he was making me do that.

"There are three main areas of concern. First, physical violence by my wife against Rachel, second, what I can only describe as mental cruelty by her against Rachel, and third, violence towards me in front of the children."

"Jesus, this is my mother he's talking about!"

This time John came over and crouched beside her.

"I know, lass. I did warn you, and there's more - a lot more. Are you sure you want to go on?"

Bess didn't hesitate.

"Oh yes. I can't stop now." She fixed him with her gaze. "I know it's early but I could do with a gin and tonic."

He smiled grimly and walked towards the house.

Manton's head didn't lift from the page.

I remember asking him again whether I was going too quickly for him. That's the teacher in me. He gave a small frown and said, "No, that's fine."

"Taking the physical violence towards Rachel, this has occurred on about five occasions that I know of over the last, what, three and a half years. I can't remember the exact dates, but I can give you some more details later if you want them. I'm not talking of normal punishment, here, which I accept may occasionally be necessary. But Stella attacks her, by striking her on the upper body, usually the arms. When it happens it's a quite indiscriminate rain of blows. Rachel puts up her hands to defend herself and on each occasion I've had to step in to stop serious damage. The last occasion was the summer of this year. Rachel wasn't wearing anything on her feet and Stella actually tried to stamp on them. This sort of incident always occurs after a prolonged period of difficulty with Rachel and it seems to me that Stella's frustration simply boils up inside her, eventually spilling over. My major concern is the effect it has on the children. John is usually present. They're both terrified, screaming and crying. It takes me half an hour or so just to calm them down."

It was quite a statement and I watched him continue to write. Soon he looked up with no comment. Remember, son, at that stage of my life I was a communicator and it has to be two-way. I needed feedback in order to progress to the next step. Manton gave me nothing. Yet - this is strange - I remember not wanting to ask him; not until I'd finished, anyway.

"Anything else on the physical side?"

"Isn't that enough?"

Of course he made no comment.

John returned with the gin and tonic, ice chinking in the glass.

"Your mother would kill me if she knew I was feeding you gin at this time in the afternoon."

"You should see how much she puts away."

She took a deep swig. There was just enough gin to give it bite. She paused to watch him pick up his shears before going back to the journal. She desperately wanted to continue with her grandfather's story 37 years ago and learn more of the child who was to become her mother. But instead she saw that her uncle was frustratingly changing the timezone, again!

Chapter 7

Friday 10 May 2013 - Lincoln

So, you're probably wondering how the hell I got to this point; being chased across Italy by an intelligent thug the size of a Silverback, to being holed up in a respectable spa in rural Hampshire, reading extracts from what appear to be my father's memoirs. Well, there are a few reasons I guess and stupidity is certainly high on the list. It actually started 10 days ago - I know that at least – in my favourite drinking house. Something I've reflected on over the years is that most of the real changes in my life - innovations, inspirations, certainly disasters - start in a pub. What that says about me is probably not on the plus side but, hey, it's who I am and I live with it.

As usual, the place was crowded. When the man walked in, though, there was an almost imperceptible drop in the buzz of conversation as people turned and stared. It wasn't because he was a stranger. It was quite simply because he was wearing a suit, a white shirt and a tie. This was *The Coal Scuttle* and no one, not even the undertaker, wears a tie.

"Betcha the next round he's a copper," said Brad, who, having been arrested four times - for assault, failure to produce a driving licence and two counts of drunken disorderly - was probably the best qualified amongst us to judge. No one took the bet.

"As far as I'm concerned," continued Brad, between mouthfuls of mint and lamb flavoured crisps, "suits are for weddings, funerals and James Bond, not for getting hammered on a Friday night."

The three of us raised our glasses dutifully and chorused our saying of the month, "Amen to that." We'd just started on our third pint, preparatory to going out on the town. Where I come from it's what you do with your mates on Friday nights and I'd been doing it now for ten years; since I was 16, in fact, when I'd had a mate run up a false ID as being an 18 year-old student at Lincoln University. We didn't so much go on the pull these days as have a good laugh after a hard week. Besides, one or all of us usually had a girlfriend. Although not on Friday nights. It was understood. Although, to be honest, I was getting a tad tired of the process. And I'd recently become aware that drinking to excess left me depressed and even aggressive, both normally alien concepts to me. But mates are mates, through thick and thin, so we stuck together.

"It's your round anyway, you tight-fisted bugger," said Jude. "Besides, if he is a member of the constabulary, he's after you, Brad, no question," and we all just grinned at that because we knew it was probably true. People in Brad's world were defined by various arbitrary criteria and when he drank he could be one of the most irresponsible men on the planet. He was on first name terms with every bouncer in Lincoln, despite the fact that a few of them had scars as testimony to his acquaintance. The year before last, the Lincoln Bouncers Association had asked him to speak at their annual dinner, as chief antagonist. Neither Jude nor I were there but, apparently, he took the piss out of every one of them individually and it was one of the wittiest and dirtiest speeches they'd ever heard.

"You're very thoughtful tonight, Jonno," said Brad, raising his voice to be heard against the general hubbub. I tried to brush the remark aside by smiling knowingly and saying nothing. The last time I'd thought about the future I'd got pissed on my own in a downtown pub and had woken in a strange bed, beside a startlingly ugly women, desperately hoping we'd both been too drunk to have had sex. She couldn't remember either.

"He's missing Julie," suggested Jude. "Regretting the day she left his bed. Mind you, who wouldn't?"

Fact is, I wasn't and, to be honest, I was glad to be on my own for a while, not having to worry about keeping a demanding female happy.

Bess looked round for her uncle. He'd nearly finished the hedge and sensed her look up.

"You know, if I didn't already know Jonno was you I certainly could have worked it out from this point."

"Which point?"

"The Coal Scuttle."

He raised an eyebrow.

"The bit that describes your misogynistic attitude towards women. Is that what I am, a demanding female?"

Maddeningly, he smiled.

"They certainly want to get their own way, women that is, girlfriends or nieces."

She looked at him with what she considered to be her scornful face, then simply stared at him for a while.

"You know, it's funny but, sometimes I think the right woman for you is, paradoxically, going to be the one who challenges you."

"Very deep. Too late now, though."

"Well, you're right there at least; at 41 you're definitely over the hill."

"I'm thinking of becoming a lawyer," I said eventually, just for something to say.

Jude scoffed.

"Jonno, lawyers are two cums short of a kumquat and have the morals of an international banker. You'd be terrible."

"Absolute shite," echoed Brad.

"Thank you for your support, gentlemen. Are you saying I couldn't cut it?"

"Oh, no," said Jude, "you'd run intellectual rings round 'em but they'd cut you up anyway because you'd play fair and they wouldn't."

Which was a backhanded compliment if ever I heard one.

A burst of female laughter made us look over involuntarily, so we spotted the suit as he emerged from the crowd and gingerly threaded his way across the room towards our table, desperately trying to avoid spilling his pint on the grey pinstripe. He seemed completely unperturbed, as he took us all in, until finally, to my complete surprise, settling his gaze on me.

"Evening, sir. Would you be John Stafford by any chance?"

Interesting, I thought, that even though you may have nothing to feel guilty about you cannot help a frisson of fear flickering through your chest at being asked for your name by a policeman. Because Brad was right, I was sure of it.

"Yes," then feeling I ought to show some assertiveness, "And who are *you?*"

"Inspector Foster. Sheffield CID."

"Sheffield?" The fluttering in my chest increased. "My sister?"

"No, sir, it's not about her; no members of your family have been hurt, as far as I know."

"Do you have any identification?" asked Jude using his best toff's accent.

"I beg your pardon, so I do."

An Irish brogue. Quite broad. He transferred the beer to his left hand and reached inside his jacket. An impressive looking card flopped out of a leather wallet. He had a cheeky grin that curled the edges of his mouth and I wondered if he exaggerated the accent for effect.

"Would you mind if I sat down?" He didn't wait for an answer, just dragged a chair out and plonked himself. "Been on my feet half the day, so I have." He sipped his beer slowly, ignoring – probably relishing – the effect he was having. He smacked his lips in satisfaction and looked around the table, then back at me.

"Would you mind introducing your friends, sir?"

He was clearly in no hurry and I knew the way my mates would expect me to respond.

"Sure. This is Brad Pitt and Jude the Obscure."

Everyone grinned, including Foster, who scratched a spot behind his left ear in a distracted kind of way. He was about 40, I suppose, hair cropped short like my own, although Foster's choice was probably an attempt to disguise a premature bald patch on the top of his head. He was also overweight, a substantial gut spreading over his belt. There was an alertness about him, or maybe it was simply that I was well into my third pint and Foster had only just started his first. A fat, gold ring crouched on the third finger.

"Inspector, I'm anxious to know what this is about but I'm also curious to know how you found me."

He nodded.

"Wasn't easy, I have to admit. I had your address, of course, from your driving licence records. When you weren't in I thought to myself, he's lived in Lincoln a while, Friday night, probably out with the lads. When none of the neighbours knew which pub you frequent I tried them all, starting with your local. It wasn't until *The Dog and Duck* that I got lucky." He deepened his smile and took another swig. "Barman's an interesting fellow, so he is; pockmarked skin, built like a Leinster number 8. Anyways, let's just say we know each other from Sheffield. You could say I ….. persuaded him to tell me where you might be."

We all knew big Arthur from *The Dog*. Not even Brad would mess with Arthur and we also knew there was no way he would finger me unless Foster had something very serious on him. The inspector was simply letting us know that he might seem like one of the boys, but he had fangs. I looked at Brad and Jude, their faces like stone.

"Very impressive, Inspector," I said. "You're obviously a very competent officer. But we've never met and Jimmy there," I flicked my thumb at the bar, "wouldn't give you the time of day, so how did you know it was me."

The smile lessened a tad.

"Well, I have a copy of the photo from your driving licence but, I have to say, it doesn't look the remotest bit like you. It was more family resemblance you might say."

That threw me and Foster knew it as he watched my face. And then, of course, it was obvious.

"My father."

Foster nodded and I thought for a moment. He'd already said no one was hurt. I could feel Brad's and Jude's eyes on me.

"I need to ask you some questions about your father, sir." I looked round at Jude, who nodded slightly. "I noticed some chairs outside. Would you mind?"

The showers had passed through that afternoon and it was now a balmy evening. Folk were strolling along the canal, enjoying this most English of cities. All the chairs had been taken, so we stood and leaned on the new balustrade. Terns swooped after scraps on the water, spraying sparkles of sunlight and adding to my sense of unreality.

"Brad Pitt I can see, but Jude the Obscure?"

"His real name's Thomas Hardy. Local barrister."

Foster nodded as if he understood but the real story was more complex. He'd been nicknamed after Thomas and I had dragged Brad along to an adaptation of the Hardy novel at the local theatre and Thomas, not noted for his brevity, had come out with a longwinded explanation of the play's themes. Brad had shaken his head and said: "Thomas Hardy? More like Jude the fucking obscure himself." It was a moment of brilliance and the name had stuck.

"Barrister, huh?" said Foster. "Useful fellow to have in your camp, I dare say?"

"Jude and I were at school together. We've known each other a long time."

"What school would that be, sir?"

"Causton Manor".

"Would that be a private school?"

"Yes, it would."

"And your other friend now. What does he do?"

The last thing I wanted to do with Foster was talk about Brad and to avoid that I knew I had to step out of what Jude calls my 'passive zone'.

59

"What's this about, inspector?"

He looked away. A family group was throwing bread scraps over the water and the terns were taking them straight out of the air.

"Have you spoken to your father recently?"

"About a week or so ago."

"Text, email?"

"Maybe two weeks."

Foster raised his hand in a kind of question.

"That's quite normal is it, you speak to him about once a week?"

All too common at the moment I thought, since our recent spat. Until then, unless he was abroad, Dad phoned two or three times a week. Ironically, I'd actually phoned him yesterday and got voicemail only. I hadn't really focused on it until now and, suddenly and surprisingly, the minor flutter in my chest expanded and seemed to place a grip on my lungs.

"Inspector, I'm giving you no more until you tell me about my father!"

I amazed myself at how assertive I was being. Foster noticed the change in his interviewee and looked away before fixing me with a steady gaze.

"We think – we only think at this stage, we have no evidence mind – that your father may have committed one act of murder and another of arson in the Sheffield area."

So, thought Bess, her suspicions were right; he is a murderer.

A look of incredulity must have shown on my face because Foster rushed on.

"We're simply following a line of enquiry at this point, sir. Nothing concrete you understand."

This was simply not possible. The relief rushed through me and I felt myself smiling.

"You're following the wrong line of enquiry, Inspector. My father wouldn't commit arson, let alone murder."

"Nonetheless, sir, humour me if you would." Foster seemed unphased by my obvious scepticism, his face now very serious as he squinted over the sparkling canal. "About a week ago, on Saturday 4 May to be exact, the ex-Principal of a local college had her house burned down. Fortunately, there was no one in it at the time but the house was gutted. All her personal belongings went up in smoke, so they did. And, two days later, a Sheffield businessman was murdered in his home." Foster was looking me straight in the eye.

"Two incidents, completely unconnected it seems, and the connection with your father only came out by accident really. In fact, it's only the apparent indication that he *is* connected with both individuals that points the finger at your father at all."

I shook my head.

"You've lost me."

Foster indicated a table that had become free. We sat down and took a sip of our beer. His glass was nearly empty.

"I was initially only involved in the murder inquiry, you understand. With that we felt that revenge was the most likely motive."

"Revenge?"

He hesitated, drained his glass and looked at me with very clear eyes.

"His name was Townsend." He paused briefly to gauge any reaction. "And he was a local gangster - drugs, money-lending, prostitution - you name it, he was into it. We're pretty sure he's been involved in a number of killings over the years but haven't been able to pin anything on him. Not even a GBH. So, we started to look at who'd be interested in a revenge killing." He shook his head. "The list is as long as Paddy Murphy's dick, so it is, and it's taking a while to follow the leads. Your father's not the only suspect." He held his hand up again. "But, to cut a long story short, one of the links in Townsend's records shows that he leant money to a Nicholas Goodger, at the customary exorbitant rate of interest. Familiar story. Goodger's marriage broke up. He lost his house, kids and, eventually, his job. He needed money desperately, thought of a business venture and borrowed dosh off Townsend. He started to pay it back but the business began to fail and he missed some of the payments. Townsend refused to give him more time, the pressure got too great and he committed suicide. At least that's what the coroner said and I'm inclined to believe it. Your father was a good friend."

He paused and got the attention of Sharon who was clearing up empties. He gave her a twenty pound note and ordered two more pints.

"How do you know my father was a good friend?"

"It's mentioned in the report of the inquest."

"Is that all you've got to connect my father? The fact that he was his friend?"

"On the Townsend murder, yes. I have to admit, I wouldn't have made the connection to your father at all, except I happened to overhear a conversation between two colleagues investigating the fire. Revenge seemed the only motive for that, too, especially since, a week before the arson, the ex-Principal received an anonymous email stating that, very soon, she would live to regret her conduct as Principal of the College. She took no action on the email until the fire. There are a few candidates and, bless my soul, one of the possible was a colleague named Stafford." He paused briefly. "They called it redundancy. But she says she forced him to resign. There's usually more to these stories than emerge initially, so there is."

He watched me consider that and I thought back.

"When was that?"

"Fifteen years ago."

That was about when my father stopped seeing me. At the time, I thought it was because he didn't wish to see me anymore but I now know it was because my mother refused to allow the visits. It took him two years in the courts to resurrect them. When you're ten you tend to believe what your mother tells you.

"Anyways, that's the connection. Now, it's a long shot, I know it is, but suddenly we had the same candidate for two apparent acts of revenge, that happened within a few days of each other. Can you see the way my mind is working, sir?"

I shook my head in denial, mainly for him but, and this came as a surprise, partly for myself.

"It's nothing but a coincidence. And I'm sure my father had nothing to do with either incident."

Foster looked away and his eyes followed Sharon as she walked to our table with the drinks. He picked up one of the pound coins from his change and folded it into her hand, as if he'd known her a while.

"I'm much obliged to you, darling. You keep that to yourself, now, do you hear?"

She beamed her thanks before giving me a quizzical backwards glance.

"Well that may be true, sir, or it may not. And your faith in your father does you credit, so it does. But you've got to remember, I'm a policeman. Have been for 20 years, although most of it across the water it has to be said. And experience has taught me never to believe in coincidences. Never."

"Surely the fact that you just happened to overhear the conversation about the arson was a coincidence."

"No sir, that's chance. Not the same thing at all. Besides, now, there's also the fact that your father seems to have disappeared off the face of the earth."

That *was* strange, I had to admit, but not unprecedented. "He's not answering his phone, landline or mobile, and his daughter and ex-wife haven't a clue either. Mind you, not that your mother and your sister see him at all." Foster's eyes narrowed. "Your mother was inclined to believe my speculations about him."

"They were divorced ages ago. As far as my mother's concerned, if the stock market takes a dive it's my father's fault."

Foster nodded.

"That's the impression I got. So, I'm looking for some objectivity, so I am. Your sister says you're closer to your father than she is?"

"I guess so."

Actually, that was certainly true. Dad and Rachel didn't really talk at all.

"She says you're much more likely to know where he is, too."

"I guess," I said.

"Then let me come to the main point of my visit, sir." The genial bonhomie had completely gone. "Have you any idea where your father might be?"

I thought about that, I really did. Not that I'd have told Foster if I'd known.

"I'm afraid not, Inspector." I started on the pint he'd just bought. "Cheers!"

He glared at me before taking out his notebook. A boat's horn sounded suddenly and we both looked round, but it was only two barges exchanging greetings. And the terns still danced on the water.

"How would you describe your father?"

The sudden change of tack caught me off guard and I thought for a bit.

"Soldier, teacher."

"Hmm, the first thing you said was 'soldier'. Would you say he was capable of violence?"

"In self-defence."

"Ever seen him hit anyone?"

"No."

"Ever hit you?"

"No."

Foster flipped back through the pages of his notebook.

"Army for 10 years; Paras. Resigned commission in '84. Captain."

He paused.

"You've omitted that he was decorated for his conduct during the Falklands War."

"You're right, I did omit that. Shows he's not a stranger to violence now, though, does it not?"

"I guess, like tens of thousands of other demobbed soldiers in the UK."

Foster was consulting his notes again.

"Breveted Major during the Falklands but it wasn't confirmed when he got back." Foster, still concerned with his notes, didn't notice my sudden disquiet. "Did he resent that?"

I didn't answer immediately and Foster looked up.

"Until you just mentioned it, Inspector, I didn't know," and I had an unexpected insight into my father.

"He never told you."

Feeling inexplicably guilty at my lack of knowledge, I said nothing. And not wanting to meet Foster's enquiring gaze I looked away, at the reddening sky, wondering what sort of response I'd get if I raised it with my father. I suspected there was a story there and, yes, I imagine he did resent it.

"Did you know he was arrested in '98?"

"What for?"

"The charge was assault."

"The victim?"

"An Adam Nasmith. Nasmith ended up in the Northern General Hospital, Sheffield with a fractured jaw and four fingers broken in his right hand, not to mention various cuts and bruises."

"Yes, I do remember. That was self-defence. Dad was going out with his wife – she and Naismith were separated - and Naismith didn't like it. So, he took a swing. He hit Dad twice before he retaliated."

"That's what your father told you?"

"Yes."

"And you believe him?"

"Of course. My father may not be an angel inspector but, as far as I know, he's never lied to me."

Foster looked doubtful.

"Pretty stupid thing to do, though, wouldn't you say; taking a swing at an ex-Para?"

I could see his point.

"Dad was teaching at the time. Maybe Naismith didn't know about the Paras. Anyway, he was much younger than Dad as I recall. Maybe he thought Dad was past his prime."

"Very good, sir. What does your father do for a living now, if you don't mind my asking?"

"I don't think he has a full-time job. He does some part-time teaching, here and there. His Russian is very good."

"Russian?"

"Nothing sinister, Inspector. His mother was Russian. His father was in the Diplomatic Service and met her while stationed in Moscow."

Foster was writing furiously so I took a long swig of beer.

"Any other languages?"

"His French is more than passable. And before you ask, he used to spend long summers in Brittany as a child, with a friend of his father's."

Foster continued to write.

"And he lives in Devon, on his own?"

"Yes, although I can seldom get him there. He lives on his boat in Cornwall most of the time and he goes abroad a lot, so I use his mobile number."

I drained my glass whilst Foster continued to write. I was bored with this conversation. I wanted to get back to Brad and Jude, tell them what had happened and seek out my father.

"The trips abroad? What's that all about, now?"

"Holidays, I guess."

"You seem to have to guess a lot, Mr Stafford. Would it be true to say that you're not particularly close to your father?"

That felt like an accusation.

"I suppose you could say that. We used to be, at one time. But recently we don't seem to communicate as much."

"Why's that?"

I shrugged.

"Just grown apart."

He seemed to consider that.

"That recent lack of willingness to communicate, it come from you or him?"

I could feel myself beginning to resent this conversation.

"Probably me."

"Any particular reason."

"No. We've just grown apart. He lives 350 miles away, we live our own lives, have our own circle of friends."

And that was all true but it wasn't the reason; not really. When Dad lived in the United States I spoke to him far more and we'd always had our own lives. No, it was mainly that I was less willing to share mine now than I'd been in the past. And, of course, we'd had a few disagreements recently. Nothing major. Just minor things. Plus, whereas he'd normally meet any mention of my mother with stony silence, the last time her name had slipped off my tongue he became openly hostile.

"That's because she's an evil bitch!"

"Dad, I don't want you saying that!"

"You'd agree with me, if only you'd open your mind a little."

"Look, I've told you before, I don't want to know what happened in your sordid past."

"I know. You're afraid of the truth disturbing your comfortable little life, where everything's rosy in the garden." He'd sighed. "I can't say I blame you for that but you'll regret it one day."

I became aware that Foster was talking to me.

"I'd be obliged if you'd tell me your father's email address. Maybe we can contact him that way."

I hesitated and Foster smiled.

"That's very interesting, sir, if you don't mind my saying. You're convinced of your father's innocence, yet you don't want to give me his email." He had that amused look on his face and I felt like a kid who'd been caught out in a lie. "Besides, I'm sure your friend inside will tell you that it's a serious offence to withhold evidence in a murder inquiry."

"My father is innocent, Inspector, have no doubt of it. But I'm just going to get my friends in on this, anyway."

They both spotted me immediately, of course and I signalled them over. They pointedly picked up their empty glasses and came outside. It was my round. Foster rose as they got to the table.

"Grand to see you, gentlemen, grand. Take a seat now won't you." Just in case you didn't know this was his meeting. "Your friend was having difficulty remembering something and he wanted your assistance."

I turned to Jude.

"He wants me to give him my Dad's email address. Do I have to?"

"What's he accused of?"

I rubbed my chin. These were my best mates.

"Arson and murder."

Jude pursed his lips.

"Well, right now, Jonno, no you don't have to tell him. But, if you refuse he has the option of arresting you and charging you for withholding evidence.

You'll be interviewed under caution and then you'll have to tell him what he wants to know or you'll be committing an offence." He glared at Foster, who studiously continued to look away. I could see that Brad had already pencilled him in for Judgement Day. "He'll probably arrest you and take you all the way to his station in Sheffield. My advice would be to give him the address because he'll get it anyway."

Foster turned back with that infuriating grin.

"Very sensible advice, too, sir, if you don't mind my saying."

I gave him the email and he wrote it down.

"That's my card. Just in case you remember something or your father contacts you." He paused. "By the way, what do you do for a living, sir, if you don't mind my asking?"

Again, the change of direction. I suppose it was part of his interview style.

"I'm a systems analyst." He stared at me vacantly. "I'm a computer geek, Inspector."

"Well paid, I imagine. DVLA says you drive an almost new Audi Quattro, top of the range."

"I get by and I'm a bit of a car nut."

Foster stood and I followed him up.

"I'm grateful for your help, sir."

"I'm sorry you've had a wasted journey."

He nodded at us all.

"Goodnight to you, gentlemen."

Again, no offered hand.

"Inspector," I called and he turned. "Didn't the gangster's killer do everyone a favour?"

The smile was nowhere to be seen.

"It's true that, apart from his family, I don't know of anyone who's losing sleep over the death, sir, if you take my meaning. But we can't go around taking the law into our own hands now can we? Besides, how do we know there aren't others?"

"Pompous, Irish git," said Brad, when Foster was out of earshot.

I sat down, trying to consider everything; observing incongruously that the landlord had switched on patio fairy lights that leant an ethereal glow to the scene. I'd never noticed them before.

I took out my smart phone and tried both my father's numbers. I left a voicemail on each and went onto my gmail account, sending him a message to contact me, all while my two friends sat patiently. So I told them what I knew. If I couldn't tell Brad and Jude, I couldn't tell anyone. It didn't take long.

"So what do you think?" asked Brad when I'd finished.

The cloud had suddenly parted and they were both squinting into the setting sun. The surrounding tables were also now empty and sparrows were landing on them, searching for crumbs.

"He didn't do either crime and they have no evidence whatever."

"Yeh," said Brad, "fuck 'em."

But I wasn't as confident as I sounded. I thought about what I knew about my father and whether he was capable of killing anyone, other than in battle. To be honest, now I focused on it, I wasn't sure. So I watched the birds for a while and my friends waited silently with me, sensing my mood. There was something I was missing. I let my mind go loose, as Sharon came out to clear away again and the sparrows scattered in a flurry of tiny wings.

"He could have phoned you from Sheffield easily enough to get that information," said Jude.

That was it!

"He can't find my father so he wants me to do his job for him."

"And are you?" asked Brad.

I looked into his face. The sun must have finally set behind me because he seemed indistinct suddenly.

Extract 2

"And the, er, mental cruelty towards your daughter?"

I looked back to the reassuring facade of the church. There would be no reaction from him. I simply had to accept that. Just tell it as objectively as you can, I thought.

"This is an area I find very difficult to put into words but Stella has never shown any genuine affection for Rachel. For a period of 5 or 6 years she's never kissed or cuddled her daughter. This is not just from my own observations but also from what Rachel's told me."

The phone rang and he snatched it up.

"I said 'no calls'," replacing the handset loudly. "My apologies. Please continue."

"My wife takes no interest in Rachel's activities at school or outside. It was always me who went to see Rachel's teacher at the end of term, went to school activities, saw the headteacher, wrote notes when she was ill. Until now that is. For the last three months Stella has done much of this because she now teaches at the same school the children attend - a private school - and it would look unnatural if she didn't. It's still me, though, who encourages Rachel with her music and I always take her to recorder and flute lessons. After I've put the children to bed, Stella goes up and kisses John goodnight but she never does the same to Rachel."

"How do you know this?"

The question was unexpected but I could see the relevance.

"Because I'm often still sitting with Rachel when she comes upstairs."

"She might not come in because you're there."

"I don't think you understand, or perhaps I haven't explained it properly. Generally speaking my wife's ire is against my daughter, not me. She doesn't really have an issue with me, *per se*. Besides, I was sitting with Rachel recently, in her room and we stopped to listen to Stella walk up the stairs and kiss John. She said: 'Do you know she's never done that with me'."

I didn't tell him, son, because he wouldn't have appreciated it, but her voice was flat, unemotional, as if it were an acceptable part of her life and that was that. Manton studied me for a few seconds.

"Anything else?"

"How much more do you want? There's masses. Stella has persecuted Rachel. In every argument between the two children she always, without exception, takes John's part. Every night I get home Rachel is standing by the front door in punishment. Stella expects me to immediately take issue with Rachel. I'm expected to be my daughter's enemy every time I come in the door and I know damn well it isn't always Rachel's fault."

"How do you know?"

"Because, damn it, I'm often there when the confrontation takes place!"

I'd raised my voice but it seemed to have no effect on him. The church clock said 1120 and it had started to rain.

"I've asked Stella to improve her relationship with Rachel, many times. Her reply is always the same, that the problem is not her but Rachel. I do accept that Rachel can be a difficult child and there have been times when I've taken Stella's side but she wants me to do it all the time, simply because she's my wife."

He pulled over another blank page and the pen rushed over it before halting abruptly.

"Have you tried anything else to change your wife's behaviour towards your daughter?"

"Are you kidding? On more occasions than I can remember I've suggested we seek professional help as a family unit; marriage guidance and psychiatric help."

"And her response?"

"Always refuses. I have seen some psychologists, with whom I've discussed matters as far as I could. One said that if what I told him was true, then my wife did need professional help and he suggested I try and persuade her to attend a family counselling session."

"And she refused?"

"Yes. I took Rachel to another educational psychologist, hoping to get something done by initially concentrating on *her*. After all, it's my wife who says the problem is Rachel. But, after several visits, he said she was a perfectly normal 9 year old. Stella didn't come and refused to have anything to do with it."

"Yes," and he shook his head very slightly. It was the first sign of any reaction.

Chapter 8

Friday 10 May 2013 - Northwest Atlantic

Over the Labrador Basin the sun was still high, as the elderly lady heard the big man beside her curse loudly. She tut-tutted her disapproval but he ignored her, just as he'd done the entire flight. Slowly, he brought his gaze back from the window, closed his eyes and swore again, even more loudly. It must have been through frustration because he was clenching and unclenching his huge fists and she knew she should remain quiet from now on.

Janelle was crossing her long legs and settling down for a well-earned iced-tea when the signal panel above one of the microwaves dinged and the light by seat 26H started blinking. God, no peace for the darned wicked! She glanced round to see whether anyone else was interested in responding but all other cabin crew were studiously reading. Even Rita had suddenly picked up a book and she hadn't read anything but Hello magazine since 6th grade.

The man in the window seat had his head turned towards her. She remembered him, of course, from when she'd served lunch, because you couldn't help noticing the scar that stretched vertically from an inch above to about two inches below his left eye. Now that eye was looking at the name badge on her chest.

"Can I help you, sir?"

"I've just seen what looked like a distress flare off to starboard. I need to speak to the Captain straight away."

She was stunned for a moment, then became aware that her jaw had dropped.

"Distress flare?" she heard herself saying.

"Yes, Janelle, we may not have much time."

The English voice was calm and firm but even so. She put on her best Georgia smile.

"Sir, we are 35,000 feet above the Atlantic Ocean. Are you really sure that …..?"

He started to stand up, excused himself for brushing passed the old lady in the next seat and rose to his full height in the aisle. If he was intending to intimidate her it worked.

"Janelle, if you won't notify the Captain, I'll knock on his door. It'll create a full security alert and everyone will be inconvenienced."

The eyes were boring into her now, jaw set. She was aware that everyone in the nearby seats was looking at them.

"Okay, sir. I'll go tell him. Please sit down."

"I'll wait here."

Feeling she'd totally lost control, Janelle turned and walked back down the aisle, knowing she was going to be about as popular as a hog roast at a bar mitzvah.

"Heads up," she said maliciously, passing her lounging colleagues, "we may have a problem. Rita, make sure that big guy in the aisle doesn't move forward."

She scooped up the laptop that contained the passenger manifest, took a deep breath and lifted the mic on the flight deck intercom.

"Rick, this is Janelle."

She imagined Rick remembering the security protocol for that flight. If she preceded her name with his there was no risk.

"Say again."

"Rick, this is Janelle. I need to see you."

"You can bring in those legs o' yorn any time, darlin'."

The captain removed the lock and Janelle opened the door. He'd swivelled round in his immovable seat, so he was actually sitting on the chair arm; not an easy thing to do in the cramped cockpit of a Boeing 777, but it did enable him to look back at her with a wide grin. She knew he was only trying to impress the new co-pilot, who *was* looking at her legs. They'd probably been talking about her.

"This is no time for your childish jibes, Rick. Save them for your wife!"

"Whooh!" said Rick, winking at the co-pilot.

"There's a guy in 26H who claims to have seen a distress flare."

The grin disappeared from Rick's face.

"Distress flare?"

"That's exactly how I responded. He insists on seeing you."

Janelle pulled down the spare seat, behind and between the pilots' chairs, and opened the laptop. Rick knew what she was doing and waited patiently.

"Where away?" asked the co-pilot.

Janelle continued to look up the occupant of 26H. Now even Brits had to complete detailed visa forms on-line she'd know within seconds who he was.

"Janelle," insisted the co-pilot, "where did he say the flare was?"

She looked up, then, and saw a not unattractive face.

"Um, starboard. He said, 'off to starboard'."

The co-pilot stood up, looked through the window and wrenched his head round to the right.

"Nothing," he said after a few moments and Janelle dragged her eyes back to the computer screen.

"Okay, who is he?" asked Rick.

"English. Accent confirms that. 59 years-old, educated at Oxford and Sandhurst. What is that, Sandhurst?"

"Military academy, like our WestPoint," answered Rick and Janelle watched him swap glances with the co-pilot. "So he was an army officer."

"Correct. Left in '84. Gives occupation as ..... 'sailor'."

Another glance between the pilots.

"Damn!" said Rick. "We ought to get him up here."

That was the last thing she expected.

"Rick, you know company policy as well as I do."

"Yeh, yeh."

But he did hesitate and she waited while he considered.

"Where is he now?"

"Standing in the aisle waiting. Rick, I don't advise it; he looks like a rough character."

"Does he look like an Islamic terrorist?"

"No but that's not ..."

"He can't have any weapons and he's nearly 60 years old for Christ's sake; what's he gonna do, take on the both of us?"

"Frankly, he looks like he could."

Rick stood up and she cursed herself for fuelling the stupidity of male pride.

"Get the door."

He walked off the flight deck to the beginning of the seats and looked at the man in the aisle for a few seconds, then signalled him to come forward and she noticed the limp for the first time. It wasn't a pronounced limp. Actually, it was hardly a limp at all but she was trained to recognise such things. He didn't acknowledge her as he passed and she followed him and Rick into the cockpit, noticing another livid scar across the back of his head, clearly visible through the short-cropped hair.

Hearing the click of the door lock behind her, she watched his reaction, his size and presence dominating the space. Most people are in awe when they get on the flight deck for the first time but he was just looking around, taking in everything, relaxed, like he was on tour.

"Please take a seat, sir," said Rick. "As you can see we're a bit short of room up here."

Seated, the visitor's knees were jammed up against the central console. He could have reached out and touched the switches and Janelle saw Rick assessing him. Since there were no more seats, she leant against the bulkhead behind Rick's chair, so she could observe everyone's faces.

"Thanks for allowing me up here, Captain."

"You're welcome. You sure this was a distress flare?"

"One can never be absolutely sure but that's what it looked like and I can't think what else it could have been. I've seen distress flares before, although not from 35,000 feet it has to be said."

He glanced up at Janelle as he said it and she expected him to smile, but he didn't.

"It was orange, about 40 degrees from the nose and I'd say about 3 miles off." He looked at his watch. "In 20 seconds it will have been 7 minutes ago. I'm sure you have your exact position on the GPS display there, plus you know your track and speed, so you should be able to work out a fairly accurate position of the flare."

There was silence for a few seconds while everyone waited for Rick's response.

"If you can't make the calculation, I can," suggested the visitor.

Rick grinned broadly and winked at Janelle. She knew what was coming now and groaned silently. Playing the dumb Southerner was his favourite rôle.

"Oh, I think we can handle it." He nodded at the co-pilot. "Us southern pilots do get a little training in navigation."

The man's mouth creased a little and she realised that was his version of a smile. Then it was gone. The co-pilot started to write furiously on a pad, occasionally consulting an electronic display and using the on-board calculator.

"You live in the UK, sir?" asked Rick.

"Yes, most of the time, on my boat in Cornwall."

Rick nodded thoughtful.

"What sort o' boat?"

"Sailing sloop, 42 feet, long-keeler."

He watched the co-pilot as he talked.

"No kiddin?" said Rick. "Mine's a Waterline 45."

"Nice boat."

"Yeh. Fin keel. Faster, more manoeuvrable".

"True but not so stable up-wind in a big sea. Sailing's a compromise. Depends on your priorities and the waters you sail."

"True enough."

Janelle had no idea what they were talking about but sensed the combative nature of the exchange.

"How far to the nearest Coastguard station?" asked the big man.

"Er, about 200 mile."

"I have it," said the co-pilot suddenly and handed Rick a slip of paper.

He said it humbly, it seemed to Janelle. She moved her legs slowly to gain his attention, then gave him the benefit of her obscenely expensive dental work. Rick put on his headset and flicked a switch on the console.

"This is Delta Flight DL65 calling Halifax Control, over."

Nothing.

"Halifax, this is DL65."

"Go ahead DL65."

He grimaced at Janelle and she knew what he was thinking. "Nothing but damned Yankees this part o' the world".

"Halifax, we have a reported sightin' of a distress fla'ya at the following position: 53 54 48 north, 49 19 34 weyest." He turned to his visitor. "What time was that?"

"1417, Eastern".

"Time 1417 Eastern. Over."

"Copy that DL65. We'll alert the Coastguard and they'll handle it."

"Much obliged to ya Halifax. Out"

He turned round.

"Coastguard will co-ordinate any rescue. They'll probably send out a spotter plane and, if they see something, a chopper will follow. They'll also, then, notify all shipping in the area of that waypoint. If their boat has any flares left when the plane comes over – if it does fly over, bearing in mind tidal drift and the unlikely possibility that our calculations are completely accurate – maybe they'll be spotted. But to be perfectly honest with you, their chances are slim."

"I know. But at least visibility's good. What's the weather forecast?"

"Good."

The space seemed smaller again as the man got up.

"I'm grateful, Captain. If you hear anything before Atlanta will you let me know?"

"Sure but it's unlikely they'll get back to us."

He just nodded, waited patiently for the door to unlock and walked to his seat.

"Janelle, those legs o' yorn are startin' to disturb my sensibilities. Now get up yonder and don't disturb me again." Rick leant back in his seat and closed his eyes. "I'm fixin' to rest a spell."

She smiled shyly at the co-pilot and he smiled shyly too.

***

Back in his seat, the man rested his head and closed his eyes. But he couldn't sleep. He'd already planned the next few days but his obsessive nature made him go over it again and again in an attempt to find a flaw, a possible weakness that could be exploited by opponents. But, apart from what he'd just done, which could bring unwanted publicity, he found none. He'd thought about suggesting to the captain that he wanted his name kept out of it but that might have created the very curiosity he was trying to avoid. You couldn't plan for the unexpected, of course. You simply had to deal with it. Just like he'd done five nights ago.

He'd done his research: large house, six bedrooms, three baths, four reception. He hadn't been able to decide on the point of entry, though, until he had details of the alarm system and for that he'd needed entrance to the house.

So he'd merely snipped a media cable, climbed a pole and answered an angry call to the company which installed the entertainment system. Within an hour he was in. The reconnoitre not only enabled him to get the complete layout and occupancy of the house but, most importantly, the name and address of the alarm installer. A break-in at their head office on bank holiday Friday and he'd secured the details. No, getting in wouldn't be difficult. It was the dogs that were the problem.

He hated dogs. Pound for pound they're much stronger than humans. Knives work but not against the charge of an adult, male Doberman. Even if you're lucky and your knife pierces a vital organ, the dog might still damage you. He wouldn't have stood unarmed against a single Doberman when he was in his prime and there were two of them guarding this place, roaming free. He was downwind and so far they hadn't smelled or heard him.

He didn't like dogs but he didn't really want to kill them and had considered tranquilizer darts, using a crossbow but the drug would take too long to immobilise the target. He'd thought of poisoned meat but he'd never have got close enough before the dogs started barking. So his old Glock 17 had come out of storage; the one that had 'gone missing' while he was on exercise in the Congo. The one that would give him 18 months in clink if it was ever found in his possession. It had last been used house clearing at night, so had a torch that clipped to the underside of the barrel. But silence was the key here and British gun legislation makes it very difficult to buy a silencer legally. The World Wide Web is a wonderful thing, however, and a private dealer in Gloucestershire had supplied not only the suppressor but also the special Glock threaded barrel needed to fit it. Good 9mm Parabellum cartridges, with a pressure ceiling of 42,000psi, were available from the same dealer. He'd worn a beard, dark glasses and a small pillow under his waistband. He'd also spoken with a Yorkshire accent. No loose ends.

He waited another few minutes, feeling the dark around him and revelling in it, allowing a cinnamon smell to capture him. He flexed his limbs again, felt their strength and, grasping the lowest branch of the cedar, began to climb.

Moving slowly he carefully felt each branch before placing weight on hand and foot, wary of puncturing the thin, leather gloves on jagged bark and leaving traces of blood. When he judged he was about ten feet from the ground he paused and settled himself in a fork between two large limbs, leaning back until he felt comfortable. He removed the Glock from its holster, adapted to accommodate the precious silencer. Then he briefly switched the light on and off, to make sure it was working, flicked off the safety and peered into the gloom to allow his night vision to return.

He was ready and waited for the alertness to come, as it always did: butterflies in the gut, increased pulse rate and sudden, heightened awareness.

But nothing happened. Nothing. Just the confidence and the small challenge; that was all.

That confirmed it. He'd always known that when these senses failed to appear - when he couldn't revel in them - it would be time to retire and disappear into obscurity. Well, he was going to retire all right but simply fading away was for others. Before pensioning himself off, there were deeds to be done and the unpredictability of animals could mean this part of his strategy could go badly wrong. He was still sure he'd thought it through, though, and his age had been part of the calculation. So he lifted the dog whistle from around his neck.

It's considered that the very top end of human hearing is 18 KHz, although not many people can hear at that high a frequency and those that can are usually young teenagers. It's thought that dogs can perceive sound at up to 45 KHz but he didn't know how old these dogs were and dog hearing, like that of humans, can deteriorate with age. So he'd set the whistle for 25 KHz as a safe bet and blew once for two seconds.

Nothing happened. He listened for a full minute, doubts rushing in. Had he set the whistle frequency too high or too low? Had their master used a similar signal for a 'stay' command? Maybe their curiosity was outweighed by their comfort or lack of courage. No. He blew again; two quick bursts this time.

And then he heard them, padding across the grass. The main thing was they weren't barking, simply curious. The sounds stopped as if they'd paused at the edge of the little copse, perhaps unsure of an exact bearing, so he whistled again and, from a distance of 30 feet now, they couldn't fail to pinpoint him. There was a low growl and he saw one of them, a dark shape, moving slowly towards him. A small yelp from the edge of the wood told him the other dog was cautious, holding back. Clever. Probably the older, giving instructions. Pity the dogs were separated but he'd just have to deal with it because the dog's eyes would be much better attuned to the dark than his and he knew that he'd soon be spotted.

He raised the weapon and just that small movement led the dog to pause at the base of the tree and look up with a louder growl. He flicked on the light to see a mouthful of teeth and immediately shot the dog through its skull. The sound of the bullet crushing bone was louder than the noise made by the Glock. But now he had to move quickly before the other could bark and to avoid that he had to make himself a target.

He jumped down. Part of his brain registered a sharp pain in his right knee where there was an old injury, but there wasn't time to think about it because, even before he'd settled in a crouch and raised the weapon, the remaining dog rushed him in a snarling fury of speed. And it didn't falter, even with the sudden glare of light in its eyes.

The shot entered through the mouth at point-blank range and killed instantly. But the charging dog had already left the ground and, although the force of the bullet pushed the head up, it wasn't enough to slow the animal's 40 kilogram momentum. He was bowled over onto his back, feeling another sharp pain; this time by his left shoulder.

Pushing the dog off, he wondered why it had become suddenly pitch black, then realised the Doberman had jogged his balaclava so that it covered the eyeholes. He repositioned it, switched off the light and, still crouching, waited again for eyes to adjust, as well as for signs of movement. That last bullet would have exited the back of the dog's skull and could have smashed through a window, setting off the alarm but had probably buried itself in the side of the house, or travelled over the roof, to drop harmlessly in a field. The best laid plans. He didn't spend more than a few seconds reflecting on the knee. He'd known for a while the weakness was there. Instead, he listened for sounds reappearing in the undergrowth as nature went back to normality.

After five minutes there was still nothing from the house. He flicked the light on again and examined the ground behind him, interested in what it was that had caused the pain in his back. But it was only a tree root, smooth with no jagged edges; no blood for DNA testing. The dogs' blood would be all over the ground and his clothing, of course, but that didn't matter. He'd polished the cartridges earlier so finding them in the torchlight was not difficult and he popped them into his pocket.

Picking up his bag, and with the Glock in his other hand, he walked, or rather limped, out of the wood, crossed the croquet lawn and paused beneath a small window. He placed the gun in its holster, delved into the bag for a one-inch wood chisel and got to work on the window.

It was PVC, double-glazed and not alarmed. Not alarmed because it didn't open. It was just a piece of glass, designed to let light into a cloakroom off the lobby. It was therefore not considered a security risk. He'd noticed it on his reconnaissance as TV repair man.

Slowly, meticulously, he worked on the tough PVC, starting at a lower corner, forcing the chisel between beading and rubber by hammering softly with the palm of his hand. Then he levered, separating the two layers. After a short while he had enough PVC to grasp with one hand. The next part, he knew, would make a noise, as the whole lower beading was ripped away but he wasn't bothered about that. Outside the dogs were dead and, inside, the solid, oak cloakroom door would seal off the sound; another reason he'd chosen this window. He pulled and discovered that the rubber surround must be fairly old because it had lost some of its cohesion. There was now straightforward access to the two vertical struts and the remaining horizontal and these were quickly removed. A swift levering with the chisel on the upper horizontal and the whole window was forced away from the inner beading.

He placed the window on the grass and moved back to the edge of the copse, watching and listening for any sign of movement in the house. He waited ten minutes more but the only sounds still were tiny ones in the undergrowth as wildlife was drawn to the smell of blood.

He'd always known that getting his shoulders through the 60x60cm square window would be a squeeze but he managed it, corner to corner, head-first. He opened the cloakroom door and again listened but there was just the tick of an antique grandfather clock and the remembered smell of expensive carpet. A small standard lamp shed enough light to see across the hall and halfway up the stairs.

The DSC Alexsor alarm system was based on movement only, through wall-mounted motion sensors, cameras and floor pads but it was effective enough. He knew where the wall motion sensors were and the cameras, because those had been visible when he'd made his visit, but he had no idea about the sensor pads under carpets and rugs. The pads were left up to the customer to place where he saw fit and there was no record of them at the installer's office. Each one contained its own small battery and wifi, which sent a wireless signal to the main control panel by the front door. As soon as he stepped out into the hall he was sure a battery operated wall sensor or underfloor pad would do just that. Then, unless he crossed that space and entered a four-digit code within 15 seconds a number of things would happen. First, the wifi control panel would send an alarm, via a mobile phone network, to the 24-hour security monitoring service in Nottingham, for which the resident had paid extra. That service would then make a call to the house, also via a mobile system. If that call wasn't answered within 30 seconds a loud alarm would sound and the security service would contact the local police.

So, acquiring the security code had been essential. The system allowed each resident of the property to programme in their own numbers and he'd no idea what those were either. But there was always a master code, used by the installers whenever they carried out repairs or upgraded the system, kept in their offices.

Sure enough, as soon as he was halfway across the hall a red light began to flash on the console. Swiftly he entered the master code and a solid green light replaced the red. Without stopping he withdrew the Glock, crossed the hallway and ascended the stairs, listening the whole time. He passed two Constable prints and a huge family photo of four adults and half-a-dozen children. He'd seen it before.

At the top, he opened a door and, moving swiftly, walked to the bed, shone the torch on the lone, sleeping figure and simply shot the man once through the head and once through the heart.

He crouched, found the two cartridges and extinguished the light, focusing on the open door. He didn't think there'd be anyone else in the house, or that they'd have heard anything if there were, but he couldn't be sure. All he wanted to do was get out of there as soon as possible but he waited beside the body, listening and watching the landing for a shifting shadow, as the green, digital numbers of a bedside clock went from 3.37 to 3.42.

He stood, tested the knee and moved quickly to the door, then descended the stairs and exited via the front door. Avoiding the dead dogs, he crossed the wood, ascended a boundary wall and dropped carefully onto a lonely, country road, where the sudden complete absence of wind gave him pause. But there was just the call of an owl, way across the valley.

40 minutes and six fields later he arrived at his car. He extracted a large, plastic bag from the boot and placed all his outer clothing, including gloves, shoes and tools, into it for later disposal. The Glock he placed under the driver's seat. Half-an-hour later he was turning onto the M1 and heading south, frustratingly observing speed limits.

For the first time since perching in the tree he allowed himself to examine his feelings. Despite the fact that he'd needed to make that kill for a while, there was no particular sense of satisfaction. Nor was there remorse. After all, it wasn't as if it was his first time. He did, however, feel hungry. To his left, a grey dawn was emerging and he began to think of a motorway service station as an attractive proposition, with its fried breakfast and strong coffee. A 50mph average speed limit came into view so he reluctantly set the cruise control and slowly headed for Nottingham Services. Two down, five to go.

Bess became aware that her uncle was looking at her in that totally relaxed, contented kind of way he had. He was sitting on the ground, fortuitously in a patch of sunlight, languidly drinking beer from a bottle. He could do that so easily, without realising it. She took a sip of the fresh coffee he'd placed by her side.

"Okay, I have questions and I want you to answer me this time. Who's the dead man if not the gangster or, perhaps more important, who's the cold-blooded assassin, if not my grandfather?"

He turned and considered her.

"You have to read it, lass."

"No. it's him. It has to be."

"You seem very sure."

"Why else tell the story?"

He nodded.

"Okay. I shouldn't be so dismissive. You're coming to this for the first time." Well he did warn her didn't he? "Yes, the dead man is the gangster and, yes, the killer is your grandfather."

With that he just looked away as if dismissing her. She felt a strange gap appear between them and thought about how she felt, sitting here in the comfort of a sumptuous country garden, confirming that her grandfather was a murderer; an assassin even. Okay, the victim was a gangster but did that make a difference? And there was the issue of her grandmother. She felt she couldn't deal with it all now, but she was beginning to understand why it had been kept from her when she was younger and why no one ever mentioned her grandfather. But then there was the younger grandfather, the one struggling to cope with his marriage.

"I have another question," she said. "Who wrote this stuff?"

"Which stuff?"

"The stuff on the plane and the break in. You weren't there."

"It was a collaboration. Dad wrote the original draft; I topped and tailed it. He was far too wordy."

She watched his grin and thought about that.

"And how do you know it really happened like that?"

"He promised me all the facts would be true."

She was sceptical.

"And you believe that?"

"Yes. And his impressions of what he saw. I asked him to put that in, too."

"So the dogs and the whistle, the shooting, the discussion with the captain, the stewardess crossing her legs to get the attention of the co-pilot; all that happened as he describes it?"

"No. It's true for all the material where he's the viewpoint character, like on the break in, but with the plane stuff I rewrote what he sent me, removed him as the viewpoint character and looked at it from the view of the stewardess, to make it *more interesting. But all the facts in there – what he and the captain said and so on - are as he gave it."*

That had the ring of truth, so she nodded to acknowledge it and went back to her reading.

Extract 3

"You mentioned a third area. The, um, violence against you," said Manton. I knew what he was thinking.

"I know, sounds odd doesn't it, a husband complaining of his wife's violence? Even more odd in my case. I'm six-two, weighing in at fifteen and a half stone and I'm still pretty fit I guess. She's five-four and the most unfit woman I've ever known. Any court would laugh at me, I'm sure."

But he shook his head.

"It depends. It's a lot more common than you think. The problem for the man is usually that he's too chivalrous to hit her back, which I suspect is the case here."

I remember thinking perhaps he wasn't as bad as I'd thought.

"Well, I don't know about chivalry, exactly, but certainly she knows I won't hit her back. She even hit me on the head with a saucepan once and I let it go." He looked up. "After that I suppose she assumed she had *carte blanche*."

"A saucepan?"

"Well that's what Rachel said it was. I didn't see it because Stella came up from behind while I was on the couch. It was certainly large and metallic."

"Any damage?"

"Not really. Just dazed for a while. To be fair, I've been hit harder than that. I was in the Paras for nine years."

He nodded solemnly.

"And she stopped after the one blow?"

"Yes and it was a one off. The usual thing is for the attack to be towards Rachel. The argument, usually about Rachel, gets to such a point where Stella loses her temper and her control and she simply lashes out at me. She always surprises me, even though I know she's going to do it. That sounds weird doesn't it?" Miraculously he grinned and it threw me for a few seconds. "She might get in the first blow, before I put my arms up and then I can defend myself easily. Eventually, she gives up when she realises she's hurting herself more than she's hurting me. But then it's not the physical violence, as such, which is the problem but the effect it has on the children. They see their mother laying into their father in a total frenzy and it scares the shit out of them. They scream and cry and it takes me a long time to calm them down."

There was a long silence while he continued to scribble and I looked out of the window, as the clock struck 1130. Eventually, I felt him look up.

"So, Mr Manton. What shall I do?"

He pursed his lips.

"Will she leave the house?"

I shook my head.

"We've been through all that."

"Then I think you have only one option - you must get a court order immediately, banning her from the marital home."

"Sounds a bit drastic."

"Well, the only other realistic alternative is for you to take out divorce proceedings, with custody, but she'll still be living in the same house and it could be very difficult for you, especially if your wife is how she appears to be."

I wasn't sure what he meant by that but I was clear about my ultimate objective.

"I'm not too bothered about a divorce. I'm not planning on remarrying. But I do want to remove my wife from Rachel and preferably from both children."

"In that case I recommend the court order. I know it sounds drastic now but it's later you need to think about."

He lifted his head and peered at me over his specs. It was as if he was saying, this is the way you have to be, Mr Stafford. This is my world. There is no room for sentimentality.

"Will I have any trouble getting it?"

"Would Rachel be willing to talk?"

"I'm sure she would."

"Then, although there are no guarantees, in this case I believe so."

You know, son, if I look back on my life, there are key moments when fundamental decisions are made. The secret to a successful life is to recognise those moments when they stare you in the face and to make the right choices. Later, I realised I should have done exactly what Manton suggested. Not taking his advice was, without doubt, the single most important mistake of my existence. But all I wanted was to get out of that antiseptic room. It had been like going to confessional without getting absolution.

I didn't get forgiveness from Kevin, the College Chaplain, either. I'd arranged to meet him for lunch at a pub and he wanted to know everything that had transpired.

"I didn't like him," I announced, finally.

"You don't have to like him. He's good at his job. That's all you need."

I shook my head.

"This man will be in charge of the rest of my life. Surely, he needs to show some empathy."

I remember Kevin running his hand through sparse hair in frustration. He was younger than me, small and skinny. My army chums would have called him weedy. And he was, physically. But he had the mental force of a bull. Maybe that's what having God in your back pocket does for you.

"You have to trust the professionals," he said. "You have to accept that, to some extent, they will take over parts of your life. But you have to trust them. If you want to see this through, you have no choice."

Part of me said he was right; the desperate part, the part that craved a solution. But I was wriggling, reluctant to take the first step and trusting complete strangers with the rest of my life was a huge one.

"Where did you leave it with him?" he asked.

"I said I'd think about my options and let him know. Christmas is coming in a few weeks. The kids are looking forward to it. It doesn't seem like a good time for breaking up the family."

He nodded at that.

"I know," he said, "but there's never a good time.

Chapter 9

Saturday 11 May 2013

350 miles maybe but I had to find out what was going on. Besides, the drive gave me time to think, about my father and our deteriorating relationship. The constant rain and lying water on the M5 made no difference to the four-wheel drive and the powerful Audi ate up the distance.

It was true what I'd said to Foster and it was something I shared with my father. We were both car nuts. "When buying a car, son, stick to German or Swedish and you won't go far wrong." He'd narrowed his eyes and bit his lip wryly because we both knew he was being pompous. He did it for effect. It was a kind of joke between us. He'd do his pompous bit and I'd smile to let him know I'd noticed. "The Germans may not know how to make a decent sausage," he'd continued, "but they're the best engineers in the world."

"And the Swedes?"

"Close second, but they're totally unrivalled at boat-building."

"Would you say you had a simple view of the world, Dad?"

He grinned sardonically, which is as close as he ever got to actually smiling.

"I try damned hard to, Son. Here's some simple questions for you, since we're discussing national stereotypes." I remember thinking it was rarely a discussion. "French food is the best in the world. Simply thinking about it makes me salivate. The French also produce the finest wine, the greatest cheese, or at least some of it, and they have the most beautiful language in the world. No question." He raised his eyebrows. "And that's not to mention the women. Anyway, is it that which makes them so bloody arrogant? Because they know all this and feel over confident about themselves?"

"You're generalising."

"I know but you have to in arguments."

"Are we arguing?"

"Don't keep interrupting; just listen to the master."

It was my 18th birthday and he'd flown from America especially to be with me. I'd defied my mother and we'd driven out to the depths of rural Lincolnshire, to his favourite pub, so he could buy his son his first legal pint. We'd sat outside in the April sunshine and I'd been forced to listen to him enthuse about the wagtails making their nests in the reeds by the river, as well as his many other pet subjects, like Bush's chronic handling of the American economy and his suicidally bellicose foreign policy. In those days I wasn't interested in such things. I was much more concerned with how I could break up with Shannon so I could go out with Lisa and the fact that apple tree blossom kept falling into my beer. But I'd listened patiently, making the occasional comment to pretend interest because, despite the fact that it was my birthday, it was really his day.

"American food, on the other hand, and this is even more of a generalisation, is usually pretty bland, their Californian wine is appallingly fruity and paradoxically expensive, they have only one major type of home-grown cheese, which they modestly call 'American' and the way they've bastardised the English language is a travesty. Yet, Americans are even more arrogant than the French." He'd pulled his face into another grin which now looked like more of a smirk. "What does that tell you?"

"Is all this still rhetorical or do you expect an answer this time?"

"No, what do you think?"

He'd sat back and took a swig.

"I don't know."

"Come on, you've got an IQ of 144 and we're only on our second pint."

I had tried to think of something witty and amusing but it was always the same. In my own space I could usually think of anything but put me under pressure and I failed every time.

"Give up. What do *you* think, Dad?"

He sat forward and studied me.

"You couldn't care a shit about any of this nonsense could you?"

"What can I say, Dad. You're more worldly than I am."

If she could continue to place the murder stuff to one side for the moment, which anyway happened 15 years ago, this was absolutely fascinating stuff. She'd begun the day thinking it was going to be a regular, comfortable visit to her uncle's cottage. Yet, quite suddenly, she was getting an insight into the relationship between her uncle and his father. And she was finally learning about her grandfather, for God's sake; this bogeyman of the family, this ogre, whose name dare not be spoken. It was as if she were being offered a window into the past to understand the present and, all of a sudden, she felt a clarity about Uncle John that she hadn't known was missing. She even knew why he was using shears when he had an electric hedge-cutter in the shed.

I was approaching Exeter, so I pulled my mind back from the past and slowed down, because the police sometimes set up speed traps about here. Dad had warned me about them a number of times.

Thinking of warnings, my father had issued a number of those. Actually, that's not really true. He didn't *warn* me exactly. Now I thought about it, he seldom gave advice, as such. He was opinionated, yes, but the arrogance was an act, not part of his character. He did give his views on things and left me to take it or leave it. Sometimes these homilies were worth listening to. The woman thing was one such. I remember when I was about 19 and having a bad time with my current girlfriend, so I phoned Dad across the Atlantic.

"What you have to remember, Son," and he'd paused to allow me to laugh at the pomposity, "is that all women are flaky. All women, without exception. Frankly, life is a lot less stressful if you can live without them. But if you can't do that the key is to find the ones that are less flaky than others."

Here we go again. All women are flaky. Bess felt a pang of disappointment. Her first thought had been correct; her grandfather was an ogre.

I thought that was bollocks at the time. Within the year I'd reluctantly accepted its truth. All the girls and women I'd known had let me down, sometimes in more ways than one, usually unexpectedly, and in a way, it seemed to me, that a man wouldn't. A girlfriend might get into a mood over inconsequential issues, or take me to task over something trivial I did, or more likely didn't do, months before, which was so unimportant I'd forgotten it. More significant, women were, in my experience, disingenuous. And they lied. Christ, did they lie!

Maybe all men think that, thought Bess, which is ironic because it's what women say about men. It was no good, she had to say something.

"All women are flaky?" she called out indignantly.
He looked round, thinking.
"You're the exception, lass. Honorary man."
"Is that meant to make me feel better?"

"Your relationships with women will be the most difficult part of your life, and I can't help you with the details. You'll simply have to figure it out." He'd grunted loudly down the phone and the Georgia crickets seemed to pause. "But good luck with that one because I've never managed it."

"This is not encouraging, Dad."

"You're more intelligent than I am."

"This is true but shouldn't you be instilling confidence in me; equipping your offspring to cope with the rigours of modern life?"

He paused to think. I could hear bullfrogs croaking and a plane droning its way to Atlanta.

"You'll be fine. Experience is the best teacher. All a father can do is love his children, always tell them the truth and nudge them in the right direction, in the blind hope that they won't fall over too often. Besides, if I did suggest what you should do, would you take my advice?"

I sped up the hill on the A38, the Devon Expressway. I knew from experience that, traffic permitting, it would take me about 45 legal minutes from here to Dad's house. I knew he wouldn't be there – he was more likely to be on his boat, 50 miles further on difficult roads – but the cottage was only a small diversion and I might pick up some clues. Dad still wasn't answering his phones or his email and a feeling deep in my gut told me that something *was* wrong. It was the lack of a text or email that disturbed me most. Dad always checked these frequently during the day. Not only were we car freaks, we were both techno freaks as well.

The rain had stopped by the time I reached Ashton Gorton. The cottage was small - just two bedrooms – and so was the well-tended, low-maintenance garden. It nestled into a grassy bank on a hill overlooking the river far below, as if it grew there. As I stepped out of the car I felt a sudden chill. I told myself it was because of the breeze that had crept up the hill, stirring flower stalks and carrying a fresh scent. The BMW was gone, of course, and all windows were closed.

I knew where the spare key was kept, though, and was soon inside, retrieving a pile of mail from the mat and placing it on the kitchen table. It was all junk mail and bills. "Let's be honest, John, apart from birthdays and

Christmas, when do we get personal stuff through snailmail these days?" The fridge door was ajar, but the towel placed at its base for defrosting had long since dried. The freezer was switched off. I examined the rubbish bin under the sink to find it completely empty.

I ducked my head to avoid the low beam and moved into the living room, sunshine streaming in, revealing dust on a table top. Paintings from Dad's travels and photographs from his past lined the walls. I stared at a framed representation of myself that was propped up on the mantle. It was a digital photo I'd emailed during my last business trip to Florida. He must have printed and framed it. I was on the beach at Miami and it made me realise how much weight I'd put on since then. I'd started a fitness regime after Julie and had lost nearly a stone but I still needed to lose another one to reach what Dad called my 'fighting weight'. Two awards he gained in the USA were also on the mantle.

There were only two photos of himself, both in groups. One was an old army snap where he was surrounded by about 30 grinning guys, raising the Union Jack at Port Stanley, or was it Goose Green? He was the smiling figure in the centre, arms around two comrades, both with sergeants' stripes. His size dominated the picture, but it was his youth and vitality that struck me, before the burdens of life had taken their toll. At that moment he hadn't a care in the world. He must have been about 28, the prime of life. He'd just won a battle and could achieve anything.

The other photo was much more recent, of the two us, taken during a 5-day trip to Venice. Of course this one showed the livid scar. It was about 8 centimetres long and traversed the left eye. It had appeared suddenly when I was about 12 and I remember asking him, in that insensitive way pre-pubescent males have, why they hadn't made a better job of it at the hospital. He said it had happened at sea, when a broken shroud had whipped across the foredeck and it was several days before he could hit port. I believed him, then. Now I wasn't so sure.

As I looked at the picture, I realised it had always been Dad's physical appearance which had dominated my childhood impressions. He'd always been sporting, playing rugby and cricket from an early age. Now, like an insurance policy into pending pensionhood, fitness had always been important to him and he worked bloody hard at it. He wore it, too, as part of his vanity, like an old cloak. I knew that the only time he'd been in hospital in the last 20 years was when my sister had had an appendectomy at the age of 16 and he'd given her a treasured copy of Tolkien. "Pure escapism," he'd said, and then, "The only people to want reality in hospital are masochists and the self-important," with the wife he'd divorced years before smoothing the bedclothes and pretending not to listen. His hair was still cut to within a quarter inch of his scalp, although it was the inevitable grey. But it was there still and I was grateful for that.

I replaced the frame and climbed the stairs, checking the drawers and wardrobe. I couldn't tell what shirts and sweaters were missing, let alone jackets and suits because, frankly, I hadn't taken much interest in my father's clothes. But nearly all his underwear and socks were gone. His uniforms were still in the chest by the foot of the bed.

Back in the living room I sat on the desk chair perched in an alcove that was used as an office. I switched on the desktop computer and, while I waited for it to boot up, opened the desk drawers. His cheque books were still there, but the passport was not. This, in itself, meant nothing. Dad often travelled in the UK with his passport. It was a good form of identification. And there was a joke he'd made last year: "Besides, you never know when you might need to flee the country." Then, in the bottom draw was a brand new, green, cardboard file, with 'John's file' written in large letters across its front. I'd never seen it before. For the first time since seeing Foster I got that queasy feeling in my stomach.

Inside were statements from four banks. One was a current account. The others showed huge deposits, totalling nearly £450,000! I was stunned. Where the hell did all that come from? Finally dragging my eyes away from the accounts, I found insurance policies, a mortgage, the deed to half a house in the United States, registration documents for his boat and a will. He'd tidied up his affairs and did not expect to return.

"Fuck are you doing, Dad?"

I examined the will and looked closely at the date but it was signed and witnessed years ago, shortly after Dad had returned from the US. Everything was left to me, apart from a small amount to my sister and a large bequest to someone in America. Details of that person could be found in a codicil lodged with an attorney in Atlanta, Georgia.

"And who the fuck is that?"

I focused on the computer monitor. The system software required a password but I knew all my father's passwords, just as he knew mine. There were no secrets there. But the computer told me nothing. There were no revealing emails and he'd wiped all his Web history, so I couldn't even see the sites he'd recently visited.

I sat back in a kind of daze. What was this all about? Was he really taking revenge on people from his past? If so why now? Where had he gone and why hadn't he said anything? Resentment surfaced for the first time and I pushed it down.

I glanced at the time. 12.30. I wasn't hungry but I could certainly do with a drink, so I walked to the local. I wanted the normality of a bar, with the casual conversation of nothing in particular. This was something I'd learned in childhood, when, on many visits to Dad, we'd walk to the nearest pub, play pool and talk to the locals. I can now see how important those days were for me. I was a shy child – oh, was I shy - but those lunchtimes in *The Rose and Crown* and *The Nag's Head* taught me that men are friendly, interesting and sometimes even fun. Now I can walk into almost any strange pub and feel at home. So long as I stay sober and don't take up with strange women.

I was still on my first pint and two of Dad's mates were telling me about the dire traffic situation in the village, when my phone rang.

"This is Inspector Foster."

I tried not to sound surprised.

"What can I do for you Inspector?"

"Do I find you in a pub again, sir?" Foster could obviously hear the unmistakable background conversation. "Wouldn't be *The Angler's Retreat* in Ashton Gorton by any chance?"

I hesitated. I resented Foster knowing where I was and knowing that his manipulation had worked. I could deny it but what would be the point?

"It's what you wanted isn't it, for me to do your detective work for you? Wouldn't your superintendent authorise the trip? All you have on my father is a coincidence – sorry, chance - which is a country mile from where you need to be."

There was a long silence. Someone was telling a joke nearby and I knew the burst of laughter at the punchline would drown Foster, so I walked outside, taking my beer.

"Well, you might be right, sir, and you might not. But since you are down there, do you mind telling me what you found."

It was couched like a polite question but I knew I couldn't lie openly.

"He's not here."

"I know that, sir, or you would have let me know you'd found him, would you not?"

It was now my turn to be silent.

"Anything else, sir?"

"He's packed up for a trip."

"I know that, too."

"How do you know?"

"Because at 15.20 yesterday afternoon, he flew out of Manchester Airport bound for the USA."

I was stunned for a few moments, then realised the pieces were now beginning to fit together. I felt short of breath suddenly so sat down on a trestle table.

"Mr Stafford, are you still there?"

"Yes."

"What I didn't realise at the time," continued Foster, as if completely unaware of the confusion he'd caused, "was that when we were talking in that charming little hostelry in Lincoln last night, your father's plane was cruising over the Atlantic Ocean, heading for Atlanta Georgia."

Suddenly it all made sense.

"Bearing in mind my hypothesis about your father, would he have any enemies in America?"

Oh, yes.

"I know he has friends there, Inspector. He lived there for three years. I don't know about enemies. His wife lives there and her family."

"That a fact now? American citizen is she?"

"Yes."

"Get on do they?"

"Well, he moved back to the UK."

I was already thinking ahead. There was no point in going on to the boat now. Fortunately, I'd packed enough for a long trip. I did it automatically and, again, I'd learned from my father. "This travelling light business is a crock of shit, son. Always pack as much as you can carry. You never know when you might need stuff, including your passport."

"Tell me, Inspector, will you be talking to the authorities in Atlanta?" I asked.

"I expect so, sir, yes. Not that they can detain him you understand. As you quite rightly say, we have nothing more than speculation and the fact that he's on the run. That's not against the la ...."

"He's not on the run!"

"Well you might be right, sir, and you might not, but one thing is for certain; he's flown 4,000 miles without telling his only son he was leaving; someone with whom he normally speaks frequently."

I wanted to end this conversation.

"Is there anything else I can do for you, Inspector?"

"I don't think so, sir."

"Then I'll bid you good day."

I took a couple of deep breaths. I'd finished my beer without noticing, so I took the glass back inside, said farewell to my two drinking companions and walked up the hill. Once in the cottage I made six calls, using the house phone. This was all his fault so it could go on his bill.

The first call was to book myself on tomorrow's Delta flight from Manchester to Atlanta. Being a Sunday it was booked solid. The only available seat was in First Class, which cost me a king's ransom but at least my long legs wouldn't be jammed up against the next seat like they normally were. The second was to my father's favourite aunt, who lived 10 minutes from the airport and in whose drive my, and my father's, car was always left before our trips across the Atlantic. She didn't let me down. The next call was to my boss, from whom I asked for a week of my annual leave. He wasn't happy. The fourth call was to Jude.

"So, you're flying across the pond."

"Yeh."

"You sure you're doing the right thing?"

"I'm not sure about anything but I've got to go. I can't explain it, Jude, but I've got to go and find him. I've got to stop him doing these things and I've got to understand it. Besides, what else is going on in my life?" To which he said nothing.

The fifth call was to Brad.

"You want me to come with you?"

"Brad, you're penniless!"

"Sure, but my new credit card isn't."

"They've given you a credit card?"

We both laughed and I was sorely tempted. Brad would be good company, so long as he stayed sober because I couldn't risk alienating the local cops. But, and I couldn't explain why, I felt this was something I had to do on my own.

"I'll phone you if I need you."

The final call was to my mother.

"What do you mean you're going to the US after your father?"

I imagined her standing in front of the fireplace, her favourite position when admonishing one of the children. She'd peer at me or my sister as if we were drunken drivers arguing about our fine, one of many my mother imposed during her fortnightly stints on the bench. Her back would be ramrod straight, hair pinned back in a bun so tight that at least there wouldn't be enough loose flesh for the familiar frown. Nevertheless, at these times, she always managed to look down her nose at me, even though she was at least several inches shorter. There were certain advantages to communicating by phone.

"Something's happening to Dad and I've got to find out what."

"The police think he killed a man and set fire to a house. Frankly, knowing your father, I'm inclined to believe it." I suppressed a sigh. "Honestly, I don't know why you spend so much time with the dreadful man."

"I know you don't."

I imagined the nose lifting even higher.

"You seem to become more rebellious the more you see him."

I let the sigh come this time. I was so used to this shit. It was part of a ritual we had to conduct whenever my father was mentioned and I was getting more than a bit pissed off with it.

"Look, Mother, we've been through this more times than you've been to educational conferences." I imagined the frown appearing across tight forehead. "I'm 26 years old; old enough to make up my own mind. I like him, he likes me, we have things in common, we get on." I paused, realising that not all of that was true, so I put some steel into my voice. "What is wrong with that?"

I knew she'd change tack abruptly and could almost see the hand appear, to be drawn across lined forehead. If I were there she'd shake her head, then sit down tentatively, as if feeling faint. The little woman, struggling against all odds to bring up her ungrateful, youngest child, a son who treated her so cruelly. Force hadn't worked and now it would be sympathy's turn.

"Nothing, I suppose. I just feel, darling, that he's such a bad influence upon you. His language, for example. You do see that, don't you?"

Normally, from this point, I'd just humour her, like I'd done all my life. But right then appeasement was not part of my mood.

"No, mother, frankly I do not." I knew her so well. She'd now be trying the weak smile and the eyes would be blinking rapidly, as if forcing back emotion. "It's not going to work, Mother."

If I were there she'd gaze at me for a while, as if her son were lost to her. She'd tried her best, God knows. Still maintaining the pretence. At all costs maintain the pretence. When she spoke it was as if she were making a great sacrifice.

"I see he has more influence over you than I."

"You're becoming paranoid about it, Mother. I'm going to the US for a bit and that's an end to it."

"I'm surprised you even bothered to tell me!"

The mask slipping for once.

"I had to tell you. You are my mother."

Bess paused to think of her grandmother. Uncle John was implying that she contrived her behaviour, like an actress, but everyone had always said, hadn't they, what a wonderful person Gran was?

He was still cutting the hedge. She'd always known how he felt about his mother of course but, at the moment, there was no substance to it.

There was one final thing I had to do before leaving. Using his computer I sent another email:

Dad

I'm at the cottage and I've found my file. You've settled your affairs, for Christ's sake! What the fuck's going on? Where did all that money come from? And who's the person in America you've made the bequest to? I'm sure it can't be Darlene or any of her family. The police say you've committed arson and murder and flown across the Atlantic to get away, or to kill someone else. It's 2.00pm Saturday. I'll be at Dorothy's tonight. Catching the Delta flight to Atlanta on Sunday. Meet me at the airport. Whatever it is, we can sort it out together.

Love Son.

Extract 4

After the lunch with Kevin I did a few hours at college and went home early, so I could be there when you and Rachel returned from school. The rain had cleared by mid-afternoon and the sun shone from a cold sky. We played football in the back garden. Since you were only 4½ I doubt you'll remember it. But I recall every kick, every call of joy and disappointment, every look and glance, even the blackbird that pulled worms by the pond and the chestnut mare with the white blaze that grazed in the neighbour's paddock. And your voices against the chill silence of winter. I remember those voices like it was yesterday. You see, I was conscious of the fact that this might be the last time we'd play free like this, without a sword above us.

I played in goal and the two of you took turns trying to score penalties. Rachel graciously allowed that you could take your kicks closer in than her but got increasingly frustrated when you began to score more goals. She started to demand that your penalty spot be taken back a metre or two. I could feel myself welling up every so often and let in a few goals I shouldn't have while trying to hide my emotions. Every time you scored, you'd put your hands up in triumph and Rachel would place her wrists on her hips and scowl. She was always so competitive; you less so.

I managed to engineer the score so it was 9-all – always first to 10 remember – and declared the game a draw. Amidst howls of protest I said I wanted to talk to your mother, so you should stay in the garden for a while.

She was peeling potatoes, a look of suppressed anger on her face.

"Have a nice game?"

She resented me playing with you while she cooked. I'd suggested many times that we reverse the rôles but she always rejected the idea with an irritated shake of the head. She never played with you. Certainly not in those days. Didn't know how to. Yet she resented *me* doing it. It was almost like, because she couldn't, I shouldn't. Now, I think it was also because I was playing with Rachel and Rachel didn't deserve to be played with. Whatever the reasons, her whole demeanour right then provided the motivation I needed to screw up my emotional courage, something I was then pretty short on.

"Saw a solicitor today."

She went very still. The only sound was Rachel's voice, carrying clear through the window.

"He said I should get a court order banning you from the house."

There was no reaction. Just that stillness. Then, slowly, she seemed to fold into herself, head almost disappearing into hunched shoulders, before exploding with rage. The potato peeler hit the edge of the sink and rebounded onto the window. To this day I don't know how it didn't break. I saw you and Rachel look up, then glance at each other but you made no attempt to come in.

"You can't do that! How can you do that, after all we've been through?!"

The words were spat out.

"I am thinking about what we've been through and particularly what Rachel's been through."

"Rachel! Rachel! You can't think of anything else but Rachel!"

She stormed into the front room and I followed. She was standing by the mantel, still kind of hunched up, silent, thinking.

"We can't go on like this, Stella."

"I'll kill myself." She looked at me for the first time, with that look of determination she has. "If you take my son from me I'll kill myself."

"You're crazy."

"Yes, I'm crazy. And I'll kill you and I'll kill that fucking Rachel."

I remember bizarrely thinking that's the first time I've heard her swear, before focusing on what she'd actually said. My mind was swimming, desperately seeking a way to calm her, but I couldn't find one. In the end I just walked away.

Later, when I'd supervised your bath, I read you both a story, as normal. You were so buoyant, so seemingly happy, so looking forward to Christmas. There'd been no incidents between your mother and Rachel that day and, when I kissed your sister goodnight, I made a decision. I'd wait til the New Year before deciding what to do.

Chapter 10

Sunday 12 May 2013 – Atlanta

Although it was only ten in the morning, the heat and humidity were already high, as Stafford exited the air-conditioned SUV. He spotted Hartley from a long way off, his tall, thin frame and blond curls all too familiar. The bright, red polo shirt, with diagonal yellow stripe, however, was not and was something he would never have imagined Hartley wearing. His arms were white, of course; he'd always been wedded to his desk, where he could impress potential clients with elegant, colonial surroundings and French polish, as well as good old American painters, such as the impressionist Colin Campbell Cooper and two Henry Farnys of Native Americans; all to demonstrate his equality and diversity, as well as support for the local culture. He and Stafford had almost identical upper middle-class backgrounds but Hartley had maintained his Home Counties accent, despite living in the Deep South for 25 years. "Good for business, old boy. Still impresses the Cousins, Yankee or Dixie." Yet here the man was, like an introvert at a party, on a school playing field covered with brightly-clad, diminutive children playing that most American of sports.

Stafford continued slowly and looked around. He'd already clocked the Lincoln Navigator parked to his right and glimpsed the two occupants ostentatiously staring at him through the surprisingly non-darkened glass. They were mere back-up, too far away from their master if anything went seriously wrong, placed deliberately to warn him that escape was futile. He scanned field margins as he walked. Half the onlookers were women and most of the men were accompanied by children, virtually all of them wearing team-shirts. So spotting the young man on a hillock to his left leaning against an old cedar was a piece of cake. He'd tried to disguise himself by discarding the suit jacket, which lay incongruously on the brown, dusty grass, doubtless covering his holstered revolver and getting dirty. But he couldn't disguise the fact that he was wearing a long-sleeved white business shirt, dark blue trousers and shiny, black shoes. He could imagine Hartley shouting at him, "For God's sake, this is a baseball field; take off that bloody tie!" And six yards to Hartley's right was an obvious ex-military type, in jeans, trainers and padded, green anorak; the latter to disguise the holster in his armpit. He must be sweating like a priest in a brothel, thought Stafford. The man wasn't looking at Hartley, though, or at the kids, but across the field, at a lone women peering through binoculars. If you were a parent, why would you bring binoculars to a kid's baseball game, when the field itself is less than 80 metres across, and why would you stand on your own, on the other side, away from the social action?

Hartley's back seemed to stiffen and he looked up, across the field towards the woman. Green Anorak actually touched his ear, as if adjusting a receiver. Stafford remembered Hartley liked to be called Colonel.

"I'm impressed, Dick. Sunday morning and you've got five operatives covering your back." Hartley turned quickly, as if surprised to see him.

"Tom!"

"Either I'm a dangerous bastard or you have too much money."

Stafford shook the offered hand and waited for the grasp of his forearm. The politician's grip that assured warmth and familiarity. The condescending smile was also recognizable. But the hair wasn't. Now he was closer, he could see that the trade mark yellow had become grey, just like his own. Time gets us all.

"You haven't changed a bit," lied Hartley, examining him closely. "Looks like you've had some sun back in the old country."

"Wind."

Hartley paused then snapped his fingers.

"Of course, the boating. How long's it been?"

"8 years."

"Has it really? Extraordinary."

Hartley kept smiling at him. Anyone looking on would believe he was genuinely pleased to see him.

"So why the muscle?"

Hartley shrugged his shoulders.

"Could be because you *are* a dangerous bastard, could be I've got money to burn, or maybe it's that I don't underestimate you. You know me. Don't trust anyone. Least of all ex-employees who turn up out of the blue and demand to see me on a Sunday morning." He glanced over at a huddle of red shirts about 20 yards away. "Or maybe I'm just getting paranoid in my old age."

"You were always paranoid. Are they armed?"

The smile disappeared suddenly and the eyes narrowed. That was another thing he remembered; the mannerism of switching instantly from hot to cold and vice versa.

"I should bloody well hope so."

Hartley looked away again. The children couldn't have been more than four or five years old and the huge helmets, contrasting with tiny bodies, made them look grotesque and misshapen, like goblins from a Disney cartoon. A red goblin was 'battering-up', practicing his swing with the little bat, just like he'd seen them do on Turner Field. The first ball went well wide and Hartley uttered a gasp.

"Are those the right helmets?" asked Stafford.

Hartley delved into a tracksuit pocket and extracted a tin of small mints, a practice he'd adopted after giving up smoking 20 years earlier. Stress reliever. He popped the sweet without looking and without offering one to his guest.

"The helmets went missing after an away game on Wednesday. Health and safety means they have to wear bloody helmets, so we borrowed some from the school's football team."

The second ball went straight through the batter, who didn't move a muscle and Hartley gave an even louder exhalation of breath as the umpire chimed, "Strike one!"

"Grandson?"

Hartley turned and glared for a few moments before nodding and Stafford juggled this knowledge. It wasn't that he hadn't imagined, before now, that this ruthless individual actually had a family. It was just that family was clearly no longer compartmentalised, as if he'd shifted into another stage of life; or maybe he'd simply accepted the inevitability of modern American culture, where everything is interrelated; where to show your 'feminine side' is considered cool.

"How's business?" asked Stafford.

He knew the answer, of course, considering the increasing number of conflicts around the world but it was an attempt to get the conversation on track. Hartley continued to look intensely at his grandson but he did turn his head slightly, as if he'd misheard, unable to hide the natural arrogance on his face.

"What do you want, Tom, a job?"

"Too old."

"I don't know, you look as if you can still handle yourself." Hartley still didn't turn. "And you've clearly still got your marbles. I always have a need for the more cerebral type."

The boy made an attempt at hitting the third ball but it was on the low side and he missed it by a mile.

"Strike two!"

Hartley cursed and shifted position. Stafford decided to get in quickly, before the boy was out and grandfather's mood deteriorated further.

"I want to buy something off you."

"Ordnance?"

"Passport."

Out at the crease the little grandson straightened the ill-fitting helmet and bravely squared up for his last delivery. A hush descended over the gathering and Stafford thought it would be all too much for a five year-old; his whole family, the whole team, were willing him to hit it. His entire future in the side might be dependent on this one hit. Maybe the boy was hoping the pitcher would miss his target, which would reverse the pressure, since they would both then be on their final ball. Then, if the pitcher threw the last one out, the boy could stroll to first base, triumphant, having faced it all down.

When it came, the ball was hip-height and straight as a dye; perfect delivery. It was missed by another mile and the grandson was out. He smashed his bat on the ground in a fit of rage and trudged angrily off the field, bursting into tears as he approached a tall blond in figure-hugging jeans. For some inexplicable reason everyone clapped, including Hartley and, sycophantically, Green Anorak.

"Unlucky," said Stafford.

Hartley turned, then, and gave him his full attention.

"Any particular passport?"

"French would be best. English or American would do. No Russian this time. I'll leave the name up to you."

"And you're going to need it *before* you leave these shores?"

"Yes."

"So, you have some business over here."

"Correct."

"You working for another agency?"

"It's not that kind of business; it's personal."

Hartley's expression didn't change.

"Any of the authorities interested in you?"

"Not yet."

"Okay. It'll cost you $3,000." Stafford hesitated. "You think that's a lot and for old time's sake I ought to let you have it for less?"

Stafford still said nothing. Hartley fished out another mint and looked away, at the family group.

"My dear chap, let's be candid. You were one of my best operatives and you were able to think on your feet when the situation changed, which of course it always bloody did." He shook his head as if thinking of his current crop. "So, I was genuinely sad when you put up your feet. No question. But, and this is the point, it was purely a business arrangement, I think you'll agree. You did jobs for me and I paid you bloody well for doing them. Bloody well."

At last, thought Stafford. This was the boss he knew and loathed. But it was the one he could deal with, like you would any tradesman. Even when he'd lived in Georgia several years ago, no more than 18 miles from Envisage's offices in downtown Atlanta, he'd made no attempt to get back in touch with Hartley, socially or professionally. It was meant to be a new start and, as far as he knew, Hartley hadn't even known of his domicile in Clayton County.

Stafford simply nodded in reply because, in fairness, what had just been said was perfectly true.

John was walking back up the path and she waited for him to arrive.

"Hartley's company, Envisage; what did it do exactly?"

He looked into the distance.

"The best way to describe it is it was a small, independent, intelligence unit. Large corporations and governments would pay it to take care of issues that they, themselves, couldn't or wouldn't deal with. I say large corporations because they were the only ones able to pay the huge fees Envisage demanded. I understand it wasn't simply field operations. It had analysts, too."

Bess followed his gaze, to the normality of the neatly trimmed hedge and beyond, to the badger wood.

"These field operations, were they military?"

"I'm sure they were, sometimes."

"And did they involve killing people?"

"Military operations usually do." She sought out the comfort of the wood again. "You having a problem with that?" he asked.

"I don't know. I've had so many shocks today. I need to think about it."

So she dropped the open manuscript onto her lap. Despite her uncle's prevarications, the indications were that her grandfather was a killer. Until now, though, that had been different; retribution on a gangster. Or even personal revenge on an ex-wife; that was also different somehow. She'd kind of put them to one side because the story was paramount.

"Killing people for money," she said. "That's different from killing for personal revenge or a sense of injustice or fighting for your country. Isn't it?"

"Maybe."

Certainly, she thought. Suddenly, the tale had taken another unpleasant turn and there was a foul taste in her mouth.

"When did you know?"

"About Envisage?

"Yes about Envisage."

"Not until later. It was a part of his life he kept from me."

"So you didn't know at the time all this happened?"

"Hadn't a clue." He continued to watch her, a non-committal gaze on his face. "You told me you were ready for this, lass. You sure you can handle it?"

Now she wasn't so sure. She wasn't sure at all.

"Yeh."

He squatted down and placed a hand on her forearm, believing every word she said, like he always did. He might not trust other women but he trusted her. He patted her arm before getting up and continuing to the shed, to put the shears away on their allotted nail.

She picked up the journal, needing to transport back to Georgia. Whatever the journal threw up, she had to know.

"I said I want to buy it from you," said Stafford.

"So you did," back to gazing at the family gathering, "so let me avail you of the process. Passports are not completed in house. As soon as I have the photo I'll need to pay someone to get it done. $3,000 is the going rate, to me, so I'm letting you have it at cost. That's for old times' sake. Anyone else they'd pay double. It'll take 48 hours, from tomorrow mornin'. So that'll be Wednesday mornin' then."

To Stafford's pleasure a slight Southern drawl had crept into the last two sentences, then the sound of a baseball being struck made him look over the field, to see one of grandson's teammates drop the bat and speed towards first base in a trail of dust. Hartley's gaze hadn't left the small group huddled around his grandson.

"Fair enough," said Stafford, "but, since it's a business arrangement, I need it sooner than that. I'll pay $4,500 for it to be completed within 24 hours from tomorrow morning. Here's the photo."

Hartley turned and stared down at the small, white envelope for a moment, then it disappeared into the back pocket of his Wranglers. He turned towards the fence, trying to get the attention of the family gathering and Stafford was able to give Green Anorak proper consideration. He was about 35, 5 feet 10 maybe and about 15 stone of gym muscle. He would have taken Stafford in and seen a man who looked as if he'd done the rounds. But he'd also have seen an old man, who'd be slow. So anorak just chewed gum contentedly and stared back, confident of his own physical superiority. Stafford knew the type well.

"You must have arranged a bank account over here," said Hartley, almost to himself.

Stafford didn't think that warranted a reply. In fact he'd had an American bank account for 13 years. A mobile phone started to burble. Hartley suddenly realised it was his and a hand dived into jeans' pocket. Stafford looked to the game.

"Doug! What can I do for you? ..... Yes ..... ha, as a matter of fact I do ..... did he really ..... extraordinary .... indeed ..... no need, he's standing right beside me."

Suddenly Hartley had his full attention.

"What time's his flight? ..... Okay, let me know and I'll have someone pick him up at the airport ..... I'm sure that can be arranged ..... and you."

The phone disappeared and Hartley stared at him.

"You going to tell me who that was or do I have to guess?"

"Before I say, I need to remind you of that confidentiality agreement you signed way back. It's still legally enforceable."

Stafford shook his head.

"Don't start treating me like an idiot, Dick. You and I both know that contract was never legally enforceable. The last thing you want is to take me to court, with all the subsequent publicity. People might actually find out what you do."

He felt Green Anorak moving towards him and so did Hartley.

"Leave it, Wade," said Hartley. He looked back at the family group. Finally, they were looking in his direction and the little grandson looked as if he was about to run over. But now Hartley didn't want it. He took Stafford's arm and steered him back towards his car, telling Anorak to stay where he was. Stafford stopped and looked back, forcing Hartley to drop his arm.

"Ever heard of Doug Reed?"

"No."

"Let's say he holds a very senior position in the CIA. He's also my main client."

"So how come he knows me."

Hartley looked into his eyes, the way very few people can; with the confidence and self-belief to know that you have enough power to deal with anyone, including the man standing in front of him.

"He has a very important acquaintance from the oil business. Augustus Bramble. Apparently, you saved his son's life, day before yesterday."

"I did?"

"Something about a flare?"

"Shit in a bucket!"

He'd totally forgotten about that. So, it'd been worthwhile after all. Amazing! But now, what he'd feared all along was about to happen. He just fucking knew it.

"He wants to meet you tomorrow morning, to thank you personally."

"Bramble?"

"Affirmative. He's flying in from Houston, early."

"Sorry, I have business tomorrow."

Hartley had completely abandoned his public demeanour.

"Tom, maybe you didn't hear me correctly. Reed is my main client. Besides, there's your passport to think about."

"Grandpa?"

Stafford stopped and looked back to the fence, now at least 20 metres away. A little boy with yellow hair had his face pressed against the wire. Hartley must have heard the cry but ignored it; merely gazed back into the hostile glare.

The main concern was how the CIA had known where to find him but there are always clues out there: a description of his military background on the visa, for example, and Bramble could have got a physical description from someone on the plane. He was well aware he didn't exactly look like an accountant. Also, the CIA have extensive files; once Reed had a name he could find out most things. Then, of course, there's the fact that he flew into Atlanta, which is where Envisage is based. Plus, Reed would have a file on

Hartley too and be able to see immediately they were at Sandhurst at roughly the same time. The phone call was probably speculation but logical.

"I'm keeping a low profile. I don't want publicity."

"That'll be made plain."

"Grandpa!"

Still Hartley remained fixed on Stafford.

"And the passport?"

"Tomorrow morning at 0900. Free of charge."

Stafford reached into the top pocket of his shirt and handed over a card. It simply said: Tom Stafford, SAILBOAT DELIVERIES, anywhere in the world, plus it gave mobile and email.

"Are we done?"

Stafford held the glare for a long time.

"We're done, for now," said Hartley, eventually.

Stafford glanced over at the wire fence but the grandson had given up. He felt Hartley watching him all the way to the vehicle.

Bess was struck by the contrast between the two views of her grandfather John was presenting. One struggling with his marriage - vulnerable and lacking in confidence - with this self-assured individual 20 years later. It was like they were two different people.

"You said you topped and tailed the stuff written by your father."

Her uncle looked up from his book and nodded.

"How much is it him and how much you?"

He didn't answer for a while.

"Good question. Of course it's 15 years since I wrote it, so difficult to remember details. To be fair, I think there is a bit of me in there. Some things I changed more than others, of course. But, apart from the stuff on the plane, I don't think I changed much. Just bits. All the conversations and his feelings I left as they were. I might have taken out or added a word here and there to avoid repetition and make it read better but, for the most part, it was an editing job."

"What about the Extracts?"

He shook his head and met her eye.

"I didn't change those at all. He wrote that stuff to me, as an explanation for his actions, and I didn't feel I had the right to change it. Besides, including the Extracts as part of the book wasn't part of our agreement. That was something I decided on, so they had to stand alone and untouched as part of his story."

That made sense to Bess and so typical of her uncle but it didn't totally explain the two different characters she was seeing. Maybe it was simply that her grandfather was at different stages of his life – 20 years between them – and that everyone changes that much. That normally we don't notice as we grow up with people. Maybe the events in 1992 were so traumatic that in themselves they changed him; hardened him, to the extent that he was prepared to kill his ex-wife. But then why wait 20 years to do it?

She could see that her uncle was about to take her back in time again. She knew it was going to be painful but she had to find the answers.

Extract 5

You won't remember that Christmas but it came and went much like every year. Too much food and drink, too much money spent, too many expectations, most of them unfulfilled. You got *The Flying Scotsman* to add to your Hornby trainset and we spent many hours in the play room. I also took the stabilizers off your bike. I ran along beside you in case you fell but you took to it first time, without so much as a wobble. Rachel read a lot and I read a lot to her. There was the odd eruption between her and your mother but nothing serious. It was as if Stella realised she had to behave, if she wanted to keep you.

By early February, I'd started to think that maybe, just maybe, this was rescuable. God, how naive I was back then! Almost the next day, war broke out. It was a long, wet Sunday, I remember, and we had to stay in all day. Even if I knew what started it, I've forgotten now. I do recall there'd been continual tension between your mother and Rachel. Then Stella started to harass her.

"Why should you have a chocolate bar when you've been a perfect little bitch all day?" "You deserve nothing." "Go away; get out of my sight!" And, when Rachel came and sat on my lap, because she really hadn't been a shit all day, "And get off your father's knee. You don't deserve it. In fact, go and stand in the hallway, and don't take a book with you!" And so it went on. And on and on. I remember asking Stella to ease off but it would just make her worse. "You're always on her side! Why are you always on her side?" Something, or someone, had to give and Rachel suddenly lost it.

"I hate you! I hate you!" she shouted, tears springing from her eyes.

"Oh, you hate me do you, you ungrateful little bitch."

Stella rushed towards Rachel, who backed up against the wall. I was far too slow and she'd hit your sister a few times before I got there. I placed myself in the middle and your mother started to hit me instead, all the frustration of the last two months in those blows. Soon, though, her brain got the better of her rage, as always, as she realised the futility of hurting herself more than she was hurting me. She stopped abruptly and stormed into the kitchen.

Rachel was sobbing and you were crying, too. You were both terrified. We all sat on the couch and hugged each other and I made innocuous, meaningless statements, like:

"It's all right. It's over now."

But actually, my chest was full and I was more frightened than I'd been on the Falklands, when we attacked the entrenched Argentine positions at Goose Green.

I took you into the play room in an attempt to get your mind on something else. Rachel came, too, holding my hand tightly. For once, she was content to simply watch quietly, while we played with your trainset. After a while I'd established some semblance of normality and we went back into the front room to watch TV. At one point, Rachel looked behind her to see if her mother was listening, then whispered in my ear.

"Dad. Can we get away and live somewhere else? Just you, me and John?"

I realised then what I should have seen before; what my 9 year old daughter had already grasped. I had to get her away, before it was too late. I put her to bed early; the same time as you, as it happens.

"You realise, Rachel that, if we leave, we can't take John."

"Why?"

I looked at the frightened face, wondering how I could tell her that, whilst her mother would have little problem with losing her daughter, she'd kick like a mustang if I took the apple of her eye.

"She doesn't have a problem with John," I said.

She was silent for a short while, twisting her hands in the flowered duvet.

"And if we take John she'll come after us," she said

"Yes."

"But if you only take me she won't."

I said nothing but she looked up at me then, such a sad look in her eyes I could have wept.

"All right," she said quietly and we schemed to leave home.

I guess I wasn't thinking straight, son. I was just desperate to save Rachel from any more cruelty; to get her to safety. And to do that I was prepared to leave you, knowing that no harm would come to you. At that moment, I was prepared to leave you behind.

Using the public call box down the lane, I phoned the College Chaplain. Remember, son, this is early '92, still in that wonderful era before mobile phones took over our lives. Kevin agreed to put us up for a couple of nights, while I got a small flat somewhere. Then I waited until about 10 o'clock that night, until Stella had fallen asleep on the couch like she always did. I crept upstairs and woke Rachel quietly. She was already dressed under the covers. I retrieved the small case we'd packed earlier and hidden under the bed, before gathering my daughter in my arms and creeping down the stairs.

I was as quiet as a mouse and I don't know what woke her, but we were just about to drive off when Stella suddenly appeared in front of the car, white nightdress blowing in the breeze.

Rachel seemed to gasp. I locked the doors and waited, hoping she'd come round the side and attempt to get in, but she just stayed in front of the car.

"What is she doing?" asked Rachel.

"I don't know but we can't move off while she's there."

I used the horn and edged forward and, eventually she moved away, shouting, "Go then!"

We bunked down at Kevin's dark, oak-panelled house.

"She won't hurt John?" he asked.

"No. We've talked about this, Kev."

Together with his wife, Rachel played the piano in the morning. Your sister was radiantly happy, John. When you think about her now, and how she was during those tragic years, you'd find it difficult to believe how joyful and full of hope she was on that bright morning. But she'd forgotten to pack certain things: clothes, toys and Jasper, her favourite cuddly. At midday I arrived back at the family home with a list.

You ran out to meet me. Maybe you remember it. Maybe not.

"Daddy, where have you been?" you asked, rather indignantly.

I stooped and took you in my arms and realised, in that moment, that I couldn't leave you; that I loved you more than life. In the same instant, of course, I realised that Rachel's dreams had just come crashing down.

I didn't handle the next few hours well. In fact, I went upstairs, got into bed and sobbed my guts up. Stella came in once in that time, saying something; I don't know what. I simply balled at her: "Get out!" and she did.

Later, much later, when I'd summoned up the will, I went to retrieve your sister. She was desolate. I tried to explain that I couldn't leave her brother. That he was part of our family.

"But, Dad, you promised we could get a place together; just you and me."

"I know I did, Darling. I'm sorry."

But I don't think, to this day, she's forgiven me.

"You can't bring out John as well?" Kevin asked.

"Stella would never agree to it in a million years and would probably carry out her threat to commit suicide."

"But Tom, I've said to you before, you can't be held responsible for her actions."

"And I've said to you before that I don't agree with you. I don't want my children growing up thinking I was responsible for their mother's death."

Bess had never been close to her mother, not in the way her childhood friends had been with theirs. Never able to discuss conflicts at school, menstruation, boyfriends. Her mother had always been more concerned with her own issues: her increasing size, the obnoxious neighbours, the injustice of having to survive on benefits, upping the dose on her anti-depressants, and Bess' absent father, who Bess had seen so infrequently since her birth. She'd always known her mother was mixed up - the constant sanity of Uncle John had been a comforting perspective - but now, for the first time, she was beginning to understand. And those endless arguments going back through the years were starting to work on her conscience.

She felt Uncle John placing one of his large cardigans over her bare shoulders. She hadn't even been aware of his approach.

"It's getting a bit nippy," he said, "so I'm fussing."

"Thanks." She wrapped the garment around her, like a blanket.

"Can I stay the night?"

"Can't put it down, hah?"

"Well, you said I can't take it with me and it will take a while. Wordiness is a family trait it seems."

The grin remained on his mouth.

"You can always leave it and come back another time."

She wasn't fooled.

"Very amusing. This is my family history, for which I have waited my entire life!"

He laughed loudly and a pair of pigeons flew out of a nearby alder.

"You'd better phone your house mates first. When are you due back at uni?"

"They won't notice I'm not there. Stop fussing."
"Give them a call".
"Yes, Uncle."
"There's a good niece. Spag bog for supper?"
"Great!"

She pressed speed dial and watched him walk slowly back to the house, broad shoulders swaying.

Chapter 11

Sunday 12 May 2013 – Atlanta - pm

By the time the big Boeing touched down I was beginning to seriously question my earlier conviction about coming to America. I'd had time to examine my earlier motivation, supposedly to prevent my father taking revenge on people, if that was what he was doing, for his own sake. How arrogant was that? Besides, whilst that motive was true in part, I was forced to recognise that the journey had less to do with a selfless act and more to do with my personal ambition; by using my father as an excuse for self-indulgence, to take a break from my dull life and add some interest before I died of boredom. So I wasn't feeling too good about myself as I headed for the exit. And to make matters worse I had no plan, other than to blindly hope Dad was going to meet me at the airport. And my mood was soon to deteriorate even further.

First-class passengers were let off first so, theoretically, I should have been well up in the queue for Immigration, but two things conspired against me. The first was a damned priest who I'd reluctantly befriended on the flight. He was struggling up the gangway with a giant, framed painting of Christ surrounded by angels and, since I was half his age and twice his size, I felt obliged to take it from him. This meant that I had to walk at the pace of his elderly sister, which was just above crawling speed and all the passengers of our plane had passed us by the time we reached Immigration. And that was the second problem; the fact that it was Hartsfield Atlanta, the busiest airport on the continent, and the International Arrivals Hall was already teeming with scores of long queues, from planes arriving every two minutes.

I knew that American customs were the slowest on the planet even before 9/11. "These days", Dad had said, "getting through Hartsfield immigration is the most mind-numbing experience of the modern world". I had puzzled over why quotes from my father kept ringing in my head and was beginning to resent the fact that his proclamations were proving to be true. So when, after over an hour, I finally stepped over the yellow line towards the booth and the priest called his refrain - "May God be with you, my son" – I wasn't in a happy place.

And the customs official didn't even glance at me. He was examining a computer monitor and fiddling with a mouse, contemptuous of the huge queues in front of him. It was a full 15 seconds or more before he looked up and asked for my papers.

"Have you been to the United States before?"

"This is my fourth visit."

"And what is the purpose of your visit?"

Only now did he really look at me, through black-rimmed spectacles, his dark, expressionless face covered in the pockmarks of childhood acne, although partially obscured by a goatee beard.

"Visiting relatives," I said.

He looked at me for a while before turning and running my passport through a code-reader. He waited, staring at his screen, then turned to me slowly, as if his neck was mechanical.

"Relatives?"

"My step-mother and step-sisters."

His gaze had not wavered.

"Go with this officer, please."

I turned to see a diminutive black woman, with golden brown hair and masses of bright-blue eye shadow, approaching the booth. She took my papers, including my passport.

"Would you follow me, please, sir?"

I have a self-awareness when I'm getting angry, partly because it's an emotion I don't feel very often and partly because a nerve twitches in my left temple. It was the lack of a reason that pissed me off most, as if I were a mere passport number. He didn't care a shit and in a way it was a form of contempt.

"Sir?" asked the woman.

I threw the ignorant customs official what I hoped was a venomous glance and nodded at the woman, then fumed for another hour, being completely ignored, in a room which was like a cheap hotel foyer, lined with slashed, vinyl bench seats, a chipped plastic counter and blank walls.

The tall man who came in, even to my untutored eye, had policeman written all over him. In place of a gun, though, a cell phone hung pretentiously from a thick leather belt. His goatee beard was the only hair above the collar of his denim shirt. He removed his shades and narrowed his eyes as he sought me out, then showed some identification at the desk and retrieved some documents.

I stood as he approached. We were of a height and I could feel him appraising me, as I had him.

"Mr Stafford?"

"Yes."

"Captain Taylor, Clayton County Police Department."

He held out his hand and I childishly left it alone. He nodded.

"I understand. You have a nine hour flight, take an age through immigration, then have to wait a further age for me, right? And I'm willing to bet my Braves' season ticket to a hog pie that no one in this shithole has offered you so much as a cup o' coffee. Am I right or am I right?"

"You're right."

"You're pissed. I'd feel the same. Here's your passport, by the way."

I felt contrite, suddenly.

"Thanks."

"What's your first port o' call?"

"Well, the first thing I need to do is retrieve my luggage from the turntable in the main concourse, if it's still there, then ….."

"It never got there. It's right outside the door. Searched o' course."

"Of course. In that case I'm heading for the nearest bar."

His face lit up like a beacon.

"Mind if I join ya?"

"I thought you weren't allowed to drink on duty."

He waved his hand in a gesture of dismissal.

"Nah. I got a driver up top. Besides, I'm off dooty."

I started to walk to the door, then stopped and looked at him.

"So I could simply walk away from this."

"Absolutely," he grinned and I couldn't help smiling back.

"I came in a bit of hurry and haven't had a chance to buy dollars, so what if I said the beer's on you."

He laughed this time.

"I've heard about you Brits being tight-fisted but I thought you at the very least stood ya own round."

"We do. I'll visit a *bureau de change* on the way. Incidentally, ….." I stopped and held out my hand. "Sorry about the hostility earlier. My name's John Stafford."

He chuckled as we shook hands.

"Rick Taylor."

As we entered the crowded underground train that would take us to the main terminus, he placed a finger over his lips, so we travelled in silence.

"How *are* the Braves doing this year?" I asked as I changed my pounds sterling.

He pushed his lips out and puffed in disgust.

"Not good, not good. Lost 7 to 4 against Detroit Tigers two weeks ago and that comes after a losing streak." He shook his head. "Defensively we're weak. You seen the Braves play?"

"My father took me, when I visited, twice. You won both times."

He squinted at me and nodded.

"Yeh, those were the days." A pause. "I still take my two boys, though."

We passed two bars in the busy concourse before finally reaching the one of his choosing and taking two bar stools in the corner. I swung round and took the place in. Everyone was well-dressed; no men who get their hands dirty during the day. One young woman close to us, in an olive-green suit, was flicking through a fashion magazine. A pretty bartender walked towards us before her face suddenly lit up.

"Hey, Rick!"

"Hey, Vicks, what's noo?"

"Nothin'." She turned her mouth up at one corner. "My life is wonderfully but boringly normal."

She looked at me in a quizzical kind of way and I returned her gaze. There was something about her face that was unexpected and I couldn't work it out. Everything seemed a little shortened and stretched out at the same time, like it was never constant.

"Who's your friend, Rick?" she asked.

"Oh, he's too young for you Vicks. Besides, he's a Brit and they prefer brunettes."

"You're a pig," she said and laughed at her own joke. "So, what's your pleasure?"

"Two cold ones. Large."

"Comin' up."

Taylor looked at me, suddenly serious.

"A year ago she was a druggie. She's clean at the moment, I think, but I like to drop in now and again to see how she's gettin' on and just to let her know

I'm keeping tabs, if ya know what I mean."

The beers arrived and I drained a quarter in one gulp, then drank some more. It was 'American pisswater' as my father calls it, but as far as I was concerned, at that moment, my father's views could go hang; it was nectar. Besides, the beer was here and he wasn't.

"Okay," said Taylor, fingering his goatee, "to business."

"I take it this visit is courtesy of dear old Inspector Foster."

"The very same," mimicking the Irish accent.

"All I've done recently is talk to policemen and priests."

"Priests?"

"Forget it. What do you know so far?"

"Okay. Good place to start. According to the Inspector, your pa is suspected of killing a British businessman and burnin' down a teacher's house. The Inspector would like to speak to him in relation to both felonies, although he has no evidence to arrest him at this point." He looked up with intelligent brown eyes. "Correct so far?"

"Yes, except that the so-called businessman my father is supposed to have killed was a Sheffield gangster."

"I did not know that." He paused. "Thank ya. Sheffield?"

"It's a large town in Yorkshire."

"Yorkshire?"

"In the North," I added.

He nodded, as if that was sufficient explanation.

"Your pa then flies to the US to, according to the good Inspector, possibly commit similar crimes over here. The Inspector believes he is on a revenge spree."

"He does believe that."

He stared at me for a while, his tongue licking his upper lip and the bottom of his moustache. The woman in the green suit was flicking magazine pages more quickly, irritated, as if resenting the fact that American airlines now required passengers to arrive three hours early for international flights.

"You follow him across to find him and ask him what the heck's goin on. Correct?"

I drained my glass.

"Correct."

Taylor nodded slowly and fingered his beard. I caught Vicks' eye.

"Same again?" I asked him and he drained his glass quickly, smiling.

"I've heard that too about you Brits; that ya drink like fish."

"Same again, please, lass."

She looked surprised.

"Hey, you really are a Brit."

"You mean Captain Taylor doesn't usually tell the truth?" I asked.

She thought about it.

"Yeah, I guess he does."

"Drinking beer is part of my religion," I said to Taylor. "An American Army friend of my father's told me once that he liked to have joint manoeuvres with the British because the first thing they do is set up the beer tent."

He laughed. I looked over at Vicks and saw she was watching me. When I looked back Taylor had a serious expression on his face.

"He was in the army your pa, wasn't he; Captain?"

"Yes."

"What unit?"

"Paratroopers."

"Tough outfit?"

"One of the toughest."

Vicks arrived with the beer and I decided it was time to state my case.

"Look Captain, I can see the way your mind is working, so let's get something straight." He was nodding. "My father knows how to kill a man, obviously. He did it in the Falklands with a gun and he could probably do it close up with a knife and his bare hands, too. Knowing how to kill was obviously part of his soldier's training, although we've never talked about it. I also think my father is capable of killing in self-defence. But that's as far as it goes. I do not believe he's committed these crimes he's suspected of," I lied. "Something is going on, though. He hasn't contacted me for ten days. That's rare. And he's flown here without telling me where he was going. That's unprecedented." I paused. "I'm here to find him and, as you say, discover what the heck it's all about."

He stared at me for a while, nodding and fingering his beard. Beyond him the woman threw the magazine down on her table and folded her arms. Her glass was empty.

"Well, that's mighty fine. Mighty fine." He removed a small notebook from his top pocket. It looked exactly like Foster's. "Your pa has family here I believe?"

"He married an American citizen in 2005 and lived here, of and on, until 2008, before moving back to the UK."

He didn't write down the information so he clearly already had it.

"Did the partnership end amicably?"

I stared at the woman in green and thought back on my conversation with Aunt Dorothy the previous night in Manchester.

"What's this all about, chuck?" she'd asked.

"I want to know what happened in America. Everything. I know he would have talked to you about it."

She looked immensely sad.

"His wife turned out to be crazy woman, who treated him like dirt and took all his money. He also lived with step-daughter from 'ell. He'd get Darlene to agree structure for 'er daughter, but she'd give up on first sign of disagreement. Your father were left to deal with rebellious teenager on 'is own. So are lot of people you might say but there were so many things." She shook her head. "When he tried to get Permanent Residence, US Immigration treated him like leper. After 3 years, he had to come back to UK after Darlene withdrew petition." Dorothy suddenly became more agitated. "She were terrible woman. I could tell that when I met 'er. I don't know how your father stuck it for so long. In fact I don't know why he married 'er in first place."

"I think he had other things, outside the house," suggested Terry, with his usual dose of oil on troubled waters.

"Yes, he did," said Dorothy, calming down and patting his hand on the couch beside her. "What was that charitable organisation 'e were member of?"

I'd remembered the awards on the cottage mantelpiece.

"Kiwanis," I said.

"That were it! Kiwanis." Dorothy gave me the benefit of her full set of dentures. "He spent a lot of spare time with them. I think that's where most of 'is friends came from."

"Do you know any of their names?" I'd asked.

She'd looked bereft, as if she'd committed an unforgiveable sin.

"Sorry."

I'd looked up at a family photo taken on a hill in Derbyshire. My father was there, walking with his woman of the time – a tall, leggy blonde - and I tried to get inspiration from it.

"He helped her with her real estate business, didn't he?" I'd asked.

"He did. Unfortunately, she were so disorganised that business never really took off. Tom weren't qualified realtor, so there were limit to what 'e could do, like. He ended up subsidising business out of 'is own capital and rescuing Darlene from poor decisions."

Dorothy had shaken her head sadly and I wondered how she knew all this and I didn't. Because she'd shown an interest.

"The craziness thing. How did that manifest itself?"

"Lots o' ways."

"Can you think of an example?"

"Let me see now." She'd put a finger to her lips. "Yes. Doesn't seem much, out of context like, but your father got award. I forget what it were called. As part of work of his ..... Kiwanis club he set up junior branch of that club, like, at local university, amongst undergraduates. Apparently, local Kiwanis crowd had been trying to set one up since Jesus Christ were a boy and your father came along and was catalyst in getting it going. Anyway, there were to be ceremony at university to mark formal chartering, I think that's what it were called, which Tom also organised. A lot of important dignitaries were expected to attend, including regional Kiwanis President, 'ead of university and local congressman. Darlene *were* invited but she refused to go, which were probably just as well, since she's got no social skills like." Dorothy grinned disarmingly, aware she was showing her prejudices. "Anyway, as you can imagine, this were very important night for Tom, and Darlene announced she were goin' to wreck it. She searched 'ouse for framed charter because without it ceremony couldn't take place. Fortunately, Tom had kept it in 'is car. She then threatened to turn up and shout insults at your father. He were convinced she were crazy enough to do it and that thought did wreck night for him."

"It was the Emory Award; the one they gave him," I'd said. "It's on his mantelpiece. He was proud of it."

"Yes." She paused. "There were lot of things like that."

I think she meant Darlene's behaviour.

"Then, of course, there were theft."

"I remember. She stole his car."

"Bit more than that. Day before 'e were due to leave, she stole 'is passport and plane ticket as well."

"Mr Stafford?" asked Taylor.

"Sorry. No, I don't think it ended well."

"Still married?"

"Yes."

"Children?"

"Two step-daughters."

He studied his notebook.

"I've got an address for your step-mother on Indian View Trail, Jonesboro. That still current?"

I recalled the address from the letter in the green file.

"As far as I'm aware."

"Would you say you were close to ya pa?"

I hesitated, just as I'd done with Foster. I'd always thought we were close but I was now beginning to question that confidence. Two days ago I'd known little of these problems Dad had had in America, nor of the battlefield promotion to major which was later rescinded, nor of this person who was so important in his life as to warrant a special bequest in his will.

"Yes," I said, "I think we're pretty close."

"Does he know you're comin?"

Again I hesitated because I didn't want to give him any vital information concerning my father but I didn't want to be caught out in a lie later either.

"Yes, I emailed him."

"Would he a got that?"

"Oh, yes. He has a smartphone and, if that isn't working, he has his laptop with him. He always checks his email."

"So, he could have come to the airport to meet ya, right?"

"Yes."

He grinned.

"And I've screwed that one up."

"Correct."

"In fact, he could be watching us right now."

I felt a constriction in my chest because Taylor was absolutely right.

"He could," I answered and willed myself not to look round. Taylor didn't either; just watched me.

"Where ya stayin? I'll drop ya."

I had to get rid of him. Any chance of seeing Dad depended on it.

"That's very kind of you but this was all done in a rush. I didn't have time to book. I need to hire a car, too."

"Not with that amount of alcohol inside you you don't. What city do ya want to be in?"

"Jonesboro."

"Well, I could take you to a good hotel or I can recommend Ma Paisley's place. It's a B & B; very comfortable."

"And somewhere you can keep tabs on me?"

He laughed out loud and Vicks glanced over at him.

"Yes." He said, as if it had two syllables. Ye'es. "Ya know, John, I like ya. So here's the thing. You are a welcome visitor to this county and your father, as far as I am aware, has not committed any crime over here."

"He hasn't committed any crime in the UK, either."

"Well, it's true we don't know for sure that he has. So, there ya go. I would just like to speak to him, man to man, like we're talking here. So, if you contact him, I'd be obliged if you'd give him my details."

It was my turn to nod.

"Fair enough," I said. I liked him better than Foster.

"In the meantime," he glanced at his watch, "it's 7.15pm. By the time we get you to Ma Paisley's it'll be 8 o'clock. That's well gone midnight UK time. You'll be too tired to do anything tonight."

I knew he was right and I knew I had to go with him. I paid the tab, leaving a big tip and Vicks gave me a rewarding smile. I scanned the faces waiting for arrivals in the main terminus but didn't see Dad.

Pretty soon, we were cruising down Tara Boulevard, its alien advertising hoardings mocking me. I felt very alone, all of a sudden. What was I doing here? What could I do? I wanted Dad. I wanted him to be here with me, telling me that none of this was true.

Extract 6

One thing that attack on Rachel did determine; I had to be rid of her; we all had to be rid of her. I remember a day in mid-February, standing outside Manton's office, pacing the car park, drumming up the courage. Men are such emotional cowards.

"I'm going for divorce, with custody of the children as part of it."

He wasn't writing anything this time but looking straight at me and nodding solemnly.

"It could be expensive."

"I don't care how expensive it is. Just rid my children of my wife."

"You know what my advice is," he offered. "After what you've just told me I could apply for the court order tomorrow."

"I know but it's too harsh and she'd probably end up committing suicide."

"What makes you say that?"

"She's already threatened it twice."

He shook his head, very slightly.

"And you believe her."

"I think she's capable of anything."

I told Stella as soon as I got home, while you and Rachel were playing outside. She collapsed on the couch.

"Please don't do it, Tom, please. I love you."

"Maybe," I remember saying, "but you don't love Rachel and you never will. That's the problem."

She was quiet for a while.

"I'll agree to the divorce if you take Rachel and leave John. Don't take John, please."

"I'm not separating the children."

Her demeanour changed instantly and I could see the hate in her eyes.

"Well I'm going to get a divorce from you and Rachel," she said.

And so a wretched seven month period began, where we were both living under the same roof, the proverbial daggers drawn.

Chapter 12

Monday 13 May 2013 - am - Jonesboro

Ma Paisley's dining room was all lace and chintz, vertical striped wallpaper exactly matching the three piece suite. Fake oil lamps (at least I assume they were fake) hung from all four walls and the ubiquitous Vivaldi's *Four Seasons* played softly from hidden speakers. One wall was dominated by a gargantuan tapestry, spelling out the words, 'In God we Trust', and seated right underneath it was a middle-aged couple, their smiles almost as wide as the breakfast table.

From one of the stripy chairs a white Pekinese hissed at me and Ma Paisley looked round. She turned and rushed towards me anxiously. Actually, that's not strictly true. Ma Paisley couldn't really rush anywhere on account of the fact that she weighed at least 300lbs. But she did kind of slither quickly, throwing hips forward and swinging arms as a counterbalance.

"Was the shower okay, honey?"

"It was fine, thank you, Mam."

I knew how to address American women. I'd heard my father do it.

"Well, you sit yourself down now, darlin," guiding me to a chair. "I'll get your breakfast right away."

"Mornin," said one of my table companions, his eyes taking me in like a salesman.

"Morning."

"Great mornin, init?" he continued.

"It certainly is."

"The Lord blesses us with his bounty," chorused his companion, her smile beaming across the table through lips so red I couldn't look at them. Unsure whether the comment required a reply, I simply smiled back.

A truly giant waffle arrived, on which four pieces of streaky bacon stretched hopefully, thin lines of what may have been meat vaguely discernible between the fat. Ma Paisley was just about to poor Maple syrup over them when I stopped her.

"Ya don't want syrup?"

"No, Mam, thank you. We don't do sweet and savoury together," I said by way of apology.

"Ya just gonna eat it like that?"

"Yes, Mam." Actually, I wanted some HP sauce but knew there wouldn't be any. "Some black coffee to go with it and I'll be fine."

I got up from the table as quickly as I could. I had to find my father and to do that I needed a car and an internet connection. I'd tried my mobile earlier and, despite organising a roving tariff before I left, I wasn't yet connected to a network. What's more, there was no wifi; I'd discovered last night that as far as Ma Paisley was concerned the World Wide Web was an organisation of crooked international bankers. So using the house-phone I dialled three local car rental companies until I found one with a 4x4. I didn't know where this journey was going to take me but I'd be prepared.

***

Augustus Bramble stared at the door through which Tom Stafford had just left.

"Colonel", he said, "what is it exactly your company does?"

"Well, Mr Bramble, let's say we, er, provide solutions to problems that others can't."

"Or won't, right?"

Bramble swung round in the silence and fixed Hartley with an intensity that could have cut diamonds. In most respects he was unprepossessing, being small, fat and bald. But he did have a Maharajah beard of bright red, streaked with grey. He also had startling cornflower eyes that commanded attention and he knew it.

"Right?"

"Right."

"And that includes causing mayhem and destruction."

"Only if necessary."

"And it often is, right?"

"Right."

Bramble nodded.

"What about problems that require intelligent observation as well?"

"Our specialism."

Despite the clear difference in their backgrounds, Bramble recognised a likeminded soul; a fellow businessman, who would do anything for a sale.

"Do you have something in mind, Mr Bramble?"

"Call me Gus, everyone does. Is Stafford still on your books?"

A slight hesitation.

"In my business, Gus, no one is ever completely off the books."

Bramble paced over to the leather couch and sat down.

"Sit down Colonel," as if it were his own Chesterfield and Hartley did as he was bid. "I run an oil company. It's called Legacy Oil. We're not in the same league as Exxon Mobil, or Shell or BP. We had a revenue of a mere 37 billion last financial year."

He paused to let Hartley attempt to look uninterested and was amused to see the Colonel actually licking his lips, like a child staring at a cookie jar.

"Now, when it comes to acquiring drilling licenses, the oil business is no different from any other; the big boys get the prime sites, such as those in the States and Saudi." He shrugged. "I'm not complaining. That's the way it is. You have to get yourself to the position where you are one of the big guys." He grinned with a mouthful of perfect teeth. "But until that glorious day we have to purchase licenses in other, often less stable countries. At Legacy we drill mainly in Africa: Nigeria, Tanzania, Angola and," he raised red eyebrows, "in Libya. And it's there we have a problem - midstream - the pipeline to our extraction point near Tripoli."

Hartley leaned across to a ceramic jug. It was probably a pre-Revolutionary antique, worth a small fortune, thought Bramble and bought simply to impress potential clients. He had a few pieces of his own, bought for exactly the same purpose.

"More coffee, Gus?"

"No. We'd been trying to get into Libya for a while and were looking to purchase some drilling licenses in certain undeveloped fields. Trouble was, in a secret deal, the new National Transitional Council guaranteed France 35% of all new oil contracts and, shortly after, the newly formed General National Congress of Libya froze any more issues of oil drilling licenses."

He paused to ensure he still had his listener's attention.

129

"So what did you do?" asked Hartley.

"Plan B. We noticed that, in October 2011, the British company, Heritage Oil, purchased a 51% stake in a Libyan outfit called Sahara Oil Holdings, which already held drilling licenses and rights. Smart move, we thought, so we copied. And imitation is the most sincere form of flattery, right?"

"Right."

"Pretty soon we were pumping oil. Everything was working fine but we hadn't calculated on the Sovs."

"The Sovs?"

"Yeh. What you have to appreciate, Colonel, is that Libya is not governed by the General National Congress or its executive branch. It's run by the militias, hundreds of the bastards, virtually none of which were disbanded post-Gaddafi and new ones are sprouting like mushrooms in horse shit. The police and the army are completely useless. Totally, fucking useless!" He raised a finger. "And our pipeline has been locked off by one of these militias. So we sent someone in. Before he was beheaded he reported that the militia controlling the pipeline were being financed by the Sovs. Because they didn't help in the civil war, they have little influence in Libya. But they do want to cause mayhem and destruction."

"The Russians?" asked Hartley.

"Yeh, the Russians! Who do you think I've been talking about?" He brought the bushy red eyebrows together and fixed Hartley with a look of venom. "I want Stafford to sort it out." Slowly Hartley placed his cup on its saucer and returned it to the ornate tray. "That a problem, Colonel."

"It's just that I know Tom is not in business at the moment. I have other operatives who could do the job for you, although it does sound like a solution will be difficult."

"I thought you said no one is ever off the books."

"That's true but ....."

"Doug Reed emailed Stafford's personnel file while I was on the plane last night. Not only does he speak Arabic, he's also fluent in Russian and French. Did you know that?"

"Yes I did?"

"That could be very useful, bearing in mind who we're up against. Now I've met him I know he's the man I want. I may not know much about your business, Colonel, but I do know men." He shook his head. "Besides, it's fated. I'm a religious person, Colonel. It's too much of a coincidence that this man recognised that flare for what it was, had the courage to report it, save my son from certain death and, to top it all, be the perfect instrument for solving my problem in Libya. May the Lord be praised!"

"Praise him," echoed Hartley but a nerve had started to twitch in his cheek Bramble noticed.

"You don't agree that Stafford is the man for the job?"

"Oh, I agree with you there. When it comes to my business, as you put it, there are two key qualities that an operative should possess: an ability to think on his or her feet and, if necessary, complete ruthlessness. Tom Stafford has both in spades."

"And he's done this kind of thing before."

"Not exactly like this but similar. A number of times, actually."

"Could I see his operations file."

Hartley shook his head vigorously.

"Absolutely not. It's commercially sensitive and confidential."

"As a potential client I'm glad you said that but I don't see your problem."

Hartley took a deep breath.

"The problem is that Tom moved out of the business some time ago and went his own way."

"Colonel, I thought of approaching Stafford myself but I suspect he would benefit from your logistical resources for an operation such as this." Hartley nodded slowly. "This pipeline blockage is costing me nearly $100,000 a day and that's not including lack of revenue. I'm prepared to offer you half a million to unblock it."

The crack of a smile creased Hartley's face for the first time.

"I'm afraid it will cost you more than that, Gus. Expenses for this trip would be high. It would need a team, vehicles and plenty of ordnance, all of which would need to be purchased in North Africa."

Bramble grinned, too, took out his phone and dialled. It was answered after only two rings.

"Doug, Gus."

"I know who it is Gus. Even though it's a scrambled phone your name comes up on the display."

"Well that's wonderful Doug. If we can just move along here. I have a problem, as you know, with my pipeline in Western Libya."

"Gus, I've already told you that we can't help you with that. We can' be seen to have the United States interfering in Libyan ....."

"I know you said that but my problem is the Sovs have gotten involved."

"Russians, Gus, Russians. No one calls them Soviets anymore."

"Yeh, yeh, well the point is I've found the man for the job. The beauty of it is he's not even American, he's a Brit. You won't have to deny a thing."

"You're talking about Stafford."

"How'd you know that?"

"I sent you his file, remember?"

"Right. Anyway, not only has he done this sort of thing before, not only does he speak Arabic and Russian, but now I've met him I know he's my boy. All I want from you is intelligence. You'll be working through the Colonel here at Envisage. He'll provide logistical support. What do ya say?"

There was a long silence.

"Doug?"

"Put your cell on speaker."

Bramble pressed a button and Hartley moved over.

"Morning Doug."

"Dick. What do you think?"

"Well, I don't know enough about it to verify its feasibility at this point. But as to whether Tom Stafford's the man for the job I would say 'yes'. The problem's going to be persuading him of the fact," he glanced at Bramble, "and I suspect it will take a lot of money to do that."

"Well, that's down to Gus. Okay Gus, I'll help you with the intelligence. But as far as anyone else is concerned, including any member of the Administration to which I belong, this is a private deal between you and Dick, and I have absolutely nothing to do with it."

"Thanks, Doug. Understood. Speak to you soon."

Bramble returned phone to pocket and turned to Hartley, who'd already moved back to his comfortable couch.

"How much will it take?"

Bramble watched him smooth the crease that ran down the middle of an immaculately cut trouser leg, then look up with a self-satisfied smile.

Bess saw her uncle was leaving for the house, so she quickly asked the question that had been bothering her.

"This part, with Bramble and Hartley; you must have made it up. Neither you nor your father were there."

She could see his eyes moving slightly from side to side, a mannerism she'd noticed many times before, when he was thinking hard or finding it difficult to remember something.

"Must have done. It had to happen something like that because of what happens later. I guess I inserted it to try and explain why Dad was asked to do the Libya job and, probably, to give some idea of the character of Bramble."

That seemed unlikely to her, unnecessary, but she said no more.

***

A police car cruised by as I drove the jeep out of the parking lot. Was it my imagination or did the officer look me straight in the eye? There had to be somewhere locally with a broadband connection for Christ's sake; this was America! After much searching for a computer shop I turned off into a tiny, outdoor shopping mall, with a car park that could have held every vehicle in Jonesboro and still run the county show. Mirage shimmered on distant tarmac and, like Lawrence of Arabia, I set out across it, feeling like I ought to have brought a packed lunch. And there, in the distance, was a Jonesboro Computing sign.

From behind the main counter a man about my own age, wearing a turned round baseball cap, smiled his welcome.

"Can I help you, buddy?"

"Yes, my smartphone isn't working and I'm looking for somewhere in Jonesboro where I can get wifi for my laptop."

"Hah, this is Hicksville, USA, buddy. Some of the sports bars offer it. Where you from?"

"I'm from the UK."

"No kiddin. Tell you what, just to show we treat our visitors well." He moved to a spare table. "Just sit yourself down there. You can hook onto mine. No password needed."

"Thanks."

"You're welcome. I'm fixin to make some coffee. Ya want some."

It seemed churlish to say 'no'.

"That'd be great, thanks. Black, no sugar."

"Comin right up."

I logged on and downloaded my private email, clenching my fist in the hope that he'd sent one. And there it was, fourth in a list of seven. It was an email address I'd never seen before - 'Beauwolf1' – so mockingly pompous, it couldn't have been anyone but him.

Hi Son

Sorry about all this. Hopefully, things will become clearer for you. You looked great at the airport, by the way. Fitter than the last time I saw you. I wanted to walk over and hug you but I wouldn't have done it, even if you hadn't been with the cop. It's not time.

I know you have masses of questions, and I want to answer them, but it's better if you discover most of the answers for yourself. That way you might understand what I'm doing, maybe even empathise with it a little. Maybe not. You were always an independently-minded bugger. Always fair-minded, even if it involved criticising me. And you do it so politely. Do you remember that time when we went to collect your sister's rental deposit from her ex-landlord? You were about 13. Afterwards, you looked at me and said: "Don't you think you were a bit hard on him." And, when I thought about it, I realised you were right. .....

"Here's your coffee, Bud."

I looked up and thanked the man, taking a sip and managing not to grimace.

"Great," I said.

..... You have better judgment than I. I don't mind admitting it. You're more able to consider perspective and speculate from it. That's one of the reasons why you're never happy with the girl you're with. She always fails to live up to your expectations. Sometimes you have to go with what your gut tells you. You'll make mistakes but you, more than anyone I know, will learn from them.

So ask around, Son. Visit Darlene and see what you think. She's still alive! 8040 Indian View Trail.

Remember this, though, I love you. I'll check in again later.

Dad.

I expelled air and read it through again. From a factual point of view he'd told me nothing, for Christ's sake! Absolutely, fucking nothing! He was dangling me on a hook, like one of his damned fish! And he'd asked me no questions; just suggested I visit his wife. What the hell did he think I was over here for, to make fucking social calls?! All this time waiting for him to contact me and, when he does, I'm no better off. Worse. By refusing to deny the allegations he was tacitly accepting them.

I placed my head in my hands. Feeling angry with my father was a new phenomenon and I could feel a pain starting over my left eye as I went through the other emails.

Three were spam, which I quickly deleted. One was from my mother demanding I contact her. The other two were from Brad and Jude, making jokes about policeman. I realised, then, how much I missed them. I banged back some non-committal replies and thought about a response to my father. It would serve him right if I simply ignored him but what would be the point?

Dad

You need to meet me and you need to talk to me. That's why I'm here, damnit! Townsend sounds like a total arsehole but what about this principal? What happened there? Why are you in Georgia? Who is it you're taking revenge on over here? I assume that's what you're doing. And why now, Dad? This stuff happened years ago. Speak to me!

John.

PS: Captain Taylor, of the Jonesboro Police Department, would like to speak to you. I said I'd pass on the message. Seems like a nice guy.

I drank as much of the coffee as I could bear, logged off and headed for the door. I was still the only other person in the store.

"I really appreciate that," I said to the guy, "and the coffee was great."

"You're welcome. Any time you want to get your email, just come on in and log on."

"That's very kind of you but I'm hoping my smartphone will be working soon."

"How long you staying?"

I hesitated.

"That depends."

"Well, maybe you'll fancy a beer sometime." He gave me his card. "I'd like to hear about Europe. Give me a call."

I'd noticed that before; Americans think of Britain as if it were part of some United States of Europe. I want to say, "How the hell should I know what's happening in Europe, I come from the UK." But here was a total stranger holding out a hand of friendship, so I stayed silent and smiled my gratitude.

"Sounds good."

Extract 7

The divorce and custody processes began reasonably enough because I started seeing Helen, the keep-fit teacher. She knew I was married, of course. So was she. But her marriage was barren of affection and interest, and she was beginning to realise she'd never really loved her husband, whom she'd married when 17. Anyway, she said she sensed something in me and wrote a letter. There was a number and I phoned. Temptation, you see, son. Gets you in the end. The chance of some female company. Someone sympathetic to talk to. I told her everything. She became my liferaft in a crashing sea and, to be honest, I don't think I could have gone through that time without her. It was, after all, 20 years ago and I wasn't as mentally strong as I am now, nor as knowledgeable. I saw her about twice a week, although I didn't actually 'know her', in the biblical sense, until after the custody hearing. If your mother found out about her I wanted to be able to say truthfully that it was not a sexual relationship. As such, I had not committed adultery. No, I saw her for the company, for some peace in a crazy world, because there was some shit going down, son.

It really started when Stella first saw a solicitor because, that night, she began making up to Rachel. I guess the solicitor had asked her: "So, how are things between yourself and your daughter?" and she'd most likely answered truthfully. And the solicitor had probably said: "Well, Mrs Stafford, if you want custody of your son, possession of the house and the bulk of the family finances, you'd better improve the relationship." Accordingly, she set out, coldly and cynically to do just that. It was sickening to watch and the most difficult thing to take over the next months. It was what Rachel had always wanted, of course; a mother who gave her positive attention and, apparently, love. How could I tell your sister that what she was seeing wasn't real? That her mother had already offered her to me in a deal that would have split the family in two?

So, I gritted my teeth and ploughed on and I still felt in those early months that the initiative was on my side. Three days after my first affidavit was submitted, listing the reasons for the divorce, mainly the terrorising of Rachel, Stella came home in a rage.

"I'm changing my solicitor!" she shouted and we all walked around on egg shells for a few days.

Kevin was adamant.

"They have to talk to Rachel."

"Who?"

"The Court Welfare Officers, of course!"

"So far they haven't even contacted me."

The next phase in your mother's campaign meant a complete change of tack. Threats hadn't worked, so now it was sympathy's turn. She pleaded with me every night after you and Rachel were in bed. I found it so difficult that, sometimes, I just had to go out and hope she'd fallen asleep on the couch before I got back.

Since the day I started the proceedings, I'd slept in the study. I bought an MFI single bed and mattress, which was surprisingly comfortable. One night she attempted to get into bed beside me. You'd think I'd have succumbed; after all I'd been celibate for a while. But I had such contempt for her it wasn't even a possibility. Eventually, I manhandled her back to her room and the next day put a lock on the door.

The next night she collapsed on the floor after you and Rachel had gone to bed. Just collapsed. I phoned the doctor and she spilled the story to him. How she couldn't cope with my actions.

"You're taking the children away from her and she can't handle it," our doctor said.

I saw myself painted as the ogre and didn't like it. When she was asleep I went round to see Kevin.

"You must tell people now," he said. "You have no choice."

So, the next day I saw the doctor and told him about your mother's treatment of your sister. He was gobsmacked and called in the Health Visitor and I had to tell the story all over again. It was the first time I'd told anyone in authority and it felt really good. They decided they'd have to tell Social Services, to which I willingly consented. It's impossible for you to imagine the relief I felt. At last, I thought, someone official is going to help me and the very next day I went round to see the social worker in her office, full of expectation.

She picked me up from the communal area but didn't shake my hand.

"I'm Claire Saunders and I've been assigned as your case worker," she said, in a manner which suggested she wished she hadn't.

She was about 35, I guess and small, with thick-rimmed specs and frizzy, ginger hair that stuck out from the sides of her head in wedges. That sounds like I'm expressing certain prejudices and maybe I am, but I'm also being factual. She wore a shapeless, brown shift, that terminated at the knee, below which she had green Wellington boots - I kid you not - with traces of mud on the heels. As I followed her to her office, I forced myself to keep an open mind. I was still maintaining that approach when I told my story for the third time in two days and she rarely made eye-contact.

"Of course, I'll have to speak to your wife."

"Of course. You do realise she'll deny everything."

"We'll see."

She arrived at the house that evening, wearing the same wellies, although she did take them off at the door. I took the children into the garden so the two women could talk. I came into the kitchen once, to get some drinks. It was April now and the evenings were getting warmer. I overheard Stella saying: "Oh yes, they have a lovely home here. I just don't understand all this." She sounded so reasonable; so believable. But I didn't interrupt. Perhaps I should have.

Claire Saunders, wellies back on, came out to see me and I sent the children inside. Again, she refused to make eye-contact and I knew what was coming.

"Mr Stafford. Good of you to give us time on our own. Stella denies your accusations."

"I told you she would."

"Yes," looking away into the field, where the chestnut blaze innocently grazed. "I shall have to consider everything that has been said to me," biting her lip.

"You don't believe me, do you?"

She didn't answer but she did look at me, then, like a soul gazing at a dying man and my heart dropped into my stomach.

She turned to leave and I called after her.

"Have you been a social worker long, Claire?"

"No, actually only a few months."

You'll have gathered by now, son, that I was not surprised by this news.

"What did you do before?"

She stopped and looked back.

"I was a nun," she said. It was the first and only time I saw her smile.

I remember not being very communicative that night and both you and Rachel sensed it. I didn't read to either of you and you didn't push it, for which I was grateful.

"She didn't believe you, did she?" purred Stella, like a cat that's stolen the cream.

Later I went round to Kevin's for support.

"I'm frightened, Kev. All of them thought I was lying. She's so believable. She's so good at it."

"Stella?"

"Who else?!"

"I know. Are you sure you can win, John?"

I can't remember my response but I recall his next question.

"What will you do if she wins?"

"She won't win. I simply can't countenance it, Kev."

"But you have to. What will you do if she does?"

"I don't know. Take them away, to another country; start a new life. I just don't know."

Chapter 13

Indian View Trail sounds idyllic. In fact, it's in the middle of a pretty rough sub-division in South Jonesboro, among several similarly named streets, like Cherokee Walk and Sioux Trace. Most of the houses were in need of repair and a coat of paint, front lawns were generally bare of grass and concrete driveways were littered with discarded bicycles or ancient, wheelless trucks propped up on repair ramps. Garages were single, mostly open and mostly full of surplus junk that families had forgotten years ago. Netless basketball hoops hung from walls at odd angles and a small group of black kids listlessly played baseball in the middle of a dusty road, wooden planks strategically placed in front of storm drains to prevent ball loss.

8040, from where I stopped the car, looked comparatively smart. For a start it was all-brick and had what looked like a new roof. The house side, door and window frames were painted with a pastel yellow, that wasn't faded, and the green grass out front had been mown recently. A smart, black Acura stood in the driveway. So, she was in. I felt nervous, suddenly. What could I say to her? What was my plan? Dorothy's words were still echoing in my head after she'd told me about the car theft.

"I think there were threats from her side of the family."

As I drove up to park behind the Acura I noticed a few things I'd missed from a distance. To begin with, the car had a large scrape along one side, from the front wing to the boot. The damage looked old; rust spots showing through bare metal. Also, a deep, unguarded trench stretched halfway from the front door to the road, a muddy spade almost buried in surplus red soil. To the side of the house that was visible, a woman's bicycle lay on its side, on top of a pile of rusted yard signs proclaiming 'Bentley Properties – Home for Sale'.

A silver lizard darted out of my way as I stepped up to the front porch and pressed the bell. Nothing happened, so I hit the knocker. I felt the sun hot on my shoulders, then Darlene opened the door in white T-shirt and black tracksuit bottoms. A pair of what looked like brand new Nike trainers sat on her feet. She'd put on a few pounds since I'd last seen her, 7 years ago, and she looked older; much older. Her long black hair was grey at the roots and, not expecting visitors, she wore no makeup. The baggy T-shirt had 'Christians for World Peace' written on it in red. There was no recognition in the distant eyes.

"Darlene, it's John." I waited but there was still nothing. "Your step-son."

She drew in breath sharply, hand flying to mouth.

"John!"

I smiled weakly.

"I'm sorry about the surprise visit but I didn't have your number."

Shock still registered on her face as we stared at each other. Finally, she snapped out of it.

"Come in. Come in"

I expected a sudden drop in temperature as I entered but the air-conditioning was obviously switched off. The front door opened straight onto the living room and I noticed immediately it's bare, white walls and well-worn couch. An ancient TV – a model discarded by most Brits 10 years ago - crouched unhappily in a corner, surrounded by an untidy scattering of DVDs. There was no decoration, or plants, or adornment of any kind, apart from a few photos, in extravagantly ornate frames, perched on a low, dusty dresser. One was of Darlene and my father at their wedding. Beside it was a pile of business cards. Darlene was smiling up at me, still in confusion.

"Well! Well!" She turned to what looked like a kitchen. "I've no beer I'm afraid but I have Diet Coke."

"Water will be fine, thanks."

She scratched her arm, looking embarrassed.

"Well, I have a problem with the water. Did you see that trench out front? Well, I have a fractured pipe and the water leaked out." She didn't speak with a real Southern accent and I remembered she was from Indiana. "The water bill was so high I couldn't pay it, so the water company cut off my water. Can you believe that? I can't shower or even make a cup o' coffee." I didn't quite know how to respond to this, so I just shook my head in what I hoped was a sympathetic way. "I'm making progress on the trench but I'm just so busy, I can't do it all. Did you want that Diet?"

"That'll be fine. Thank you."

I followed her into the kitchen, the draining board and one work-surface covered in unwashed dishes.

"And you can't even wash up."

"No!"

The word held all the anguish of a woman hard-done-by. She opened the cavernous fridge on nothing but Diet Coke cans and cracked two open. While she did so I strolled to the window and looked out on the back garden. The window was open, presumably to create a through draft to the open window in the front. A tasteful deck, with attractive lamps, led onto long grass, from which more discarded yard signs protruded in confusion.

"There you go," as she passed the can to me. "Well, it's great to see you, John. Are you on holiday or what?"

"Kind of." Change the subject. "Can't Samantha and Wendy help you with the water leak?"

"Well, Wendy lives with her boyfriend most of the time. I told her I did not approve of her doing that, outside the sanctity of marriage. I'm very particular about that. But she went ahead and did it anyway."

Darlene looked indignant but frankly that was something I couldn't blame Wendy for. She was 15 when I'd last seen her and a total pain in the arse but in her position I'd have left this house in a heartbeat.

"But can't her and her boyfriend help you dig?"

Darlene examined the vinyl floor of black and white squares.

"I guess."

She said it like it was a question that had not occurred to her.

"What about Samantha and her boyfriend?"

We'd moved through to the living room and she sat down on a well-worn chair. It rocked back immediately and a foot rest shot out from its base with a thump loud enough to make me jump.

"Well, Samantha married Josh, a year or two back now, but I am not yet a grandmother." So, she'd married him. Darlene was smiling to herself. "But I am hopeful."

And I'm sure they're going to bring a new baby round here a lot, I thought.

"But can't they come and help you with the water leak?" I persisted.

"I guess." Then a thought seemed to occur to her. "But even when I've fixed the leak, I've still got to pay the bill."

"How much is it?"

"$643."

I swigged the Diet Coke. I'd forgotten the metallic taste.

"How long have you been without water?"

"Umm, about a week, ten days."

"And your daughters know that?"

She'd finally twigged where I was going with this and looked uncomfortable. In fact, she put her head down, got up and rushed out of the room.

"Shit," I said under my breath. What the fuck was I doing? This was not why I was here. But what *was* I doing here? I waited 10 minutes, staring at those blank walls and cursing my father. Finally, Darlene came back, dabbing her eyes with toilet tissue. She'd added some eye-makeup and her previously white face was less pale. She'd also changed her T-shirt. This one was plain, sky blue and tight-fitting.

"I'm so sorry about that. What must you think of me?"

"It's all right. I'm sorry I upset you." I hesitated as she looked at me in a kind of sheepish way. "I guess real estate is tricky at the moment?"

"Hmm," she smiled. "Your father used to use that word; 'tricky'. I do miss him."

She looked into the distance, as if remembering some past experience. I had to raise the matter of Dad at some point, and this seemed an ideal opportunity, but I wasn't ready for it yet.

"So, real estate is going through a bad time," I persisted.

"Yes, it's so hard at the minute. As you probably know we had the Credit Crunch and the economy was in such a bad way. The bottom has fallen through in the property market across the whole country and it's even worse locally. There are so many realtors around here and Clayton County is a desert for selling houses. There's simply no value in them. So many blacks have moved into the area that many white folks are in negative equity." Darlene looked at me hard. "I am not racist, John, but they do bring the value of your property down so. There's no doubt about that."

I didn't know what to say, again, so I kept quiet. There was a sound from outside and I looked up to see the French windows in the dining area slide open and a young woman step through. Her face was in shadow and, as I stood up, she rushed towards me, then stopped suddenly. Her expression, once full of anger, changed to surprise.

"Hello Samantha," I said.

"John!" Well at least *she* recognised me. "I thought you were your father."

"Why would you think that?" knowing what the answer was going to be.

Samantha was petite and pretty, I'd always thought but, as I watched, her face took on a look of absolute loathing again.

"Because he's just beaten up my husband!"

I took a deep breath, my mind full of questions. Darlene had stood, hand to mouth.

"Tom is here, too?"

Samantha was still looking at me.

"You're not surprised," she said.

I always thought she was the intelligent one of the family, as well.

"Where's Josh now?" I asked.

Samantha's hateful gaze hadn't left me.

"In the car," she said eventually.

Thinking the Jeep was Dad's he'd obviously decided to stay in the car and send his wife in by the back door on his behalf. Real brave. Darlene was flapping her arms like a mother hen.

"Bring him in! Bring him in!" she said.

Samantha finally dragged her eyes away from me and stalked to the front door. Well, at least he's still alive, was my main thought.

Josh tried to hold himself erect when he came in, to his full six foot six, but he failed, the pain of his injuries inclining him forward. Apart from his height and what must be 19 stone weight, there was nothing I recognised about him. Seven years ago he'd had dreadlocks; some throwback to his Caribbean heritage. Now his hair was cut as close as mine. And his face was unrecognisable. With its natural darkness, combined with the dimness of Darlene's front room, I couldn't make out the details, but it looked a mess of swollen flesh and blood. The main pain seemed to be from his side, though, which he was grasping with both hands. Darlene was speaking through a hand clasped to her mouth.

"Oh my God! Oh my God!" and then, "I have no water. Oh my God!"

"Just get a clean towel, Mom!" shouted Samantha and Darlene rushed off.

"What happened, Josh?" I asked.

Darlene had returned with the towel before he answered.

"He kicked me when I was down," he mumbled through puffy lips.

"What happened," I persisted.

Samantha, dabbing ineffectually at the blood, shot me another look of venom.

"He phoned and asked to meet me," continued Josh. "In the games field behind this sub-division."

"Go on."

Samantha gave me that look again.

"It's hurting him to talk, can't you see that?"

"He called me an arsehole," said Josh indignantly.

"Is that when you went for him?" I asked.

He looked up at me and I knew the answer. He must have been so confident. And then, incongruously, I felt angry again. Really angry. There was more than Josh behind it, I knew. I also knew how destructive my anger could be and was usually able to control it.

"You stole his car didn't you? And I suspect there's a lot more you did to him. You are an arsehole."

He must have felt my contempt and launched himself off the couch. Samantha and Darlene both screamed, "No!" I planted my feet and braced myself, amazed there was no fear. "First rule, Son; always get in the first punch." I was just about to throw a right when he collapsed at my feet, spurting blood all over Darlene's beige carpet. She still had hand to mouth and seemed to be hyperventilating. Samantha dived on top of Josh, full of concern. I moved to one side to give her room but my anger was still there, fuelled by adrenalin.

"I'll tell you another reason you're a fucking arsehole," I said. "And this goes for you as well, Samantha, and your little shit of a sister. Your mother's been without water for ten days, for fuck's sake! Ten days! Have any of you lifted a finger to help her repair the leak, or pay the bill?"

Darlene suddenly burst into floods of tears and Samantha screamed at me.

"Can't you see he's hurt, you bastard? But you don't care do you?"

"Neither do you, it seems. He should be in hospital."

"He won't go to hospital, you bastard!" Samantha screamed.

"He won't go to hospital because then the police will become involved and they'll start to wonder why and how a man of his size and age – what is he now, 29? – came to be beaten up by a smaller man, twice his age. They're also going to find it difficult to believe that my father attacked Josh. In fact, they may even laugh at your precious husband."

"Get out," Samantha breathed

Josh was staring at me, his head still on the carpet, saying nothing.

"Oh, I'm going. I really don't want to be with this dysfunctional family a moment more than I have to. But remember this; my father owns half this house," Darlene moaned, "so I've as much right to be here as you."

I walked slowly over to the pile of business cards and took one.

"I'll phone you later, Darlene," I said.

She'd stopped sobbing and was just staring at me with wide, frightened eyes. I hesitated. There were still questions but this was clearly not the time, so I simply walked out into the warm, life-giving sun.

I backed the Jeep out of the driveway and accelerated up the road. But at the junction I stopped. I was breathing heavily and my heart was thumping. Losing my temper was something I did once in a blue moon, although I'd long suspected that my calmness – my submissiveness – was a truce, not a trait.

I had to think about what had just happened. Besides, where the hell was I going? I turned left and pulled into the side, leaving the engine and air-con ticking over. About 25 metres away, the same group of kids was playing baseball in the road. They glanced at me briefly before resuming their sullen game.

Christ, what a fucking mess? Samantha had been right, of course. I didn't care what happened to Josh. It bugged me that she'd been right and it concerned me that I didn't care. I really didn't care! Was it because Josh had gone up against my father? He stole Dad's car, after all. Did he think he was just going to get away with that? But there was more. I didn't really care about Samantha's feelings either. She must have been part of the conspiracy to steal the car. In fact, it wouldn't surprise me if she'd been the brains behind it. Darlene I did feel sorry for. That might be a mistake, of course. She'd been part of the theft and, since talking to Aunt Dorothy, I knew there was much more. But, at the moment, I couldn't help it. She just seemed pathetic and I wondered, not for the first time, why the hell Dad had married her. They just didn't fit.

I should tell Captain Taylor about this incident but I wasn't going to. I was sure Dad was in hiding, paying cash for everything and the police wouldn't find him easily, if at all, but there was no point in making it more difficult for him. Samantha would probably take Josh to the hospital, anyway, and then Taylor will eventually know, but Dad will have taken that into account. That he'd come out of the skirmish unscathed I had no doubt.

I'd calmed down now at least and began to disbelieve I'd reacted the way I had. It was an old dilemma: do I accept my frailties or try and change them?

An argument seemed to have developed in the baseball game and, eschewing the air-con, I let down my window to listen and get some kind of normality into my thoughts. Apparently, the dispute was a classic one about a base call. The batsman was claiming he was in and the baseman that he was out. It was just starting to get personal, when a small, mangy dog, seeing his chance, shot out from the front yard, grabbed the ball and ran off passed me like a bat out of hell. The batsman stamped his foot in disgust and everyone just stared after the disappearing dog. I couldn't help laughing. More than anything else, at that moment, I wanted to chase the dog, retrieve the ball and join the kids' game.

So, in my quest, if that's what it was, to find my father and stop him taking revenge on people, if that's what I was doing, how far had I come? Absolutely nowhere. In fact, I was no nearer contacting him in Jonesboro than I'd been in Lincoln. Worse, I'd found myself actually agreeing with him over Josh. So, what was his next move? Would it be on Darlene, or Wendy my other step-sister, or someone else I knew nothing about? The only way I could find him was by pre-empting him, by working out where he was going next and getting there ahead.

I picked up my phone and looked at Darlene's business card for Bentley Properties. There was a landline and a cell number. I dialled the landline, which timed out to an answer system after four rings. I hung up and tried the cell. I got the message: "This number is unavailable at this time." I dialled the landline again and then a third time before Darlene finally answered.

"Bentley Properties."

"Darlene, this is John."

"John!" then nothing.

I wanted to tell her to lock herself in the house, but if my father wanted to get in he could. He even had a key to the front door, for Christ's sake!

"Darlene, is Wendy at work at the moment? I thought I'd pay her a visit?"

"I don't know whether it's her shift or not, but she works at *Chick-fil-A*, on 41."

She obviously hadn't worked out yet that Dad could be thinking of revenge on Wendy, too, although it wouldn't be the same treatment. I was sure beating up young women wasn't his style.

"Thanks," I said and hung up.

The sign outside said *Chick-fil-A* sold chicken in many forms, yet there were no pictures of chickens; only a sign which boasted enormous black and white cows. I guess it was the same kind of American logic that called a bun full of beef a hamburger and named toilets 'bathrooms', even if the only thing you could do inside them was take a piss. I squeezed into a packed car park, between a small Chevy and a pickup the size of a house. It was right round the back, so maybe Dad wouldn't see it. I wasn't intending to talk to Wendy. What could I say to her? "You may be in danger from my father." I don't think so. I simply wanted to lie in wait in some way and see whether he turned up. It sounds pathetic when I put it like that but what else could I do? I took my time walking to the front door and, by the time I entered the cool interior, my shirt and trousers were sticking to me. I really did need to go shopping for some shorts and thinner shirts.

I scanned the restaurant for Dad, then, drawing a blank, looked at the staff. I know I last saw her a while ago but I was sure I could spot her if she was working. And there she was; a tall, hefty brunette with large nose. She was one of two servers and I got in line. She wasn't expecting to see me and I thought she probably wouldn't recognise me, but she might if she heard my accent. Could I mimic an 'American'? Christ, I'd watched enough Hollywood movies. I was the next one up when Wendy was called away to clean tables and I breathed a sigh of relief.

I ordered a chicken bun thing with a side salad and a glass of iced water, then sat down in a corner where I could watch the door. The food was surprisingly good. I wolfed it and settled down to wait.

Wendy paid me no attention, just cleaned tables in a desultory kind of way. I noticed that, like her mother, she'd gained a fair amount of weight since the last time I'd seen her, but then they seemed to be fitting in with a national trend. On the table nearest me sat the 'Family Lard'; two adults bulging obscenely out of their shorts and T-shirts. Their two children were equally obese. Annoyingly, like so many things at the moment, it reminded me of something Dad said.

"The average life expectancy of the American male is less than that of a Puerto Rican."

"You're kidding!"

I'd been genuinely shocked.

"No."

"Why?"

"It's not an easy answer. Lots of reasons." He'd frowned and looked into the distance. "But the main ones are probably their health system, which sucks, connected with the most important motivating factor in the US, which permeates their culture from top to bottom."

He'd paused and given me that enquiring look of his and I'd thought hard.

"Greed?"

He'd pointed at me.

"Yes. I wasn't going to say greed but, in a way, you're right. It's the power, the pull, the sacredness of the dollar. Everything in American life seems to be subjugated to making more money, usually regardless of the consequences."

"But that's what capitalism does doesn't it?"

"Well, that's one definition of it, sure, but America takes it to a whole new level. In 2008, when I still lived over there, the official figure was that about 40 million Americans didn't have health insurance and a lot of liberals believed the real figure was much higher."

"But I don't see the connection with the Sacred Dollar."

"Be patient, I'm getting to it. Who do you think makes money out of the US health system?" He ticked a list off on his fingers. "Doctors, insurance companies, the drug companies – it's more costly to buy drugs in America, where most of them are made, than virtually anywhere else in the world – and food and drink companies, to mention just four. Why should you encourage people to lead healthy lives when you profit more from them being unhealthy? The Sacred Dollar. Why do you think the right-wing in America kicked like mustangs at Obama's attempt to bring in universal health insurance? Because they control or own the organisations that make the big bucks."

"Whereas in Britain," I'd suggested, "the state largely pays for health care at the point of delivery, so it suits the taxpayer and the government to encourage people to eat healthily."

"You've got it."

I remember thinking at the time that there was a flaw in the argument but I couldn't work out what it was and I couldn't figure it out now either. I felt frustrated suddenly and the whole American venture seemed overwhelmingly pointless. What the hell was I doing here? I picked up my leftovers and dumped them in the receptacle, then left without even glancing at Wendy.

The heat made me break into another sweat before getting in the car and I nearly drove off before noticing the note pinned under the windscreen wiper. It contained two webmail addresses, together with usernames. One had a password attached and the following message:

I'm concerned the authorities may monitor our emails. I assume that you had to give the police your email address, which means they could also have mine as well. I've created new webmail accounts for both of us.

Of course he'd followed me. Any notion that he was going to simply turn up at a fast-food restaurant and walk in while I was waiting for him was laughable. I dug out my phone but there was still no signal. I could contact Dad by wifi email and that was it. He was controlling the play and the only way I was going to talk to him face-to-face was if he wanted to. I felt rebellious, unwilling to play the game according to his rules. He obviously wanted me to access the email account, so I wouldn't; not for a while anyway. Instead I went shopping.

***

Stafford covered the phone and swore loudly as he watched the Jeep pull out of the parking lot and head for Downtown Atlanta. He knew exactly how this conversation would go.

"Let me make myself clear, Dick. I'm not interested. I have other things to do."

"I appreciate that, Tom. Maybe Bramble will take a delay while you finish your business over here."

He didn't want to mention that he was finished in the US, although not in Europe. Four down, three to go.

"Give it to Green Anorak."

There was a slight pause.

"Ha, you mean Wade. He isn't suitable for this job and you know it. I'll pay you a cool million. Half now, straight into your Swiss account today and the second half on successful completion."

Stafford swore again but this time out loud.

"You're unbelievable. You have no idea what you're asking me to do here. Enter a completely lawless country, where there are several civil wars going on, travel through those conflicts probably hundreds of miles into the desert, persuade by force or otherwise a local militia to unblock an oil pipeline and secure a future flow. We don't know who this militia is exactly, what their demands are, how many there are, nor how they're armed. And this militia seems to be controlled by some Russians. There are so many imponderables it's laughable. And you think that paying me a million is going to tempt me?"

"I've considered the potential difficulties." Hartley always reacted when his professional competence was called into question. "What may help is the CIA has offered us intelligence assistance and they might be able to help with some of your questions."

"You must have someone else on your staff with the required skills, who speaks Russian and Arabic."

"You know very well I don't."

"Then you're slipping."

"Maybe. How much do you want?"

"Want of what?"

"Money."

"You're not listening, Dick. Not interested. Besides, I have enough money."

"One and a half million," suggested Hartley.

"For fuck's sake!" and then into the silence, "How much is your client paying you?"

A further pause.

"2 million."

"That means three at least and you wanted to pay me one, when I'm doing all the work. You're not only a liar, you're a fucking crook."

Stafford held out no hope that insulting Hartley would tempt him into hanging up; not where this much money was involved. Besides, the man had pressure he could bring to bear and it would be coming soon.

"I may be a crook but I'm good at my job. I get things done and I've put a lot of money into that account of yours in the past."

"And I have enough."

The theatrical sigh was deep.

"I didn't want to do this Tom but this job is important to me." Here it comes. "I'm sure customs, maybe also the police, would be interested in the details of that passport you received this morning. Unless you can get another quickly, and I very much doubt you can or you wouldn't have come to me in the first place, you're not leaving the country in a hurry."

"There are ways."

"Yes there are but they take a while and I know them too."

Christ he really didn't need this! He was done with it, retiring! He watched the traffic travelling freely on Tara Boulevard and thought how wonderful it would be just to join the flow, pass the towers of Atlanta and slide up to the mountains for a day. In fact, since he knew where John would be going later he might as well do just that.

"I know you might think that," Hartley paused, "that taking me out of this equation might solve the issue for you, Tom, but it wouldn't. The Agency would find you and you'd end up going anyway. At least this way you're being paid for it."

There was a long pause while Stafford thought hard. He simply had to play along until he was out of the country.

"Here's what's going to happen. I'm making no commitments at this point but there are conditions."

"Of course."

"First, I want that intel, such as it is, and as much up-to-date info on Libya and your client's operation as you and the CIA can muster. Second," he pushed buttons on his smartphone. "You writing this down?"

"Yes."

"If I do this and I'm not guaranteeing I will, the earliest I can arrive in Libya is ..... Tuesday 28 May. That's two weeks' time and it's not negotiable. If Bramble doesn't like that it's tough shit. I have things to do and you have a lot of prep. Talking of which, there's one thing you don't need to think about, additional men. If by some remote possibility I do this I do it on my own?"

"Fine but what do you mean, *if* you do it?"

"Third, I will however need a good Libyan guide. Local knowledge is everything. Maybe the CIA will help you with that one. Fourth, I want a Landrover in Tripoli. A Toyota Landcruiser will do but it has to be in good nick. New would be good. It also needs to be fully loaded: arms, provisions and electronic equipment, including two satellite phones from two different networks. I'll send you the details later. Do you have any contacts in Tripoli?"

He imagined Hartley writing furiously and took some satisfaction from it.

"No but Reed might."

"Okay."

"Anything else?"

Stafford thought hard.

"I'll arrange my own transportation but there is something else. I don't know what you've promised Bramble but I want you to change the arrangements you've agreed with him. Explain that you haven't finally agreed that you're going to do it. I need more data."

"I can't do that."

"The amount he's giving you is for solving the problem. I can't guarantee that. At the moment I don't know what I'd be getting myself into and the problem might simply not be solvable. Some problems aren't. What I may be able to do is make a recommendation but he'll have his own analysts who can do that. Why would he pay you 3 million for something he can do himself?"

Hartley said nothing this time.

"So, whatever you've arranged with him you need to change it now. You ....."

"He's already advanced me a million."

"Ha, well I never said you weren't a clever Dick. Pay it back."

"I can't do that."

"Yes you can. Turn over a new leaf. If I accept the job, you make a new deal with him and pay me £375,000, plus expenses. But remember, I may not go to Libya. Completion may simply be a recommendation and it may not solve all Bramble's problems immediately."

Silence for about five seconds and Stafford waited.

"He won't like it."

"Then make him like it. It's your problem. Since you're insisting it's me that goes, you shouldn't have accepted his money without consulting me first."

"It's not me that's insisting on you, it's him." More silence. "All right."

"Then we're done. I'll be in touch."

"I'll get the supper on," said Uncle John as he passed her.

"You know, you're like your father in some ways."

"What do you mean?"

"He's a planner. Sees the whole picture."

"Really?"

"Yes, don't be modest. It's what you do. I can see it's inherited."

He was smiling.

"Thank you, lass. You don't often give me compliments." Still smiling he put on a slight frown. "In fact, I can't think of the last time."

"When did he learn Arabic?"

"Hmm. '83 I think. Lebanon."

"Lebanon? So the British Army was stationed there, during his time."

"I think so. Can't remember the details. I must have been no more than a teenager when Dad told me. A British contingent was sent out to help the Americans and the French stabilize the situation after the assassination of the Lebanese President. Forget his name. The Paras weren't there. If I remember rightly Dad was part of a special forces detachment. It was his French which got him the posting. While he was there he decided to learn the local lingo, too. Bit of a polyglot, the old man."

She thought about that.

"Does being able to speak only four languages qualify you as a polyglot?"

"Only four? Hmm, don't know. Of course he probably did a few jobs for Envisage which enabled him to expand his knowledge of other Arabic dialects, so, if each dialect is sufficiently different to count as a separate language, maybe it's more than four."

Bess put the journal down and thought more broadly about Envisage. She hadn't really accepted the notion that her grandfather was a murderer. Not really. She'd read it and her uncle had confirmed it, yet she'd refused to validate it in her mind. It was as if, until this point, she was reading a novel and there would be a sudden, wonderful twist at the end which would dispel all previous beliefs. John was about to leave again.

"Granddad was a professional killer wasn't he."

He said nothing for a while, then.

"I wouldn't describe him like that. He sometimes had to kill because killing may have been a necessary part of the overall goal but he was a lot more. Once he played the part of a computer executive in Western Russia. He also headed a hit team into Somalia, taking out a local warlord."

"Did you resent the fact that he'd kept this part of his life from you?"

"I went through a phase of resenting it. Now I understand. Incidentally, apart from me, you're one of only two people in the country who does know, so let's keep it that way."

"So the fact that everyone else in the family dislikes him must be because of something else."

"Must be. I'll get your bedroom organised, too."

Extract 8

Life at home now entered a new phase. One night, when I came down from putting you and Rachel to bed, she turned on me:

"If you think it's been nasty up 'til now, think again. Now it really starts. I've got a new solicitor and he's going to have you for breakfast."

The confidence in her voice was terrifying and, soon after, her first affidavit arrived. To say it was a pack of lies would be an understatement and there seems little point in listing them here. Suffice it to say that it was a description of 13 years of blissful happiness, within an idyllic family, marred by only a few discordant notes; the sort of things that happen in every home. Of her treatment of Rachel, of course, there was nothing. She was completely puzzled and devastated by my motives in taking this action. As preparation for what was to come, it was nothing short of a masterpiece.

"I'll put the children to bed from now on," she said that night. "After all, I'm going to be doing it for the rest of their childhood. I might as well get used to it."

I could have argued and insisted I do it but she wouldn't have given in. It would have meant arguing in front of you and Rachel, or Stella and I putting you to bed together and, to be frank, I couldn't bear to be in the same room as her. So, I let it go. Another mistake. When she came down she had a look of triumph on her face.

"I'm going out," I said.

"Going to see your fancy woman, are you?" That threw me and she saw it. "You're pathetic. Do you think I don't know all about her?"

"You're bluffing."

"Am I? Helen isn't it? Keep-fit teacher? Let's see," she put a finger coquettishly to her mouth and smiled into the distance. "She makes you feel good about yourself; isn't that what you said?"

I left, stunned and headed for Kevin's house, where a wane light burnt in the window, reflecting moving images off the polished, wooden walls. He looked surprised to see me.

"I thought you were seeing Helen."

"Something's come up."

"You'd better come in."

I stood in the middle of the dark living room.

"Tracy in?" I asked.

"Yoga."

I turned to face him.

"Stella knows about Helen."

He gasped.

"How did she find out?"

"That's what I'd like to know. Helen and I have been so discreet, but Stella knew her name, her job and other stuff, too."

Kevin was looking away, his mouth slightly open, eyes wide.

"What sort of stuff?"

"Well, the sort of stuff I've only said to you, Kev. So what's going on?"

Even in the shallow light I could see the colour drain from his face and he collapsed into a chair, looking at the floor. When he spoke it was in short gasps.

"I don't believe he's done it. How could he do that? I told him in confidence."

"Told who?"

"Mortimer Holroyd; the Vicar of St Paul's Church." He risked a quick glance at me. "He's also Chaplain to your wife's school."

I was struggling to assimilate this new information and remembering what I knew of Holroyd.

"I know he's Chaplain to St Paul's School. He made a pass at my wife at one of the social events."

Kevin nodded.

"He has a reputation as a ladies man. But he shouldn't have done it. I told him in a priestly confidence. It's sacrosanct! You cannot break a priestly confidence!"

"Well, your pious fucking priest obviously couldn't care a flying fuck for your priestly fucking confidence because he's told Stella everything you told him, probably because he wants to get in her knickers!"

Kevin started to sob. I turned away, willing myself to regain control. This had to be thought through.

"What happened?" I asked.

Kevin blew his nose and crushed the tissue in his fist.

"Stella had obviously gone to him for support." He flicked his eyes up at me for a moment. "Reading between the lines, now, she knew that you were talking to me, so she went to him to see if she could get any information."

"And she got it," I said, cruelly and he stopped talking. "Go on."

He took a deep breath.

"He asked to see me. Remember, Tom, that in terms of the hierarchy of the Church, he is technically my boss." I said nothing. "He asked me what was going on between you and Stella, so I told him about Stella's treatment of Rachel. He asked whether there was another woman and I told him about Helen and how important the relationship was to you."

"Jesus! Did you tell him that the relationship didn't start until after I'd decided on the divorce?"

"Yes, I told him that."

He was looking at me again, gaining confidence.

"Well, he either doesn't believe you or he wants to get in my wife's good books so much he doesn't care about the priestly fucking confidences! He sounds completely immoral."

Kevin grimaced and I could see a fresh set of tears coming. Instead he shook his head in disbelief.

"I have to agree with you. I can't believe he's done it."

He was contrite but I didn't feel like letting him off the hook that easily.

"You do realise what this means?"

He was keeping the tears at bay now but only just. He screwed up his face. "Of course I do. I've given her the one weapon she needed to crush you."

Succinctly put, I thought.

"Well, either you or Holroyd has. What's his address?"

He gave it and I turned to leave.

"Where are you going?"

"I'm going to beat the shit out of him."

Kevin stood up then.

"You can't."

I turned at the door.

"And why's that?"

"Because you'll go to jail and you won't get custody of your children." He paused and so did I. "But there's another more urgent and, indeed, more ironic reason. He's not there."

"I'll wait."

"You'll wait a long time. You see, he was admitted to hospital this morning. He's had a heart attack."

Looking back, son, I can see that it was a good thing he did have the coronary. Kevin was right about that. I'd have put Holroyd in hospital and had a criminal record these past 20 years. Another irony, as you'll soon find out, if you haven't already because I don't know when I'm going to send this to you.

Anyway, back to the story. Feeling frustrated and impotent, I went to see the Bishop. He was sympathetic and disturbed by what I had to tell him and said he would talk to Holroyd. However, I held out no great hopes that the Vicar would fall from grace. How do you admonish a man recovering from a heart attack? In fact, a few years later, I heard he'd been promoted to Canon Holroyd. So much for the morality of the Church of England.

Chapter 14

Monday 13 May 2013 – Jonesboro – pm

Over 5 hours later, I arrived back at the computer shop. My smart phone had decided to work - I had a phone signal and 4G - so I could have accessed my email through it. But I wanted Randy's friendly face. As I got out I looked round for a police car, which I'd been doing all day. But there was still no sign of a cop. Not even a non-police car had followed me into the car park entrance, at least 400 metres away. I was wearing new summer clothes and couldn't believe how cheap they were. I'd walked round two shopping malls, had a pretty good meal at a fast food outlet called 'Wendy's', which I thought was slightly ironic, and spoke to some interesting guys in a sports bar. I was glad to see that Randy had customers but he still signalled to me that I should sit down.

I accessed my normal email account first, but there was nothing new. So I logged onto the new account Dad had given me, using the new password. It contained one message. The email said: *John. Herewith. Love Dad.* Expecting more patronising bilge I double-clicked on the attachment and it opened as a *Word* file.

OK, Son, some explanations. I guess you deserve it! You've spoken to Darlene, Sam, Josh (I hope he was mashing his words!) and Wendy. What did you think of them all? A shower aren't they? The more time goes on the more I wonder why on Earth I married that woman. Seems unbelievable now. One of my many mistakes in life. When you think about marrying someone, son, make sure you live with them for two years first. In other words, don't do as I do, do as I say! Knowing your sense of fair play I bet you felt sorry for Darlene. Did you warn Wendy or were you just lying in wait for me?

Josh came at me, by the way, although I wanted him to, I admit it. I thought if I rile the bastard sufficiently he'd go for me. No regret. I've been waiting years for justice and it feels good. Better than letting injustice fester. A sense of injustice is a terrible thing, son.

You asked about the college principal. Long story. She was a married woman wanting an affair. I didn't, not with her anyway, even though I was single at the time. Then it was one of the oldest stories in history - a woman scorned, hell hath no fury – she hit me with everything she could: jobs with impossible timescales, designed for me to fail, criticisms galore and ganging up with her cronies on the senior management team. We used to have stand up rows. She even found a fellow conspirator, also a married woman I'd rejected, although they might not have known that about each other. Together they cooked up a scheme whereby the second woman would complain to the principal about me. In the end the Principal boasted she had enough evidence of my duplicity to go to the Governors with a request for my sacking. The alternative was for me to resign. I refused, saying I'd welcome a hearing. She and the Chair of Governors worked out a redundancy deal and I took it.

That was when I stopped seeing you, if you remember. I think I've mentioned this to you before. I had no income coming in so I couldn't afford the child maintenance or my share of the school fees. I wasn't worried that you or your sister would suffer unduly, since your mother was on such a high salary and her new husband was pretty well-healed, as well. Anyway, in retaliation, your mother refused to let you see me. Legally she couldn't do that but the custodial parent has huge power. I didn't see you for quite a while, before I got the visits restored and it wasn't easy. I had to go back through the courts and through court bloody welfare officers.

I can feel your mind working. Okay, that was a pretty shitty thing for the Principal to do but does her action justify the burning down of her house? Apart from her suffering, it means her family suffering, too. .....

"Hey, how's it goin, Bud?"

I pulled myself away from the screen and looked round at Randy, noting the now empty store behind him.

"To be honest with you, Randy, it's been a shit day."

He showed me his teeth.

"I'm fixin' to get a beer shortly. You're welcome to join me."

I realised, then, I was tired and just wanted to go back to my room to sleep. But I knew I couldn't throw this hospitality back in Randy's face.

"That sounds good. Cheers. See you in a minute."

..... And that is the real question isn't it? Can it be justified? Well, I've long held to the view (I don't think we've talked about this before) that modern, post-industrialised societies gloss over some serious ethical issues – particularly those committed against men - as 'part of the rich tapestry of life', whilst severely punishing relatively minor indiscretions because they have economic consequences. Steal in order to feed your drug habit and you're put in jail. But a man can have his career wrecked, with all the consequences of that, because of a woman's jealousy or sheer bloody-mindedness, and she gets away with it, partly because there are no legal mechanisms for dealing with it. If a woman claims sexual harassment, the first action is to believe her. The man is assumed guilty until proven innocent. If I'd claimed that the Principal had deliberately engineered the professional differences between us because of my rejection of her sexual advances, most people would have laughed at me.

So, the question is, should people just get away with that, like they always have? Well, not always have. Historically, when our society had very few laws and even less ways of enforcing those we did have, people were killed for relatively minor indiscretions, and in those days you *could* get away with it. And maybe that's what I'm returning to; a kind of atavistic justice. Why should arseholes get away with monstrous actions because they don't break the law?

And the Principal's family, who also suffer as a result of my actions? Well, that did cause me some concern but if her family blame her for the ills that have been done to them, then maybe that's part of my motive, too. Am I being heartless? Possibly. She's knows it was me now, by the way. And I want her to know. She also thinks that I haven't finished with her and I want her to think that, too. I want her to fear me and regret the immoral actions she took against me.

This was serious shit, but it didn't affect me the way I'd have expected it to. In fact, I didn't feel any emotions at all. It was as if I was anaesthetised against it or made myself be. He had to justify it, of course. Jet lag was hitting me in waves. I looked up. To my left, Randy was shutting down his systems.

Heady stuff, huh? You probably think your old man's finally cracked. Maybe I have but I have a deep sense of injustice, John, at many things that have happened to me in my life; things about which I could do nothing at the time.

Anyway, enough of that. There's someone I'd like you to meet while you're over here. It'll get you away from all this unpleasantness and draw you out into the real America. Lizzie Anderson lives in the North Georgia Mountains; the way you drive, about 10 minutes or so from Jonesboro! 2483 Deer Mountain Road, Blue Ridge, Georgia.

Take care, son. Love always.

Dad

PS Check inside and outside your Jeep for bugs, including under the bonnet, before you leave for the mountains. If you find an electronic device that you think shouldn't be there, change your car. In any event, dump the police tail. I don't want them finding Lizzie.

Slowly, I sat back in the chair and ran hands over my face and hair. I wasn't sure I could deal with these issues now. I knew they'd keep surfacing, though, until I finally confronted them. Suddenly that beer with Randy seemed like a good idea.

We were just about to exit the front door when I noticed it was blocked by Captain Rick Taylor, looking decidedly less happy than the last time I'd seen him. The angry, brown eyes looked momentarily at the laptop cradled in my arm, before settling on me again and it suddenly occurred to me that Dad had been right. Taylor knew where he could find me and not because he'd had someone following in a car.

"I think we'd betta have a talk, Mr Stafford."

Behind him, a police Sergeant was leaning casually against the 'red on black' and pointedly had his palm resting on his sheathed hand gun. Taylor had one too, this time. The very last thing I wanted to do right then was talk to Taylor but, yet again, I knew I had no choice. I glanced back at Randy.

"Sorry, mate," and he raised both hands in the universal gesture of peace.

"It's beer time, anyway, Captain. Let's go."

Taylor didn't move.

"I'd rather you came down the station."

"Are you arresting me?"

He hesitated.

"No."

"Then I'd rather we talked over a beer."

I risked a smile and, eventually, he nodded, indicating I should get in the police car.

The sports bar was the same one I'd visited earlier and some of the guys were still there. They said 'hi' as I ordered my Bud Lite. About ten monitors showed the same college basketball game amongst the massed neon of beer adverts. Taylor levered himself into a booth alongside a window, facing the door and I placed the laptop beside me on the bench, hoping he wouldn't think about it. The emails were all conducted on webmail and would not be traceable but I'd stupidly, stupidly saved Dad's attached file to my hard drive, and a sustained search would find it. Taylor had fixed his hypnotic gaze on me.

"It appears your pa has been kinda busy," he said by way of an opener.

I nodded.

"So, you've got my card, why didn't you call?"

"I thought you'd find out soon enough, when Samantha took Josh to hospital."

"Oh, I found out a lot sooner than that, Buddy. She done what you should o'. Called the police as soon as you left the house and reported the assault."

Smart girl, I thought. Knowing the cops would find out eventually, she'd pre-empted them, making Josh look like the innocent, as well as the aggrieved, party.

"It's now gone beyond claims of innocence, Mr Stafford." I noted he wasn't calling me John any more. "Your pa has committed a serious assault on an American citizen, an offence which carries a jail sentence. If you know where he is, you need to tell me now, or *you* are committing an offence."

Taylor's brown eyes bored into me, his lips set. In the face of his asperity I could feel my own anger starting to rise again but I kept it down and spoke in what I thought would be a reasonable tone.

"Do you really think that if I knew where my father was I wouldn't be there right now? Why do you think I came to this country, to help him harm people?"

"I don't know, why did you come? At first I thought it was to stop your father but Samantha Pesant said you agreed with the assault on her husband and that you called Mr Pesant," he reached into his top pocket and took out his notebook, "an asshole. Is that correct?"

"Yes, I did call him an arsehole but that doesn't mean I agree with the violence. The day before my father was due to fly back to the UK, in 2008, Pesant, in concert with his now mother-in-law – and no doubt masterminded by the lovely Samantha – broke into my father's home and stole his car, passport and travel documents. I think there was some other shit going down between Dad and Pesant that I don't know about."

"All important facts you omitted to mention at the airport."

I looked outside into the car park, at a biker in full leather gear and tassels, riding a large Harley, roar in and park right outside our window. Taylor's gaze, I knew, had never left my face.

"Perhaps I should have told you. But he is my father." I met his gaze again. "Besides, those facts are on record somewhere in your police station."

That threw him and he fingered his beard for the first time.

"He reported the theft?"

"Within hours. I don't know all the facts but I've been told by my great aunt – and she wouldn't lie if the lives of her grand-children depended on it – that your officers were really helpful. That under Georgia law what belongs to a husband also belongs to his wife, even if they're living apart. He asked them whether that also applied to his passport, which technically belongs to the British Government, and was told that they didn't know. However, the legal advisor to the department was due in the following day, by which time Dad was due to be on his way to the airport."

He was fingering his goatee some more, looking out at the biker placing his helmet on the handlebars. He had a thick, black beard and a red do-rag on his head.

"What happened?" he asked.

"It's third hand information but this is how I understand it." He nodded. "Part of the dispute was about an insurance cheque, paid out on property destroyed when Darlene's car burnt out. The cheque was in my father's possession but neither Dad nor Darlene could cash it until it was endorsed by both parties. Dad wanted to place the cheque in his account, take what was his as replacement for his burnt laptop and give Darlene a cheque for the balance. Darlene, as I understand it, wanted the cheque placed into her account and refused to give Dad any money at all. Stand-off. Until the theft. Dad had no choice. Darlene kept the car and he exchanged the cheque, duly endorsed, for the passport."

"And I guess your pa resented that, huh?

"Wouldn't you?"

He stared at me for a while.

"Anything else you want to take the opportunity to tell me."

"I think there was a lot of other shit flying around but I have no specific knowledge of it."

"Do ya think he'll go for Darlene?"

"I don't know. She's clearly culpable but I just found her pathetic."

He looked out the window and I followed his gaze. Traffic was moving slowly on Tara Boulevard, perhaps conscious of the occupied police car crouched in the car park.

"I believe Pesant made the attack on my father. He practically admitted as much to me."

He nodded.

"Off the record, I think so, too. I've seen him. But I think your pa provoked him into it, don't you?" I stayed silent. "Don't you?"

It was obvious anyway.

"Yes, I suspect my father wanted to beat the shit out of him. That's one of the reasons he's here."

"You bet your sweet ass that's why he's here, just as good ol' Inspector Foster suspected. Well, he kinda did beat the shit out of him, didn't he? Three broken ribs, badly bruised kidney and I don't think he'll be sitting in the family photo shoot for a spell."

I kept a straight face while he looked at the bunch of drinkers at the bar.

"Why were you at the computer shop?"

He knew the answer.

"Checking my emails."

"Anything from your father?"

"No." He seemed to accept it so I asked quickly. "How did you know where to find me?"

He fingered his beard.

"I had you followed."

"No you didn't. I've been watching my back all day." His expression didn't change. "You've got a bug on my car and I'm not sure that's legal."

He smiled for the first time.

"Oh, it's legal, buddy. This ain't good ol' liberal England, ya know."

He moved to the edge of the bench and stood up.

"Don't leave town," he said as a passing shot. Any request for a lift back to my car was clearly a waste of time. At least I could now fire up my laptop and delete that file.

But Taylor didn't leave the car park and he'd be able to see what I was doing through the window. So I simply left. The guys at the bar were debating some hot issue and only the biker, sitting alone, looked up.

It was nearly dark as I left the building but the traffic on Tara was still heavy and, like most American highways, no account was taken of pedestrians. I weaved between cars that waited in three lanes at the light, then risked life and limb racing vehicles on the other carriageway. The journey was about a mile and a half back to the Jeep and I took my time, thinking what I had to do the next day. I was tired and my brain wasn't working well but I'd figured it out by the time I got in the car.

"Supper in two minutes!" John called from the house.

Good timing, thought Bess, as she wrenched herself away from a warm North Georgia to the cool of a Lincolnshire evening.

"Fine!"

She looked around for a page marker and decided on a much-used beer mat that seemed to live on the garden table. She'd seen it many times before, without really noticing it.

He'd lit a wood fire, as he often did on chilly, spring evenings and the large room he used for both living and dining was already warm. Insects flew in the open window and floated high on hot air. The smell was fruity. Bright paintings hung from an old-fashioned picture rail, like bunting. The house always had that lived-in feel that her mother's lacked. Some of what he thought was her favourite music played low from hidden speakers.

It wasn't just the cold that had prompted him to light the fire, she knew. It had given him something to do while he was thinking. He continued to look at her, like he'd done for most of the day; questioning her in some way. Normally, conversation between them just flowed but not this night. The journal was between them on the table, in more ways than one, and she knew she had to finish it without too many questions. Pointing her fork at the meal she said:

"You always do this well."

"Well, thank you, mam," he replied in a Southern American accent. "You are most kind. And the second compliment today. I am indeed honoured. How far have you got?" finally asking the question.

"You're just left the sports bar, heading back to your digs. Taylor's just given you a bollocking. You describe it well."

His eyes searched her face, as if not sure whether she was genuine or whether there was something behind all the flattery.

"Some writers say it's more difficult to describe real events," he said. "That reality gets in the way of entertaining prose."

She decided to change the subject.

"Why did you call it Cold Eating?"

He shook his head.

"Amongst your expensive university studies you've obviously never heard of the Spanish proverb, 'revenge is a dish best served cold'."

She grinned.

"Actually, I have heard of that. I thought it was English."

He just watched her finish eating.

"Go on. I know you want to get on with the journal. I'll make the coffee and I'll do the washing up, too."

Music to her ears.

"How is it you're the only person in the known universe without a dishwasher?"

"This a trick question?"

"I'm going to buy you one."

"I'll send it back."

"You are so bloody stubborn!"

He just laughed. She drained her wine glass, grabbed the journal and settled into one of the two armchairs by the fire. She felt full and comfortable and realised that, at that moment in time, she couldn't think of anywhere else she'd rather be.

Extract 9

The ensuing weeks set into a pattern. I was increasingly cut off from you and Rachel. Your mother did everything with you now. I could have muscled in but thought the arguments in front of both of you would have been damaging. Your mother ceased to include me in meal times, so I began to fend for myself in that department; a lunch in the canteen at College and a sandwich when I got home. Even so, I started to lose weight.

Finally, the Court Welfare Officers asked to see all of us, in their offices. We waited for a long time in an interview room, while, I later learned, we'd been observed through a two-way mirror. Stella couldn't be so selfish with you here, so Rachel held onto my knee for a while. You came and sat on my lap, for which I was grateful.

Someone took the two of you off and Stella and I were interviewed together, by two men. I wanted separate interviews but they wouldn't allow it. We were asked a lot of completely irrelevant bullshit about our childhoods and families. Stella tried to suggest that the death of my mother, three years earlier, was significant and they pounced on it like cats on dinner scraps.

"How do you feel you were affected by that, Mr Stafford?"

"Not significantly. I wasn't particularly close to my mother and I hadn't seen her for over a year when she died."

"Hm. Why weren't you close do you think?"

I could feel myself getting annoyed.

"Why are you asking all these ridiculous questions about my relationship with my mother? She has no relevance here. In fact, why are you focusing on me at all? It's her you ought to be asking questions of," flicking my thumb at Stella, "and why she's terrorising my daughter."

I remember them smiling condescendingly. The whole thing was a complete waste of time. Later, they came to see us in the 'family home': "Just to see how you are in your own environment." What they saw, of course, was a complete fiction, where everyone, especially Stella, was on their best behaviour.

"When are you going to speak to Rachel?" I asked them as they were about to leave. It wasn't the first time I'd suggested it and they didn't give me an answer this time either.

Then, of all the events that happened in that period, the one that made me most angry swung in from cow corner. In a fresh affidavit, she accused me of sexually assaulting Rachel. At first, I thought I'd misread it, then I couldn't believe it. I knew she was completely unscrupulous but this went beyond that. She knew exactly how I felt about child sexual abuse. When I challenged her, she refused to talk about it. Even if I was to forgive her for all the other stuff, I could never forgive her for this.

As it turned out, though, it was the one big mistake she made in her campaign. Later, in the custody hearing, my barrister was to quiz her ruthlessly on the accusation. Why were there no signs, either physically or psychologically? Why had she not mentioned it before, to either doctor or social worker?

"You're making a very serious accusation here, Mrs Stafford. Where's the evidence? Persuade the court that this accusation is anything more than a figment of your rather disturbed imagination, in a sordid and disgraceful attempt to paint your husband in a bad light."

She had no real answer to that, of course, and, in the end, her statement amounted to a vague worry about the future, if I gained custody of the children.

Your sister must, even now, be completely unaware of this accusation. I've never told her and Stella certainly wouldn't have mentioned it. I wonder what Rachel would think of her mother if she knew.

By the way, I've kept all the affidavits, so you can check them at any time. They're in one of several yellow files marked, 'Legal', in the cupboard off the lounge.

Chapter 15

Tuesday 14 May 2013

At 6.00am Ma Paisley's dining room was all but deserted. There was only the Pekinese to open an evil eye and silently watch as I tip-toed towards the window to the ever-present hiss of air-conditioning grates.

A police car was parked right outside, a sleeping officer at the wheel. Did that mean Taylor had decided to remove the bug on my Jeep during the night? Maybe the police presence was just a less than subtle warning. Either way, I'd already decided what to do. "When you're in a no-win situation, son, just change the rules. Do something different and unexpected: sacrifice your queen, turn off onto a side road, plunge through brambles and suffer it." Well, I wasn't sure about the brambles but I was certainly changing the play.

I placed $60 under a vase of gardenias in the centre of the dining table and left quietly by the back door, carrying my valise and laptop. I was wearing a fresh golf shirt and my new shorts, together with thick, breathable socks, rolled down to ankles inside my hiking boots. I felt good, as I always did on those rare occasions when I rebel. It's kind of liberating.

There was no fence out the back; simply a faded white post with a pink ribbon on it, signifying the edge of Ma Paisley's property. The ground was hard, brown and dusty as I skirted some scrubby trees and, with the sun in my eyes, headed for Tara and an early Marta to the airport. It would be at least an hour or so before anyone stirred back at the house. I'd told Ma Paisley to wake me at 7.30 for an 8 o'clock breakfast and there was only the two of us on the premises last night.

The bus, a noisy, rattily affair, was nearly empty as I paid the driver and placed my luggage on an unexpectedly new, chequered seat. Across the aisle, a middle-aged black man in faded Levis was reading the sports pages of *USA*

Today. From where I sat, the headline read: 'Under fire' above a picture of Barack Obama. Politics and conflict always rage in the background.

It was 6.40am when I arrived at Hartsfield and walked as quickly as I could without drawing attention to myself. I estimated it would be 7.15 at the earliest before Ma Paisley discovered the money under the vase and would know I'd absconded. It would probably be later but I decided to play safe with 7.15. She'd check my room and immediately phone Taylor, probably dialling his private cell phone. He wouldn't know, though, whether I'd left at 7.00am, 5.00am, or even midnight. I reckoned it would take him 10 minutes to get organised, before he started to check the taxi companies. Drawing a blank he'd probably think of the Marta but that wouldn't help him. He'd know I either needed a new car or was catching a plane. He'd phone all the car hire companies in the area and check the airlines. Eventually, someone on his team would phone Hertz at the airport. But all that would take time. It was early in the morning and it would take a while to get a team on the phones. I reckoned I had at least 30 minutes from the moment Taylor knew I'd done a bunk to him getting through to Hertz, whose phone is always busy. So I could allow myself at least another hour before I had to be away in the car. Taylor couldn't put out an 'All Points Bulletin' on me, or whatever it's called. I wasn't a murderer or a bank robber. In fact, I hadn't committed any crime at all, as far as I was aware. So, once out of Clayton County and through Atlanta, he wouldn't find me. Unless, of course, he was brighter than I thought he was and worked out immediately what I was doing and where I was going. Then I was buggered.

Fortunately, Hertz was only a short walk from the bus station and it took no more than 15 minutes to complete the paperwork on another 3 litre Jeep I'd booked on my mobile phone late last night. Despite the hour, the glossy blond on the desk was bright and smiley, looking at me in that direct way women do sometimes when they're interested in me. In normal circumstances I might have enjoyed flirting with her. She handed back my passport, documentation and the keys to the 4x4.

"If you'd like to go outside to the Hertz stand, sir, a bus will be along shortly."

"A bus?"

"Yes, sir. It'll take you to your car."

I looked at my watch.

"How long will it be?"

"Ten minutes, at most."

And so it was. At 7.15, right about when I'd estimated Ma Paisley would be discovering the cash under the flowers, I was driving out of the Hertz lot *en route* for Interstate 75, which would take me through Atlanta towards the Blue Ridge Mountains.

Hell of a name that, isn't it, the Blue Ridge Mountains? I can see, now, the term may hold a certain romanticism for you; not a concept I take to readily and at the time I didn't think it. I have to admit, though, I did feel good. The sun was shining, I could forget my troubles for a while, I had a powerful vehicle around me equipped for the terrain and almost anything could happen. And, as so often it does when you're not looking for something, it pops up completely unexpectedly.

The journey took me over three and a half hours because I stopped a few times. The first was to drive up a deserted track about four miles to see whether I was being followed. It had belatedly occurred to me that Taylor might have inserted a bug in my luggage. The diversion took me about 25 minutes but it was worth it for the peace of mind.

The second stop was for breakfast. I'd missed an evening meal last night and was starving. And America is, of course, the greatest country in the world for finding somewhere to eat, at any time of the day or night. They call it comforting and, in a way, it is. I decided on a Waffle House near Jasper. I ordered the steak and eggs, and, on the advice of the waitress, had the hash browns 'scattered, smothered and diced', which, as far as I could work out, simply meant bits of onion and tomato mixed in. With two pieces of toast on top, a cup of strong coffee and a plastic 'glass' of iced water, I felt like a new man. I took my time over the meal, enjoying the freedom. I even phoned the first hire car company to say where they could recover their vehicle and that they could charge my credit card.

The satnav showed that the start of Deer Mountain Road was 25 miles off the highway, uphill the whole way and round numerous twists and turns. Eventually, I spotted 2483 painted on the base of a bottle-green lamppost that marked the beginning of a pine-needle track bending through a lime-coloured wood. Any house was not visible.

I felt nervous, belatedly realising that Lizzie, whoever she was, might not want to be found; so I stopped and got out, and my face was immediately massaged by a warm breeze. In a tall birch, a bird of startling blue proclaimed its territory and a pair of chipmunks scampered up an adjacent pine. Deep and distant, a woodpecker hammered for grubs. There was a scent of pine needles and freshly cut wood and I reluctantly admitted that maybe Dad had something in this nature thing.

Returning to the car I continued down the seemingly endless drive, until it turned sharply and the trees vanished to reveal a quite stunning vista, of countless ridges of tree-covered hills, vanishing into a distant, blue haze.

When I was growing up, my father would often stop the car to look at a view and my sister and I would mock him. "Stop the car, Dad. Look at the view! Look at the view!" He'd then protest. "But can't you see? It's beautiful." We'd be merciless in our scorn. "Yes, Dad, we know it's magnificent. But we have somewhere to go, remember?" In those days, to arrive was more important than to travel. But now I stopped the car and just looked. Dad must have seen this view, as well, and I'm sure he'd have paused right here. I don't know why you've sent me here, Dad, but I'm sure part of it was to look at this. And, yes, it is spectacular.

I wrenched myself away and continued down the track, which opened up into a wide flat area of baked earth. Squatting over the edge of a cliff, with the valley below, was a two-storey cabin, fringed by a small, flower garden. Parked outside was a large, dust-covered, Toyota Landcruiser, the *crème-de-la-crème* of 4x4s. Lizzie knew her vehicles and my respect for her went up before I'd even met her.

I was still nervous, though, as I stepped out to a cacophony of cicadas - louder than I've ever heard - and the fresh-cut wood smell was stronger. I looked at the house. Any occupier must have heard the Jeep a while ago but no one came; only the biggest dog I've ever seen. It emerged from the front door at a gallop, barking loudly and raced towards me.

When I was a child I was bitten in the leg by a dog and have never taken to them. In fact, to be perfectly honest, big, vicious dogs scare me rigid and fear swept through me. Instinct said jump back in the car but somehow pride held me to the spot. Someone was almost certainly watching. "A dog won't attack you if you stand your ground, Son. Make eye contact with it, point at it, shout at it, do anything but run because, if you do, it will chase you down." It was nearly on me when I pointed at it and shouted at the top of my voice.

"Stay there!"

It stopped in a growling, snarling swirl of dust and we stared at each other for a few moments, the dog issuing a low snarl though huge teeth and me trying to look contemptuous. After about ten seconds I squatted down, tried

174

to look friendly and put my hand out. "Come on, boy." The dog changed its demeanour immediately and came over, head low, tail wagging. In a few moments I was stroking his head and he was licking my hand. If only I had the same effect on humans.

I stood and looked round, at the fruit trees and the goats ranging freely amongst them, and at a swing chair in the shade of two pines about 40 yards away. In the chair, quietly observing me, was a woman. I would have expected her to get up when I spotted her but she just sat there, gazing back. I looked round at the house, half expecting someone to come up behind me but there was no one there. Courage, John, it's just a woman your father wants you to meet. Slowly, I strolled towards her, pretending confidence, a small dust cloud rising at my passage and the dog happy to pad along beside me. I could see that she would be tall when she stood and slim. Her face was shaded by a wide, straw hat, with a blue ribbon tied round it, which flapped gently in the breeze. She was wearing jeans and a rough denim shirt.

I was about 20 yards away, maybe less, when she seemed to stiffen and, when I took off my shades to see her more clearly, she stood up suddenly, a book dropping from her lap into the dust.

She was a woman of about 40, I guess. But then I'm crap at guessing women's ages. Long, curly, yellow hair poked out from underneath the hat in a completely unruly way. I knew there were straighteners these days, which could have done something with it, but I also instinctively knew this woman would scorn such things. It was the confident, couldn't care a damn way she looked at me, with huge, blue eyes shining out of a fair face.

"You look like someone I used to know," she said.

The voice was soft and northern.

"If your name is Lizzie, then I'm not surprised."

Her eyes had widened at my accent and she broke into a smile so wide her whole face lit up.

"I knew it. You're Tom's son."

I nodded, then her smile lessened. The eyes seemed to dim but her lips were still parted. She came forward and grasped my hand in both of hers, as if she'd known me all her life.

"Has something happened?"

"He's still alive, if that's what you mean."

She examined me further.

"Is he well?"

175

"As far as I know."

"But something has happened."

"Yes."

Still holding my hand she continued looking at me and I couldn't look away. She had a kind of strength.

"Why are you here?"

I shook my head.

"I don't know. Dad emailed me to say that, since I was in Georgia, I should visit you."

She nodded very slightly.

"Your father did tell me your name but I've forgotten."

"John."

"Yes." The wide smile returned, wide and genuine. "Well, I'm very pleased to meet you John."

I felt awkward.

"Lizzie, until yesterday I didn't even know you existed."

"No," she said, the smile lessening again and she dropped my hand. "You'd best come to the house," and she walked passed me. I stooped to pick up her book - a novel by Bharati Mukherjee called *Holder of the World* – and obediently followed. I'd already decided I'd follow her anywhere.

"Would you like some iced tea?" she asked when we entered the front room.

"That'd be great, thanks."

"Although, if you're your father's son, I guess a beer would be better, right?"

I laughed.

"A beer would be better."

Why do houses in the Southern US have so few windows and those they do have are so small? It makes their rooms so dark and it took me a while to adjust to the lack of light. When I did I saw that it was a small and sparse room with rich rugs on a wooden floor; dark, hardwood furniture and a rocking chair beside the empty grate of a wood-burning stove. The entire back wall was given over to bookshelves and I examined them while Lizzie was gone. They contained a cornucopia of novels - some classic, some modern - travel books and history. I noticed immediately that one whole shelf contained nothing but books about art and I wondered whether that was what Lizzie did, paint. On a small table by the rocking chair lay a large hardback, nearly two inches thick, called *The God Delusion* by Richard Dawkins. I picked it up. A frayed leather bookmark showed a place three-quarters through.

"Your father sent it to me for Christmas. You can't buy it in this country. It's great but a bit heavy for me. Small doses only."

Lizzie was carrying two bottles of *Sam Adams* and looking at me with those large eyes again.

"Straight out of the bottle okay?"

"Absolutely," I replied and hefted the book. "You have the same views about religion as Dad?"

I wouldn't have thought it possible but her smile deepened and she looked away.

"It's how we met. At a Humanist meeting in Atlanta. We were all concerned about the evangelical Christians and the religious fundamentalism that has such a grip on this country." She indicated a chair and sat down on the rocker. The beer was like nectar. "Tom got up and spoke. I was mesmerised. His voice was so modulated and it had a resonance." She talked with such reverence, as if recalling a meeting with the Archangel Gabriel. "And he marshalled his arguments so well. And, of course, he has that British accent. Like you, but not like you."

"I was brought up in the North, Dad in the South."

She continued to examine me with those wide eyes.

"If this embarrasses you, I'm sorry but, seeing you is like looking on Tom when he was a young man, a long time before I met him. It's fascinating and spooky, too. It's like I've been taken back in time. You are so like him, did you know that? Of course you do. It's not just your looks but the way you talk, your mannerisms; everything."

I smiled back to show her she'd not offended me.

"So I've been told. I mentioned to him once that in 30 years' time I'm going to dread looking in the mirror."

She laughed and so did I. She kept gazing at me, though, in a way I've never been examined before and I felt myself wanting some respite.

"But there are differences" she continued. "Tom said you were better looking than him. I thought at the time that was simply modesty talking but I can see he was right."

I *was* embarrassed now and willed myself not to blush. It was one of those statements to which there is no answer. If I accepted it I'm arrogant, if I protested I'm calling her and my father liars. She seemed to appreciate my dilemma and laughed again.

"He also said you were more perceptive than him."

"Dad exaggerates a lot," I finally blurted out and she didn't laugh this time.

"I'm so glad to meet you, John Stafford."

It was said with such feeling that I warmed to her even more. It was no good; I had to ask.

"Were you and Dad …..?"

I couldn't say it.

"Lovers? Yes. Oh, yes. He's the love of my life. The tragedy of my life is that I was married to someone else."

"Was?"

She looked away again, still smiling faintly.

"Your father had already left his wife when we met but I was still living with my husband. Finally, I decided I was going to leave him and live with Tom." She paused. "Then it all went wrong. My husband got sick. He needed me, more than he'd ever done before. Tom's wife, what was her name, Darlene?" I nodded. "She wrote to INS withdrawing her petition for Tom's permanent residence and he had to go back to the UK before they threw him out. If I were a Christian I'd have thought God was punishing me for my sin of infidelity." She laughed ironically and took a swig of her beer. "My husband eventually died two months ago."

"I'm sorry."

"It's okay. I now know what they mean when they say, 'it was a blessing in the end'."

My mind was so full of questions, but I waited.

"I emailed Tom, expecting that we could finally get together but he didn't reply. I tried again with the same result. One afternoon, about a month ago, he phoned. He was very ….. unTomlike. Very ….. guarded. He said it was just a bad time for him at the moment and he'd send me a message soon."

She paused.

"Are you that message, John?"

I didn't know what to say.

"What has happened?" she asked and I decided to tell her, everything. I looked away to gather my thoughts and noticed the dog lift its head from the rug, ears pricked. Lizzie noticed, too. All I could hear were the cicadas and the faint tick of a clock.

"What day is it?" she asked.

"Tuesday."

She laughed suddenly.

"I'd forgotten," she said and stood up. "Well, this will be interesting."

"Someone's coming?"

"My daughter."

She was shaking her head slightly, still smiling to herself.

"Does she know about you and Dad?"

"No."

Finally, I heard the sound of a vehicle approaching. The dog jumped up and barged through the screen door. He wasn't barking this time.

"I was going to tell her when Hugh died but the right moment never seemed to come. And then, when Tom made no attempt to contact me, I thought, well, there's no urgency."

I stood up, too.

"I'm sorry, I'm making things awkward for you," I said.

She came over and held my upper arm with both hands, the ever-present smile lighting her face.

"I'm so glad you're here, John," then she went out to greet her daughter. Since the door was open I could see her standing in the shade of the porch through the screen door and I could hear clearly, too.

"Who's here, Mom?"

Lizzie said nothing.

"Mom, you been holdin' out on me?"

When I caught sight of her I could see that she was tall, too, with long, chestnut hair tied in a ponytail, face tanned lightly by the sun. She was about my age and quite beautiful. I was so taken by her looks that she was on the porch embracing her mother before I focused on the light brown uniformed shirt, with a sergeant's stripe on the sleeve, and the revolver nestling in a holster by a shapely right hip. Christ, Dad, what the fuck are you doing sending me here?! Another part of my brain, the one that keeps working in the background, told me that my estimate of Lizzie's age must be way off beam.

Lizzie came in, glowing.

"Darling, I want you to meet a new friend of mine. Charlotte, this is John Stafford."

While she waited at the door for her eyes to adjust, I tried not to glance at the sidearm. I was struck by the lack of embarrassment at the pause, as if it was part of the family ritual. Eventually, she stepped forward, looked up at me and put out her hand, which I took gratefully. It was a strong grip for a woman. I couldn't discern her eye colour but the eyes seemed dark and as hard as bullets.

"Pleased to meet you," I said, trying to sound indifferent.

"And I you ….. I think," turning and looking inquisitively at her mother.

I noted the Southern drawl but it was that 'I think' which made me smile to myself.

"We're drinking beer, darling. You?"

"Yeh, beer. Fine."

She sat down on a couch and examined me in a completely open, almost arrogant, way. In most cultures it would be considered somewhat forward, for a woman to look at a man so openly, especially a beautiful woman. But I knew this one, like her mother, couldn't care a fuck about that. Again, I felt a little uncomfortable and asked a question to hide it.

"Are you city or county police?"

"County."

It was said abruptly, with all the warmth of a winter wind.

"I must confess I don't understand the functional difference between the two."

"Your accent is British."

She made it sound like an accusation.

"Yes."

"So, to what do we owe the pleasure of ya visit, Mr Stafford?"

It was becoming increasingly clear to me that my visit was not a pleasure to Charlotte.

"I'm sure your Mum will explain."

"Yes, I will explain," said Lizzie, coming back into the room. She gave Charlotte her beer and walked over to me, gripping my arm again and smiling that smile. Charlotte noticed the intimacy and continued to glower at me. "Why don't we all sit down," said Lizzie. "I think we need to talk."

Lizzie sat in the rocker and I in a lounge chair between them. There was a silence, which I thought Charlotte would break but she had the good sense to look at her mother and wait. The dog came over, made eye contact with me and sat by my leg, so I stroked his head.

"I've been meaning to tell you this for a while, darling, but the opportunity never seemed to arise." She laughed at herself. "Or perhaps I was too frightened to tell you. You can be quite disapproving."

Lizzie smiled at her daughter to soften the words.

"I had an affair, while I was still married to your father. There, I've said it. He was an Englishman named Tom and I loved him very much. Still do, as it happens. This young man is his son." She turned and gave me the full warmth of her smile. "His surprise visit came less than, what, 20 minutes ago, yet I feel I've known him all my life."

I understood exactly what she meant. Charlotte turned to me, then back to her mother.

"Well, I knew you'd tell me, sooner or later."

Lizzie kind of gasped.

"You knew?"

"I guessed. Was it about five years ago, when I was away at college?"

"Yes. But how did y .....? Silly question." Lizzie turned towards me again. "She notices everything. Always has. Every small nuance. She's just met you, yet I bet, without glancing at you again, she could describe you in every detail, from your boots to the tip of your head."

"You're embarrassing me, mother."

"I am aren't I? And that's the first time I've seen you blush in a long while, my darling."

"Mom!"

I watched Lizzie enjoying herself hugely and turning the tables on her daughter at the same time. It tends to be a national trait that Americans wear their heart on their sleeve, but Lizzie took it a whole stage further. She was simply the most open person I'd ever met. Combined with her innate affection and sense of fun, I could understand the attraction for Dad. Here she was, telling her daughter of a solemn family secret, yet she refused to take it seriously. The dog placed his head on my leg, so I stroked him absentmindedly and waited. Charlotte waited, too.

"I felt guilty. Of course. But I couldn't help myself. Tom was just the most exciting man I'd met in my entire life. Charlotte, you should know that I was going to leave your father to be with him. Then it all went pear-shaped, as you know. Hugh got sick and needed me. Tom went back to the UK. When your dad finally died I expected Tom to fly over. But he never did." She looked round at me, again, the mouth still smiling but the eyes pleading. "Then, out of the blue, his son arrives. Can you tell me why, John?"

I wasn't sure whether she meant why I'd come or why Dad hadn't contacted her but it was probably the same question.

"How do you know he is his son?" asked Charlotte.

Lizzie and I smiled at each other. Charlotte noticed, of course, and looked at her mother in fury at being excluded from yet another intimacy.

"Just trust me, darling. He is." She gave me her attention again. "So, John, I'm thrilled that you're here but fascinated to know why. And why now?"

"I'm sorry Lizzie. I'd tell you if I had an answer but I don't."

For the first time, not even the hint of a smile appeared on her face. I stood up and walked to the window without realising I was doing it but distantly aware that the breeze had got up, creating little dust swirls across the yard. In the distance, a massive, black cloud soared over the western mountains. Why wouldn't Dad want to come over for such a woman? Because there was no future in it? Because he didn't want to hurt her?

"Maybe it's got something to do with why I'm in the USA."

"Why are you here?" demanded Charlotte.

The dog appeared beside me and started wagging his tail. I reached down absentmindedly to stroke him and he sat at my feet. It gave me something to do because I didn't know how to say what I needed to. Lizzie seemed to notice my discomfort.

"John, Charlotte and I need a few words. Why don't you sit on the porch for a spell. We'll be right with you."

I grabbed my beer and moved out, porch boards creaking under my weight. Thunder sounded in the distance and goats started streaming from the orchard into the yard. Well, I'm here, Dad, but I still don't know why. Out over the hills a bolt of lightning seared the black sky. Several seconds later, thunder rolled in again and the goats started to enter the barn, so I sat on a cane chair and watched them for a while.

The swing door sounded and Charlotte came out with another beer. She handed it over and then sat directly across from me

"Thanks," I said. She may not be friendly but at least she had good priorities. The dog came over and placed his head on my knee again, so I stroked him.

"He likes ya," she said.

Maybe her mother had told her to be nice.

"He does seem to. Any idea why?"

"Mom and I were just talkin' about that and the way you tamed him when you arrived. She thinks he recognises you as male and maybe he sees you as his new pack leader." She shook her head. "Myself, I think he senses something in you, some affinity, but I don't know what. God knows, he never gives me any attention."

It seemed that she was trying to be friendly.

"Aren't there any other dogs around here?"

"Not really. It's pretty isolated. Occasionally, a dog comes visitin' but he soon sees 'em off. The only time he's ever wanted company before now is when old Jes Pritchard's bitch is on heat, bout ten miles over yonder." She waved her hand in the general direction of the distant mountains. "Then he just disappears for several days. Eventually, he comes back with his tail between his legs, hungry as a hog."

"Sounds like a good life," I said. "What's his name?"

"Patch."

I examined him.

"But he hasn't got a patch."

"That's my mother's sense of humour for ya." I laughed but she didn't. The swing door sounded again and Lizzie came out, beaming broadly, of course, and carrying two more beers.

"I know it's only mid-day but this is a special occasion. Besides, it looks like some weather's coming in and I just love to drink beer on the porch when it rains. You okay, John?"

"Yes, thanks."

Lizzie sat down next to me and I saw the two women look at each other. They'd been talking, obviously, and they deserved some explanation. The trees in the orchard were beginning to sway in the increasing wind.

"I don't know where to start," I said. "And I have a couple of concerns. One is I don't want to upset you any more, Lizzie. The second concerns you, Charlotte."

"Me?"

"You're a police officer. The police are involved in this case and I'm keeping things from them, about my father."

Lizzie looked concerned but Charlotte's expression didn't change.

"What are you saying, exactly?" she asked.

"I'm not sure. I just know I have a story to tell your mother but I'm not sure it's a good idea for you to hear it."

Charlotte was silent and still for a while. Then the hostility was back in her eyes.

"Well, listen to you. You've known my mother five minutes and already you're claiming exclusive rights. ..."

"Charlotte!" Lizzie trying to intervene but to no avail.

" ….. Who the hell do you think you are? This is my family home and there's no way I'm leaving here right now!"

I had simply been expressing a concern and looking for reassurance, I suppose. Gorgeous or not, every instinct told me to get up and drive away from this woman. On the other hand, I'd probably handled it badly and now felt stupid to have mentioned it.

"What Charlotte means, John, is that she's not a police officer while she's here. Isn't that right, darling?" smiling at her daughter.

Charlotte's glare hadn't left me.

"Darling?"

Charlotte dragged her eyes from me to look at her mother's smile.

"Yes, Mom."

I nodded at Charlotte.

"And you, Lizzie?"

"You are such a fine boy, John. Don't you worry about me. You go right ahead."

I finished my beer and started on the second. Patch's eyes followed every movement. How much more simple and uncomplicated life must be for a dog. Until a short while ago I was in control of my actions. I looked at Lizzie, so open and sensitive and trusting. I spoke directly to her.

"Back in the UK the police want to talk to Dad on suspicion that he committed a murder and an act of arson. He's admitted both actions to me in an email." I glanced at Charlotte. "I've destroyed the email and I'll deny everything in a court of law. They're both revenge attacks, although Dad calls it justice. The murdered man was a Sheffield gangster. Dad then flew to the US and I followed him, in total bloody naivety as it's turned out, to try and catch up with him and to stop him doing these ….. acts of revenge." That was the truth, I thought to myself, if not the whole truth. "But he won't talk with me, either in person or on the phone. Only by email. Since being here he's assaulted his stepdaughter's husband and put him in hospital, so he's now wanted by Clayton County police, too. I'm also in trouble because I didn't report the assault to a certain captain of police and he told me not to leave town, which I've obviously done."

While I was speaking, Lizzie's eyes hadn't left me but, when I paused, she looked away, at the solid wall of rain rushing across the yard. An incredibly loud crack of thunder resonated around us as rain began hammering on the porch roof. Patch crawled closer to me and I reached down to comfort him.

Within seconds the gutter was flooded and water began falling off the roof in a solid curtain. Lizzie was still looking into the distance, not seeing the rain at all.

"So, Tom is in Georgia and he didn't come to visit," she said.

I hardly heard her above the noise of the storm.

"He sent me instead. I guess he doesn't want to implicate you in the whole thing."

"But why send you? You said so yourself, you didn't even know I existed until yesterday. Why tell you about me now? Why send you at all?"

"Maybe he wanted you to know and it would have been too painful for him to tell you face-to-face."

Charlotte's eyes hadn't left me and I felt under scrutiny, as I always do when I lie. I feel the whole world can read my mind, or my face, and I just knew Charlotte was having no trouble reading me. Jude had laughed about it once. "You have to believe in the lie to make it work, John. I do it for a living. You couldn't do it to save your puritan life."

"But why now?" asked Lizzie. "Why is he doing this revenge thing now? It's been four to five years since he was here."

I could say I don't know, that I'd asked myself the same question countless times, but they'd both think I was lying. The yard suddenly lit up in a flash of forked lightening, accompanied instantaneously by another roar of thunder, as the rain continued to test the porch roof. To my surprise, Charlotte spoke.

"I've learnt from much experience that you cannot keep things from my mother. She will eventually get them out of you, no matter what. Sometimes it takes a while but she will always get there." She looked over at Lizzie, who still seemed distant; shell-shocked. "Sometimes, it would be better for her if she did not know certain things but she just has to know everything. It's part of her character."

Could she be trying to absolve me from blame? Somehow I doubted it but I steeled myself anyway.

"Your questions are the same ones I have and I really don't have the answers." I met Lizzie's eye. "In fact, I think you're asking three questions here and we're getting confused between them. This is speculation on my part but, as to why he hasn't been in touch since your husband died, it may be because he knew he had these things to do first. I think he has elements of his life, past conflicts, that he needs to tidy up before he can settle down. If that's the case then maybe he will get back in touch. But if he does, you won't be living together in the US or the UK. He's already a wanted man in both countries. As to why he's sent me to meet you, I'm not sure. Maybe he wanted the two most important people in his life to know each other but I'm simply guessing."

The skies thundered again and neither of them even blinked, just stared at me. I was coming to the question I didn't want to think about and I took a deep breath. On cue, Patch nudged my leg, as if to give *me* comfort.

"The final question, 'why now?', has always been there for me. It could be for a number of reasons, of course, but meeting you, Lizzie, has given me a possible answer, as, I think, may have been Dad's intention. If he doesn't come back for you, after he's finished this current business, there can be only two reasons that I can think of; another woman or an incurable illness." I rushed on. "I've found no evidence of another woman and if I was my father, I'd fight hell itself to be with you. But he wouldn't want to put you through another lingering death." Lizzie looked away again, her inner gaze far away. "My logic is often crazy and I'm going to find out the truth right now."

I extracted my smartphone. There was a good 4G signal and I started texting.

Dad

I'm with Lizzie. You have to tell me the answer to this question and you have to tell me now. Do you have a terminal illness? Is this why you're doing this revenge thing at this time and is it why you haven't been to see Lizzie? Don't keep us in suspense, please. Its not fair on her or me.

Son

Soon, Lizzie began to sob quietly. Charlotte got up to comfort her. I'd never felt more wretched and powerless as I did at that moment, as the rain continued to fall in torrents and Lizzie sobbed into Charlotte's shoulder. Where are you, Dad? Are you out there now, defying this fucking storm? I tried to contemplate a world without him and couldn't manage it.

Lizzie stopped sobbing, eventually. We all stayed silent and, after a while, the rain stopped, just as suddenly as it had started, and the sun followed right behind. The yard became a steaming quagmire, with little rivulets criss-crossing it. Birds began singing again and so did the cicadas. Lizzie looked up and, predictably, smiled at me. My phone beeped with a text message and they both stared at me as I hit the screen.

Christ I'm sorry son. I should have thought you'd think that one up. No, apart from the fact that my knee's fucked, I'm fine. Love to Lizzie.

I must have grinned my relief because Lizzie nodded.

"Told you my logic is often faulty. He sends his love."

She just looked into the distance and still it meant we didn't have an answer to the why now question. Lizzie and Charlotte seemed to have forgotten it, though, so I didn't push. In fact we just sat there on the porch a long time, talking inconsequentialities: what I did for a living, why the British loved village cricket so much and the incomprehensibility of the game to Americans, the beauty of the high woods and Lizzie's painting of them. It felt comfortable, as if we knew it was what we all needed. Even Charlotte thawed a bit and talked about the nature of policing in North Georgia. When she spoke I saw a vulnerability in her gaze, and I thought that the only way she could handle real emotions was to hide behind an icy exterior. And I unexpectedly felt sorry for her, in the same way I would for a struggling child. I realised, then, that she hid the same helplessness as the rest of us. At one point Patch lifted his head and seemed to sniff the air. Then he got up and loped off into the woods behind the barn, returning after half-an-hour or so, looking pleased with himself and lapping a whole bowl of water.

"Can I see the paintings?" I asked.

"Sure, later perhaps. You are staying the night aren't you?"

There was nothing I wanted more.

"That'd be great, thanks."

I reached down to stroke Patch and looked out across the sun-baked yard, which held no sign of the deluge. I thought how astonishing that was. In the UK it would have taken half a day or more for the land to dry out, even in high summer. In the distance, the hills weren't shrouded either but sharply outlined against a Mediterranean blue. I brought my gaze closer and looked out over the yard, at the deep woods. It looked so appealing, an escape from my reality. I stood up and so did Lizzie.

"What will you do now?" she asked.

"I don't know. Take stock? I need to take a walk and think. Is that all right?"

"Sure. Take patch and you won't get lost."

"Great. Come on, Patch."

He'd got on his feet when I had and now jumped off the porch with alacrity. So we walked off into the woods behind the barn.

Looking back, I can see that this was the moment at which I most felt like giving up. What was the point of it all? When you reach 26 years of age you think you're finally a man, but you're not really. You lack the coping mechanisms that come from experience. I'd put on a brave face for Lizzie but all I wanted was to lie down and take my mind away somewhere, anywhere. The only time I can remember feeling so low before was when I was five and Dad had just moved away from home. After a visiting weekend he'd bring my sister and me back in the evening and I'd feel a tearing in my chest as I'd realise he was shortly to leave me again for another two weeks. I wouldn't cry, though; not while he was still there. I'd wait until he'd gone, then be inconsolable until eventually falling asleep on a sodden pillow. Later, much later, Dad told me he would stop the car at the end of the road and also sob quietly to himself.

Patch led me down what was little more than a goat path through another lime green wood. Small pink, lilac and yellow flowers reached for the sun, which slanted through large cracks in the canopy. It was marginally cooler in the trees, although there was no breeze. I could hear no birds singing but the cicadas, of course, were relentless. I sat down against a thick tree and looked around me. Patch came padding back, tongue hanging out, oblivious to anything but the sheer joy of the moment.

"He's not here is he, Patch? I thought you might have smelled him earlier. But if he was here he's not any longer."

I was tempted to shout for him but resisted. If he wanted to see me he would. Instead I got up and followed Patch for an hour, with the sun on my left, down into a rocky river valley, walked alongside the stream and back up the hill, this time with the dipping sun on my right. Apart from dodging the muddy bits where the sun had not penetrated, it was an easy, pleasant walk, with the sound of woodpeckers echoing through the woods. Slowly, I stopped thinking of Dad and began to focus on myself; on how fit I felt and on the sheer wonder of the life around me.

Supper was "simple Southern fare", according to Lizzie, with apricot chicken, green beans and roasted potato thins, followed by Key Lime pie. It was all delicious. "French wine is something I learnt to appreciate from your father, but it's expensive round here, so you'll have to make do with the local variety." It was sweet and fruity and frankly awful, but I drank it and said nothing. Charlotte was silent during the meal and thoughtful. She seemed to have lost her hostility to me at least but there was a troubled look on the beautiful face and I'd noticed her mother giving her searching glances. The meal was finished when Charlotte asked me that same question.

"What will you do now?"

"I don't know." But I thought about it some more. "In a way my priorities haven't changed. I still want to stop him doing what he's doing but I want to see him more. To talk to him. But I don't know his next move." I looked at Charlotte. "He can't leave the US, can he?"

She shook her head.

"Your captain of police will have notified US Customs. As soon as he shows his passport he'll be detained."

"But he must have known that would happen. Knowing him he would have a plan for dealing with it."

She nodded.

"So what's his next move?" I asked. It was a rhetorical question and they both knew it. I turned to Lizzie? "Can you think of anyone else over here he fell out with."

"No, he seems to have got on with everyone, except Darlene and her family."

"I need to send him another text."

"You need to do something else, too," said Charlotte, "and that's call Clayton County Police Department and check in. If you don't they're likely to alert customs about you, also. No need to tell them where you are. Use your cell phone."

"I appreciate the advice, Mam."

She smiled at me for the first time and I felt an unexpected glow in my chest.

"Too late to do anything tonight," said Lizzie.

So, in that hot, sultry dark, we sat out on the porch to the resonance of the cicadas and watched the turning stars, brilliant in the clear mountain air. And, by a kind of tacit agreement, we did not mention my father.

Bess looked up. The fire had died but John had closed the window and the room was still pleasantly warm. Beside her, the coffee he'd provided to keep her awake had long gone cold and her uncle had finally fallen asleep in his armchair.

She studied him for a while. His head had fallen forward and his breathing was slow and heavy. She'd always thought she knew him well but that wasn't really true. He knew her well and that wasn't the same thing. She'd never really thought about it before but he'd never really opened up to her, revealing his deeper fears and emotions. But then why should he? In fact, perhaps the relationship had worked because of that. But now, reading the journal, she could see a depth to him that probably no one else had even glimpsed, apart perhaps from Brad and Jude. His fear was that the reading would change their relationship. What he meant by that was that it would change the way she thought about him. But what new negatives had she discovered? His anger, maybe. She hadn't been aware of that before. But who was it that said, "Anger is in all of us; the secret is to let it out every so often"? Probably half of history's bloody philosophers.

She stretched her legs and yawned deeply. She was tired, too, but she'd read another chapter, maybe two.

Extract 10

Andrew Manton called me to a consultation with the barrister he'd chosen. Colleen Sixmith was her name. In high heels, she was almost as tall as me but considerably prettier, with a body to die for, and I remember thinking that a lot of men probably already had. She had black hair, tied back in a red ribbon and an equally dark suit that showed every one of her ample curves. It must have cost a small fortune, because there's no way Sixsmith could have bought clothes 'off the peg'. When she spoke it was in a clipped, Home Counties accent, in between drags on Rothmans. She must have smoked four in the course of our short meeting.

"I've been through all the paperwork, Mr Stafford, including the affidavits." She took a deep drag and blew smoke at the ceiling. "We don't have the Court Welfare Officers' report yet, of course, but, in the meantime, there's one thing of which I'm certain." She fixed me with eyes as green as emeralds. "The Chaplain must testify. We have no evidence that your wife's treatment of your daughter is any more than a story you have made up, in an attempt to gain custody of your children. But you've been talking to the Chaplain about it for years; is that right?"

"Yes, he can verify everything."

"Correction, Mr Stafford. He can verify that you have told him what's been happening. He cannot verify that the abuse has actually taken place. Correct?"

"Yes, I suppose so."

"Nevertheless, his evidence may be enough to persuade the Judge that it isn't simply a story you've made up since you met this keep-fit teacher."

Her gaze left me while she dragged on her cigarette and lifted her head to blow smoke at the ceiling. She wanted me to look at her profile.

"Will he testify?"

"I'm sure he will."

"Good, then he should write an affidavit and be prepared to give evidence in court. If you leave Andrew his telephone number, he will contact this cleric for an interview, just to make sure he says the right things in his statement."

I left Manton's office with a sense of optimism that I hadn't felt for a while but that only went as far as a busy corridor at College, where I bumped into Kevin.

"What do you mean they want me to testify?"

He rubbed his lips nervously and I felt another worm of doubt stir in my chest. I got the impression he avoided me for all the next week until I met him in almost the same spot. He saw me, looked shifty, smiled weakly and wanted to walk passed. But I stood in his way, ready to confront him.

"You've seen Manton?"

He was looking at the floor.

"He thinks I should not testify."

"What! That's not what he said the last time I saw him."

"I had to tell him what you said to me, that night when the social worker didn't believe you." He looked up at me. "Do you remember? I asked you what you would do if you lost the custody hearing and you said that you would take the children out of the country. I'd have to go on the witness stand and if I was cross-examined about it I'd have to tell them. I'd also feel obliged to put it in my affidavit."

Yet again I was stunned by the perfidy of the clergy. He made to walk away but I grabbed his arm.

"That was a throw away remark said in a moment of stress and you know that. You don't have to put it in an affidavit and even if you were forced to reveal it under cross-examination, the disadvantage of that, compared with the advantages of you testifying about Stella's abuse, is nothing!" Some students were walking past, so I paused and lowered my voice. He tried to use the diversion to wriggle away but I held him easily. "This is about your job, isn't it? It's about your career. The official Church line, from the Reverend fucking Holroyd downwards, is that I'm lying and you don't want to be tainted by giving evidence in my favour."

"Let me go!"

"Oh, I'll let you go, you snivelling little shit. You were my best friend in this place, Kevin. You were my confidante and I told you everything. I trusted you and you've let me down."

I released his arm but he stayed still now, so I simply turned and walked away.

It won't surprise you to learn, son, that I didn't see much of the Reverend Kevin Orton after that but it did mean my list of allies was decreasing rapidly. In fact, I'd started to gain enemies; lots of them. Neighbours I'd been friends with for years would abuse me on the phone. New affidavits of support for Stella, from people we'd both known socially and professionally for years, would appear daily, citing my faults and praising her wonderful qualities as a person and as a mother. One of them, interestingly enough, was from Mary Holroyd, wife of the esteemed Vicar of St Paul's. Stella even managed to dredge up an affidavit from a colleague at my previous college, with whom I'd never got on. All the abusers and accusers were women I noticed. Not a man amongst them. I don't know whether that was significant or not. I do know that the Head of St Paul's School, was asked by your mother to pen an affidavit of support and he refused. For that small gesture I was thankful. My only really close friend now was Helen. If I'd been sensible, I would have given her up but she became my only support in this turmoil and I clung to her. But, in truth, she was more than that. She was my 'Yorkshire lass'; uncomplicated and caring. In my time of weakness, it was just what I needed.

Chapter 16

Wednesday 15 May 2013 - am

Sounds carried easily in the wooden house and I hadn't heard Lizzie and Charlotte moving about by the time I'd shaved and showered, but Patch was all over me to be let out. The dawn had a chill to it, so I went back and donned a sweater before walking into the mist. Patch shot off to the woods while I dialled Dad's mobile number, but it rang out to voice mail yet again. He still wasn't ready to speak to me so I wrote a text.

Dad

Lizzie is a remarkable woman and I can see what you see in her. She still loves you. God knows why! You're such a stubborn bugger. Do you think she wouldn't understand what you're doing? Is that why you're ignoring her? You're a cruel bastard. I think she and I will stay in touch, whatever happens. Look we've got to meet. There's no way you're going to leave America. Your passports too hot. So where do you go now? I'm heading back to Jonesboro this am. Will text you when I get there and where and when we can meet.

Love Son

I sent the message, thinking how predictable it was that, whilst much of the UK was still barren of 4G coverage, it worked fine in this remote area of North America. I logged on to my new email but there was nothing, so I tried my regular email, to find a slew of messages, including one from Brad, telling a joke about a blonde on her way to Atlanta. It was good to hear from him and I banged a quick reply about how gorgeous the women were in Georgia, because that's what he'd want to hear.

Patch came back as I finished. I squatted by him and together we smelt the air. The fresh pine smell was back. I stood and looked at the distant hills, their tops piercing the mist the sun would soon burn off. And I have to admit it was a strange, pleasurable sensation, simply standing here, soaking it up and I thought that at any other time I might even have felt a joy at being here on such a morning. So, I stripped off the sweater and just stood there, leaning against the Jeep, letting the sun bathe me in the escape.

The spell was broken by the swing door creaking and I looked round to see Charlotte slowly descending the steps, her dark brown hair still shower wet and glistening in the sun. I found myself staring and looked away quickly. When she got up close she was smiling, exuberant. Steady, John.

"Hey," she said, stopping in front of me.

"Hey."

We just looked at each other, both feeling awkward.

"Look," she said, "I think we kinda got off on the wrong foot, yesterday."

I wondered whether this was her or her mother talking.

"We did. I said the wrong thing."

"I was hostile."

We both looked away, slightly embarrassed.

"What's your plans for today?" she asked.

"Back to Jonesboro."

She gave me that rare smile again.

"Mind if I tag along?"

That surprised me, then suspicion took over.

"Why?"

She shrugged.

"Maybe I can help."

I waited but she said nothing more.

"Is this your idea or your mother's?"

She looked away and bit her lip.

"It was her suggestion but I'm happy to go along with it."

That had a truthful sound to it and I couldn't see Charlotte doing anything she didn't want to.

"What about your work?"

"I got time owin' and I can claim personal business. After all, it is, isn't it?"

"I guess so."

I knelt down to stroke Patch, in two minds. The prospect of sharing a journey with this woman was almost irresistible and the fuzziness in my chest was lingering. On the other hand, my brain must rule. It was hard to see how she could help, our personalities tended to clash and I'd feel I had a spy in the camp. Yet again, and again infuriatingly, another conversation with my father came to mind. "You need to look for three things in women." I'd felt that he wasn't pretending pomposity on this occasion. "First, beauty. Don't believe all this bollocks about looks being unimportant. That's a crock of romantic shit. Of course, beauty is in the eye of the beholder and she has to be beautiful to you." He'd raised his finger dramatically. "Second, intelligence. The saying, 'lust lasts longest', apart from being difficult to say after three pints, is also bollocks. Before you know it it's gone in the morning. But if she has a mind that can keep pace with you, son, you won't get bored." He'd stopped and grinned. "A trait I have noticed in you, by the way." The index finger was raised again. "Third, and most important, sensitivity. It's also the most difficult to define, but If she has no sense of your needs and feelings, or those of other people, if she tends towards coldness and indifference, drop her like a brick." He'd given a kind of guffaw and I'd felt everyone in the pub look over. "In fact, I've been with a few beautiful, intelligent women with the sensitivity of a brick." He'd grimaced again. The thing was, he seemed to be describing Lizzie's daughter, unless, of course, I'd misread her. Maybe last night, at the bottom of two bottles of wine, when I saw glimpses of vulnerability, was the real Charlotte Anderson.

"You don't seem too keen on the proposal," said Charlotte.

"My father's wanted by the police. What if we find him?"

She nodded.

"There's no need to worry about that. I'll just pretend I'm not a police officer." She pursed her lips. "Besides, I've promised my mother."

Why was I hesitating? I knew I wanted her to come and I didn't have to force the smile.

"Okay, be good to have you along. Have you thought through the practicalities?"

"Handling practicalities is what I do. We have a light breakfast, then you follow me while I take the Cruiser back. I speak to my Lootenant, you drive me back to my place, I pack a bag and we go."

And that's exactly what happened. Much to Charlotte's irritation, Lizzie hugged me and kept hold of me. She made me promise I'd come back soon and I was glad to do it. I stroked Patch, who was quiet and Lizzie held onto his collar as I drove away. She looked so forlorn and I felt a powerful backwards tug as I followed the Cruiser up the lonely track.

At the police station in Blue Ridge, Charlotte told me to wait in the car but I rebelled by getting out of the Jeep and leaning against it, soaking up the sun again and trying to look nonchalant. Two motorcycle cops, carrying their helmets and laughing at some joke, stopped and peered at me, chewing gum in that slightly amused, indifferent way American cops have. They were about my age and as alike as peas in a pod.

"You here on business, buddy?"

"No, I'm waiting for someone."

"And who might that be?"

"Sergeant Anderson."

They looked at each other and guffawed.

"You with DD?"

"DeeDee?"

They laughed again and glanced at each other mischievously.

"Yeh, Sergeant Anderson; DD."

"I don't get it."

They were enjoying themselves hugely. One of them looked behind.

"You gotta guess, buddy."

"Okay. Um, DeeDee, Double D? Bra size?"

They guffawed again and one of them pointed a finger.

"Not bad, buddy, not bad. Could easily a bin."

"So, you going to give it to me?"

"Delicious but Deadly."

I laughed with them and they appreciated it, coming a little closer in a conspiratorial kind of way.

"Where ya from?"

"I tell you what," I said, "you've got to guess, buddy." They stopped chewing and their eyes narrowed warily. "But I'll give you a clue, it's in Europe."

The silent chewing resumed again and continued for several seconds, until one of them said:

"Australia."

He was perfectly serious. Somehow I managed to keep a straight face.

"Fraid not. It's the UK."

"UK?"

"You know, Britain."

They looked at each other and shook their heads.

"England," I said.

"Ah, England. Sure, buddy. The Queen and all that, right?"

"Right."

They both came over and stood either side of me, leather gloved hands on the roof of the Jeep.

"So, how ya come by these parts?"

To my immense relief, Charlotte walked out of the building. The cops, looking the other way, didn't see her.

"Well," I said, as if thinking hard, "it's a long story."

They just nodded and chewed gum, waiting for me to continue.

"Aren't you two meant to be on patrol?" said Charlotte.

They turned round sharply, smiled and made an imaginary gesture of touching the hats they weren't wearing.

"Yes, Mam."

As they moved off, one of them turned and winked at me.

"Take care, bud," he said.

"What did you tell them?" asked Charlotte when they were out of earshot.

"Nothing. It was just a bit of male bonding."

"Hm. Anyway, I thought I told ya to stay in the car."

"Well, that's just it, Charlotte" I smiled. "You may be able to give orders to those two but I prefer to be asked nicely."

I waited outside again at Charlotte's house, which was set back between a bridal shop and a 'Souvenir Emporium' with a small Union Jack in the window. Astonishing. Across the road, a large but faded sign was plugged into the red brick wall of a grocery store, which read 'Red Man Chewing Tobacco', around a Native American with a massive headdress of feathers and, at the bottom, 'Warning: This product is not a safe alternative to cigarettes'. And I thought what an amazing understatement that was for a product that has almost certainly caused the death of more Americans than were killed in their civil war. And, in fact, most of the buildings in this pleasant little street, where birds chirped and weeds grew in cracks, were probably built before the Civil War. It seemed like a quiet backwater, the 'old town' of Blue Ridge, half a mile from the brash Appalachian Highway, with its supermarkets, MacDonald's and Chamber of Commerce. The street had a warm feel to it and I felt like strolling, but I didn't want to incur any more of Charlotte's wrath.

Though when she came down her front steps she took my breath away. Hefting a haversack on her back, that thrust her breasts forward in a plain, white T-shirt, and wearing denim shorts that showed brown legs almost as long as mine, she looked fabulous. Even the hiking boots looked delicate on her and I was powerfully reminded that I hadn't been with a woman for quite a while. She saw me looking and gave a broad smile, as she shrugged out of her backpack and I placed it in the boot.

We travelled in silence for a long way. The lack of conversation clearly didn't bother her but it did me, so I decided to break the ice.

"I think your mother is an amazing person."

"Yes." I felt her looking at me. "She took to you like you were the son she never had."

"I imagine your mother is warm towards everyone."

"Not everyone. You should see how she treats the grocer's boy when he's three hours late with her delivery."

I laughed. She *did* have a sense of humour. We were right up behind another battered pickup, doing 65mph. Huge wagons were thundering passed us.

"She's very different to me isn't she?" she asked with a certain reservation and I thought I'd better be careful.

"I think we're all different from our parents."

That made me think of Dad. Amazingly I hadn't thought about him for at least an hour.

"Hm. Maybe. Incidentally, I know I'm a police officer in Fannin but we passed the county line a while back. If you want to speed up do it."

I checked my mirrors and accelerated passed the pickup, taking the 4x4 up to 80 and holding it there. I'd noticed on the way up that, compared to my Audi, the Jeep was like driving a boat.

"Just don't get pulled over," she added. "That could be embarrassin."

"They can hardly give me points on my British Driving Licence?"

"That's true. *I* certainly wouldn't know what to do with it and I'm in charge of traffic. Probably issue a verbal warning and let you go."

We both smiled. I thought I'd successfully steered the conversation down a safe channel but Charlotte had a relentlessness about her.

"You liked Mom but you're not sure about me, are you?"

That threw me and I hesitated.

"It's okay. Most people don't like me. I'm used to it. It simply doesn't bother me."

I glanced over. She really meant it.

"You certainly have a lot of confidence."

"Well, my mother saw to that. We may be different from our parents but we are what they make us, right?"

"Yes. But how do you mean?"

"She never criticised me. Always praising my abilities, telling me I was good at this and excellent at that. Great in one sense. It gave me a huge confidence in myself but it blinded me to my faults."

I felt her looking over, expecting me to respond. But I chickened out and instead decided to defend Lizzie.

"I'm sure you're right about your mother's influence," I ventured. "She certainly had an effect on me and I've just met her. But do you think that's the whole story?"

Christ, what was I saying? Every instinct told me to change the subject. Charlotte crossed her legs and the movement gave me an excuse to look down at them. I felt her looking at me again.

"How do you mean?" she asked.

"How do I mean?"

"About my mother's influence not being the whole story behind my personality."

"Oh, I don't know. Life is never quite that simple is it?"

It was a pathetic thing to say.

"You're bein disingenuous, John, although you're doin it for valid reasons, I know. You're either tryin' to protect me from your thoughts or you're afraid to tell me. Either way, you're wrong. I told ya, I'm tough. So tell me."

I turned to her, uncertain.

"Look, Charlotte, we've got a journey to make together and we need to get on. I'm simply trying to stop us falling out."

She nodded.

"I can see that's one of ya qualities. We won't fall out. I promise. Just tell me."

There was nothing else for it.

"I've known you less than 24 hours. Whatever I say is going to be based on very little evidence."

"My mother says you're one of the most perceptive and sensitive men she's ever met. I hate to admit it but she's always right about people."

That made me feel good.

"But I'll be guessing, you understand?"

"Okay," she said, a little frustratedly. "You'll be guessing," making a fair fist of my English accent.

The traffic had eased in front, so I pulled into the inside lane and reduced my speed, gathering thoughts.

"I think your confidence also comes from your looks. You're gorgeous and you know it. I bet boys have been trying to get in your knickers since you were a kid."

I looked over and she smiled.

"You don't have to try with men, so you don't. The whole thing makes you appear cold and indifferent, especially with your work colleagues. You're more intelligent than them, as well, and deep down they know it and resent it. They also resent the fact that you're honours degree entry and you've been promoted over them at such a young age."

She was staring through the windscreen, a faraway look on her face. I waited, hoping she'd let me stop..

"Go on."

I overtook a truck, its exhaust belching black smoke over the cab. It gave me time to think about what I was going to say next without giving offence. Quoting the 'delicious but deadly' joke would have bolstered my point but I dismissed that idea as soon as I thought of it. I already felt guilty about laughing at it.

"It's a typical male reaction. Not only do they resent your mind and your promotion, they can't stand the irony (which they don't understand, by the way) that they fancy you. On top of that they resent the fact that you're unobtainable. You'd have to be an exceptional person for them to like you."

Even though I was watching the road I could feel her looking at me.

"What else?"

"That's it. I think all this makes you very independent and distant when dealing with people, which makes you appear cold and aloof; almost arrogant. The proverbial 'ice maiden'. But it's more than an appearance. I think there's a substance to it. From what I've seen, unlike most Americans, and certainly unlike you mother, you don't deal with emotions as such. You must have them but you don't seem to show them the way other people do."

I glanced over. She wasn't smiling any more but she wasn't grimacing either. A small silence developed.

"That's a lot of firm opinion from someone aged only 26."

"Hey, you're right. I'm probably completely wrong and being way too simplistic. I don't really know you. In 26 years' time I'll probably have completely changed my mind."

"Are we still going to know each other in 26 years?"

She reached forward and adjusted the air-conditioning. After all I'd said, she could still focus on whether it was too cold. Whatever her faults may be, she was an amazing woman.

"Not if you keep doing things like that," I laughed.

"What?"

'It's okay. Doesn't matter."

"What?!"

"Well, ….. there are two people in this car."

She twigged suddenly.

"I should have asked you about the air-con."

I was smiling still but she wasn't.

"It's kind of polite," I said, "but I wouldn't have argued with you. It is getting cold in here."

She sat back and stared through the windscreen again, remaining quiet for a long time. When she spoke, it was as if from far away.

"You were right in everything you said."

"It's not important."

I felt her looking at me.

"So, my physical charms are lost on you?"

"Now, Miss Charlotte," I tried my Southern accent, "who's bein disingenuous this time. You bin observin' men looking at you since you were knee-high to a racoon. You know I ain't no different."

It worked. She was laughing, although probably *at* me rather than *with* me.

"Pretty good," she said. "Not quite accurate but not bad."

I saluted.

"Thank you, Mam."

After a short while she asked.

"Tell me about your pa. He's the real mystery man here, isn't he?"

"My father's no mystery." I had a sudden thought. "Is that why you're making this trip with me, because you want to meet him?"

She thought about it.

"Partly. Any man my mother is crazy about I wanna meet."

Then another thought struck me.

"Shit!"

"What?"

"I haven't phoned Taylor. My phone's right there, with his card inside the cover. Could you dial his number for me?"

Charlotte complied silently and handed me the phone. I pressed the speaker button so she would feel part of the conversation. We were approaching a turn off the highway. Huge, smart, permanent signs advertised Waffle House, Red Roof Hotel and Dawg Gas.

"Captain Taylor, please."

"May I ask who's speaking?"

"John Stafford."

Right before the interstate exit the proprietor of Dawg Gas had erected a more temporary, handwritten sign, using red paint on a white board: 'Unleaded Regular, $3.79 and nine tenths'. Nine-tenths?

"I'm putting you through right now, sir."

"Mr Stafford. Good of you to call."

I ignored Taylor's sarcasm.

"You're welcome, Captain. I just thought I'd check in to let you know I'm still alive."

"Well, that's mighty fine of you, mighty fine." Charlotte chuckled. "But it's not *your* death that concerns me."

"Any news of my father?"

"No, it's been mighty quiet here since you left town. Where are you?"

"Travelling back to Jonesboro on the ....."

I looked enquiringly at Charlotte.

"515."

"515," I repeated.

"Who's that with ya?"

I glanced at Charlotte again and she shook her head.

"A friend. We've just passed a town called Ellijay."

"Ellijay, huh. Been visitin North Georgia Mountains have ya?"

"Yes. I had to get away."

"Ahuh."

"I'll call you and tell you where I'm staying tonight, in case there's any news of my father."

"Well that's mighty fine of you, sir. Mighty fine. Is this your cell phone?"

"Yes."

"Don't change it."

Then he hung up.

"I thought he'd be mad," I said.

"He likes ya. I bet everyone likes ya."

"I think the Bentley family might disagree with you about that."

Charlotte was quiet for a while. I glanced over and found her looking at me intently.

"You must be really worried about your father."

That took me totally by surprise and, inexplicably, I found myself welling up. Instantly I forced the tears back, embarrassed, praying she hadn't noticed and concentrating on the road. After a few moments she reached over and touched my forearm and I looked over to be greeted by a shy smile. It was an intimate gesture and I thought, then, that we'd maybe crossed a barrier. Ahead, the highway seemed to stretch into infinity, as it disappeared into another blue haze and I began to wonder whether beauty really was its own reward, or whether I was actually starting to like her.

***

Josh Pesant had suggested Stafford enter the wetlands by the west gate, which would give him an easy walk on a well-maintained path to Shamrock Lake; a distance of no more than a mile. But he walked in through the unmanned north gate, passed a crooked sign claiming 'Clayton County Water Authority water recycling habitat' and set off south-east through the woods.

The wildlife heard him coming, of course, and kept their distance, apart from one deaf wild turkey, which noisily squawked its way through the undergrowth and a herd of white-tailed deer that imperiously passed him in the distance, one male carefully watching him the whole time. He crossed two rushing streams and consulted the GPS plotter on his smartphone only once, bisecting the designated path about 100 yards west of the Lake. Ignoring the rendezvous point, he kept going through the wood on the opposite bank for a further 150 yards, until he found a good observation post, surrounded by bushes, with a clear view across the corner of the water. The sun was to his back and unlikely to reflect off binocular lenses. He was two hours early.

And why wouldn't he be? He couldn't believe that even Josh could be so stupid as to think he wouldn't be a little suspicious. "You whooped me Tom. I want another go. Just you and me. Round two." He had to be acting on his own because Samantha would know that Stafford would never be fooled by it. So, he settled himself into the undergrowth, sporadically exploring movement on the lake, where the occasional turtle had enough of sunning herself on floating logs and slipped into the cooling water. He'd hoped to use the wait to observe the local bird life but, puzzlingly, there was none. There were mosquitoes, though, lots of them, so he rubbed some insect repellent into the exposed areas of his face, neck and hands. When he lived in Georgia he'd become acclimatised to them. They were still biting at the end of the three years; you simply didn't notice them any more.

Josh arrived about an hour before the agreed time, holding his side. He had two companions in tow, both wearing camouflage gear. Stafford examined them through binoculars. One of them removed a revolver, broke the shaft and seemed surprised that there were actually bullets in the barrel. He looked nervous and had a puzzled frown. The other had a pistol, checked the firing mechanism competently and proceeded to scan the horizon across the lake, including Stafford's hidey-hole. Seeing nothing he replaced the handgun in his pocket but continued to look. Josh seemed to give instructions and the two disappeared into the undergrowth, leaving himself kicking dirt in the clearing, for all the world an innocent, vulnerable man.

Stafford had thought that Josh intended to hold him at gunpoint, get his mates to tie him up and give him a beating. But he wouldn't use his bare hands for that. He'd have brought a baseball bat and there wasn't one. So, the intention was clear and the man with the pistol would probably be the one. The other looked too incompetent and Josh didn't have the guts for it.

If it wasn't for the mosquitoes, it would have been quite pleasant waiting there, in the shade, for nothing to happen, as he contemplated the next few hours. The stupid idiot had changed the rules. This was a deception that could not be tolerated; not in his present situation. Three months ago he might have let it go but not now.

Scanning the lake he finally managed to find a family of Pied-billed grebes and watched them for a while, diving for crustaceans. And then, a wonderful Cooper's hawk, soaring on an updraft, eventually disappearing over his head above the canopy. Josh must have looked at his watch a dozen times, kicking the dirt in increasing frustration, before finally calling his gang and walking off the way he'd come.

Waiting ten minutes, Stafford left in the opposite direction, moving swiftly. He knew where Josh and Samantha lived and was determined to get there first.

Extract 11

So, the day of the custody hearing arrived. I hadn't slept all night and it must have shown because both Manton and Sixsmith raised their eyebrows when I entered Manton's office for the pre-hearing briefing. Neither of them stood, or even greeted me, and there was an air of despondency in the room. My barrister was wearing the same, figure-hugging suit and high heels. Only the hair-tie had changed.

"Help yourself to coffee," said Manton.

The presence of Sixsmith had obviously shamed him into showing some hospitality.

"This CWO report is useless," said Sixsmith.

"I know."

"It's non-committal and even tends to side with your wife, if anything, suggesting she has a more positive attitude than you."

"I know."

"But the major problem is that they have not talked to Rachel, despite repeated requests to do so by Andrew and yourself." She looked at me in an accusing kind of way, as if she regarded it as my fault. "We must challenge the report. Do you agree, Andrew?"

"We have no choice."

And that's what happened. We walked the short distance to the court in the June sunshine and Sixsmith challenged the Court Welfare Officers' report straight away.

"They have had four months to conduct their investigations and, frankly your Honour, it is disgraceful that, when Mr Stafford's whole case is based on his wife's abuse of his daughter, the CWOs have not interviewed the daughter."

And the judge accepted the argument.

"Are the Court Welfare Officers present?" he asked.

Off to my left the two tentatively stood up to hear their fate.

"Ms Sixsmith is quite correct. You have been lax in your duty. This is not the first time this has happened in recent months and I am of a mind to put an end to this pussy-footing. Why did you not interview the daughter?"

"It's not our practice to do that, your Honour."

"Not your practice!"

The judge looked at them as if they'd stolen the Court Welfare Fund and one of them shifted nervously from foot to foot. I didn't feel sorry for them. The judge glanced at his watch.

"It is now 10.55am. I want you to go outside and phone your boss immediately. I don't care what he's doing because I want him in this court, standing where you are, in no more than one hour. If he is not here there will be serious consequences. Is that clear?"

And, within the hour, he was there, gazing up at the judge like an errant schoolboy. Apart from anything else, it made me realise how much power these judges have.

"I am telling you that your officers will interview Rachel Stafford as soon as possible. Do you understand that, sir?"

The Head of the Court Welfare Service bowed his head in subservience.

"Your honour."

"Good. This hearing is now adjourned. My clerk tells me that the next available date is not for three months. It can't be with me, though, I'm booked up. It will be under a different judge."

Result, you might be thinking but it was all a waste of time. If they'd spoken to Rachel earlier, she'd have responded differently. But Stella had had time to work on her. Her mother didn't hit her any more and she didn't punish her unnecessarily. On the contrary, she took her out for trips and bought her treats, like lipstick. I could see that Rachel was still slightly wary but the relationship with her mother, as far as she was concerned, was now completely different. What Rachel now saw was something close to the mother she'd always wanted and, whereas I'd been pushing for her interview with the CWOs, now I feared it. I felt that our whole future was dependant on this one meeting; on the capricious nature of a troubled 10 year old.

When they finally came, right at the end of August, they asked Rachel nothing about the abuse. They simply put the question: "When your parents split up, do you have a preference as to who you would like to live with?"

"No," she answered, "I have no preference."

Before that fateful answer your mother took you both on holiday for a fortnight, to your grandfather's place in Spain. When you returned, I took you to South Devon and we stayed in a B & B in Ashton Gorton, my introduction to the village in which I was eventually to settle. You had a great time, rowing up and down the river, playing football on the beach and hunting for crabs in those wonderfully clear rock pools. In fact, looking back, it must have been a great summer for you.

For me, it was naturally a difficult holiday; pretending everything was fine but always conscious of the notion that it might be the last extended period the three of us would spend together. But the sun did shine that summer, mercilessly and without feeling.

Chapter 17

Wednesday 15 May 2013 - pm

A few hours later Charlotte and I were enjoying a late lunch in the Atlanta Bread Company, a few miles from Jonesboro. 'The ABC', is more like a sit-in delicatessen than a fast food outlet; a kind of bakery café. You can get almost anything on any bread you care to name and there's a variety of cheesecakes for dessert, something for which I am particularly partial and something which I was trying to stay away from while I was on the diet. As a first course I'd gone for something relatively simple and was tucking into avocado, with tomato, onion and Provolone cheese, on French. Charlotte, more used to the complexity of American menus, had been adventurous and gone for the hot pastrami on rye, with Swiss cheese and spicy mustard. It was all delicious. The brick walls were decorated with massive murals of famous American writers and Bach played in the background. In a world where the demand for healthy, tasty food was increasing, it was a classy concept I could see taking off in the UK, if anyone was to think about it. In the queue for the counter I'd texted Dad.

"89." The counter clerk called the number of the next order and I watched a suited man fetch it.

"So, we just wait here?" asked Charlotte.

She ate her bun delicately, I noticed, holding it with unvarnished fingertips and taking small bites, whilst the only way I could eat my sandwich was to grasp it fully in both hands and drop slices of avocado on the table.

"Yes. I gave him until 2.00pm, so we've got another 40 minutes."

"Did you mention me?"

"No."

"Do you think he'll come?"

"No."

"So what happens if he doesn't? What do we do then?"

Across the aisle, two teenage lads were looking at Charlotte, as they had been, off and on, since we sat down. She'd completely ignored them.

"90."

"I've been thinking about that and so far I haven't come up with anything." I took a sip of chilled orange juice and shook my head. "I don't know anyone else who's pissed him off over here. I have no idea what his next move is."

She finished her sandwich and opened the ABC crisps, which came with every order.

"Maybe he's finished over here," she said.

"Maybe."

"Well, he's done his thing in the UK. He's fired the house of a principal of a college and killed a gangster. Over here he's beaten up his step-daughter's husband. So where else has he been in his life?"

I shook my head, as if I didn't know the answer, but actually it was at my own guilt. I felt like I did when Foster had asked a similar question.

"He's been on holiday all over but the only place he's ever lived abroad is the US."

"91."

She took a deep breath and looked over my shoulder at the mural. Her eyes were hazel I decided.

"So, tell me about his army career. Was any of that out of the UK?"

"Yes, quite a bit and, of course, he fought in the Falklands War."

"The what?"

I smiled and her face seemed to harden, as if she thought I was laughing at her.

"I'm not surprised, as an American, you don't know about it. Besides, it took place in '82, before you were born."

She seemed appeased.

"So what happened?"

I dredged up my knowledge of the Falklands dispute, based on what I'd read and heard.

"Do you know where the Falklands are?"

"Not a clue."

"Okay, short geography lesson. They're small islands in the South Atlantic, about 300 miles from Southern Argentina. Basically the middle of nowhere. The Argentinians call them the 'Islas Malvinas'. Britain colonised them in, I don't know, early to mid-19th century, mainly because of their strategic proximity to Cape Horn."

"So what happened?" she asked again, clearly interested. Every other woman I'd known would be yawning at this point.

"Well, the head of the Argentinian Junta, one General Galtieri, decided to divert attention from his failing economy by picking at an old sore, the British occupation of the Malvinas, thus uniting the country behind him against a common enemy. It's a strategy as old as the hills. Rulers have been doing it since forever."

"As in Homer and the Greeks, right?"

"Right, and as in Machiavelli and Swift and Shakespeare and Orwell and a lot of other writers. In real life, it's one way Putin's managing to keep his internal popularity. American presidents are not averse to the technique either. The thing is it works. In the General's case it gained him popular support, right up to the point where he lost the war."

I looked away to gather my thoughts and, interestingly at this point, four military personnel sauntered in and joined the queue at the counter.

"Since there was only a token garrison on the islands, the Argentinian invasion was a piece of cake. To be honest, most Britons hadn't a clue where it was either and the British Government, I'm sure, would have liked to just forget this remote outpost of British colonialism 7,000 miles away and kick it into the Southern Ocean."

"So why didn't they?"

"The inhabitants got in the way. They didn't fancy the idea of living under the yoke of a military dictatorship and wanted to remain British. So, Margaret Thatcher, waving that good old flag of self-determination, decided to send a task force to the South Atlantic to regain the islands. My father was part of that mission as a Captain in the Paras, the Parachute Regiment."

I paused.

"It was bloody. My father doesn't talk about it but I know he lost a lot of men. He got a couple of gongs, one for bravery under f .... "

"Gongs?"

"Medals. And, I learnt the other day, he got a battlefield promotion to Major as a replacement, presumably, for the death of his company commander."

Charlotte had a puzzled look on her face and I knew what was coming.

"Didn't you say yesterday that he was a Captain?"

"The brevet rank of Major was never confirmed by Headquarters. He finished as a Captain."

She still had that confused look.

"Do we know why?"

"No. Maybe a superior officer didn't like him, or ….. Of course! Someone must have blocked the promotion. Someone, maybe, who had a grudge against him. Charlotte, you're brilliant!"

"Of course I am," she smiled.

"You know, lass, I really am going to have to teach you modesty."

Looking back, I can remember that she slowly rested her chin on her hand and looked into my eyes.

"That should be interestin'," she said.

But, at the time, all I could focus on was the fact that I'd found another possible target of my father and, if I could find out exactly who it was, I just might get there ahead of him and force him to speak to me. Then the uncertainties crowded in and I must have looked depressed.

"What?" Charlotte asked.

"There are still huge unanswered questions."

"Such as."

"Well, how am I going to find out who this person was? Who is it that makes decisions like that in the British Army? Are they made at regimental level or higher up? If this person doesn't live in the US, as a wanted man how is Dad going to leave the country? Simple stuff like that."

"99."

I'd obviously missed the other numbers. Amazing how they simply become part of the background, like the cicadas.

"Okay," she said, "let's deal with the issues one at a time. First, your father leaving the country. I've been thinkin' about that. He can't leave on his passport. That's for sure. Taylor would have seen to that. How long would he have been planning this?"

"He could have been planning it for months, maybe years."

"Okay. Time enough then to get a false passport."

"How does he do that?"

"I don't know. It can't be easy, especially since 9/11, but I've heard it's possible, particularly in Europe. Not cheap, either, of course. He'd have had to spend your inheritance." She grinned briefly. "He'd add to his chances if he didn't fly direct to the UK, also. Maybe, using the false passport, he could cross the Mexican border by road. Controls are less there than at an international airport and certainly less at Mexican airports. He actually has many options."

She talked like she ate, with a kind of delicate reserve. There was no animation, no exaggerated movements, no excitement. It was almost like she was a professional actress reading a script for the first time.

"Providing he has a false passport," I said.

"Yes."

"What if he doesn't?"

She looked away to the mural again. The hazel eyes had green flecks in them I noticed.

"Then he has to stay here or leave the country without a passport." She said logically, looking at me now. "He sounds like a resourceful guy. US Customs look for illegal immigrants crossing the Mexican border but hundreds still cross every day. It's gotta be a cinch for someone like your father to go the other way. Then he can use his genuine passport to fly to somewhere in the Caribbean and from there back to Europe. If not Mexico, there's always Canada. That border has to be one of the most unguarded in the world." She paused. "What?"

I was impressed and must have been looking at her in a different way.

"Nothing," I said. "Thanks, lass. You may be right."

I tried to put myself in Dad's shoes.

"In fact," I said, "the hardest part may be getting back into the UK. Let's suppose he manages to get to, say, Amsterdam. He'd be worried about flying to a British airport. They'd be looking for him there and the checks are good. He could, though, take a cross-channel ferry from Rotterdam or Zeebrugge, across the North Sea to Hull." Charlotte was looking blank. "Sorry, I think I may have lost you with those European cities."

She looked slightly uncomfortable for the first time and gave a weak smile.

"Don't worry, carry on."

"Well, I doubt the authorities would have thought to cover that route and the checks are minimal compared to airports. Once in Hull he can catch a train to Manchester and pick up his car. Either that or he can get off the train somewhere *en route*, away from the port, and simply hire a car." I shook my head. "He must have thought all this out in advance because he knew the trouble he was about to get into. He's been one jump ahead of me the whole time."

"6!"

I sat back and looked around, checking whether Dad had slipped in by the back door. I looked out onto another massive car park but it was just full of stationary cars and a few innocuous individuals walking between them. My watch showed there was still time to go. Charlotte had gone into one of her studied silences and I was grateful. Draining the last of my juice I said:

"Okay, if he needs to leave the country, that takes care of the passport issue. So how do we find out who wronged him in the army?" I was talking rhetorically again and Charlotte knew it. "I don't know who makes those kinds of decisions, about confirming brevet ranking. I've got a feeling it's made above regimental level but I just don't know."

"What's a regiment exactly?"

"Of course, you don't have regiments as such, apart from a few exceptions. In the British Army the regimental system is still the basic unit of organisation; has been since time immemorial. Each regiment is divided into battalions. The Parachute Regiment has four, each of about 500 men. Para 1 is connected to special forces and Para 4 is a reserve unit. Para 2 and 3 are the two main operational forces."

"How come you know so much about it?"

I grinned ruefully.

"I was going to follow my father into the Army. Officer training. I was very serious about it."

"What happened?"

I had to think about that because to be honest I wasn't sure. I know my mother wasn't too keen on the idea, to put it mildly, and I was living with her at the time. Dad was keen but he wasn't a major influence on my life right then. I shrugged.

"I changed my mind."

She just nodded solemnly.

"So tell me about the Parachute Regiment."

"The Paras are the main airborne infantry element of the Army. There's a very tough selection process, an even tougher training programme and, of course, they tend to operate with minimal or no support, quite often behind enemy lines and against superior numbers." I paused. "Shit, I sound like a regimental promotion vid. But it is considered an elite unit. Most of the recruits into British special forces come from the Paras."

"What was your pa's role?"

"Each battalion is commanded by a Lieutenant-Colonel and divided into 4 companies, A, B, C and D, plus a support company, each led by a Major. Each Company is further divided into about 4 platoons, each headed by a Captain. My father was one of those."

"So, he was in charge of, what, 30 or so men."

I was impressed again.

"Yeh, about that."

"So, when the company commander was killed, the battlefield promotion was between him and probably three other men."

"I see what you mean! We may not be looking for a hostile battalion Colonel, but a rival Captain who may have queered Dad's pitch with headquarters. You're not just a pretty face, lass."

She didn't return my smile. Maybe the saying didn't translate into Southern American, or maybe she thought I was being patronising, which, now I think about it, I probably was. She opened her mouth to say something, then seemed to change her mind and closed it, settling for a steady glare. I remember thinking that although our relationship seemed to have developed I could be wrong. I sensed she was still going to be hard work and I wasn't sure I had the energy to devote to her at the moment. All I could think of was how I could get the information about Dad that I needed. Who would he have talked to about it? My mother? They were still married at the time. I glanced at my watch and looked round.

"He's not coming," I said.

"Maybe I've put him off."

"No. If he was here he'd have spotted you and phoned or texted me to ask who you were. Or maybe he'd know who you are. He's probably seen photos of you."

I watched a grossly fat woman waddle from the counter. Despite my preoccupation I couldn't take my eyes off her as she spread her truly massive backside to test the strength of her seat before fully descending.

"I need to phone my mother," I said. "But I don't want to do it in here. We might argue," I added by way of explanation. "I won't be a moment."

She just looked at me as I got up and made for the car park. It felt better out of the air-conditioning. Something that I'd embraced on arrival I was now seeing as kind of dehumanising. With the sun on my face some of my confidence returned, which I always needed when dealing with my mother. It was past 7.00pm in the UK so I dialled her home. While I was waiting for the connection I noticed that my arms and legs were starting to go brown.

"Hey, Mum."

"John! Why haven't you called?"

"I've been busy, Mum." I had to put her in a good mood. "I'm sorry I haven't phoned before. How are you?"

She ignored the question of course.

"What's happening over there? Have you found your father?"

I'd learnt over the years that the best way to deal with my mother was to tell her as little as possible for her to get her teeth into.

"No."

It was not difficult to put disappointment into my voice. I had to handle this carefully. Any question about my father was likely to cause her irritation.

"But I do have some clues. Mum, can you remember back to when Dad was in the Army?"

There was a long silence.

"Mum?"

"Of course I can. I'm not likely to forget a decade of sub-standard accommodation in Germany and bloody Chelmsford. Christ, bloody Chelmsford! South Essex is the back of beyond."

I crashed on.

"Do you remember whether there was anyone in Dad's company or battalion he really disliked?"

Another silence but I let it develop this time.

"There were quite a few people he didn't get on with, if that's what you mean. Your father never learned the value of compromise."

"Anyone he particularly disliked?"

I held my breath.

"As a matter of fact there was. Another Captain in his company. Hated the ground he walked on." It couldn't be this easy. "I met him several times, at those crushingly boring mess dos. Seemed a very nice man to me. Always polite. Well brought up. A gentleman."

Whatever my mother's faults, there was nothing wrong with her memory. I took another deep breath.

"Can you remember his name?"

"Jeremy, I think. Yes, Jeremy."

"Second name?"

"Um, Baxter. Jeremy Baxter," she said with a certain pride.

I let out a silent breath.

"Thanks, Mum." I had to change the subject quickly. "You know the weather here is absolutely gorgeous. The real humidity, apparently, doesn't come until later in the summer."

I should have known it wouldn't work.

"He is doing these things, isn't he, your father?"

There seemed no point in denying it. Word would soon get back to Foster about Josh. It would give her a further stick to hit him with but one more wouldn't make any difference.

"Yes."

"And is Jeremy Baxter his next victim."

"I don't know. I'm merely looking at possibilities."

"John, I don't want you involved in this anymore. You have to ....."

"Look, Mum, I've got to go."

"No ....."

"I'm parked at the side of the road and I'm getting strange looks. I'll call you later."

I hung up, knowing I'd never hear the last of that one. But I didn't care. I was on a mission. For the first time, there was a small chance I could get in front of Dad and I was going for it. Because I'd finally worked out why I felt this imperative to stop him? It wasn't because I disagreed with the notion he'd posed, that people should not get away with the injustices they do to others. I hadn't worked out an answer to that one, as he had, but then I didn't feel his burning sense of injustice. No, it was for him. That was why I was doing it. Living his revenge would eventually destroy him. I had to stop him for his own sake. Was that arrogant? Yes, of course. But he was my father.

The phone rang. I saw it was my mother and let it ring out. I needed to phone Brad and wanted to do it out here in the sun but knew I couldn't leave Charlotte on her own any longer.

"19!"

She caught sight of me and I was grateful when she smiled. I levered myself carefully between table and bench. The last time, I'd hit the table with my knee and spilt her juice. She raised her eyebrows inquisitively.

"I have a name but we're not there yet. I have to make another call."

The tables had thinned out around us, so I switched to the speaker so that Charlotte wouldn't feel left out. Across the room, the orca woman was still eating.

"Bradmondo! What's occurring?"

"Jonno, you bastard! How's the Land of the Free?"

"Hot, and the women are even hotter. Well, one in particular."

Charlotte fluttered her eyelashes.

"You bastard. She with you now?"

"Yes."

"Put her on."

"You think I'm stupid enough to let you speak to her."

"You bastard! Darling, if you're listening, whatever he says to you he's lying. I'm the good-looking one. And my dick is bigger."

Charlotte laughed out loud.

"She likes me, Jonno."

"She's appalled by you, Brad. She's laughing out of embarrassment."

He laughed loudly.

"Brad, I'm glad you're in good heart because I need a favour."

"Ah, ha."

"What have you got on at the moment?'

"Well, I have a meeting with Stephen Spielberg tomorrow morning. He wants my latest play. I'm debating whether compromising its artistic integrity is worth ten mil". Charlotte was laughing again. "Then I've got a Swiss banker flying in this afternoon to back my commercial development of Lincoln's new county cricket ground. But I can keep them waiting. What do you need?"

"Are your powers of research still finely tuned?"

"To perfection."

"So you're primed with pen and paper."

"Hold on." I could hear Brad's ancient, pay-as-you-go mobile hitting the table like the brick it was, then a small silence. "Go on."

"Jeremy Baxter."

"Okay."

"He was an officer in my father's regiment, the Paras. He was certainly there in '82 and probably for some time before and after that. I want to know everything you can find out about him; when he joined the Paras, when he left, what rank he left with and when and how he got his promotions. My father, whose name is Thomas, was breveted Major in '82. I need to know whether Baxter had anything to do with it not being confirmed. I also need to know where Baxter's living and what his situation is. Any other background information you can find out about him would also be appreciated, especially whether his name is on any official documents concerning my father."

"Is that all? Just a sec."

While I waited for Brad to catch up I glanced over at the obese woman. Her wooden chair was showing a definite bow in the middle. Across the table, Charlotte was completely still, looking at me with no expression that I could discern.

"Is it true what the police think about your father?" asked Brad.

"Yes."

"And Baxter's his next victim?"

"Possibly. So don't go close to Baxter. Do all your research from a distance. And Brad, you'll have expenses, especially if you travel to Chelmsford. Give me your bank account details. I'll transfer the ….."

"I don't need your money. And why Chelmsford?"

"You'll find out why Chelmsford, and Brad, you're skint. What are your account details?"

He growled.

"I'll put it on my new credit card."

"Okay but I'll pay you when I get back. I appreciate this."

"No worries. I'll get straight onto it, sir. Oh, and bye darling! Remember, whatever he's giving you, you get more for your buck with me."

Charlotte laughed again.

"Bye, Brad," she said.

"Baby, I just love your accent."

"Love yours, too."

I felt a twinge of jealousy and decided to cut in before the conversation got out of hand.

"Cheers then mate." I said.

"Cheers old buddy," in an attempt at an American accent and I pressed the red button.

"Sorry about that," I said. "He has an ego the size of Everest."

"He sounds fun."

"He is. He's also a good mate."

Charlotte nodded sombrely and over her shoulder I noticed the huge woman reach behind her and shift her weight, as if retesting the strength of the chair. It was definitely bowing now. I was just about to point this out to Charlotte when my phone rang. I looked at the display and got a bad feeling.

"Captain Taylor," I said and Charlotte raised her eyebrows.

"Where are you?"

The voice was harsh.

"In the Atlanta Bread Company at Morrow."

"Stay there," and the phone went dead.

It took a few moments for Charlotte to realise that Taylor had hung up.

"What?" she asked.

"He's coming here now and I don't think it's good news."

I could see her mind working behind the eyes.

"I'm not going," she said.

"I don't want you to, lass, but I don't want him finding out about Lizzie, either."

"You'll have to lie about me," she smiled.

I just knew she was going to say that.

"Look, it's not that I have a problem with lying persé, it's simply that – as you've already discovered – I'm not very good at it."

"In which case we'll only tell a small lie. We'll be perfectly honest about me; what my real name is and that I'm a police officer in Fannin County. He can check that information anyhow. But we kinda distort the truth about how we met, which was walking on the Appalachian Trail. Chance meeting. He asks about specifics, which he won't, make up some story about tripping over a tree root or something. There's no reason to mention the connection between our parents at all."

I nodded. Sounded easy enough.

I glanced over at the obese woman. She was feeling behind her all the time and adjusting her position. I dragged my eyes away from the imminent disaster and watched the car park, while the counter clerk continued to shout her numbers. Charlotte was looking into the distance.

"Would you believe I've never been out of the country," she said with her deadpan face and I realised she was still thinking about Amsterdam and Zeebruge.

"Why would you?" I said to console her. "You've got every kind of climate right here in North America. And you're not alone; 60% of Americans don't have passports."

But she didn't seem appeased.

"How many countries have *you* visited?"

"A few," I lied. "Brits tend to travel a lot."

She looked at me vacantly, which I now recognised as her sad look. I screwed up my courage.

"Why don't you come over and visit this summer?"

She looked at me enquiringly for a few moments.

"I'd like that."

This was accompanied by a small smile and I hoped I wouldn't regret my recklessness.

But right then Taylor arrived, flanked by two uniformed officers. They were a Laurel and Hardy cliché; one a tall, thin Caucasian, the other a short, rotund Mexican, with a full, curled-up moustache. For the second time a firearm was attached to Taylor's belt. He spotted us as he came in, although he strolled to the counter, apparently in no hurry. But he pointed towards us and the two officers sauntered over and plonked themselves at the table across the aisle, no more than six feet away. Both of them were steadily chewing the ever-present gum and trying not to stare at Charlotte. Taylor, carrying three iced teas, met my eye and I got the distinct impression this was going to be a long session. I remembered my English manners and stood.

"Captain, this is Charlotte Anderson."

He ignored both of us; just gave out the teas to his men, placed his own on the table and levered himself onto the bench beside Charlotte, without jogging the table.

"We met yesterday, in the mountains," I babbled.

She gave him the same initial scrutiny she'd given me but he didn't so much as glance at her.

"You can say anything in front of her, Captain. She knows everything." I looked down at the table. "I kind of unburdened myself."

He inclined his head toward her without taking his eyes off me.

"You have any connection with his pa, Mam?"

"I didn't know of his Pa's existence until I met John yesterday."

It was a clever answer. In any event, Taylor seemed satisfied with it and continued to glower at me.

"You heard from your Pa recently."

"No."

Everything about this interview told me something serious had happened. Taylor continued to glare.

"What is it?" I asked, eventually.

"Mr Josh Pesant was found today, lying beside his vehicle, outside his house, with his throat slit."

"Shit!" I said. He was examining my response. "Dead?"

The tall uniformed officer across the aisle scoffed loudly.

"Well, yes, dead," continued Taylor. "You get your throat slit by a professional assassin, you die, instantly. The only suspect for the murder is obviously your pa. Not content with beating the shit out of Pesant, he comes back for his life!"

I looked away from the hard eyes. Whether Dad had intended to kill Josh from the beginning I didn't know but it certainly worked for him. It enabled him to really punish Darlene, of course, by making her life and that of her family sheer misery. The grief caused by Josh's death would be huge, principally for Samantha but the knock-on effect for Darlene and Wendy would be immense, especially if Samantha blamed them for Josh's death. Wendy might not feel any guilt but I suspect Darlene would. I'd always seen Dad as a clever man but not a cruel one and suddenly it had all changed again. I couldn't care a rat's arse for the Sheffield gangster and I couldn't get worked up about burning down the Principal's house either. The assault on Josh I even ended up agreeing with. But killing him? I didn't even feel like challenging Taylor's portrayal of Dad as a professional assassin.

Bess looked away and took a deep breath. He's right. This murder is different. Gratuitous. Josh had had his punishment, part of which was to leave him frustrated and impotent. But Granddad had chosen to kill him and that seemed brutal and unnecessary. Or was it? Could Granddad have simply walked away from the lake, knowing that Josh wanted to kill him and having to look over his shoulder the rest of his life? But he was going to have to do that anyway, wasn't he, with the police after him in two countries? She just couldn't make the judgement. It was all getting too complicated.

Maybe she was examining it too narrowly. The big debate, surely, and one she and John were yet to have, is whether taking a man's life is justified under any circumstances. Before today she would have said definitely no. Now, she wasn't sure about that one either and she didn't think her uncle was. But John was asleep in his chair so now clearly wasn't the time.

She was very tired but she had to finish the chapter.

Charlotte's eyes, for the first time, held a touch of concern. When I spoke it was as though someone else was speaking.

"What can I do for you, Captain?"

I didn't think it possible for his face to harden any more but it did.

"I'm gonna ask you one more time. Do you have any idea where your pa is? Just bear in mind before you answer, that if I later find you lied to me about this I will slap you in jail so fast your Limey teeth will rattle."

"If I knew where he was do you think I wouldn't be there right now?"

"Do I take that as a 'no'?"

I could feel the anger again. It was almost becoming a friend.

"Yes, you can take that as a 'no'!"

I felt the tall officer stiffen before Taylor asked the next question.

"Where were you between 11.00 and 12.00 this morning?"

"He was with me," said Charlotte quickly. "In an SUV, driving from North Georgia to Jonesboro."

Taylor shifted his position on the bench, so that he was half turned towards her and they finally made eye contact.

"And what do you do exactly, Miss Anderson?"

"I'm a police officer in Fannin County, on vacation."

His tongue snaked out to touch his goatee; a gesture I remember him making only once before.

"That a fact? And what do you do, *exactly*, in Fannin County Police Department?"

"I'm the sergeant in charge of traffic."

"Mighty fine, mighty fine. Graduate entry?"

"Yes."

"What's ya degree?"

"Criminal Law."

"Ha, that a fact now? That a fact? So what's ya connection with this Brit."

He flicked his thumb at me.

"We met by chance and," she paused and glanced at me, "found we liked each other. The fact that I'm a police officer is a coincidence."

He continued to look at her for a few moments before shifting position and facing me again.

"How do you communicate with your pa, laptop or cell?"

My heart hit my stomach.

"Laptop, mainly."

"You don't use your cell phone?"

"I phone him. He never replies. I text him but again he rarely replies."

"Navigate to the texts you've sent to your pa, then hand me the phone."

I did as he asked, knowing there was nothing of value. I could feel Charlotte's gaze on me but I kept looking at Taylor, scrolling through and seeing that I was telling the truth. His face was still a mask.

"But he does send you emails, right."

This was the question I was dreading.

"Yes."

221

"You get your email on this?"

"I can but when I'm with my laptop I tend to use that."

"And where is your laptop?"

"In the Jeep."

"Go get it. Officer Zackary will accompany you."

The tall Caucasian stood up. I hesitated and not just because of the way Taylor had put it. My laptop was my most valued possession. I did most of my work on it and, along with my smartphone, conducted a lot of my personal life on it, too. But he had me and he knew it. I quickly thought through Dad's emails. They would confirm his crimes, of course, but the police knew anyway. It was the violation of intimacy I resented.

"That's my property, Captain. I'm not sure I want to do that."

Taylor smiled for the first time.

"Sergeant Anderson, as an expert in criminal law, would you kindly tell Mr Stafford here the extent of my powers, under the Georgia Code, in a murder investigation."

Charlotte looked seriously concerned for the first time.

"You don't have any choice, John. If you refuse he'll forcibly search you at gun point. He'll find the keys and get the computer anyway. He might even throw you in jail for good measure, for obstructin' justice."

Taylor had looked at me the entire time, so I looked straight back into Taylor's eyes, silently showing my displeasure. Perhaps he was just doing his job, although I didn't like the way he did it. But, if it had to be it had to be. I simply had to accept it, the way Dad had had to accept Darlene extorting the cheque. At least I'd destroyed the *Word* file, so there was no electronic link to Lizzie. I took a deep breath and reached into my shorts' pocket, extracting the car keys, then threw them to the cop who was still standing. He was so surprised he dropped them.

"It's the white Jeep," I said. "Under the passenger seat."

Officer Zackary picked up the keys and looked at me with grievous bodily harm in mind.

"Do it," said Taylor and Zackary reluctantly moved off.

There was an awkward silence, while Taylor drank his tea and stared at me.

"I want a receipt," I said, still feeling belligerent.

"Oh, I'm not sure I want to take it away, Mr Stafford; at least not at this time." He watched my reaction with amusement. "I just want to look at your email. I'm sure you'll help me with the passwords." Taylor looked under the table. "There's no power outlet here."

"There's enough juice in the batteries."

"In which case, why don't we place it on that counter over there by the door? Then we can all see it, nice and cosy."

Having connected, and on Taylor's instructions, I entered my email, but only my old account. There were two new messages and both were Spam.

"There are messages in the Inbox from my father," I said. "I'll leave you to it."

I took Charlotte's arm and guided her back to our bench. Looking back I saw that one of the officers was keeping us under observation but he wasn't within earshot.

"There's a more recent account," I said.

"What?"

"There's a more recent email account. Dad pinned the address under my windscreen wiper. And if I know Dad, there's a message waiting for me."

"You'll have to tell him. If Taylor finds out you withheld it, your feet won't touch."

"It's webmail. There's no way he can know."

"You don't understand. You're playin' with fire. What do you think's gonna happen now? When we leave here the police are gonna be over you like a fly on shit. You won't get any privacy."

"What about in my own bedroom?"

"Well, yeh, you'll get that, but they burst in on you when you're accessing that withheld account and you are in jail, bud."

I looked away and abruptly, incongruously, remembered the gross woman but somehow, in all the activity, she'd gone and I hadn't noticed. The chair was still intact, although with what looked like a permanent sag.

"29."

"If I give him that email account, Taylor will find out about your mother. Do you want that?"

Charlotte looked down at the table before looking at me again.

"No but it won't be the end of the world. She had nothing to do with the homicides."

"The police may tell Darlene about her."

"True but I would say that's the least of Darlene's troubles."

I couldn't help being impressed with her capacity to hold a bland facial expression, so you didn't know what she was thinking. It was like moods passed her by. But it was more than that. She kind of withheld herself and watched you. Before I thought she was like an actress; now I realised it was the opposite, as if she were part of an audience at a play.

"I was thinking of the effect on Lizzie when Darlene contacts her, which she will." She just stared blankly. "Also, there may be an admission from Dad that he murdered Josh."

"There's no doubt about that anyway, is there?"

I ran my hands through the stubble on my scalp.

"And there's another besides," she said. "I have to consider my position now. If there is any information on that email account which might give Taylor an idea of your father's location I am duty bound to tell him. Your father has committed murder on US soil and I am a police officer."

Given my record with women I shouldn't have been surprised but I was, which just goes to show how bloody naive I am.

"So what happened to pretending not to be a police officer?"

Again, her face still held that neutral pose.

"That was before the homicide. John, I have no choice."

I suppose it was as close to pleading as she could get. At least she wasn't pretending she was acting on my behalf.

"You don't know that it will contain that information," I said.

"No. But it may contain a clue. That's why Taylor wants it? Please tell him, John."

It was definitely a plea but her look was the same.

"So what are you saying to me, Charlotte, that if I don't tell him you will?" She said nothing. "Knowing that if I refuse I'll be slung in jail and interrogated."

She continued to say nothing; just looked at me with that frustratingly blank expression. With Jude or Brad I wouldn't be having this conversation. I don't know what I was more disappointed about; having to reveal the email or Charlotte's duplicity.

"You know the irony here, Charlotte; my father wouldn't be so stupid as to give a hint of his whereabouts, even to me. Especially to me. And you seem to have forgotten something; if they interview Lizzie they'll find out who you really are."

I could see her thinking about that.

"But I haven't said anything untrue."

"Misleading, though."

She didn't answer that, so I got up and walked over to Taylor. I glanced over my shoulder in the hope that she'd call me back but she simply stared at me.

"There's another email account," I said.

He turned and looked at me, then back at Charlotte.

"Now why didn't ya tell me about that before?"

"Shall I get it up?" I asked.

"Be my guest, but write down the username and password first."

I complied, then logged off one account and onto another. And there was a brand new message from my father.

Son

Sorry I couldn't make the ABC. Decided it was better to keep my head down. Somehow Josh got hold of my old email address. I guess Darlene gave it to him. Anyway, he asked to meet me again, arrived with two friends, both armed with handguns, intention clear. Fortunately I'd smelled a rat and was well-hidden. But I had no choice then. I couldn't live the rest of my life with Josh alive, looking over my shoulder for him, or one of his killers. They might even have gone for you. So, I drove to his house and waited behind a convenient fir tree halfway down the drive.

I think my revenge on the Bentley family is now complete. I thought about taking the Acura. After all, it's mine. Instead, I think it will serve better as an unpleasant reminder to Darlene of Josh's death, from which my wonderful wife will never recover. Nor does she deserve to. I imagine she seems like a helpless idiot to you. Believe me, she's not.

So, my mission over here is done. I'd like to have visited some of the great friends I left in Georgia but it wouldn't have been easy, or appropriate. Above all, I would love to have seen Lizzie. I think you know why I can't.

I promise you I will meet you soon but it has to be when I'm done. I fear your powers of persuasion more than the Grim Reaper himself. You, of course, will try and find me before then and try to stop me. It's your nature.

Take care, son. Love you more than I can say.

Dad

Taylor was a slower reader than I, so I looked out of the window and tried to crush down the emotions. Somehow, through one of the methods Charlotte and I had discussed, Dad was going to leave the country, en route to his next victim. Whether that was Baxter or someone else, I didn't know. The near-empty car park, with its huge spaces designed to accommodate American gas-guzzlers, was still bathed in sunlight. In the distant blue, a small light winked, and I saw it was a plane, queuing in its landing slot for Hartsfield. Beyond it was another plane and then another. I watched them hanging there, defying gravity, while I waited for the questions.

"So, we have a written admission of guilt."

"Yes."

"Who's Lizzie?"

Taylor's temperature seemed to have cooled a little but since he'd been close to boiling point that didn't say a great deal. I thought carefully about an answer.

"She's the love of my father's life and he hers. He hasn't seen her for five years and she has no idea where he is. And, as you can see from the email, he has no intention of seeing her."

Taylor pulled his goatee.

"Yeh, I did see that and I wonder why, if she is 'the love of his life', he wouldn't wanna visit."

Taylor continued to gaze at me in that intense way he had, brown eyes piercing and I willed myself to look back into them.

"I don't know."

"He says you do know."

"Well, he's wrong, I don't!"

Beside me I felt Officer Zackary shift his weight. Taylor's gaze stayed on me.

"Give me Lizzie's address."

"No."

I felt Zackary move closer. Taylor flicked a warning glance towards him.

"This is a murder enquiry, Mr Stafford."

"As you've said, Captain, but I'm not going to give it to you."

I felt a firm grip on my arm and a peppermint breath on my face.

"Zack," said Taylor firmly, "leave it."

But Zackary was not in the mood for leaving it.

"I don't think you heard the Cap'n, sir," said Zackary, chewing the gum, smiling the smile.

Taylor could have stepped in again but chose not to. I looked into Zackary's simple, beaming face.

"Take your fucking hand off my arm and get your foul breath out of my face!"

Zackary stopped chewing and his smile was replaced with a toothy snarl.

"Zack! Move away."

This time he did; slowly, reluctantly.

"I'll ask you again for Lizzie's address," said Taylor.

"Captain, she has no more idea where he is than I do. Believe me. My father wouldn't be so stupid as to tell her, just the same as he wouldn't tell me, for the same reasons. Now you can arrest me, slap me in gaol, have me up before the beak in the morning. To be honest I'm passed fucking caring. But I'm not going to give you Lizzie's address. She's had enough stress in her life and I don't want you giving her any more."

I gazed out over the parking lot again, feeling them all looking at me. It seemed an age before Taylor said:

"In that case I'll need the laptop."

"I'll need a receipt."

"Officer Gomez, give Mr Stafford a receipt for his computer."

It was then I realised that my defiance had been a waste of time. He was going to find Lizzie's address from one of Dad's previous emails. The stocky Mexican gave me a receipt and they prepared to leave. My anger had gone as swiftly as it had appeared and I tried a polite tone.

"There's nothing left for me here, Captain," I said. "You saw what my father wrote. He's finished, too. I need to book a flight back, probably for tomorrow. Can I pick up the laptop at mid-day?"

"You can come to the station but I can't guarantee it will be available."

They walked out then. I turned for a final glance at Charlotte, looking so delicious but deadly and staring at me defiantly. So I simply left her there, to find her own way back to Blue Ridge and headed for the nearest motel.

I found one at Eagles' Landing, booked myself in and walked to the nearest bar. Over my first *Sam Adams* I texted Dad.

Cops have laptop + email usernames + passwords! Need new webmail accounts. In bar on Eagle Spring Drv. Cop outside. Christ Dad you actually fucking killed him!

I was into my third when the reply came through, with his perfect spelling and punctuation.

Sorry, Son. Didn't think through the trouble it would cause you. Go home. Promise will speak when ready. Mine: prey8040@yahoo.com. Yours: searcher8040@yahoo.com.

"Fuck you," I said loudly and the Australian bartender looked over.

"Stood you up has she?" she asked.

"I wish," I replied but we struck up a conversation, which lasted until my sixth bottle, when I staggered back to my lonely bed, thought of Charlotte's enigmatic smile and slept the sleep of the damned.

He left her. He just left her there! He could at least have gone back and had it out with her. There might even have been some conflict resolution. But for him, she knew, it was better to avoid a problem than confront it. Which was a shame because Bess sensed he'd missed an opportunity there. They certainly liked each other. No, they fancied each other. "It's the three L-words, Lass; Love, Like and Lust. When you're young, it's all about the love and the lust. The thing is, though, you can't have romantic love without lust but you can lust without loving. Love can get in the way sometimes and liking someone is fickle. But lust is true. It's pure and uncomplicated." She remembered her uncle saying that. Now she wondered whether he was quoting his father. Did he get in touch with Charlotte again, or with Lizzie?

He was still asleep in his chair, so holding the journal to her chest, she got up quietly and slipped upstairs to her room. And it was *her room. He kept it for her, like a shrine almost, from the blue and gold flowered duvet they'd bought together a decade ago, to the posters of pop stars and bands she'd worshipped in her teenage but had now ceased to admire.*

She climbed into bed, intending to finish the chapter but, when her head lay back on the remembered pillow, she felt sleepy and began listening to owls calling across the valley. They were Tawnies, John had said. She wondered if they have Tawny owls in the North Georgia Mountains, then slept, dreaming of high, blue hills and a dog called Patch.

Extract 12

So, finally, to the final custody hearing. The fucking custody hearing, which was planned to stretch to three days and lasted two. At the last minute Manton didn't turn up. He sent a junior instead and I tried not to see him as a rat leaving the sinking ship.

Part of me wants to give you a full account of what took place; relate the arguments for and against in the style of real courtroom drama, to recount the cut and thrust of barristers duelling at the bench. But the sensible side of me, the side that wants to be without too much pain at this time, wants to avoid detail like the plague because, in the telling, this story is hard, son. This is the fourth day of writing and I want to be rid of it. I want to finish it before I reach the bottom of your bottle of Chivas.

The first day focused on Stella. She was in the witness box and answered questions from the defending and prosecuting barristers. And she was so confident. She told lies from beginning to end, of course, but, apart from the sexual abuse allegation, she handled it all with consummate ease.

"So," asked Sixsmith at one point, "these accusations your husband is making concerning your abuse of your daughter are complete fiction, is that right?"

I remember her taking on a look of sadness, as if someone had just told her of a death.

"I'm afraid so."

"Why do you say that? 'I'm afraid so'."

"Because it's not a very nice thing to have said of one. And because ….."

She hesitated, looking at the floor.

"Because?" prompted Sixsmith.

Stella placed her hand over her mouth and blinked rapidly, as if in distress. The judge smiled at her kindly.

"Take your time, Mrs Stafford," shooting a fierce glance at Sixsmith.

"Because," said Stella, eventually, "I think Tom has been under such stress at work that he sometimes doesn't know what he's saying. I think he's been mentally disturbed for a while. My family and some of his colleagues agree with me."

If I didn't know her I would have believed it. Sixsmith paused, probably wondering how she should follow that up.

"Mrs Stafford, have you ever threatened to commit suicide?"

"No."

"When your husband told you that he was going to divorce you and take the children you didn't threaten to commit suicide?"

"No!"

The reply was almost indignant and the judge nodded with a frown, as if the question had been unnecessary.

The next day was September 8th and my turn in the witness box. You know, whenever that day comes round every year I don't sleep the night before. Most people, when asked to identify the worst day of their life, find it difficult to remember. I have no such difficulty. And I do remember the very clever trick by her barrister; the way he drew me into the trap.

"Mr Stafford, this claim about your wife's abuse of your daughter," he spoke with a sort of incredulity in his voice, "it's fiction isn't it?"

"Not at all, it's very real."

He frowned to himself.

"But you see, there's no evidence."

"If the Court Welfare Officers had interviewed Rachel early enough, and had asked the right questions, there would have been evidence."

"Early enough?"

"Before my wife persuaded Rachel that things would now be all right between them."

"I see, so things are all right now, between your wife and your daughter?"

I hesitated.

"They appear to be."

He feigned a puzzled expression and looked at the judge.

"So, what is the problem?"

"The problem is that my wife is faking it. The only reason she is being nice to her now is because she wants desperately to win this hearing, so she can gain the bulk of the family capital and retain her reputation in the local community. She'd love to get rid of Rachel, indeed, she offered her to me in a deal, where I took my daughter, she took my son and we split the proceeds."

Out of the corner of my eye I saw her shaking her head slowly and I forced myself to look at her. She was smiling sadly. The judge was looking at her, too. Her barrister opened his mouth to say something but I got in first.

"I refused to split up the children so she's forced to be nice to Rachel for now. But if she was to gain sole custody of the children, she'd return to type and I fear for Rachel's safety and sanity."

He looked down at his notes.

"Do you know a Helen Worthington?"

The sudden change of tack threw me, as was intended.

"Yes."

"In what capacity?"

I'd known this question would come up but I remember my stomach turning over, nonetheless. What I should have said at that moment was the whole truth and nothing but the truth; that we were good friends and I saw her about twice a week; that she was my rock in these difficult times and that it was not a sexual relationship. It wouldn't have been too damaging. Instead I stupidly tried to play down the relationship because I knew how key it was for your mother.

"She's a keep fit teacher in one of my classes."

"So, you have no other relationship with her other than one of tutor and student?"

To be honest, son, I can't remember my exact answer, here. I think I said something about us being friends.

"So, you don't meet her outside of class?"

I hesitated, feeling the judge's eyes boring into me and I panicked.

"We may have met a couple of times, yes."

"Just a couple?"

"Yes."

He consulted his notes again.

"You drive a Saab, is that right? Registration D209 ENN?"

I had a terrible sense of foreboding, like death was waiting at the bottom of a steep slide.

"Yes."

"Do you know St Benedict's Close?"

I parked the Saab there every time I visited Helen. St Benedict's Church was a couple of streets away from where she lived. I never parked outside her door because I didn't want anyone to know we were seeing each other. My stomach turned over and I panicked again.

"I don't think so, no."

I heard myself say it and couldn't believe I had.

"It's round the corner from where Mrs Worthington lives."

"Is it?"

"Yes; just a few streets away. Since you deny knowing St Benedict's Close, Mr Stafford, you'd be surprised to learn that your car was parked there three days ago, for two hours, between 8.15 and 10.05pm."

I realised, in that moment, that I'd lost. Technically, I'd lied when giving evidence. He'd caught me out and the system would never forgive me. It wasn't a very big lie. Compared with hers it was miniscule. But the difference was I'd been caught. I felt myself coming out in a sweat and gripped the edge of the witness box for support while her barrister continued.

"Your honour, I have here a sworn statement form a private detective, showing that Mr Stafford's car was parked in St Benedict's Close, on that day, at that time, plus 4 other occasions in recent months."

I'd been followed and I hadn't noticed, but then I hadn't been looking.

"Mr Stafford," said the judge, his face like thunder, "have you anything to say?"

I knew what I had to say now.

"Yes. Mrs Worthington is a very good friend of mine. We do see each other occasionally. But it is not a sexual relationship. We started seeing each other after I took out divorce and custody proceedings. But the main part of my evidence is the truth. My wife is a child-abuser!"

"Recess!" shouted Sixsmith.

Chapter 18

Friday 17 May 2013

I walked out of Terminal 2 at Manchester Airport, to be greeted by a grey dawn, a big wind that had blown us across the Atlantic in record time and a waving Terry, standing beside his little, blue Peugeot. I was really pleased to see his open, completely honest face.

It was almost a week since this had all begun and I was close to exhaustion. Normally I sleep like the proverbial on planes; especially flying back from the East Coast during the night, when you lose 5 hours. But this time, back to flying 'economy', I was kept awake by the constant flushing of the toilet through the bulkhead at my back, children crying and the frustrating fidgeting of the landscape gardener beside me. All I could do was doze and, of course, think. Not that I did much serious thinking. It was rather like that half-time between waking and getting up, when semi-conscious thoughts enter and roust around, unbidden and uncaring. To some extent you can control them.

Strangely, I didn't think about Dad much. It was almost as if I knew I could do nothing about that issue until I heard from Brad. And I knew how I felt about my father. Pesant's murder had not affected that. I might not understand it but you don't need to understand why people do things to feel affection for them. I love my sister but I'm not sure I like her very much and I certainly couldn't live with her any more.

I did think about Charlotte a lot, which was probably brought on by a strange combination of desire and guilt. I'd decided, sadly, that beauty *is* its own reward. I can be as shallow as the next man about that. The real disappointment, though, was admitting to myself that I'd actually started to like her. She had honesty and a kind of sadness that I wanted to eradicate. And I was haunted by a sense of remorse at simply leaving her, to wonder whether I was coming back and finally realising that I wasn't. But she would have given up my father to Taylor, as well as the well-being of her own mother for Christ's sake! That I would not have believed. In the end she had shown she was the same as the others. They all let you down in the end.

So, with these maudlin thoughts I greeted Terry and hefted my luggage into the boot, including my laptop. "You copied the hard drive?" I'd asked Taylor but he hadn't answered, just handed it back and turned away.

I slept for a wonderful three hours at Dorothy's and, just before leaving, she told me, calmly and without emotion, about the results of a recent biopsy. A cancer I didn't know she had had spread to her bones and she wasn't expected to live passed Christmas. Would I please tell everyone on my side of the family, just so that they knew? The thought of telling Dad depressed me so much I couldn't face it and all I could remember about the drive back to Lincoln was continually looking in the mirror.

***

The only CIA building that most people are aware of is the impressive looking headquarters at Langley Virginia. In fact, the word 'Langley' has become synonymous with the 'CIA'. But Stafford knew there were many other CIA premises, mostly in Washington several miles away, sometimes standalone and sometimes sharing with other departments of state. The address he was told to enter into his satnav was 2430 East Street North West, Washington DC. It was the original headquarters which, when Langley was completed, was meant to be abandoned, but it never was. In fact it's now part of a complex, fronted by an attractive red-brick building, which the Central Intelligence Agency shares with the State Department.

Confident that the reach of Clayton County Police Department didn't stretch to a federal agency 700 miles away by road, he showed his real passport to the guard and drove into a crowded car park, stopping next to a Porsche Boxster convertible, with the hood down, the hazy Washington sun warming its soft beige leather. The poor man's Porsche but still a nice car.

Stepping out, he noticed that the temperature was considerably cooler than it had been in Georgia, which justified his choice of jeans and leather jacket. He was sure it wasn't fashionable but then that had never been part of his motivation. John, he knew, wouldn't buy any clothing that wasn't attached to a current fashion house. Even his underwear was Calvin Klein! Different generation and different culture but sometimes he worried about John. He knew he wasn't soft but his hardness had yet to be really tested. The unmistakeable, comforting aroma of a river came to him and he looked west. The car park was high on a bank and he could see the Potomac clearly, deep and green, only 300 yards away beyond the John F Kennedy Centre for the Performing Arts.

He walked towards the entrance and hardened his mind. This was a meeting he could do without but one that was entirely of his own making. He'd never been able to stop himself being a fucking boy scout and the weakness was always getting him in trouble. The irony was that no one he did business with would ever believe it. After Pesant, neither, probably, would John.

The handshake was dry and firm.

"Doug Reed. Pleased to meet you Mr Stafford."

But he said it in a way that implied he wasn't pleased to see him at all. Dark eyes looked up at Stafford as if he'd raped his daughter. And Reed was not what he was expecting. The CIA has strict guidelines for employee health and fitness, which everyone is expected to follow; even senior managers. There's a gym on most of their premises and they tend to cook their own, low-fat food. And, true, Reed was clean-shaven, had a dark suit, white shirt, company tie and black shoes polished to a brightness that would have blinded if they were ever allowed into the sun. But he was also obese, with a stomach that could have contained a beer barrel. He was probably about 45, yet the hair was jet black and Stafford suddenly realised it was a toupee. Matching black-rimmed spectacles sat on the podgy face. In fact, the only bit of real colour on his entire person was his mouth.

"This way please."

The tone was definitely curt, not even the hint of a smile and Stafford recognised that, like himself, this was a meeting Reed wanted to get over with as soon as possible. The corridor was lined with large battle paintings, mostly depicting the War of Independence, although Stafford noticed one which contained the battle flag of the Confederacy as well as Old Glory, so the Civil War was also a feature.

"You've been here before, I believe."

"A while ago. Maybe 7 years. Before your time I think. Your record keeping is good."

"Hmm. Actually, to prove your point, it was 8 years."

Stafford nodded and sniffed the aroma of freshly baked bread coming through an open door, then was immediately ushered into a small, windowless briefing room, with a table, six chairs and a huge, flat screen showing a map of Libya. The door slid to automatically behind him, hydraulics hissing as rubber expanded towards the floor, sealing them off from the outside world and he realised they were in what British security services call a 'secure speech' room. Anyone attempting to listen to their conversation using the incredibly powerful long-distance microphones now widely available would be disappointed. British secure speech rooms were always cold, Stafford remembered, but the CIA seemed to have mastered temperature control.

The two people present stood as he entered and he felt them examining him.

"Mr Stafford, this is Raziya Goldstein," said Reed with a certain pride, as if she were a prodigy. "Don't be put off by her apparent youth; she's head of our Libya Desk."

She was tiny - five feet nothing at most - and came round the table with quick, short steps, pulling an embarrassed smile. Yet he sensed a paradoxical boldness about her, as she threw out her hand and looked up at him keenly behind thick-framed spectacles. Stafford liked her instinctively.

"Morning," he said.

"Good morning," she replied, before pacing back round the table.

"And this is Zac Prentice. He's our oil expert. We've bussed him in from Langley especially." He paused and glanced wryly at Raziya." Although, actually, I'm told he drives a brand new Porsche, so they're obviously paying him too much over at headquarters."

Stafford knew that the Porsche he'd seen in the car park was a 4-year-old model but he said nothing. Nor, sensibly, did Zac, although his expression indicated he wanted to. He seemed even younger than Raziya. But whereas she was tiny and dark-haired, he was tall, blonde and had the look of a decathlete about him. There was a confidence in his movements, too, as he came round the table and an extra squeeze to the handshake, to reinforce a tough-guy image.

"So," said Reed loudly and everyone moved to sit down. "As you know, Mr Stafford is going to Libya to sort out Legacy's pipeline problem. It's up to us to give him as much intel as we can that might assist him in that task, although officially this meeting is not taking place."

This was said with a deadpan expression but both Raziya and Zac grinned. They already knew about the need for secrecy, of course. The warning had been for Stafford, who sat back in his cushioned chair and relaxed.

"I'm very grateful to you, Mr Reed," he said, "for arranging this meeting.

I'm sure it will be a great help to me." He could be as courteous as the next man when he wanted to be. "But I have to say, just so we're under no misapprehension here, that what I've agreed so far is to examine Legacy's pipeline issue. I haven't agreed, yet, to take the job."

To his surprise Reed pulled a small grin.

"Hmm, you seem wiser than your boss, at least. Ms Goldstein will conduct the briefing." Reed pointedly looked at his watch. "I'll stay, so long as it doesn't take too long."

Raziya, clearly used to Reed's attitude, broke into a smile and fixed her intelligent brown eyes on Stafford.

"How much do you know about Libya?" she asked aggressively.

Stafford looked at the map of Libya on the LCD display that took up one entire wall. He'd spent much of the last 24 hours online, boning up on the country and had almost made a decision. All he really wanted from the meeting was confirmation of the current political and military situation but he'd make it look good.

"Not a lot," he said. "Geographically, it's a huge country, the size of Alaska, with only six million people and the largest known oil reserves in Africa, hence its importance. The vast majority of the population lives along the northern coastal strip, in the cities of Tripoli, Benghazi, Misrata and Sirte, as well as the towns that have developed around the oil industry, like Azzawiyah. The Al-Jabal Al-Gharbi area south of Tripoli also holds a fair amount of the population. But most of the country is mountainous desert and deserted."

He paused and gave Raziya an enquiring look. She nodded and added: "The Sabha region in the Fezzan district also has a fair-sized population." She fiddled with her mouse and the large screen image zoomed into an area about 150 miles to the east-north-east of the Elephant Oilfield.

"Thank you."

She had lapsed into silence and Stafford felt he was being tested.

"Language-wise it's Arabic, although I confess I'm not sure how Libyan Arabic differs from modern, standard Arabic."

She looked up in surprise.

"You speak it?"

"I'm a bit rusty."

"Where'd ya learn it?"

"Lebanon, although I did extend it later to include some classical stuff."

She nodded.

237

"You should be fine. The past tense is used much more in the case of verbs but you'll get used to that. Many of the words are spelled differently, of course, but they're pronounced roughly the same. Some nouns have slightly different meanings, too but they tend to have the same sound. *Lauh*, for example, is spelt *lo h*, and means simply 'wood' as opposed to 'plank', but you'll get used to that, too."

She may be Jewish, Stafford thought, but she knew her Arabic. Reed was fidgeting beside him and looking irritated.

"Thank you," said Stafford to Raziya. "That makes me feel more confident about the language." She smiled again and Stafford felt he'd made a friend. " Moving on, I think we can take the political and security aspects together and it's not good. The General National Congress is not really running the country. Neither is the President, Al Magariaf, nor is the Prime Minister, Ali Zeidan, neither is the National Army or the various police forces. The country is controlled by militias. In fact the Government of Libya, such as it is, is actually employing some of the militias to keep control. A mess but I'd be grateful, Raziya, if you'd put some flesh on that skeleton for me."

She nodded.

"Yes, sir. Generally speaking you're correct. And you need to know that all the militias seem to be well-armed; the bigger ones particularly, with armoured troop carriers, tanks, SAM and rocket launchers."

Stafford thought that confirmed his decision to go in on his own. Taking a group of armed men would be provocative and futile.

"Our belief is that most of the GNC is sympathetic towards the Muslim Brotherhood and the Islamists, which make up a lot of the militias."

She fiddled with her mouse and the face of a 70 year-old man in a general's uniform replaced the map on screen.

"There is some good news. This is Khalifa Haftar. He's our guy."

Reed cleared his throat less than discretely and she paused.

"Careful, Ms Goldstein."

"Yes sir," but she hesitated. "I think it's fairly well known outside the Agency, sir, that we promoted Hafter in Chad in the 80s." She paused to check with Reed, who nodded and she turned her gaze on Stafford. "Being opposed to Ghaddafi, he was exiled to the US."

Again she hesitated.

"Where you trained him in anti-terrorism," suggested Stafford.

Everyone looked at Reed, who was silent for a long time, until.

"Yes, Mr Stafford, we did, and a few other things, also."

"And it's proved worthwhile," continued Raziya enthusiastically. "He's now effectively in charge of the army in Libya, despite the GNC's attempts to veto that decision, and at the moment is engaged in fighting jihadist groups in Benghazi and the surrounding area. In fact, you could say that the militias are starting to coalesce around two distinct movements; one led by Haftar and the other composed of Islamists. We're not sure who the leader of that latter group will be yet, even if it does coalesce. There are hundreds of these militias and they spend a lot of time fighting each other. The situation is very fluid and can change overnight."

Which again simply confirmed his judgment but he'd better show willing.

"What about the area I'm supposed to be going to?"

She looked round at the blond Adonis as if he were an insect on the sole of her shoe.

"Sure," said Zac, "Raziya, you want to get the oilfield up on the screen."

A few clicks and another map of Libya appeared, this one with all the oilfields marked in red, the oil terminals in purple and the pipelines in black. Stafford was impressed by the sheer number.

"How many are there?"

"Over a hundred oilfields. There are not so many pipelines because companies share those. And, of course, there are gas pipelines as well, which ....."

"And where exactly is the oilfield in question?"

"Er, right, Raziya?"

She zoomed in.

"And how far from Tripoli is that, by road?"

"Just over 200 miles."

Stafford glanced at Raziya and raised an eyebrow. She nodded.

"And what are the dangers en route to that oilfield would you say?"

"Manifold," she replied. "There are well armed militias throughout the region. If you got through without being ambushed I'd be very surprised."

It was now Stafford's turn to nod. At this juncture he should ask about Legacy's involvement: oilfield, pipeline, where the blockage is, and any satellite images the CIA had, but he couldn't see the point.

"Mr Prentice, what's the general situation with oil production in Libya as a whole?"

"Deteriorating rapidly. Legacy's not the only company that has ......"

"What about offshore?"

"Now that's a bit different. There are active fields still pumping oil. In fact BP is putting a lot of investment right now into what it thinks is a new field north-west of Tripoli. Trouble is, downstream the only terminals would be in Libya and they're targeted by militias."

"Show me the offshore field."

Raziya played with her mouse and they all peered at the screen.

"Where is it Zac? About here?"

She drew a yellow circle.

"Yeh, bout there."

"How far from Tunisia would you say that is?" asked Stafford.

"60 mile maybe," answered Zac.

"Is there oil off the Tunisian coast, in the Gulf of Hammamet?"

"There's some. Lundin Petroleum and Eni both drill there. But rumours are the BP field, which is closer to Libya, has much more scope."

Stafford shifted his head to gaze passed Raziya and imagined the town behind the thick wall; the sprawl of downtown Washington, with its wide, tree-lined boulevards almost absent of traffic and he became aware of the total silence for the first time.

"Do you think, Ms Goldstein, that the political and military situation in Libya will improve in the short- to medium-term?"

She glanced at Reed before answering.

"Frankly, no. I think it's going to get worse."

"Despite Hafter?"

She hesitated only to pull a small smile.

"Despite Hafter,"

Stafford nodded, pulled himself upright in his chair and placed both hands on the table.

"You've all been very helpful. Mr Reed, do you have Mr Bramble's cell number. I think I'd like to talk to him direct."

They all waited while Reed consulted his mobile phone.

**

Arriving home around 3.30pm, I phoned Jude and Brad but got no reply, so I left text messages to meet me at *The Coal Scuttle* at the usual time, then busied myself with domestic duties like clothes washing, whilst catching up on the world via SkyNews.

"Will you look at this guy," said Jude, as I walked up to our usual table. "He strolls in like Beckham, wearing Dockers shorts and boasting the tan from hell."

"It comes naturally," I replied, sitting down and sipping the beer they'd already bought me. "God, that tastes good!"

Jude turned to Brad.

"See what I mean. He's gone for a week, does he say, 'Hey, guys, great to see you?' No. All he's interested in is the beer."

"True," answered Brad, "but I want to know about Charlotte. Is she as gorgeous as she sounds?"

"Ugly as sin."

That made him pause.

"Really?" asked Brad.

I took another sip, trying to look serious.

"What can I say? Sorry to disappoint."

Brad gave his bark of a laugh.

"You lying toad!" and we all laughed.

"Good shag?"

"Never happened."

"Why not?"

"Well, we had a kind of disagreement."

Brad's mouth dropped open but nothing came out. Jude grasped two imaginary labels, as if he were wearing a jacket and looked into the middle distance.

"Your honour, this witness is being deliberately obtuse. I'd be obliged if you would direct him to answer the question. 'Kind of disagreement'; what is that exactly?"

"Well," I smiled, trying to make a joke of it, "she offended my sensibilities."

"She's gorgeous, isn't she?" persisted Brad.

I looked into my beer, still smiling.

"Yes, Brad, she's just about the most gorgeous woman I've ever met."

"I knew it! And you were out before you even got to the wicket. Man, those sensibilities of yours sure get in the way of progress. Couldn't you have shagged her first?"

We all laughed and I held up my glass to a chorus of, "Amen to that." The familiarity of it all gave me an overwhelming sense of belonging. This was *my* rock. It was where I felt at home and, just for the moment, I didn't want to think of my father. But duty is a strange thing.

"So, Brad, what have you got?" I asked.

He placed his hand on a cardboard file lying on the bench beside him.

"Quite a lot, but first a quick résumé from you is in order, I think." He looked at Jude. "Is that the right word?"

"That is the right word."

I took another swig. I'd already decided to tell them everything, although there wasn't much they didn't already know.

"I'm happy to but the police might interview you. If they do, you know nothing of certain facts, which I'll mention as I go along."

Brad was laughing.

"Now hold on, Jonno," he said, "the police are my long-standing, best buddies. I'm going to tell them everything, you know that."

I smiled.

"Okay, but Jude, as an officer of the court, it might place you ......"

He was laughing, too.

"Only you would concern yourself with something like that."

"You actually beat me to it, lass."

John strolled into the kitchen, wearing his dressing gown and running a hand over bristly hair. Bess had slept like the proverbial and woken early to rain beating against her window. Normally, she'd ignore it and lie in until eleven but not this morning. Eschewing the shower she'd crept down for a mug of coffee and the next chapter of Cold Eating.

"That's a first," he continued. "Oh, lass," catching sight of the coffee jug, "you are a beauty."

He poured into one of the small, flat cups he preferred, sat down at the table across from her and rubbed his unshaven chin in that desultory way she'd recently discovered men adopt in the mornings.

"God, that tastes good. You must do this more often."

"You don't believe in God."

He began prising the sleep out of an eye.

"We feeling argumentative this morning?"

"Yes."

"Why?"

"I don't know."

He rubbed the other eye, took another swig and yawned extravagantly.

"How far have you got?"

It was as if he needed to share the same experience as her.

"You've just got back from America. You're with Brad and Jude in the pub."

He nodded to himself, then got up slowly with his coffee.

"I've got to see a man about a dog in Lincoln sometime today" he said, then went upstairs.

"Okay. My father won't talk to me but he has admitted, through email, killing the gangster in Nottingham and firing the ex-principal's house. In America, he beat up, then killed, my step-sister's husband."

"Shit," said Jude. Brad was staring at me intently.

"They're revenge attacks," I continued. "He's on a revenge spree, although he calls it justice."

They glanced at each other, then just stared at me.

"Fuck," said Brad.

They stared at me silently for a while

"In his defence, his son-in-law did try and kill him first."

More silence.

So," said Brad eventually, pointedly placing the thick buff file on the table, "you want to get to your father's next victim before he does."

"Correct."

"Why?"

"What do you mean, why?"

"It's a simple question, Jonno," said Jude. "What are you going to do? Try and stop him killing Baxter?"

They were both looking at me keenly and I got the distinct impression they'd discussed this before I arrived.

"You two going to give me a hard time over this?" I asked.

Jude shook his head.

"We're concerned about you, Jonno. If you're going to try and stop him how are you going to do that, exactly? The only way you can do it effectively is tell Baxter your father's after him and that sounds nasty for your father, to say nothing of the danger to you. This Baxter is probably ruthless and just as skilled as your father in the art of killing people." He pulled a face. "Sorry. Didn't mean that to sound the way it did."

He was perfectly correct, of course. I hadn't thought things through. Before all this began I considered forward planning one of my skills. America had proved that wrong. In fact, I hadn't really planned the trip at all. I have a totally naive belief that I can do anything by sheer will and the power of intellect. I placed my hands to my face and blew through them.

"You're right. But I have to find him. I have to stop him doing these things. They'll destroy him. Don't you see? He's promised to see me when he's done but I can't just sit here and do nothing while the person I care for more than anyone else in this fucking world is killing people and destroying himself into the bargain."

I hadn't expected it to come out as emotionally as that. I thought they might nod in understanding but they didn't, simply looked at me in that infuriatingly concerned way they had. Finally Jude said:

"It's the path he wanted, Jonno. I know he's your father but you could ask, what right do you have to interfere with his choices?"

"I know, I know! But I can't just sit here and do nothing while he goes around killing people. Put yourself in my place – do it now - would you simply put your head in the sand and get pissed?"

I could see the dilemma in both their faces and it was a long time before Jude answered.

"No."

I turned to Brad, who shook his head and frowned.

"But you still need to think about how you approach it."

"Agreed," I said. "So what do you have, Brad."

They looked at me, then at each other, still wondering whether they'd got their point home.

"Okay," said Brad, eventually. There was a sudden animation to him. He was dying to tell me. "Finding Baxter wasn't difficult but I'll come to that in a mo. It's the connection with your old man that was the hardest thing to find." He shook his head. "The British Fucking Army is not exactly the most open and caring institution in the world. My first attempt was to phone the Army Personnel Centre in Glasgow, praying I wouldn't have to attend in person." Jude and I grinned. Currently, Brad's old banger was taxed but uninsured. "They have records of all those whose service ended between," he looked down at his notes, "1921 and 1997, which fits with your father but they were tighter than a Scotsman's wallet. All they'd do is pass on a letter to Baxter. Big, fucking deal. They did say, however, that the Regimental Headquarters at Chelmsford would have far more records, so I decided to pay them a visit, just like you predicted, you smart bugger. I let the train take the strain."

He paused and gazed over my shoulder, treating the room to that filmstar smile.

"Interesting town Chelmsford. Lots of historical significance. Did you know there are Roman ruins that date back ….."

"Brad, you bastard! What did you find?"

I knew he had as much interest in Roman ruins as I did in plumbing. He glanced at Jude with a shocked expression.

"Charming. You know, Jude, you're right. Here I am, giving up my valuable time in the dole queue, doing a favour for a mate. Do I get gratitude? No, I get fucking insults."

I smiled.

"Brad, just give me the info."

Brad grinned and held up his empty glass. Jude did the same.

"I believe it's your round old boy," they chimed.

I groaned loudly. They expected me to go to the bar but I looked up and managed to get Sharon's attention with a raised arm. I made a circle over the table and she nodded.

"On its way. So, Brad, ruins aside, how did you get on at Chelmsford?"

They were both still grinning at me.

"Well, it wasn't easy. First problem was getting through the gate, which I did partly by saying I was you and was doing research for my dad, who wants to get back in contact with one of his old muckers from the regiment. They got through to the Records Office from the gatepost and told me that I need to write in and get permission. I said I'd come all the way from Lincoln and that my dear dad was in the US right now. He'd phoned me yesterday because he wanted to visit a particular friend who he believed was living over there."

This was Brad's big moment and he was obviously going to pan it out. I glanced at Jude, who was feigning rapt attention.

"Anyway, eventually they relented and I got in."

"Didn't they ask for ID?" asked Jude.

"Glad you asked that question. I was sweating like a pig that they would and I was trying to think of explanations as to why my name had changed. Then, when they asked for ID, it suddenly came to me that it didn't matter. As far as the gate guards were concerned I was asking after my father, a mister Cresswell, and it was he who was a Captain in the Paras. When I got to the Records Office I simply told them my name was John Stafford and they assumed that had been checked out at the gate."

Jude and I shook our heads.

"Amazing," said Jude.

"Amazing," I repeated.

"Don't take the piss." He wagged his finger at us. "I tell you this was a job well done. The next step called for all my considerable charm. The girl behind the desk was, frankly, dumpy and unattractive, and not used to being hit on by someone of my obvious looks and personality."

Jude and I both laughed and Brad paused for us to finish.

"I indicated to this far from beautiful girl that I was interested in her and she responded well. Don't expect me to reveal to you two cretins how I do it but I have to say that good looks has a lot to do with it, so there's no point in you even trying.

"I also told her that I was interested in an old army chum of my dear old dad, Captain Baxter. And we looked him up. He was, indeed, in the same company, commanding another troop. They had fought together on The Falklands. Major Baxter resigned his commission in," Brad consulted his notes again, "July '85."

He looked straight at me then and I suddenly realised what he'd said.

"*Major* Baxter."

"Yes."

"He got my father's majority."

"If that means he got to be a major instead of your father, then yeh, looks like it. He was promoted Company commander in July '82, on returning from the Falklands. He became your old man's commanding officer."

"No wonder Dad resigned soon after."

Sharon interrupted us with three beers on a tray and I paid her.

"If there was bad blood between 'em – if he buggered up your dad's promotion – I couldn't find that out without revealing the true purpose of my visit."

"No, you've done well, Brad." I thought for a moment. "The rest I need to get from Dad. Where does Baxter live now?"

"Another good question. There are actually three Baxter residencies. There's the old family home, which he now owns, near Reigate in Surrey. He also has a villa in the south of France." Brad shook his head. "Haven't found exactly where that is yet." He grinned at us. "But not to worry because at this wonderful time of the year he lives in his third house." He paused dramatically. "His mother's an Iti, did you know that? When his father died in '99, Baxter bought his dear old mum a place in her home town, so she could be with her childhood friends and relations. He likes to spend spring there by all accounts, being with his mother and no doubt playing the bigshot with the locals. Speaks the lingo." Brad paused and took a deep swig. "You know I swear they need to change this barrel."

I glared at him and he couldn't hold the indifferent pose, almost spewing beer over the table as he laughed.

"Right now," he continued, "Baxter is in northern Italy, at a place called Mogliano Véneto. That's pronounced Véneto, for you two ignoramuses, with emphasis on the first syllable. It's about midway between Venice and Treviso, about eight kilometres from Marco Polo Airport and there are good road and rail links, so getting there is easy peasy." He looked up at me. "But, apart from his grey-haired old mother, I know nothing about his living arrangements. He could live alone or with a wife, or with children, or grandchildren." He paused. "Or with a bodyguard." I nodded. "Baxter is a businessman, at least he was. Retired last year at the age of 58. A real entrepreneur. Oil, arms, chemicals, real estate. You name it he was into it. When he retired he was worth 260 million quid."

Jude whistled.

"Yup," continued Brad. "Your genuine fat cat, with the morals of an alley cat, by all accounts. Traded rocket launchers to any organisation that would buy them, including, probably, so-called terrorist groups, although he always claimed he didn't. One of his companies was involved in employing mercenaries in Africa, South America and Asia."

He paused for a response but Jude and I were too stunned to react.

"How do I know all this? Well, I have all the back copies of *The Financial Times* for the last 10 years in my back room, of course." I couldn't help smiling as Brad floated a piece of A4 onto the table. "Or it could be from this article in the FT, year before last, on his retirement. It's entitled, 'Last of the Thatcher brigade'. There's even a bit about his career in the Paras." He looked pointedly at me. "The most useful thing, perhaps, is the colour photo."

I looked closely. Thin face, grey moustache, white hair brushed back from high forehead. White teeth shone out of a deep tan and ice-blue eyes stared imperiously at the camera. I tried to push away what I knew about the man. What would I think of him simply from the picture? The overall impression was one of strength and almost contemptuous power. I knew instinctively that if Dad was going up against him he'd be taking a risk and suddenly I was scared for the first time.

"Good work, Brad," I said, extracting my smartphone. "What's the nearest big town, Venice?"

"Hold on a minute," said Jude. "How's this going to work?"

"What do you mean?"

"I mean, what are you going to do and how are you going to do it?"

His voice held a touch of asperity, or maybe frustration, and I looked up. Their faces both held the same concern and I realised I had to deal with this.

"All right. The first thing I'm going to do is email my father and tell him I know about Baxter and that I'll be there ahead of him."

"Reasoning?" asked Jude.

"Reasoning that he might agree to see me first."

"Why would he agree to do that? It didn't work in America."

"In America he was ahead of me. This time I'm ahead of him. Besides, I'll tell him that I'm going to sit outside Baxter's door, so he'll have to come through me."

Brad and Jude looked at each other.

"Sit outside Baxter's door!" said Brad with some irritation. "Have I not got through to you the type of geezer this bloke is?"

Jude held up a hand.

"Let's deal with that in a minute, Brad. Do you know for a fact that you're ahead of him?"

I thought it through quickly.

"I'd say it was very likely but not 100 percent definite. His car is still in Manchester, so he hasn't flown back the way he went out. Besides he'd be picked up at any UK airport. I think the only way he could be ahead of me is if he managed to get a false passport and has flown directly to Italy."

"Is that possible, getting another passport?" asked Brad, turning to Jude

"Not my field," said Jude, "but I hear enough stuff to believe it is. How much time did he have to plan this?"

"He could have been planning it for years," I admitted and realised that was the third time I'd said that in the last few days.

Jude nodded.

"You've got to consider the false passport's possible. Which means you may not be ahead of him. Besides, as Bradmondo intimated, you can't simply park your British backside outside Baxter's house without him getting suspicious."

"I know and I wouldn't be so bloody stupid as to do that. What I said was I would tell my father that I would. He might be concerned enough about my safety to try and prevent it and agree to see me."

"Woh, sneaky Mr Stafford."

I smiled.

"Taking a leaf out of your book, Mr Hardy."

He nodded. I spoke into my smartphone and asked for a cheap flight to Venice and for an hotel in Mogliano Veneto.

"When are you going?" asked Brad.

"Tomorrow."

"I'll come with you."

I looked up. He was serious and, to be honest, I felt a sense of relief. It would be good to have someone like Brad on this trip.

"Be good to have you, Brad. Jude?"

He shook his head with another frown.

"I've got a big case on Monday and there seems little point in flying out tomorrow only to fly back the next day."

There was a BA flight from Gatwick around midday with two seats available. I booked them and left the return trip open. I found a very reasonably priced four star hotel in Véneto and booked it for two nights. I didn't think there would be a difficulty, out of season, if we wanted to extend it, which we probably would. I paid using my credit card again.

"Done," I said.

"How much is it?" asked Brad

"It's on me, Brad and I don't want any discussion about it."

He looked defiantly at me but said nothing; just walked silently off to get the next round. Jude was silent, too, as we both gazed into the imaginary distance, each with our own thoughts. I'd just got back from the USA that morning and tomorrow I was flying out to Italy. Well, father, you've certainly made my life more interesting, which I've already admitted to myself was part of my motivation for this whole venture.

"He'll be fine," said Jude. "And I think you might find having another person there very useful."

As usual, Jude was proved right.

Extract 13

It was all too late, of course. The three of us – me, Sixsmith and Manton's monkey - retired to a quiet room to consider our position.

"You have to concede," urged Sixsmith between drags on her Rothman.

"Why? She's still a child abuser! She's lied about everything, from beginning to end. I give up now, I'm implying that she hasn't."

She blew smoke at the ceiling as if she'd just created the perfect smoke ring.

"That may all be true but the fact is it's you who's been caught out in a lie and the judge doesn't believe any of your story, anyhow."

"How do you know?"

She shook her head and smoke came out of her nostrils in wavy lines.

"I've been up before enough judges. He doesn't believe you."

I knew this to be true, had known it all along, but I still wasn't going to let go. I stared at the wall and a picture of an 18th century hunting scene, where the fox ran free.

"There's another consideration," continued Sixsmith, mercilessly. "If you quit now I may persuade the judge to ignore the fact that you have lied in court. If you continue, it will probably annoy him so much he's likely to refer you to the police for a criminal prosecution. You'll be found guilty and have a criminal record for the rest of your life. You may even lose your job."

"I don't care!"

They argued with me for what must have been over an hour. I simply lost track of time. But the result was inevitable. At the end I had no choice and Stella was a grinning, strutting peacock, according to my friends in the lobby. The opposing solicitors thrashed out a temporary schedule of when I could see the children and I was back in court, being lectured by the judge about honesty and maligning the name of an innocent woman. I nearly threw up. Instead, I had a swift pint in a local pub, where I thanked my supporters and stayed at a friend's house overnight.

I met you and Rachel the next day in the garden and assured you that, although the court had decided you would live with your mother, I would still see you at weekends and every other Christmas. You seemed okay at that time and I had a brief hope that might continue. But the old cliché is right; the leopard does not change her spots. It was a constant, stressful battle to get to see you and to handle the visits. You found it so difficult, I know, when I brought you back. Rachel held up better, ironically. Until, that is, her mother started terrorising her again and she remembered past pain. I have a file an inch thick of correspondence and court documents where I tried to get to see you after the hearing. When you were 8 years old I had to go to court to get permission to take you on the Norfolk Broads for a week because your mother refused. I may have told you. That was a good holiday, though, wasn't it? And, of course, we were not to spend Christmas together again for another 19 years. Stella even started to abuse *you* at one time, I recall. You left the house, then, and stayed with a friend. And, of course, your mother abused your step-sisters, even to the extent that her new husband had to lock her out of the house one night, she was in such a rage. Pity he didn't call the police, but then I didn't either, so I can hardly blame him for that.

And Helen? Well, your mother managed to destroy that relationship, too. I know they met on at least one occasion, at your mother's request, claiming there was something of 'vital importance' to divulge. I don't know what your mother said to her, exactly, but I can guess. Helen was a simple sole, unused to the cunning machinations of someone like Stella. In the end Helen couldn't handle the strain of it and we parted.

So, there I was, 39 years old and, without wishing to sound dramatic, my life is wrecked. I certainly couldn't face Lincoln or Yorkshire any more. Too much baggage. So I resigned my post at college and took up other work. Very different work, with a company in the USA. Maybe I'll tell you about it one day.

There you have it, son. A sad, even tragic, tale of love and hate, of good and evil, although, I must confess, there wasn't much good, and where love began and wickedness ended I don't know. Make of it what you will but please, don't think ill of me.

All my love,

Dad.

It was so weird, she thought. When you read a published novel you find out all about a character, but you know it's fiction. What she'd just read in the Extracts described her family's real experience. To some extent she felt privileged. It was like she'd had the opportunity to go back in time and, as an adult, meet her mother and, of course, her grandfather. And he didn't fit the image she'd already formed of him. This … man of Lincoln … this desperate father, was a different man. Yes, he was flawed, but weren't we all? This was the man she would have loved. If he walked in now she'd hold onto him and never let go.

She glanced at the old-fashioned Bass Breweries wall clock, with its half worn-away Roman numerals and beer stains. 10.40am! Jesus! And she was still in her nightshirt; the Winnie the Pooh one that had lived permanently under the pillow since she was 15. He wouldn't have gone to Lincoln without saying goodbye. So, feeling excited but with what she thought was amazing self-restraint, she inserted the beer mat, closed the journal and went for her shower.

When she returned he was sitting at the kitchen table, reading it and, inexplicably, Bess felt jealous. He had a hard look in his eyes but it softened when he looked up and saw her.

"You look beautiful, lass."

"You saw where I got to?"

He simply gazed at her, saying nothing. She needed to ask so many questions but something in his manner made her pause. The text would give her the answers.

"More coffee?" he asked.

She just held out her cup, returning the silent treatment. Bess walked into the living room and settled into her favourite armchair by the fire. He must have lit it while she was upstairs and it was already blazing. Rain slashed against the window but she didn't hear it.

Chapter 19

Tuesday 21 May 2013

When his mobile rang Stafford was stretched on the bed listening to evening sounds through the open window: the slap of feet amplified like an echo by the high buildings, constant hushed conversations, shouts of the gondoliers as they jostled for position in the narrow waterway and, once, the screech of fighting cats. But above it all there was the sound of birds. Even though darkness had already descended, scores of them were still defending their territory. Then, quite suddenly, their noise stopped, like someone had closed a door. It reminded him of his phone call to Augustus Bramble two days ago, when Bramble had closed his study door, cutting off the party sounds beyond.

"Well now, Mr Stafford, what can I do for you?"

"Libya. Did Hartley pay you back the money you advanced him?"

"He sure did. Big surprise, I can tell you. I suspect you had something to do with it."

Stafford had looked through the window of the EuroCity train as it flashed through the Austrian countryside, at the still snow-covered Alps in the far distance, and gathered his thoughts.

"I shan't be going to Libya. It would be a waste of my time and your money."

"Go on."

"I've researched it and spoken to Reed and his experts at the Agency. It's a lawless country, with no effective government, and it's getting worse. The underlying problem isn't really military, it's political and that's not my forte. By some miracle I may be able to solve your pipeline blockage in the short term. In the medium- to long-term the same or different issues are likely to crop up. My advice is to cut your losses in Libya."

Stafford let a silence develop and watched the mountains get closer, remembering the skiing, many moons ago, when the knees were good.

"You telling me I made a mistake buyin' into that oilfield?"

"Maybe. But I have a suggestion. Go offshore in the Gulf of Hammamet and bring the oil ashore in Tunisia."

"Yeh, we've looked at Tunisia. Lot o' dollars."

"Well, if you use Libya you still might get a blockage at the refinery. But probably not in Tunisia. At the moment BP is drilling in the Gulf. They might appreciate a partner to share the load."

"In my experience the Brits are tighter than a camel's ass in a sandstorm. No offence."

"None taken."

"So. That it? Dump the oilfield and go offshore."

"In a nutshell. You'll still have the licenses to drill on land, of course, if the situation improves. Your investment in the oilfield could still pay off. And for that advice, Mr Bramble, I charge you nothing. Neither will Dick Hartley because you'll have come to the same conclusion yourself eventually. You've saved yourself a couple of million."

Bramble said nothing for a while.

"Why haven't my people told me this?"

"Maybe they don't want to tell you you made the wrong decision buying into that oilfield."

"Uh hah, you suggesting my staff are scared of me?"

"I think they're probably terrified of you."

Bramble laughed. Stafford couldn't believe he was taking it so well.

"Okay, Mr Stafford. I've got your number and I still owe you for my son."

"You owe me nothing and the number will be no good to you; I'm retiring."

He *was* retiring too. Not quite yet, though. Four down, still three to go. Beside him he felt Louise stir herself and he looked at his watch. 2132.

"Buona sera, Francesco."

"Buona sera, senor." He spoke in an excited yet hushed voice. "He arrive with girl. Two guards; one on boat - I see light before Baxter arrive - and one in passage ..... my English it so bad ..... *di fronte la torre*."

"Opposite the tower?"

"Si!"

Stafford suspected he meant the marker beacon at the end of the jetty.

"Does it have a red light on top?"

"Si!"

"So you've seen one guard on the boat with Baxter and the girl, and another man opposite the boat on the quay."

"Si"

"And that man arrived with Baxter and the girl."

"Si."

"How far from the boat is that man?"

"Um, 30 metre, senor."

"And which doorway are you in?"

"You count six from end."

"Stay there."

He turned to Louise. She was already standing, ready, a bag for her change of clothing at her feet. She couldn't have looked more like an Italian beauty if she'd tried. He knew she sometimes felt nervous before a job so he forced the crack of a smile and she beamed back.

He dressed carefully, knowing that he'd be changing into a wetsuit later. It was a 300 yard completely exposed walk along the outer jetty and he'd never approach the boat that way without being spotted. So swimming the short distance across the harbour was the only way. Even a non-swimmer could do it and he grimaced at the irony. He'd sailed nearly every ocean in the world and made sure both his children could swim like fish but had never learnt to swim himself.

Bess looked up to see her uncle standing in the doorway, wearing his wide-brimmed leather hat and long raincoat; the one with the flaps on the shoulders.

"Off to Lincoln. There's cheese and ham in the fridge, bread in the bin, plus ....."

"John, stop fussing."

Lunch was the last thing on her mind. He nodded and just walked out.

"Have a good time!" she shouted after him, feeling guilty at her abruptness.

She got herself a gin and tonic, this time with more gin, then watched his Porsche exit the drive before moving back to her chair. Rain was still slashing against the window and she gazed into the fire to clear her mind.

By contrast with the street outside the hotel, the lockup boathouse on the Campo de la Guerra was deserted and silent. He noticed something scurry away into the mist at his feet, pulled Louise towards him and they waited by the rotting gate, like forgotten lovers.

After five minutes he decided they were alone, so he opened the padlock, flicked on his torch and peered at the boat Francesco had provided. It was a sensible craft. Not one of those ubiquitous varnished speedboats so beloved by the ostentatiously rich, nor a common inflatable rib, but a battered, fibre-glass workboat, about 18 feet long, that no one would notice. It even had 'Nave Meccanico' written alongside. Boat mechanic. The 6hp 2 stroke Suzuki outboard looked similarly worn but Stafford was sure it would start at first pull. He found the blue bag in the locker and donned the wetsuit. It was a little tight but would do. In any event it was essential; the Lagoon water temperature in May is far from warm and if he was cold he was no good to anyone. He tied the knife belt around his waist and fastened the dry bag containing the Beretta to the belt, then he put his trousers, jacket and shoes back on over the suit. He might sweat up for a while but that was tolerable.

As he steered the boat carefully down the narrow passage and out into a deserted Grand Canal he felt nerves he hadn't known were there seep from his body, like forgotten gifts. Besides, being on water was such a natural element for him, so he confidently crossed in front of the target marina, steering passed some unlit cardinal buoys, to a little, private harbour on the island's south-east side. Louise, in her dark jacket, sat quietly beside him, her long, raven hair pinned back in a pony-tail to retain its shape. He'd thought of everything he could. But there was just a small doubt about this operation. He'd had to improvise at the last minute and it was his last difficult killing. How often do things go wrong when you're nearly there?

The rough, concrete slipway was empty. Louise, who'd been messing about in Cornish boats since she could walk, jumped out and helped him haul out the boat. She grabbed the painter from the bow and looked for somewhere to secure it.

"You've not sailed in the Med before have you?" he asked.

"No, why?"

"There are no tides to speak of. The boat's not going anywhere."

"Ah," and she threw the painter back into the craft. "Do I get changed now?"

"Later."

He paused to listen but the only sound was that of a light easterly shifting the leaves of a stand of trees up on the bank. Over the lagoon, a gibbous moon laid its carpet. The moon was a hardship and a blessing. It would mean unsettled vision as they moved from light to shadow along the alleyway to the quay but it would also mean that Louise's performance would be in full view, which was just the way he wanted it. 2236.

"We might as well get closer to the quay. Take my arm. If anyone sees us we're out for a late stroll."

So they left the slip and walked softly WNW on the stony sand behind the trees. After a 100 yards or so they reached a rough tarmac path, which right-angled north-east. The first stretch was easy because there was an open garden to the left, sweeping up to the old monastery, and there was enough moonlight to see their footing. Then the trees became taller and thicker to their left and flat-sided houses rose on their right, blocking moonlight and creating a black tunnel, with only the ambient lights of Venice showing small at the end.

"Wait here a few minutes," he said. "Your night vision will adjust."

She squeezed his arm and hugged him closer. Two lovers pausing for another passionate embrace.

Soon they moved into the alleyway, with just enough vision to walk carefully, until they reached an iron-grill fence. During daylight hours a small gate is open, to allow residents and tourists access to the quay, but at night it's locked. However, at only four feet in height it was easily scalable and Stafford helped Louise over before climbing himself. There was now enough ambient light from the main island for them to see what they were doing, although it was still pretty gloomy. He knew there were six electricity boxes alongside the restaurant wall to his left, but only because he'd seen them yesterday. On his reconnaissance he'd also picked out two security cameras but knew they'd show no detail in the low light. The restaurant closed at 2230, so there should be only staff still there, cleaning up. The outside dining area, which looked over the masts of the marina to the lights of Venice, was lit by a small violet glow.

"Get changed now."

***

David Tallow had been perched on the winding stair of the bell tower for a while now and his aging limbs were starting to complain. In fact, if he didn't move soon, he was sure they'd seize up with cramp.

He was about 10 feet below the viewing platform of the church of San Georgio Maggiore, from which you could get, "the most magnificent views of the whole of Venice", according to the guidebooks. And he had to agree because he'd been up there earlier in the day, with the tourists. Instead of leaving with them, though, he'd hidden in a secluded corner of the entrance building at the base of the tower until everyone had gone and then simply waited.

Tom had not been sure whether anyone would be stationed on the viewing platform. He'd just thought it would be a good position to offer covering fire of the boat less than a 140 metres below and across, and it would be the kind of thing that sneaky bastard Baxter would think of. And sure enough, around 2030, while there was still enough light to see, a man carrying a large case let himself in by a side door and re-locked it before proceeding to climb the stairs. Which was a bit of a relief, actually, because Tallow had been locked in. If no one had turned up he'd have had to abseil from the bell tower on a retrievable line and he was getting a bit old for that kind of shit.

He'd immediately recognised the man's body type and the way he moved; ex-Army for sure, probably infantry, used to a crouched run across broken ground. Early to mid-30s and fit as a butcher's dog. The high-powered rifle, its bipod stand and ammunition, as well as, probably, a big night scope, would weigh at least 25 pounds, yet he carried it as if it were a feather. He'd phoned Tom to let him know, then climbed the stairs to his present position. He really hoped the soldier wasn't ex-Para. He hated killing Paras.

He looked at his watch. 2246. Tom had been clear when they'd stood up there that afternoon.

"Can you see how you can cover the edge of the quay over the roof of the buildings, the exit to the marina, 15 to 20 metres of open water, as well as Baxter's gin palace and dozens of other boats moored on the far side of the jetty? So, as well as stationing a man up here, on his boat and on the quay, I think he'll have another on a nearby craft as a final backup, in VHF coms. If I had his resources that's what I'd do. That makes four. He knows I'm coming and he'll figure on needing four guys."

"Listen to you. He thinks you're that good?"

Stafford had shaken his head and pulled the corners of his mouth apart in his impersonation of a smile. It was a kind of pursing of the lips.

"He thinks I'm slipping or he'd have six guys."

Tallow chuckled because he knew from personal experience that, although it was said as a joke, it was probably true.

"To be honest, I can't be sure, David. You'll just have to adapt."

Then the self-deprecating modesty to counter-balance the arrogance.

"So, whatever night it is - tonight, tomorrow night, whatever - 10 minutes before the agreed time you make your move. I want *you* on the end of that rifle covering *me*."

So, at 2250, former Sergeant David Tallow removed the silenced Beretta, switched off the safety and made his move.

He sacrificed speed for quietness, feeling each foot onto the steps, as he ascended. Just as he reached the viewing platform a radio started to crackle.

"Steve, you there?"

Tallow looked over the lip. It was surprisingly light and he saw the man reach for a handheld.

"No, I'm sitting in the Trat, finishing a bottle of Valpolichelli with a gorgeous Italian bird. Where the fuck do you think I am?"

Tallow's first thought was that Baxter must have arranged a private VHF channel. He couldn't have that kind of conversation over the public airwaves.

"Yeh, well at least you've got a view, you lucky bastard."

"That's true, I've always wanted to experience the delights of Venice by night without actually being in it."

"Know what you mean." Clearly his compatriot didn't appreciate irony. A good sign. "Listen, Steve, do you think the old boy's lost it?"

"What do you mean?"

"Well, all this heat for one man."

A new voice cut in.

"..... you two shut the fuck up and keep this channel clear!"

Tallow watched the man place the radio on the floor and waited in 10 seconds of silence before stepping onto the platform.

"Freeze." He'd always wanted to say that. The man's head jumped up in shock but apart from that he stayed still. He was perched on a camp chair, peering over a rifle that was angled down at about 60°. "You move another muscle laddie and a silent bullet will pass through your skull."

Tallow moved closer and to one side.

"Now raise your hands, slowly."

"Good lad. I don't want to kill you Stevie boy so I want you to, very slowly, and without using your hands, turn round in your chair so you're facing me. Do it now."

There was a moment's hesitation but he did it, very slowly.

"Good. This is going well, Stevie." He removed a large plastic tie from a side pocket and threw it onto the man's lap. "Now pick up that tie and loop it round your hands, in front."

The man did as he was told and held out his hands for Tallow to tighten it.
"You think I'm a fool, laddie. Use your teeth."

What most people would have done is raise their hands to their mouth
so when the man did the opposite Tallow was ready. He saw a hand dash to
waistband and the Beretta coughed. He shook his head and fired again, this
time through the man's chest, just to make sure, then groaned.

"You silly English bastard!"

He replaced the pistol and rifled pockets for the key to the gate. Finding it
he put on his gloves and examined the rifle.

***

Louise was now in a cream dress that finished halfway up her thighs and
only just managed to cover her magnificent breasts. It clung to her curves as
if it had been painted on. Matching high heels sculptured her legs. In fact,
Stafford thought she looked fabulous, which was the whole point. There was
certainly nowhere she could have concealed a weapon and no way the watcher
in the end doorway was going to be looking at *him*; not even if he was gay.

2302.

"Okay," he said. "This is your time."

"You betcha."

Dropping the bag of clothes into a corner for later retrieval by Francesco,
she put her arm through his and they stepped out like late, inebriated revellers
from the restaurant and began staggering, 150 yards to the end of the deserted
quay, ostensibly to be picked up by boat outside the church. The guard in the
last doorway must have been watching couples do that for the last two nights.

Their passage was lit by several lamps stuck out of wharf buildings, so they
stopped once to embrace and add authenticity to their cover. They passed
Francesco but knew it only because of a whispered, "Good luck, senor."
About 20 yards from the end they passed a 12 foot high ornamental bronze
shell and Louise got to the business end of the script as she started to stagger
more towards the building. Approaching the doorway she almost fell and her
breasts nearly fell out of the dress as she pulled away from him and lurched
into the dark doorway. Predictably, the man's outline became visible as he
moved forward into the light, two hands outstretched to support her and she
gasped in surprise.

"*Scuzate Senor!*"

Stafford was already moving towards her, as if to drag her away, except that he made an apparently drunken lurch passed and plunged the knife into the space between the man's thick neck and chin. Stafford felt warm blood pulse over his fingers but the blade had not penetrated as much as he'd wanted. The man made an instinctive move to remove the knife, so Stafford did it for him by placing fingers in eyes and tugging hard against the flesh that had closed around the wound. Unable to cry out, the guard slumped back against the door and grasped his neck in an attempt to stem the flow, so Stafford decided to put him out of his misery by extracting the silenced pistol and shooting him through the heart, thankful that Francesco had found that second suppressor.

He grabbed Louise and pushed her into the shadow of the doorway. She was far too visible in that cream dress and the only real weakness of the plan he could see was that staff might choose this moment to leave the restaurant. So he crouched and scanned the marina for a while, especially *Vengeance*, her bow no more than 15 yards across the water. But there was just the winking lights of the main island. He found the dead man's VHF in a deep pocket, checked that it was still working and turned to Louise.

"You were brilliant," he said. "You need to stay here with the body now. Stay in shadow and don't move until Francesco picks you up. Shouldn't be long. If anyone comes along, walk round to the front of the church as if you're waiting to be picked up by boat. Can you do that?"

"Yes. I took it in the first time you told me," then she moved back into the dark.

He crouched and watched the quay again, but still nothing moved. He then stood and stripped down to the wetsuit, cleaned the knife on his victim's clothing and pushed the body well into the darkness of the doorway. He placed the VHF radio into the dry bag with his mobile and clipped it to his belt. The excitement had returned at last. He could feel it, behind the scenes.

He slipped quietly into the water backwards, thanks to some convenient steps right there in front of *Vengeance* and pushed away immediately. He'd like to have used breast stroke because it makes less sound but knew he'd tire before he made the distance, so he used plain crawl.

65 metres above him, David Tallow was refamiliarising himself with the Belgian FN SCAR-H rifle; what the Yanks call the Mk17. Standard NATO issue, this was the long barrel version, capable of accuracy up to 800 metres, or more in expert hands. Since the range here was no more than about 70 metres across and 70 down, accuracy would not be an issue. The CTS-230

digital night scope had up to 4 times magnification but he didn't need it. In fact, there was enough residual light to allow medium brightness settings which increased pixelation and therefore clarity. He'd say one thing for Baxter, he didn't stint when it came to buying equipment.

Even though he thought he'd only need one bullet, if any, Tallow released the magazine, checked it was full and reslotted. He then adjusted the buttstock to fit his long arms, pulled the charging handle to check there was one up the spout, switched off the safety to semi-automatic and peered through the scope.

He easily spotted Tom entering the water and traversed the rifle right and down, across the other boats then back to *Vengeance*. He didn't have to move the weapon far as at least half-a-dozen boats were within his field of vision and he didn't think any boat watch would be too far away. Tom was swimming to the stern, where there was a bathing platform and he disappeared down the starboard side so as to be invisible to anyone looking from the other craft.

Tallow watched as he came out of the water, using upper body strength only, then knelt on the bathing platform. He waited, looking round and probably getting his breath before standing up and disappearing into the main deck area behind the wheelhouse. And right then, from the cockpit of the third yacht down, a dark figure rose quickly, jumped onto the outer jetty and ran towards *Vengeance*. Tallow could even see the shape of the handgun he was carrying.

"Make it a head shot, if you can," Tom had said. "He might be wearing body-armour."

Tallow had thought that unlikely at the time and still did. He couldn't see that arsehole Baxter caring enough about his men to supply them with armoured vests. He certainly hadn't when he was his commanding officer and the dead man lying beside him hadn't been wearing a vest. Besides, the figure in his sights was a moving target and a head shot was going to be difficult. In any event, the H in the gun's description stood for 'heavy' and Tallow doubted if a Kevlar vest would stop a 7.62mm bullet at this range. So he aimed for the torso.

There was hardly any kick from the rifle but it wasn't silenced, of course, and the sound echoed around the dome of the viewing platform like a clap of thunder, as Tallow watched his victim arch his back in death and topple over the jetty into the icy waters of the Lagoon.

On *Vengeance's* main deck, the shot also sounded like thunder and Stafford tucked himself into shadow beside the companionway. As far as Baxter's remaining guard was concerned that shot had been fired by his own man, undoubtedly chosen for his marksmanship and Tom Stafford was now dead, probably lying on the quay and needing a disposal before the police arrived. The smart thing to do would be to get on the radio and check. The unsmart thing was to check himself. Fortunately, he chose the wrong option.

Within a few seconds a man rushed out, gun in hand. Stafford waited for him to be framed against the Venice glow then simply shot him in the head. He slumped against a facing leather seat and his handgun clattered to the floor.

But there was still Baxter. Woken from his exhausted sleep by the rifle shot, he would soon be fully alert. He might even have heard the plop of the silencer or the sound of the gun hitting the deck. So Stafford ran across the upper deck, adrenalin dulling any pain from his knee. He stopped at the top of the companionway to the lower deck and peered in, gun levelled. Completely naked, Baxter was standing by the bed, reaching under his pillow.

"Don't even think about it, arsehole," said Stafford and Baxter stopped. "Remove your hand, very slowly, and place both hands above your head."

He did it, slowly and in the meantime the girl in the bed became aware of the situation and sat up.

"You're a dead man, Stafford."

He carefully descended the companionway steps and made eye contact with the girl. She'd formed a tent with the sheet and tucked it under her chin. Her mouth was open and she was breathing in short gasps. At least she wasn't screaming which was a good sign.

"*Parla Inglese?*" asked Stafford.

She paused.

"*Si* ..... yes."

"Good. If you do exactly as I say I promise I won't hurt you. Nod if you understand me."

She nodded.

"Okay, first, remove your hands from under the sheet and place them on top."

She did that, too, with a certain alacrity actually, as if by showing her tits she gained confidence.

"You're a dead man, Stafford," said Baxter.

"You've got repetitive in your old age, arsehole. But then you were always a bit short on creativity."

He's figuring he still has at least two men outside, thought Stafford, which was good. It could make him more compliant if he thought he was going to be rescued at any minute. He turned to the girl again.

"What's your name?"

"Angelina."

"Of course it is."

He unzipped the dry bag with his left hand, removed a plastic tie and threw it on the bed.

"Angelina, you know what that is?"

She picked it up.

"I think so."

He moved back a little, beside the first en-suite bathroom.

"Arsehole, without lowering your hands, walk to the front of the bed and turn round so you're facing to port."

Baxter gave Stafford a look that could have dropped a blind-side flanker then complied.

"Good. Put your hands behind your back. Angelina come round and put the tie around his wrists."

She got off the bed and walked round to meet Baxter, still completely unembarrassed by her nakedness, and they both complied without demure. Angelina because she wanted to live and Baxter because he expected his men were going to burst in any minute.

"Pull it tight .....Good, now Angelina, go back to bed and stay there, keeping your hands on top of the sheet."

Now Stafford could remove his own handheld from the dry-bag.

"Victor 2, this is Victor 1, over?"

Three seconds while he looked at Baxter. He had to admit he looked in good shape for a 60 year-old.

"Victor 1! Good to hear your voice!"

"Good to hear yours, too. Anything else happening?"

"Not a sausage. How's the magnificent major?"

"Looking not quite so magnificent."

Tallow sniggered but Stafford got back to business.

"Shut up shop there, get down here as soon as pos and wait for Victor 3."

"Roger that."

While he speed-dialled Francesco on his mobile he watched Baxter. He'd turned towards Stafford and his eyes were flickering, as if he was realising his position might not be as secure as he'd thought. Perhaps he recognised the voice on the radio. And he must be curious as to why he wasn't dead already.

"Victor 3, you can pick us up now."

"I am here, senor."

"Outside?"

"Si, Senor."

"Good. Pick up the girl and wait for Victor 2."

"Okay."

Francesco had clear instructions. If he heard no shot he was to wait in the boat for a phone call and steer south-about the island in a stately manner. It was by far the longest route but wouldn't draw attention. If he did hear a shot he was to speed north as quickly as possible to pick them up, before a policeman on the main island, or anyone else with a little curiosity, started to wonder why it should thunder on a largely clear night, with no lightning and no rain. Baxter was saying nothing; just staring back at him with hatred in his eyes and a shrivelled manhood.

"Why haven't you killed me already, Stafford?"

He turned to the girl.

"Angelina," said Stafford, "if you describe me to the police or repeat any names you've heard here tonight, I'll know it. I will find you and I will kill you. Just say we were wearing masks."

Actually, he wasn't bothered what she said in the long term. Eventually, the authorities would work out who'd killed Baxter and his men but it would be nice to have the time for them all to get out of the country. She didn't seem scared now, just looked back at him with intelligent eyes and he suddenly saw he'd misjudged her.

"No you won't," she said. "But I won't say anything."

He'd stereotyped her as a gullible call girl. Her excellent English was a clue he'd missed.

"Thanks."

"What's going to happen to him?"

"He's going to disappear. He's not a very nice man."

She nodded and kept her eyes fixed on Stafford.

"Victor 1?" called David from the upper deck.

"Down here!"

Tallow descended the stairs and burst into laughter this time. Baxter backed off a pace.

"Well, well, well, if it isn't the magnificent Major, with a dick the size of a pencil stub and looking like a plucked chicken."

Tallow roared again and Stafford put an arm on his.

"Baxter, move," he said.

"No."

Stafford shook his head slowly.

"It's all the same to me but if you refuse to go I'll shoot you in the leg and we'll carry you."

"I'll do it," said Tallow, lifting his Beretta.

Baxter hesitated only briefly before walking to the stairs. Tallow preceded him and together they got him into the boat with Francesco and Louise, who was wrapped up in a fleece to keep her warm.

They turned south-west, away from the main island, and dropped Louise and Francesco at the landing stage they'd used before. Stafford then headed south-east. They kept going for nearly a mile, into the deep water passage, where they stopped the boat and tied Baxter's legs to the anchor line.

At first Baxter didn't realise what the line was attached to but as soon as Stafford dropped the anchor over the side he began to scream. Both men hauled him over but he clung to the gunwale for several seconds, gasping, desperate to live.

"Please Tom! I can make you a rich man."

The butt of the Beretta came down on each hand and Baxter disappeared into the deep.

Slowly, she became aware of the rain still sweeping against the windows, as if the beast was not placated. And for sure it wasn't. She put the kettle on in order to make a jug of coffee and threw another log on the fire. Of her uncle, there was no sign. That was fine because she suspected the manuscript would answer her questions.

Chapter 20

Friday 24 and Saturday 25 May 2013

Back home, I stocked the fridge for the long haul and waited. By Friday there was still no word from my father and I hadn't missed a Friday night with the lads since a stomach bug laid me low a year ago. I knew that if anyone could cheer me up, Brad and Jude could, so I went to the pub.

The Coal Scuttle was packed as usual and I sensed a mood of optimism amongst the crowd. It gave me a sense of well-being for the first time in a while. This is my world, I remember thinking; this is where I belong; not the hot fragility of the American deep-South, nor the ghost towns of Northern Italy, or even comfortable, middle-class North Hampshire, with its bournes and chalk-streams and watercress beds. No, *The Scuttle* was a microcosm of what feels right, with its shared culture, its laughter, good mates and decent beer. I almost felt like smiling.

"So, what are you going to do," asked Jude, after I'd related the notion that I believed my father was about to kill my mother and made an attempt at explaining why. But I kept it factual, avoiding the emotion and they both knew it.

"Nothing for the moment. He's promised to speak to me first. So, I wait for him to contact me and, when he does, I'll dissuade him."

They both looked at the table and I knew they wanted to look at each other.

"You're not going to warn your mother or contact the police about this?"

"It'll complicate matters. Dad might see it as me taking sides against him. Besides, I suspect he's quite capable of killing her even if she is alerted. My best hope is to meet with him and persuade him of some other course. If I can't, then I'll phone Foster."

They both said nothing, just stared at me. Eventually, Jude said: "Okay."

I could see they wanted to change the subject, to talk of something more secure, but they were reluctant and uncertain. I guess it was like talking to someone who's suffered a bereavement. How do you know the safe topics and are you belittling their loss if you talk of inconsequentialities? I grinned to make them feel more comfortable and spoke to Jude.

"Changing the subject, you haven't asked about Jonno and Brad's great adventure."

Brad guffawed and launched into the whole Italy thing because Brad could tell a tale. His literacy skills were poor, but he was like one of those story-tellers of old, who existed before men could read and write. He had an extraordinary memory for detail and could separate the significant from the trivial in an instant of flowing speech. He saw things visually and told it like that, using his hands expansively to describe a vista or a person's nose. He exaggerated the dangers and his heroic rôle, of course, and we all laughed when he described the way the pretty girl had saved us at the airport. By the second pint I'd mellowed and Jude told us of his latest case.

"My client, the man, has been married to the respondent for 18 years. Two years ago they had their one and only child. Now she wants a divorce and claims the daughter is not his."

"Poor bloke," I said.

"Yes, he's devastated."

His face was deadpan.

"Because," suggested Brad, "she wants more out of the settlement and doesn't want him hanging around after the divorce?"

"Perceptive of you, old boy. My solicitor, bless her, was suspicious and asked for a paternity test. The wife complied. My client gave her a sample of his DNA and, together with a sample from the child, it was sent off for analysis, using one of these DIY DNA things. And the result was that my client was not the father."

Jude held up a finger dramatically and I could imagine him, in his wig, capturing a jury's attention.

"My solicitor was still suspicious, suspecting that the wife had, in fact, sent off a sample of her lover's DNA instead. We go to court on Monday to request a completely independent test, conducted by a professional clinic." He paused. "Bradmondo, are you listening to me?"

We followed Brad's gaze, to three attractive women who'd just walked in. They all seemed to be in their twenties but, as I've said before, I find it increasingly difficult to judge women's ages. Wearing high heels, and skirts that doubled as belts, they were heavily made-up and had the excited, bubbly ambience of a bevy of girls out for a good night on the town. I hadn't seen any of them before.

"Choose between the others, boys, but the dark one's mine," said Brad.

I could see what he meant. The two blonds were attractive enough; one was tall and slim, with legs up to her armpits and the other was shorter and carried maybe a few extra pounds but they were both very attractive. The brunette, though, was quite strikingly beautiful and once Brad had decided on his quarry, all you could do was stand back and admire. Compete and humiliation swiftly followed.

"I'm not sure I'm in the mood for this, Brad."

"Oh, come on Jonno. It'll do you good. Take your mind off things."

And, of course, I had no choice. There were three of them and three of us. Girls always stick together. It's like they have a pact not to get separated. If I dropped out they'd drift off to find another trio and I'd incur the wrath of my mates.

Brad waved his hand, caught Jimmy's attention and pointed at himself. We watched as Jimmy spoke to the women and pointed at our booth. They looked over and whispered to each other in that way women do when they talk about men; conspiratorially, heads together, all teeth and flashing eyes. I knew that, if they decided to come over, they'll already have discussed our individual, physical merits. We waited patiently, in the sure and certain knowledge that the attraction of Brad's long, blonde hair and film-star smile would eventually pull them in.

"I expect I'll get the fat one again," groaned Jude.

"I wouldn't say she's fat," answered Brad. "Besides, look at those tits, your honour," and Jude did brighten a little.

After a minute or so, the girls laughed together, picked up their drinks and, swinging their hips in the same old way, walked slowly to our table. We stood up and Jude and I waited for Brad to take the lead, as he always did, but it was the brunette who got in first.

"Thanks for the drinks."

"You're welcome," said Brad. "Won't you join us?"

The brunette smiled.

"How do we know your intentions are pure?"

Her voice had a familiar twang but I couldn't place it. It certainly had a confident strength, as if speaking was part of her job and I guessed she was a teacher. Brad looked at me with a twinkle in his eye, as if to say this one was going to be fun. Then he gave her the full, winning smile and I wondered, for the nth time, how it was that someone who'd been in so many fights could keep such a perfect set of teeth.

"Baby, if I said our intentions were pure, I'd be lying to you. Besides, if you thought they were, well, you wouldn't have walked over here, would you. Where's the challenge?"

She narrowed her eyes and bit her bottom lip, pretending to think.

"Okay."

She stood back, though, allowing her companions to squeeze in first. Brad was between the blonds. The brunette was inside me, her right thigh against mine and her perfume intoxicating. I could see Brad was slightly irritated by the arrangement but knew he had the confidence to brush it aside. Brad could run a table like a king holds court but, again, she got in first.

"My names Becky. The leggy blonde is Shannon and the cleavage over there is Leanne."

We all had an excuse to look at Leanne's cleavage.

"My name's Brad. This is Jonno and Jude. You all have to be very careful with Jonno. Unfortunately, he has a high IQ but we do forgive him that. When he's sober he's as gentle as a lamb but get him pissed and you want to stand clear, believe me."

Jude and I grinned at each other. It was all part of the ritual and I interrupted with my line.

"Um, pot, kettle and black are words that come to mind, Brad."

He laughed it off.

"Don't listen to him, darling." This to Shannon, who was hanging on his every word. "You're going to have to keep him sober if you want any performance out of him at all."

Everyone laughed, apart from Becky. I glanced left and saw the small smile on her lips, which told me she'd immediately grasped Brad's implication. She was his.

"Now the big man on my left," continued Brad, "may look like the village idiot." Jude brought his eyes together, sucking his thumb at the same time and everyone laughed at that one, too. "However, amazing as it may seem, he is, in fact, the scourge of the Lincoln bar, a barrister of repute and, if you are very lucky – sorry, unlucky - he will quote Shakespeare at you all night. Just try and keep your eyes open."

Jude puffed out his chest and grasped some imaginary lapels, as if he were addressing a jury.

"Ladies, Romans, countryman, lend me your lugholes, for I come to bury Brad, not to praise him. The evil that women do ….."

"Yes, thank you, Jude; don't ring us, we'll ring you." It was an old joke but Brad had a way of saying it and we all laughed again, including Becky this time. "Jude is a truly wonderful man, who has only three faults. The first one you know. The second is that he has a weakness for women with large breasts. So, Leanne, this is your lucky night."

Jude bent his head and ostentatiously focused on Leanne's cleavage, his large tongue hanging out and Leanne giggled. Jude picked up her hand and became serious. Brad and I knew what was coming. We'd heard it a dozen times.

"It seems she hangs upon the cheek of night, like a rich jewel in an Ethiope's ear."

"Thank you, Jude, I think we can do without Ethiopia tonight. What you have to understand, Leanne, is that, although Jude's admiration of the female form may be a noble pursuit in its own way, it does tend to blind him to women's dark side, where they lure him into bed against his will." The laughter was infectious now. "His third weakness, and by far the worst, is that he occasionally bets on the Scummers to win. He gets off lightly because he's a mate; I just ignore him for 24 hours. Everyone else gets a red card for life."

The two blondes were looking at the table with puzzled frowns.

"The Scummers?" asked Becky.

"Man U," I said.

"Man U?"

"Manchester United Football Club."

She nodded, then spoke.

"And what about you, Brad; how would you describe your strengths and weaknesses?"

Satisfied that he'd got her attention, Brad put on an expression of humility.

"Well, baby, I have few strengths and many weaknesses, it is to be admitted, one of which is an appreciation of beautiful women and you are undoubtedly one of those."

That kind of squirming flattery always worked for Brad. Jude and I had watched it in action for over 10 years and, in fairness, had benefitted from it, although we cringed every time. But somehow I knew it wouldn't work with this woman. There was something individual and controlled about her. I felt she'd summed him up and, just for once, that the woman was playing him.

As if to confirm that she suddenly put her hand on my thigh. It was so unexpected that I jumped. Brad picked up the movement, of course, and his eyes narrowed. Then Becky ostentatiously put her arm through mine and I felt her gazing at me. I was looking at Brad, wondering how he was going to deal with it but he simply smiled and nodded at me sagely, as if to say, "I'll give you this one, buddy."

***

When I woke the next morning she was leaning against the bedroom door jamb, holding my only tray and wearing one of my shirts. It was classically corny but she looked the sexiest thing since the latest Aston Martin and given the choice I'd have been hard pushed. I propped myself up.

"I might have known you'd pick my best shirt."

She smiled and placed the tray on my lap. It contained two cups of coffee – one white, one black - a fruit juice, a boiled egg and brown bread soldiers topped with butter.

"What do you mean?" she smiled. "It's your only shirt; at least the only one with tails."

She propped herself on the bed and sipped her coffee.

"How did you know I drink my coffee black?" I asked, just to break the silence. She hesitated only a heartbeat or two as I sipped.

"You talk in your sleep."

Maybe it was the sudden hit of the caffeine, or maybe it was simply having an alcohol-free brain at my disposal, but I had one of those sudden, mind-blowing moments of insight for which Jude says I'm infamous.

"I do talk in my sleep but I don't think it would be about coffee." She had light-blue eyes and they were flickering across my face. "Dad sent you."

The eyes widened, slowly, then she laughed and shook her head.

"He said you'd guess."

The whole of last night had been contrived.

"Why?" I asked.

She stopped smiling and became serious.

"He wanted to give you a message and he's worried about your security. He thinks your email is watched and your phones are definitely bugged. Last night, while you were in the shower, I took a bug from under that table, one from a lamp in your lounge and the one from the phone. You're also being tailed. I noticed them, last night."

The conviction in her voice made me remember, abruptly, the gravity of what my father had done.

"Them?"

"Man and woman. Young and fit. They even bumped into us twice while we were dancing. They were trying desperately to look like they were into each other but they weren't. At least the woman wasn't."

"How so?"

I was trying desperately to grasp what she was saying and had just thrown out the question to give myself time to think.

"She fancied me more than the man."

"Police?"

"I think so. Difficult to be sure."

"Why didn't you simply stop me on the street? Why go through this rigmarole?"

I could feel my anger coming through and she sensed it.

"That was my idea. What could be more natural than three girls meeting three boys for a good night out? Your father told me where you'd be, I picked up Shannon and Leanne, who were up for a bit of fun, and the rest was easy."

It certainly was, I thought. What complete fucking mugs men are? I pretended indifference and broke my egg.

"I knew there was something about that accent; West Country?"

"Cornwall."

"Have you known my father long?"

"About 10 years."

"Socially or professionally?"

She thought about that.

"Bit of both."

"Was shagging me part of the bargain?"

"I asked him whether he'd mind and he said it was up to me."

"Did you shag him, too?"

She turned and looked at my picture of a naked female angel on a mountain top.

"Of course I did. I have to confess, that was part of the attraction, to shag the son as well as the father."

"And compare the two?"

She dragged her gaze back to me and her eyes came into focus.

"Not really, but it was a turn-on."

I suddenly didn't want the egg any more, so I drained my coffee in silence.

"Don't be cross," she said.

"What's the message?"

"He wants to meet you tomorrow at his favourite country pub. He says you know where it is."

"Time?"

"Opening time."

Chapter 21

Sunday 26 May 2013

The Moorhen nestles in a lush, green vale beside the River Ancholme, between the Lincolnshire Edge and the Wolds. The last time I'd been there was my 18th birthday, 8 years ago. I think I mentioned it. Then, I can remember that excitement of being with my father for the first time in over a year. Now, I wasn't sure what I was feeling as I pulled off the Market Rasen road, down the single-track lane, lined on one side by ancient bungalows and willows and, on the other, by a field of barley, thriving in the mid-day sun. I was excited; I could feel that. I was also nervous and unsure of myself, but that wasn't something new.

On Saturday morning Becky had used an appliance Dad had given her and checked my car over, suspecting some kind of GPS tracking device. She'd found it attached to the underside of a suspension bracket and popped it into her handbag.

"I can sell that," she said with a smile. "In the meantime, my car's parked round the corner. They'll follow me from now on."

"They're bound to find out eventually."

"Sure but this sort of thing is technically illegal in the UK without a warrant and I strongly suspect they haven't got one, so they can hardly give me serious grief."

She pecked me on the cheek and left, after giving clear instructions about how to detect and lose a tail. But they didn't differ markedly from my home-grown techniques used in North Georgia. When I reached Market Rasen I was sure no one was following.

I'd decided I had to have a purpose to the visit. This was partly because my father could be very persuasive. My track record was good there, though. I could be just as stubborn as him when I put my mind to it, and Dad was good at recognising those occasions and when to back off. But I did need a purpose because I knew that, if I drifted into it, emotion would take over from reason and I'd be lost. No, I'd decided what had to happen. I had to dissuade my father from killing my mother.

Now, this is not an unreasonable request, you might think. But I knew that killing his ex-wife was the final part of Dad's mission. Also, and I know this sounds crazy considering the killings, but my father is essentially a good person and, in a way, that was why I had to stop him. He did things for the right reasons, even though he sometimes got them wrong. He'd do anything for his children or a mate, regardless of personal sacrifice and would be horrified at the thought of letting anyone down. There was no side to him. He had warmth and humanity - a huge heart - which he tried to disguise. The dilemma in all this is that I knew my mother was capable of most, if not all, the things of which Dad had accused her. I'd actually seen some of them with my own eyes but I'd buried them. Oh, she appears sweet enough; has always worked hard at that. She's adored by the neighbours and most of her school staff. But, after a while, and if you stand back and watch, you can see through the sugar coating. Nevertheless, she was my mother and, in my own way, I cared for her. Maybe that's why my step-sisters saw through her before I did, because they don't.

I knew Dad would have left the BMW at Dorothy's place – he couldn't risk the car being spotted by police – and the only vehicles in the parking area were an old Landrover with *The Moorhen* written on its passenger door, a Peugeot 205, about four years old, and a brand new, 3-door Ford Focus. No one was in sight.

The pub's front door opened as if by magic as I strolled down a line of orange marigolds. In the foreground to my right a mixture of trestle tables, benches, tables and chairs were scattered about the apple trees in apparently haphazard fashion. The well-tended lawn smelled freshly mown. Further out, more willows fringed the river, just visible through an old cow-drink, but otherwise the Ancholme was hidden by its high bank.

"Two pints of your finest ale, please landlord."

He looked behind me.

"Two?"

"Two."

I looked around while he drew the beer. The place hadn't changed. I remember the landlord, or probably his father, had been in the RAF and pictures of fighter planes, long since obsolete, filled the yellow-brown walls, like stale memories. I'd taken a swig and was receiving my change when the man looked behind me again and I knew my father had arrived.

He hadn't changed either. It was only Christmas since I'd last seen him, yet, somehow, I think I'd subconsciously expected the strain of the last few weeks to have made him look different. His skin was browner, that's all. But it was the same twinkling grey eyes, shining out of the same old face and I felt a prickling behind my eyes as I went forward and hugged him, which was our normal greeting. Pulling away, he placed his hands on my shoulders and looked at me in that candid manner he had and I just looked back, unable to speak, feeling ten years old again.

"So," he said, "is this tan the result of Georgia or Venecia?"

"I wasn't in Italy long enough to get a spaghetti dinner, remember?"

He nodded.

"I sure do. God, I was scared shitless Baxter was going to catch you."

Until I read the *Word* file, I'd never been able to imagine him being scared of anything. Now I was with him again, it was like I'd read an episode from the existence of another man. He was so confident, so full of life and it was infectious. He clapped me on the shoulder, full of good cheer.

"It's so good to see you, John. Let's get this beer and sit in the garden, like we did before."

He nodded at the landlord, sipped his beer and I followed him out. Like me, he was wearing shorts and a polo shirt, with robust-looking hiking boots. But unlike me he had a small rucksack on his back. I followed his still athletic figure as he strolled, with a limp I hadn't seen before, to the far side of the garden. He sat on a chair facing the car park, as I knew he would. Beyond him, no more than 20 yards away, wagtails still flew between the reeds.

"What's with the limp?"

"Ah, nothing a few days on the boat won't take care of."

He supped his beer and studied me over the rim.

"That your Focus?" I asked.

"Ya."

"Where were you when I arrived?"

He threw his head over his left shoulder.

"Copse of willows over there. I'm glad you arrived on time. There was a cob with some cygnets who was getting ready to break my arm." He looked apologetic. "I just had to be sure you weren't followed."

"I wasn't. Becky was most insistent. And she removed a tracking device from the car."

He nodded.

"She's a good girl."

"Yes, well, maybe not good exactly."

He looked at me keenly.

"I know you shagged her."

"Difficult not to, really."

"True."

I thought about her for a while.

"Is Becky her real name?"

He hesitated.

"No, but if she chose not to give you her real name I should respect that."

"What? Do you think I'm going to try and find her? She's too old for me, Dad! And, by the way, too young for you."

He stopped, his glass halfway to his mouth, and laughed. He actually laughed.

There was a small, slightly awkward silence. I sensed we were both reluctant to get into the issues, so we drank and allowed the ambience of the day to seep into us. He leaned back, ran a hand through bristly, grey hair and breathed in deeply, smelling the air.

"What's in the bag," I asked.

"Sandwiches for our lunch. I knew you wouldn't bring anything."

"That all?"

He became serious.

"No. There's also my wallet, a bottle of water, a very tasty knife and a semi-automatic handgun." My stomach did a little flip. "It's a Glock 17, which means it can fire 17 rounds of 9mm ammunition. It's a very reliable weapon, used by armies and police forces all over the world. There's also a spare ammunition clip."

I couldn't think of anything to say for a few moments. Eventually, I said:

"Are we expecting trouble?"

"Just being cautious."

"But the gun, Dad? The police are not going to be armed. And even if they are, you don't want to be shooting policemen, for Christ's sake!"

"You're right about that. Besides, for some reason your tail dropped off last night. Not sure why. It may have something to do with the fact that .....
Becky removed those police bugs from your flat. On the other hand it may be a pure coincidence."

"So what's the gun for?"

He brought his gaze back to me.

"Like I said, I'm getting cautious in my old age. It's just in case there are any repercussions from other interested parties."

"You mean like Baxter?"

"Baxter's dead."

It wasn't a surprise, of course. In fact, in a way, it had been inevitable and I reflected how extraordinary it was that even the most outrageous acts can become normal. My father had committed his third murder – at least as far as I was aware it was only his third - and, again, I felt nothing.

"What about his associates, taking revenge? They must know who killed him."

He nodded.

"Good question. Baxter wasn't totally retired from the arms business. He oversaw a few operations a year, just to keep his hand in. His job was to meet and greet the buyers and sellers; the contacts man; the honest broker who they trusted. The day-to-day business was actually run by his second-in-command, an old school chum. There were five other staff who looked after the actual transportation, guarded the warehouses, that sort of thing. I had to kill four of those to get to him, including his deputy." He paused to watch me react, so I didn't. "That leaves two. Baxter wasn't close to any of them. They were simply hired hands as far as he was concerned. They wouldn't have the motivation or the guts to come after me. They've seen what happens to my enemies. They're probably running for their lives as we speak."

That seemed like a sensible conclusion and he exuded such confidence. Certainly *I* would have run like hell. A silence developed. He was waiting for me.

"I'm sorry I messed things up for you."

He shook his head.

"I told you before, that's my fault for not taking you into my confidence. And I underestimated you. It didn't even occur to me that you'd find out about Baxter, let alone get there ahead of me. That was pretty cool, by the way. How's Brad?"

"Er, he's fine. Still smarting at the fact that the lovely Becky, or whatever her name is, appeared to prefer me to him. He's frightened he's losing his touch."

I heard a car arrive behind me and watched him look over my shoulder, then back at his beer. We were making smalltalk, skirting the issues. Sooner or later one of us had to ask an important question but I wasn't ready yet.

"I can't believe that you followed me to Georgia and then flew to Italy."

He really wasn't annoyed at all.

"Neither can I really. Just seemed like the thing to do at the time. When you learn your father has killed someone and has set out on a revenge spree you can't simply sit back and do nothing."

"I can see that," he said and I felt a rush of impatience, suddenly.

"Tell me more about what happened in Italy," I said.

He looked at me keenly.

"You mean after you left?"

"Yes?"

But I could see his mind was elsewhere. His eyes had a distant look and I wondered whether he was thinking of the woman who waited in the Blue Ridge Mountains. So, when the question came I was ready for it.

"Before I tell you what happened in Italy, tell me about Lizzie."

I took a deep breath.

"I think she's great, Dad. Liked her immediately." He continued to look at me. "Why didn't you contact her after her husband's death."

He still looked at me, shamefaced this time, remembering, perhaps, the ubiquitous smile against blue hills.

"She's the love of my life, you know."

He wasn't talking to me particularly but some inner part of himself, rarely breached.

"And you hers."

He looked away and I left him to his thoughts because how could I go there with him? His life had been crammed with disappointments, particularly where women were concerned and then, at the very moment he finds the right one, he walks away.

I glanced to my left. A couple settled down on a bench seat, glancing at us in a surly kind of way, as if they resented the fact that we'd taken the only decent table. Perhaps we'd taken their regular spot. They were both about 30, maybe, in loose jeans, brightly coloured T-shirts and sturdy walking shoes. They were slim, tanned and looked fit, as if they spent all their life outdoors. The man placed a small rucksack on the bench beside him and my imagination began to work overtime. I dragged my eyes away from the couple and looked at Dad. He didn't seem bothered in the slightest so I decided to ask a meaningful question.

"Lizzie doesn't understand why you can't be with her. And frankly neither do I."

He nodded at the table.

"Can't blame either of you for that." He fixed me with a look of certainty. "Maybe I will be with her one day but I had to get all this stuff done first." He shook his head. "And now I'm a wanted man, all over the world, so whether we can be together is problematic."

I thought about that.

"So you put revenge before love."

He pursed his lips again.

"I suppose I did, although I prefer to call it justice."

That response didn't bode well for my purpose.

"So we come to the question that I've asked you and that Lizzie asked me. Why now, Dad? Whatever you call it, these accounts you're settling go back a long way."

"Another good question and one to which I don't have a coherent answer." He looked passed me, as if seeking inspiration. "These accounts, as you call them, have never left me; they've eaten away at me, like a cancer, and I guess I just reached a point where I couldn't bear the sense of injustice any more." He brought his gaze back to me. "I know that doesn't explain it. Nothing external happened to compel me suddenly. It's inside me, John. I changed inside, over a period of time and I know I couldn't continue as a person until I'd sorted it."

This was not good. I decided to change the subject.

"Did you ever meet Charlotte?"

He seemed to refocus, eyes questioning.

"Charlotte?"

"Lizzie's daughter."

"No. She's about your age, I think."

"Yeh."

I wanted him to ask, to get his mind down a fresh path.

"So, tell me tightarse. What's she like?"

I took a deep breath.

"Difficult to say on such brief acquaintance but she had some good qualities."

He narrowed his eyes in a mischievous kind of way and I remembered his resilience, his amazing capacity to bounce back from misfortune, as if he were saying: "Listen, chum, I've been there many times and whatever you do or say will not phase me." What he actually said was:

"Did she like you, too?"

"Amazingly."

"Well, well, well. That would be ironic; if Lizzie had you as a son-in-law."

I shook my head.

"You're jumping the gun a bit, here, Dad. Besides, there's no way it's going to happen."

He raised his eyebrows.

"Why's that?"

"Couple of reasons. To begin with, she's very different from her mother."

"How so?"

He was looking at me with a new interest.

"Do you remember telling me once that a good woman should have three things?"

He nodded in memory.

"Beauty, intelligence and sensitivity."

"Right. Well, she had the first two in spades but, what her mother has in abundance, Charlotte sadly lacks; at least I thought so but, like you, I have been wrong about women."

His eyes were skimming across my face, reading my thoughts.

"You fell out."

"You could say that."

An insect bit my neck and I slapped it dead, then drained my beer, glancing to my right. The couple were smiling, seemingly happy in each other's company. Up passed the apple trees the sun shone from a cloudless sky and I tried to relax in its warmth.

"This weather reminds me of Georgia without the humidity," I said.

He shook his head at my attempts at diversionary behaviour.

"You going to tell me what happened with Charlotte?"

"It's not important."

He bit his bottom lip as if struggling with something.

"I bet Lizzie liked you."

"She did. It was like – this seems really stupid – but it was like we'd known each other all our lives."

He nodded and I could see his eyes misting. He placed a hand over his mouth in an unfamiliar gesture.

"My round," he said suddenly and walked off with the glasses.

To my left a family with two small children had arrived and the shrill tone of small, excited voices chased a football over the grass. A girl of about 6, her legs going like pistons, long blond hair flying out horizontally, easily outpaced her younger brother. She pounced on the ball and held it aloft like a trophy. It reminded me of my own childhood. The children's mother, either in her third pregnancy or a big eater, shouted at them not to fight, threw out her diaphanous robe like an actress and plonked herself down at the next table. Then, taking out a paperback from a voluminous, canvas bag, she began to read. The children, doubtless used to their mother's preoccupation, began to squabble and this continued until their father appeared with a tray of drinks and called them over. I watched as they sipped quietly through straws, only to speed off again with the ball, their father following. The mother didn't take her head out of the book once. I continued to watch the game because it was safer than focusing on the elephants in the garden. To my right, the female hiker was staring at me in a not unfriendly manner. I turned away, embarrassed. The sun was so hot now it really did feel like Georgia.

"What was the second reason?"

Dad had returned with the beers.

"Second reason?"

"You said there were a couple reasons why you'd not be cuddling up to the lovely Charlotte."

His grin was broad again, his eyes twinkling, as if the last conversation hadn't happened and I wished, for the umpteenth time, I had his capacity for recovery.

"Oh, I just thought that every time Lizzie saw me she'd be reminded of you and that might upset her. Understandable really; I've only got to think of you and I break into a cold sweat."

I grinned crookedly to show I was joking and he chuckled. We were back on an even keel.

"Actually," he said, "I don't think she'd mind it. Having the son as part of the family is some compensation for not having the father."

"Maybe."

The truth was I suspected he was right and that hadn't been my second reason at all. He was silent for a while, looking at me, and I knew he was summing me up again, thinking about what he had to say and how he was going to do it.

"So," I asked again, "what did happen in Italy?"

He looked me straight in the eye and I realised, quite shockingly, that I'd been wrong. I'd always known that with my father what you saw was what you got. Always. But right then, just for a moment, I glimpsed something behind the eyes and then it was gone. But I *had* seen it and it was something he kept hidden.

"I'm surprised his disappearance didn't get any prominence in the UK," he said. "I know it happened in Italy but Baxter was a well-known British businessman and was probably up for a knighthood."

He was looking at me intensely

"I had to do it. I was going to, anyway, of course but after your ….. foray in Venice, he knew that I, or my son, wanted him for some reason or other and, aware of our previous relationship, he couldn't afford to take the chance your presence was benign. If I hadn't killed him, he'd have killed me, and, possibly, you."

He glanced behind me to examine more arrivals. The pub garden was really beginning to fill up and I could smell a Sunday roast cooking.

"What happened between you and Baxter?" I asked.

"You mean in the Army?"

"Yah."

Baxter wasn't what I wanted to talk about, of course, but again it allowed me to avoid the elephants, and I was curious. He grimaced.

"We were in the same class at Sandhurst and didn't like each other from the getgo. He had the confidence that comes from an Etonian education, except in his case it came over as arrogance. His natural progression would have been the Blues and Royals, or the Guards, but he chose the Paras because he wanted to appear tough. And he was, in his own way, but his toughness was based on theory rather than practice. He'd talk the talk and get his men to walk the walk, which is part of what a good officer should do, but he missed out the most important part; leading. In training, my troop would beat his, not because I was better at planning or strategy, or because my men were fitter than his. It was because he wasn't as good at leading men. I know that sounds arrogant but I don't know any other way to say it."

He was animated, suddenly..

"Do you know, there's an amazing similarity between leading a group of soldiers into battle and teaching a reluctant class of 16 year-olds?" He guffawed at the analogy. "Giving orders, using your authority, is quite secondary. It's about relationship. They have to trust you and respect you. Eventually, unwilling 16 year-olds do their English composition, or soldiers attack a fortified position, not for themselves, but for you. Baxter never understood that. For him, men were pawns in the chess game of his own personal advancement."

"And he blocked your gazette, then took the majority for himself?"

He looked grim.

"Yes."

"How did he manage that?"

He shook his head.

"Men with Baxter's background have family and school loyalties behind the scenes."

I didn't really want to know the answer to the next question but my curiosity, my fucking curiosity, got the better of me.

"But he lives in a house, surrounded by a high fence and is guarded by a huge dog and several ex-special forces personnel. How the fuck did you kill him?"

"Are you sure you really want to know."

I thought about it.

"No, you're right. I don't want to know."

He nodded solemnly and drained his second pint, then breathed in deeply, nostrils flaring, eyes everywhere, as if sensing the day for the first time. There was a calmness about him, now, as if finally accepting the inevitable. Settling his eyes on me he said:

"Is it time to talk about the elephant?"

I took a deep breath myself.

"Yes."

"Okay. Why don't we walk along the tow path?"

He hefted the rucksack and headed for the walkbridge.

So, it was on the banks of the Ancholme that my fate would be sealed, and fitting it seemed. Despite recent rain the way was dry underfoot and well-worn as we set off at an easy, ambling kind of pace. The river mirrored a startling blue and seemed companionable somehow, as it flowed low between lush, lime edges of high grass and clamorous, lilac flowers. Every so often we'd wave away a ball of gnats in languid air as we headed deeper into the margins, inhabited by warblers and coots, the latter calling their warnings as they made pit-a-pat trails across the still stream.

Dad stopped and looked back at the beer garden, still visible across the flat, green land, then resumed his stroll.

"You read the file?"

"Of course I read it."

I felt him look at me.

"So, what do you think?"

I stopped. It irritated me that I hadn't worked out an answer to the question, even though I knew it was coming.

"Christ, Dad, what do you want me to say?"

He said nothing, just resumed walking. Then:

"It's my interpretation, of course, with all my prejudices and biases. But I tried to be as impartial as I could. All the facts are true, and my feelings; those are true, too." He gave a short bark. "I'd like what life I have left to be full of love and happiness. Isn't that what we all want? But my life was never going to be like that; not since that summer."

I felt anger coming. I couldn't stop it and stopped walking again, forcing him to face me.

"Look, if it helps, I believe every fucking word you wrote. My mother can be a bitch. She fucked up your life….."

"She stole my life."

"All right, she stole your life. But that doesn't give you the right to kill her!"

"Doesn't it?"

"No, it fucking doesn't! You know, I can't believe that we're standing here discussing this; whether my father should murder my mother!"

He looked at the water, then down at the earth and said nothing, thinking about his pain and his revenge. This was where I had to challenge him. Right here and now, so I waited, like a counter-puncher. Over his shoulder, a hawk hovered above a meadow studded with poppies. I watched it for a while until, slowly, he raised his head and looked into my eyes and I knew he was still resolved.

"But we are discussing it, John. More than anyone I've killed so far, your mother deserves to die. I've been wanting to do it for over 20 years."

"And what gives you the right?"

"The right? The only answer I have is a pompous one. I think, just as a man gives life, he has the right to take it away, if the cause is just."

He was inspired by iconoclasm and the courage it took to break the mould, and I knew I would get nowhere by challenging him on that. It was part of his creed of honour, a component of his DNA, and without it he wasn't a man. Yet somehow I had to win this argument. I had some weapons in my armoury and the first was using my intellect. It was what I was supposed to be good at. I looked to the hawk for inspiration but it had gone, perhaps to stoop unnoticed on an unsuspecting vole with a hungry family.

"I know that's what you believe, Dad. You've already demonstrated you have that moral position. I don't agree with it but I accept you have it. But this murder is different." I was calm now and he sensed my resolve. Our eyes were locked, like two old adversaries defending entrenched positions. "It's different for two reasons. First, and you said this yourself, the cause has to be just and it's only your opinion it is. It doesn't even meet the eye-for-an-eye criterion. She hasn't taken a life. She's fucked up people's lives but lots of people do that, Dad. If everyone turned round and killed the person who's ruined their life we'd be knee deep in murders."

I paused while he looked away.

"On the face of it, that's a good argument, son, but it really doesn't wash. To begin with, the main reason we don't have all those murders already is because all those aggrieved people are afraid of the consequences. I'm not. But the main problem with your reasoning is that you're ignoring the fact that her actions have affected me." He jabbed his chest with an index finger. "Me. I don't care what society or the legal system might think. I've thought about this for a long time, believe me. I've sat in judgement and I have decided she deserves to die." He shrugged. "You can call that supreme arrogance if you want - it undoubtedly is - but I'm prepared to live with it."

"But in a way you've made my second point, Dad. Her actions in the past have affected you, and Rachel and me and a hundred other people, but if you kill her that action will affect me, too. She's my mother!"

I was still in control but my voice was shaking.

"I know, son. That's why we're having this conversation. That's why I sent you the file. Because this affects you as much as me; more actually, since you'll still be around to deal with the after-effects. I've obviously got to disappear." He looked away. "Give me a good reason why I shouldn't do it."

I saw, then, that reason on its own would not persuade him.

"For my sake, Dad, don't do it."

He closed his eyes for a moment or two and took a deep breath.

"Do you love her?" he asked.

"Yes."

"Do you really, John? I mean really? Do you even like her?"

I seriously thought about it but he rushed on, as if to save me from an admission.

"Does Rachel love her? You know the answer to that. Do her step-daughters love her? Absolutely not. Do they even like her? Neither of them lives at home any more and they avoid her like the plague. Laura hasn't seen her step-mother for nearly five years, even though they live in the same town. The last time I saw Laura, at Christmas, she told me the only reason her father doesn't leave your mother is because the marriage is 'convenient' and because they're so tied together financially that separation would be too taxing. No pun intended. Apart from Stella's mother, a bitter old lady if ever there was one, who's stabbed me in the back more than once, who would suffer unduly from her death?"

I had to answer that question and I turned away for inspiration, along the straight line of the river, disappearing in its new summer haze. This was not a time for dishonesty.

"All right, Dad. I may not like her, as a person, it's true. She's good at hiding her faults and I know her to be sometimes hypocritical, self-centred, money-orientated and a score of other things. And I'm sure she did all those unimaginably cruel things to you, and to Rachel, and consequently to me. But, in my own way, and I can't explain this, I do care for her. We've had some good times."

He looked at me with an uncharacteristically melancholy expression, then turned to gaze back down the track.

"Let's sit down," he said.

He had to direct me, like we were in a theatre. So we squatted on the river's edge, staring at the water. The opposite bank was dominated by a splash of yellow flowers. Beyond, a field of wheat, still more green than brown, sheltered life in its curtained keep.

"It's not enough, John. When a man comes to this stage in his life he looks back, at his achievements and failures, his loves and hates. I've achieved quite a lot, I guess. Part of that I like to think of as having some small input into you becoming the man you are. I've also had many failures." He gave another bark. "I've had a lot of those. I've loved a lot of women. And men. And I've disliked a lot of people. The balance sheet of life balances pretty well."

He lapsed into silence and looked out over the field. I followed his gaze, to a zephyr stirring the stalks.

"Most men would be content with that, Dad. You've lived your life to the full, made your contributions to it and the world is the better for your passing."

He was still staring out over the field.

"Thanks for that, son." Then he shook his head and pursed his lips. "But it's not enough, you see. There's unfinished business, and your bitch of a mother and that arsehole Holroyd are still there."

For a moment, I couldn't think who Holroyd was, then remembered; the vicar of St Paul's who'd betrayed a priestly confidence and turned Dad's life around. So, 20 years after his heart attack he was still alive. Dad was probably thinking of that now as he watched another breath of wind stirring the corn in exactly the same place as before.

"I don't care about Holroyd," I said "but I do care about my mother."

He looked at me sharply.

"That's interesting. You're not concerned about Holroyd's fate, yet his sins are less than hers. Supposing she wasn't your mother. Would you still be so protective?"

I really thought about that.

"No. No, I wouldn't be so protective. But she is, Dad. She is."

"And that's the rub isn't it," he said, looking out over the field again, as if it contained his inspiration. "I feel such a burning sense of injustice, John, one I've lived with for 20 years; more than a third of my life; more than half my adult life, for fuck's sake! Finally, I've reached the point in my psyche where I'm compelled to right that wrong, at last, at long last, and you want to take it from me!"

The emotion in his voice made me choke up. Did I have the right? If I didn't try and stop him would I be doing my duty to my mother?

"I understand that, Dad. I really do. But you used to tell us, Rachel and me, that two wrongs don't make a right."

He scoffed.

"That's stuff you tell kids to make them behave. Adult life is far more complicated."

"Maybe, but would it really be righting a wrong? The two things are not of the same weight. In a way, her sins are greater than your sin of killing her. There's no way killing her will make up for those 20 years, Dad." I could see he was thinking about that. I placed my arm round his shoulder. I couldn't help it. "You have many years left. Live them. Go off with Lizzie, hide from the authorities. Do whatever you want but live your life, Dad."

He grabbed my arm hard and tears sprung from my eyes. He turned and looked into them, then across the meadow.

"So, she gets away with it, yet again."

His voice was thick and his shoulders began to shake.

"Unless there's another way; some other way," I said.

I was aware only of him; his feel, his smell, his feelings. It was as if the day had ceased to exist and we were alone in the world, dominating it. Slowly, he raised his head and turned to look at me and I could see the tears running down his face, too. A light seemed to come on in his eyes and his head came up.

"Maybe there is another way," he said and looked at me keenly, unashamed at the tears. "You have to tell the story, Son. You have to write about all this."

"What?"

"Make it a novel but use the facts as you know them."

"A novel? I have no talent for writing," I protested.

"You have more than you know," his voice shaking with conviction. "You have the ability to do anything and you certainly have the sensitivity to write a novel." His voice was trembling and I'd never seen his eyes so piercing. "You publishing the book will be my justice. Promise me!"

So I made the promise. We'd struck a bargain.

He seemed to sag for a while as we sat in companionable silence, with only the chirp of birds to break the stillness.

"I'll help you. There are pieces of the story that only I know. I'll write them and you can top and tail them to fit the story."

Then he levered himself onto his feet.

"All this talking has made me thirsty again," he said.

We'd come about a mile and we took our time walking back. I could tell he didn't want to talk now so I said nothing. But there was still another elephant and, in a way, it was even more difficult than the first.

The couple had gone, I noticed, as we approached the beer garden and I remembered Dad had seemed completely unconcerned by their presence. I always did have an over-active imagination. The garden was completely full, though, and two waitresses were bringing out meals. The smell of food made me hungry, so we drank our beer and ate Dad's sandwiches on the edge of the green, by the willow trees. Dad wasn't a great cook but he always made tremendous sandwiches. These were homemade ham and mustard on wholemeal, just as I like them. He was quiet and contemplative, then said.

"I shall miss this. Lazy Sunday afternoons at English pubs. God, I'll miss it."

"I know." It was an opening I couldn't pass up. "We do have to discuss it, Dad."

He turned to look at me.

"What happens to me now?" He shook his head and fixed me with those grey eyes. "No we don't. I think it's best you don't know."

I wasn't sure that I understood that but I nodded because that was what he wanted.

"I can't exactly live a normal life, anyway; not with the police in the UK and USA after me. So far the Italians haven't twigged."

At his car I hugged him hard. He'd got himself together but I hadn't. Tears streamed down my cheeks in rivulets because I knew what was coming.

"I'm not going to see you again, am I?"

"Best not, son."

He tried to push me away but I wouldn't let him. Finally, I'd become stronger than him. But only physically. I gripped him tight, my body shaking with sobs I couldn't control.

After a few minutes I stopped shaking and let him hold me at arm's length, so he could push my tears away with his thumb, like when I was a child.

"I'm so proud of you, John," he said and, with that, slowly turned and got in the car.

The tears kept coming as I stood, unashamedly, and watched him drive out of my life, his hand piercing the skylight in a final farewell. As he disappeared round the bend, I imagined him stopping and sobbing, too, just like after the visiting weekends long ago.

Chapter 22

You'd be forgiven for thinking that the Ancholme was the real end of this tale; that maybe you have some romantic vision of my father sailing away and living on the oceans between the Equator and Capricorn, like an albatross, forever pining for his one true love; that I returned to my humdrum life, cracked out my word-processor and attempted to tell the whole, confusing story. Well, the second part of that is largely true.

I cut myself off from everyone for 2 days, ignoring emails, phone calls and texts. I couldn't face going back to work, so I didn't. Brad and Jude eventually knocked on my door and attempted to cheer me up, to no avail. I took to walking a lot; something which, in the past, I'd shunned scornfully as a pastime of the aged, middle-classes.

One of my problems, of course, was whether to warn Mortimer Holroyd. By not doing so did I become duplicitous in my father's crime? Was I committing some kind of crime myself by not reporting what I knew was about to transpire? Indeed, by saying I didn't care what happened to Holroyd had I in fact legitimised whatever punishment was to befall him. But in the end, I reverted to type and did nothing. I justified this by saying I'd been down that route twice and failed and, even if I did warn him, Dad would get to him anyway. Besides, I didn't think he had murder in mind. And, in a way, it was part of the bargain we'd struck.

Then my dilemma was resolved early one evening in a phone call from my mother.

"Have you seen the local paper? Of course you haven't. It will be all over the Sundays tomorrow, anyway."

She was breathless.

"Mother, calm down. What's happened?"

"It's Mortimer. He's killed him! Your father's killed him!" Despite everything, I was shocked. "Am I next, John? Am I next!"

"Why would you think that, mother?"

"Am I next, John?"

"No mother, as it happens you're not on his list."

"How do you know?!"

I took a deep breath.

"Mother, believe me, you are not on his list."

She didn't even pause to consider.

"I'm contacting the police. I shall demand protection. God, John, he's a monster! I can't believe I married him. I'm so ashamed for you that he's your father."

She hung up, saving me from doing it. I logged on to the *Lincoln Herald* website. Apparently, the police had received an anonymous call and, on arriving at the good Canon's house, had found him naked, tied to a kitchen chair and quite dead. The cause of death was not yet known and there were no further details. Reading between the lines, Dad had wanted to humiliate and terrify him and the shock had brought on a final heart attack.

It was a brutal demise, pitiless and full of malice – gratuitous even - and I thought my father may have gone too far. Perhaps being deprived of his major victim had fuelled the cruelty he'd shown Holroyd. In which case that was my fault and I do still wonder about that death.

Then Inspector Foster turned up one night. I'd taken to staying in, wading through my DVD collection as a form of escapism and I hardly heard the knock on the door. He was wearing the same suit and cheeky grin. Behind him was a police car, equipped with driver.

"Don't you like doorbells, Inspector," I said, shaking the now offered hand.

"Very perceptive of you, sir. As a matter of fact, I don't. Sometimes they don't work and you don't know that until your suspect's out the back door. A straightforward knock works every time, so it does." He looked around, taking in everything, including the film, which I'd paused. "I'm sorry to disturb you."

"That's all right. I've seen it twice, anyway. I can offer you beer or scotch. No Irish, I'm afraid."

He shook his head.

"Give me a good Scotch, anytime. And, yes, I think I will have one, if you don't mind."

I decided I really liked Foster, then. The official car outside said he was still on duty but, beer or whisky, he didn't care.

"Take a seat, Inspector."

He plonked himself heavily into my Chinese made leather couch.

"You can guess why I'm here."

"Are you guarding my mother?"

"Yes, sir, we are. But I need to ask you, is he going for her?"

I handed him the drink but he didn't sip it, just stared at me, waiting for an answer.

"What makes you think I would know that?"

He looked me straight in the eye and the smile was gone.

"I think you do, sir."

I thought for only a few seconds. He deserved an answer.

"No, he's not going for her. You can pull your men off; it's a waste of police time."

He still didn't try his drink but balanced it on his knee.

"And, to be clear, how do you know this?"

"Because he promised me he wouldn't."

Foster nodded slowly and finally tasted his Scotch.

"Very nice, sir, very nice." I think he meant the scotch. "Would that be in person?"

A little warning bell told me to be careful but I was past caring.

"Yes, we had a drink at a country pub."

"And when would that be."

"8 days ago."

He was nodding slowly and sipping his whisky again.

"To be honest with you," he said, "I was as much concerned about my men as your mother."

"He wouldn't harm your men, Inspector."

"No, sir, I'm sure he wouldn't."

It was clear he believed that about as much as he believed in Leprechauns. But he hadn't berated me for not telling him about meeting my father. And for that I decided not to rebuke him for placing the bugs on my car and in my flat. Instead, I watched his gaze wander round the room, as if inspecting my choice of décor, before finally focusing on my favourite painting. It was a mass of blue and yellow and silver and people saw the wrong things in it.

"You heard about Canon Holroyd, of course?"

"My mother told me."

He crossed his legs and settled back into my comfortable cushions, as if this would be a long session.

"Your mother says that Holroyd informed her that your father was having an affair and that's why he killed him."

He paused and waited.

"Is that a question?"

"Yes, that's a question."

"In one sense, yes."

"So, is that why your father killed him?"

I didn't like the way he put that

"Have you established a cause of death?"

He thought for a while.

"I can't tell you that."

"Okay, but would a heart attack brought on by the terror of my father's actions be a possibility?"

He screwed up his eyes and looked at me keenly.

"It might."

"Then that's manslaughter, isn't it, not murder?"

"That would be for a judge and jury to decide. They might find that your father, knowing Holroyd had a dicky ticker, intended his actions to lead to a heart attack anyway." He paused again. "Look sir. All I'm trying to do here is understand all this, so I can move on to pastures new."

I could see that.

"So," he smiled, "back to my first question. Did Holroyd inform your mother that your father was having an affair?"

I could see, then, that Foster was a good copper, fair and task orientated. He'd get the job done.

"Yes and no. He wasn't having an affair, as such; not in the familiar sense, but he was acquainted with another woman and it was a lot more complicated than that."

He increased his smile and drained his glass.

"Well, as long as your Scotch holds out, I've got all night."

I fetched the whisky bottle. It took me an hour to tell the whole story. Foster only interrupted once.

"So, until the judge ordered them to, they didn't speak to your sister at all?"

"Only when we were all present and they didn't ask the questions they should have done, about the abuse."

"Court Welfare Officers!" he said, as if it were an expletive.

By the time I'd finished we'd gone through half a bottle. Foster gazed long into the painting, his thoughts far away.

"Did the abuse continue after your father left?"

It was my turn to pause now.

"Is this off the record?"

"Absolutely not."

What the hell, I thought, perhaps she had it coming.

"After a while, yes. She started back on my sister, as Dad knew she would. She started on me and didn't get very far. I left and stayed with a friend and his mother. She also abused her step-daughters. There was one occasion her new husband actually locked her out of the house all night he was so afraid of what she might do. I left the house soon after that but I do know, from talking to one of my step-sisters, that there were more incidents."

"You know, we could bring a prosecution, even at this late date."

"You'd get nowhere. She's the respectable headmistress of the most prominent private school in the area and a JP to boot. People would clam up and you'd get pressure from above to drop it. Even if you persisted she'd wriggle out of it somehow. She's very believable."

He drained his glass again.

"You're probably right."

We sat in companionable silence for a while.

"I'll have to keep some sort of protection for your mother. She'll protest to the Chief Constable if I remove it altogether, so she will."

He'd drunk twice as much as me but the whisky seemed to have no effect on him.

"You've sussed her pretty well," I said.

"And I'm not going to find your father am I?"

"You've got more chance of shagging Keira Knightly." He laughed. "He's probably slipped out of the country already."

"Well, if he contacts you, be sure to tell him to stay out of the country. No offence."

"None taken."

He nodded and stood up. At the door he turned.

"There is still one thing that's a little puzzling. From what you say, and I don't doubt you for a moment, if you think about what she's done to him, I'd have thought that your mother, in your father's eyes, deserves to die more than any of them." This was a discussion I wanted to avoid. "How did you extract the promise that he'd leave her alone?"

"I guess I have good powers of persuasion."

He looked at me with total scepticism in his eyes, then nodded.

"Yes, of course you have." We shook hands. "Good day to you and thanks for the Scotch."

Two days later I went back to work and tried desperately to immerse myself into it, but my ability to concentrate had completely gone. Once, when I looked up, I found my boss staring at me with an expression of concern. That same day I resigned and I think he was relieved to let me go without notice.

My new spare time enabled me to think of my promise to my father. I read three 'best-selling' novels and couldn't see what all the fuss was about. Then I read a couple from the Man Booker shortlist and began to see it. But although I tried to analyse the books as best I could, I thought that maybe you needed a degree in English Literature to fully understand them. I watched the England Cricket Team snatch defeat from the jaws of victory in the one-day series against New Zealand and June slithered towards July, in this great British summer that couldn't make up its mind whether it wanted to rain or shine. From Dad, there was only silence.

Then, one bright, sunny day, a rather macabre email came, with an attachment containing his contributions to the novel. I didn't read the attachment then. Perhaps I should have done but I was completely bowled over by his comments because he listed his funeral arrangements and pointed me to the green file in his bureau. There were just two personal comments at the end.

Please ensure that your mother is not at the funeral.
I love you and will always be with you.

Dad.

I thought, for the first time, that he might be contemplating suicide, then dismissed it. Too easy. He really wasn't the type. Not that I knew what that type was but I didn't think he was it. I had a feeling of foreboding, though, and couldn't shake the notion that he was going to die. It was the way he said 'the' funeral, as if it were inevitable. A kind of impotent panic set in as I found myself in exactly the same mind-set as before, where I desperately needed to talk to him. But how? Dashing off to Devon and Cornwall would give me the satisfaction that I was doing something but it would be a useless gesture because he wouldn't be there. I phoned, emailed and texted several times a day but reply came there none.

"Dad, don't do this to me! Is this my penance for getting you not to kill Mum?"

And the more he refused to speak, the more convinced I became that something was imminent. But why? What had I missed?

So when one week later Foster turned up unexpectedly at my door, you'd think I'd have been prepared for it but all I could do was stare at him.

"Can I suggest you sit down, sir."

I did his bidding and he came and sat beside me, like an Irish mother.

"I'm sorry to tell you, that your father's dead."

I looked at my painting, like I always did in times of stress.

"According to the Italian police, your father's body was found yesterday in the Grand Canal, Venice."

He was dead. My father was dead. My head swam and I felt for the couch as if I was about to topple. Foster grabbed my arm and helped me down.

"I'll prattle on, if that's all right with you, sir, and you can tell me to stop whenever you want. According to the local police your father had probably gone for a midnight swim off the Lido beach, which is part of Venice I understand, and been caught by the current that runs between the Lido and the main island, sweeping him into the main canal. Vicious current, so I'm told. His body was found in the morning by a Grand Canal resident, puzzled by something knocking against her boathouse door. Sorry."

I stood up and Foster did the same.

"I need a drink."

"I know you probably feel like something stronger right now, sir but I recommend tea. I'll come with you while you make it."

I walked into the kitchen, switched on the kettle and made tea like an automaton. I paused when I poured milk into the blue jug I keep for visitors. Dad had brought it back from one of his recent trips abroad. It was inlaid with gold motifs and looked North African.

"Identification of the body had been possible by connecting the British dentistry and the Parachute Regiment tattoo, together with the passport and other possessions collected from a suit jacket abandoned on the Lido beach which matched the trousers your father was wearing."

I was still staring at the jug as my brain slowly switched on. It didn't make sense. He couldn't go through everything he had recently only to die. I knew, of course, that Dad swam like a rock and the notion that he might have gone for a night swim for pleasure passed credibility. So an accident it wasn't. Which left only two possibilities, both of which seemed equally unlikely. I doubted he'd been killed. He'd taken care of all that, hadn't he? Why would he go back to Venice if he hadn't? Unfinished business concerning Baxter? Had one of Baxter's henchmen been out for revenge after all? Or perhaps my certainty that he wasn't the suicidal type was completely wrong. Perhaps, while I'd been asleep, in the early hours of a Venetian night, alone and with more courage than I could imagine, my father had quietly committed suicide, knowing that any sort of life, with or without Lizzie, was now impossible. He'd known it all along, which is why he'd made no attempt to contact her. Suicide would have been paradoxically undramatic and anti-climactic and I could see irony in his grin. "Thought I'd go out in a blaze of glory didn't you?"

The kettle boiled and I made the brew.

"It wasn't an accident, inspector."

"Well you might be right, sir, and you might not. But you'll still have to go over and identify the body. I'm sorry." He paused. "I've dealt with the Italians before. They have one of the worst bureaucracies in Europe, so they do. If you want to fly the body back you might find a few obstacles are put in your way."

I couldn't sleep that night, so got out of bed in the small hours and drove to Devon to check the life insurance and Dad's instructions, which included a list of all those to contact. Then I flew to Marco Polo, to find that the Italians couldn't be more helpful. This was largely due to Foster indicating that my father might have been a little unstable and the death might have been suicide.

"I realised something," he'd said. "Not coming from Ireland you probably wouldn't understand this, sir, no offence, but the Italians are Catholic and suicide is a mortal sin against God."

In my father's case, yet more irony but I was grateful to it because they couldn't get rid of Dad quick enough. I'd already made arrangements to fly him home before I went out and, within 4 hours of my identifying the body, my father and I were soaring over the Alps, heading for Gatwick.

The cremation was a small, family thing but the funeral ceremony itself was a Humanist affair, perched on the edge of a blustery, Devon hill. It was a celebration of a life and the field was packed to the horizon. I invited Lizzie but she did not attend. Dorothy was too ill to travel but Foster took a few days off and came, as did all those on Dad's list, plus some others. I did give a reading and managed not to weep, although half the 'congregation' did. One of Dad's ex-Army mates made a speech, as did one of the locals from the cricket team, and both managed to keep their eyes dry. Everyone shook my hand and told me what a wonderful man he was.

Then it was back to Dad's cottage for the 'wake'. I'd thought about holding it on his boat in Fowey but the cottage won. Much more room and all the Fowey people came anyway. Miraculously, the sun came out and the wind died to a gentle breeze that rose up from the river valley, like a blessing. The life insurance allowed for a professional catering team and food was served in the garden. I'd provided the alcohol, which I dispensed in a small gazebo labelled 'Stafford's Beer Tent', which was monopolised equally by ex-Paras, members of Ashton Gorton Cricket Club and the regulars from the local pub in Ashton Gorton, as well as, as far as I could see, representatives from all the pubs in Fowey. Quite a gathering and pretty soon it was a loud party. Jude took over behind the bar and I spent much of the time listening to Brad holding court with a group of locals, cracking joke after joke. Foster laughed so much he had to sit down.

The beer ran out around 6 o'clock and most of the men strolled down the hill to the pub to continue the revelry. There was plenty of wine left, so some of the women stayed. But life had gone from the festivities and everyone had left by seven. I sat down on my own with a glass of scotch, on the swing chair that Dad had erected between two hornbeams, so that he could gaze down the valley.

Trees rose on steep hills from the vale, where the sun, still high on my right, warmed the river that snaked before me. I watched a buzzard soaring below and a single boat motoring down on the ebb towards the river mouth, with the promise of a sea bass or two. It was a beautiful spot and Dad couldn't have wanted anything better. I thought of him sitting here on his own of an evening, remembering his past and making his plans for the future. I still hadn't read the chapters Dad had sent, so, as far as I was concerned, he'd murdered four men and I didn't care.

Brad and Jude came over and crouched down either side of the swing, like two boulders, silent and immovable, just waiting for me.

"You know," I said, "I hope, when my time comes, I have a celebration like that."

They raised their glasses and chorused:

"Amen to that," and we toasted my father.

Chapter 23

A Monday in May 2028 – Lincolnshire Wolds

Bess had let the fire die but the sun had come out so she'd ventured into the brilliance of Uncle John's garden, with its riot of spring flowers, most, miraculously, still intact. The gale had killed off the last of the plum blossom, though, and it lay on the sodden ground like confetti. Beyond the fence, the corn still stood, green, tall and motionless in breathless air. The badger wood seemed so sharp she felt she could reach out and touch it. She dried the seats and table, brought gin, tonic, scotch and glasses out on a tray, poured herself a drink and waited.

It was late afternoon when he returned, smiling warily as he strolled up the garden path, sensing her mood, as he always does and indicating the bottles.

"You know you drink too much."

"Special occasion."

He looked at her for a while.

"Am I going to need it?" he asked.

"Maybe."

She should have smiled, she knew, to ease his anxiety but she didn't feel like it. He sat down heavily and helped himself to a generous measure of whisky, then watched her anxiously.

"So, lass," the silence getting to him. "This time yesterday you practically begged me to reveal the big family secret that's been whispered about at weddings and funerals. Now you know." He paused. "Do you wish you didn't?"

"No. You know me; I've always got to know and to hell with the consequences. In fact, when I read your description of Lizzie I knew that was a trait we share. But this is my agenda, John. It's me who still has the questions."

He nodded solemnly, took another swig and watched her.

"For me," she said, "the big thing about it all is that, in the end, he loved you more than he hated her."

He closed his eyes before replying, then stared into his empty glass.

"That's about the size of it."

The next time her tutor asked that question about love and hate she had the answer.

"And all that was true, the conversation on the Ancholme? That really happened?"

He still wasn't looking at her.

"Word-for-word."

"But you didn't publish!"

She knew it sounded like an accusation and wanted it to.

"No."

She had to say it. Whatever the consequences, she had to say it.

"But that was the bargain, John! That was how you kept Gran alive."

"So you're happy to condone all the murders."

She shook her head in frustration.

"You're deflecting! My motives are not the issue and the murders had nothing to do with why you didn't publish. You know that perfectly well! You implicitly condoned them, too. The point, here, is that that was a solemn promise you made!"

He looked up, the eyes challenging.

"Do you think I don't know that? Do you think I don't feel guilty every day of my fucking life?! Do you think I'm proud of the fact that I've let him down?"

He stood up suddenly, walking towards the fence, then stared at the distant wood. She recalled that over 24 hours ago sweat broke out on her chest when he did that. But not now. A part of her thought she should say something to lessen his anguish but, again, she didn't really want to. When he turned back he seemed calmer.

"Do you think I haven't been shitting a brick all day, knowing you'd read that chapter and knowing what you'd think?"

She'd suspected that; had thought he probably delayed returning to avoid this conversation; understood his huge reluctance to discuss the 'family secret', and his anxiety on giving her the journal. He'd been right about one thing. It *had* changed the relationship.

"But why, John? Why didn't you try and publish?"

He hunched his shoulders, sat down and poured himself another scotch.

"Lots of reasons. A purely practical one is I don't think it's good enough to publish. The ending is lame, for example."

"True but you could have done something with that. You didn't even try to improve it."

"But then it would have been fiction and not truth."

The frustration was building in her.

"You never even tried! It's a lame excuse and you know it. My guess is that it was writing this story that gave you the confidence to write in the future; made you realise that you could actually do it. That's something else you owe your father."

He was peering at her in an intense, puzzled kind of way, as if wondering why she was so much on his father's side. He tried to smile.

"You know, lass, you can be real hard when you want to be." He raised his finger. "You saying that reminds me of the time you ….."

"John! Ditch the deflecting crap. It won't work. It's not the time."

He was silent for a while, starring at the ground, as if noticing the sodden plum blossom for the first time.

"Sorry, lass. Stupid. There are lots of reasons why I didn't try and publish. At least I've justified it to myself many times." He looked up at her. "I suppose in some ways it was simple inertia, although even inertia is rarely simple. You have to realise that, by the time I'd finished the manuscript, which I wrote in my spare time, two years had gone by. Two years of peace. Things had settled down. Your Grandmother wasn't abusing anyone as far as I could see." He looked at her keenly. "She never did with you did she?"

"No." She thought quickly. "But then, when I was younger, I never saw her without Mum."

He nodded.

"Everyone seemed happy with their lives. And that's what I do, lass; keep people happy. Then I began to imagine the storm that publication of *Cold Eating* would create? Can you imagine the shit my mother would have stirred up? And what about *your* mother? Can you envisage the effect on her of having that side of her life on public view? You know she lives on the edge at the best of times. And I thought about the knock-on effect on you. Above all, lass, I wanted you to have a stable upbringing."

Bess thought about her mother. He was probably right there.

"That was when I started inviting you over for visits. You were seven."

"You were making sure you kept an eye on me, just as Granddad wanted."

She could see it. She thought about her grandmother, always a shadowy figure in her childhood, but later charming and gracious and fiercely proud of her only grandchild. Yes, damn it, she could see it! John was watching her, letting her think.

"So, she gets away with it yet again."

"My wonderful mother? Not entirely. Apart from cold politeness at Laura's wedding, I've hardly spoken to her for ..... 13 years. You see, what Dad said was true. I was the apple of her eye. She sends me birthday and Christmas cards but I don't reciprocate. I've banished her from my life and it must hurt like hell."

"I hadn't realised that. You've never spoken of her but ..... Did you confront her?"

"She's the other person whose read the manuscript."

He paused, frustratingly.

"Well, what happened?"

"We argued."

"No, really? Tell me, what happened!"

He smiled for the first time since they'd begun the conversation.

"Priorities, lass. Let's freshen our glasses first."

"Do you know you are the most frustrating person I know?"

And she was forced to wait as he smilingly poured gin and tonic into her glass and scotch into his own. He'd clearly sensed most of her hostility had gone and was enjoying himself again. She understood him as well as he understood her now. The book had helped. The diversionary tactic was partly for him to get his thoughts together but mainly to summon his resolve. John liked excitement in his life but not personal confrontation; even the memory of it.

"I know, lass; I'm a disappointment to you."

"You can say that again."

"I'm a disappointment to you."

She couldn't help smiling it was so corny.

"So, are we okay now? Drinks all right? Are you comfortable, Uncle John?"

"Great, thanks. Yourself?"

"I'm fine! Will you get on with it?"

"I bet you haven't eaten lunch. What do you fancy for .....?"

"John!"

He held up his hand.

"Okay." He took a swig and gave a big heave of his shoulders. "It's just that I don't like talking about her."

"I know."

He looked over her head, getting his thoughts together.

"After two days of giving her the manuscript I went back. I wondered how she'd be with me. Would she go for the gentle, sympathy approach or put her full venom on view. She wasn't standing by the mantle when I came in, but sitting on one of the Court's couches, holding a handkerchief in both hands, so I had my answer. She denied it all, of course, said that Dad had always been unhinged and gave the murders as evidence. I knew that any court would agree with her. She couldn't believe that I'd written it, that I was siding with him, after all she'd done for me. I said I never wanted to see her again. She stood up and moved towards the mantelpiece, as I knew she would. She became enraged and said that if I publish she'd disinherit me. I told her what she could do with her inheritance and left."

She examined his calm face.

"You saved her life."

He gave a short laugh.

"Yes I did and that's the biggest irony of all."

He looked at her intently, draining his whisky. She'd finished her drink, too but decided she'd had enough. She watched Cat walk slowly up the path, picking her way carefully between the fallen flakes as if they were glass fragments.

"It's still your agenda," he said.

Cat jumped onto his lap and he began stroking her gently.

"The family conventional wisdom is that he committed suicide?" she asked.

"That was the conclusion of the Italian coroner."

"But you don't believe it."

"I just don't know. It couldn't have been an accident because he wouldn't have been swimming, unless he fell off a wall or a boat and wasn't a strong enough swimmer to save himself. But Dad falling off a boat simply doesn't seem right to me. He sailed more miles than most people have walked. I dismissed suicide initially but I now think it's possible. He'd completed his mission and maybe he didn't fancy being a wanted man for the rest of his life. On the other hand, maybe his past finally caught up with him and he was killed. If not by Baxter then someone else he wronged. But I have no evidence to support anything. In a way it's still a mystery; a very frustrating one."

"What about your mother?"

She couldn't bring herself to call her 'Gran' again.

"What about her?"

"Could she have had him killed?" He raised his head uncharacteristically quickly. "Contract killer or something?"

"I confess, lass, I hadn't thought of that." She could see him thinking hard, then he shook his head slowly. "No, she's probably capable but it doesn't fit. By that point she must have surmised she was safe. Why take the risk? Besides, why Italy. He must have made the decision to return himself."

"Was there an autopsy?"

"Yes, in Italy."

"And drowning was the cause of death?"

"Yes."

She thought about that.

"But drowning doesn't fit with killing. It does fit with suicide or an accident, though."

"I know."

Bess thought he held a look of surprise. It was as if he couldn't understand why he didn't know the answer to the question. Then he seemed to stare into the distance for a while, all the time stroking Cat in a rhythmical kind if way.

"And why Venice?" she asked.

"Venice?"

"You just said he must have made that decision. Why did he go back to Venice?"

He seemed to become more alert and bit his bottom lip.

"I remember wondering about that at the time. Seemed strange. I wouldn't have thought he had any particular passion for the place but maybe he had."

He frowned.

"Did you ever go back to see Lizzie, on one of your many visits to the States?"

"No. When she didn't turn up for the funeral I emailed her and we kept in touch for a while – a year or two – then, well, you know how it is – or perhaps you don't - it kind of died out. Inertia is a terrible thing."

"How did you explain ditching Charlotte at that restaurant?"

"I said we had a disagreement, which, after all, was true and she accepted it."

"That's sad, that you didn't keep in touch, after saying you would."

"Yes."

A bark from the wood got her attention and she looked over the wheat field, where swallows and martins wheeled like Spitfires.

"Fox," said John.

"I thought they only came out at night."

"With the constant rain we've had, rabbits and small mammals are kept underground for long periods and go hungry. As soon as the rain stops they come out to feed, even in broad daylight. The fox knows this."

Bess looked over the sun-drenched field, passed the wood, to rooks massing on the horizon and, beyond, to the well-tended fields and margins of the next wold. She felt unsatisfied.

"It shouldn't end here," she said.

His forehead creased.

"The story you mean?"

"It shouldn't end here."

He seemed bemused.

"It doesn't. I go on, Brad and Jude go on, the fox goes on and has cubs and they go on and kill more rabbits. Above all, you go on, as your grandfather intended." He paused. "In a way, you're his legacy."

She thought about that and about the story she'd just read, as she gazed over the field.

"No," she said, with absolute certainty. "You're his legacy. That passage of time changed your life. By your own admission, you were stagnating in a dead-end job. Now, your horizons are endless." He seemed to stare at her but then she saw that his eyes were far away. Cat began to nudge his hand for more stroking and he didn't notice. "But the main thing I take from it is he sacrificed the one thing he wanted to do most in this world before he left it and he did that because he loved you more than anything. You're his gift to the world."

He had that stillness again and ideas began to form in her head.

Epilogue

A Tuesday in January 2029 – North Georgia Mountains

They were only half-a-dozen miles from the main road when they crossed the snowline. The covering was thin at first but the more they climbed the deeper it got, until the heavy 4x4 started to slide in the corners. John pressed the traction control button on the dash and the vehicle increased its speed slightly yet seemed to gain grip. Bess reckoned the snow was about 10 centimetres deep now and unbroken, as she watched her uncle out of the corner of her eye. He seemed focused on driving but she sensed the reluctance still in him.

"How do you ensure it doesn't skid?" she asked, to get his mind off their destination.

"Piece of cake in this baby. That's what that button's for. Electronic controls organise the power to each individual wheel, depending on the grip. The system senses if a wheel is losing adhesion and, within a nano second, reorganises the power ratio to the four wheels. All I have to do is steer and make sure I feather the accelerator."

"Sounds like fun," she ventured.

He gave a short laugh.

"It's quite the opposite and it makes me feel like a eunuch."

"Come on, John. Surely this trip is fun?"

She was determined to deflect his mood.

"Yes, well, we'll see what sort of reception we get. The closer we come the more I think it was a mistake. I told you, we should have phoned to warn her."

Bess smiled broadly.

"It'll be a great surprise. She'll love it," she said, realising that she sounded as if she'd known Lizzie all her life.

He didn't reply, just concentrated on driving. But Bess felt the excitement bubbling inside her. At last, after months of pressure, he'd agreed to make the trip and she was finally going to meet Lizzie and, hopefully, Charlotte, too.

The snow had started to fall again as they reached Lizzie's track. John turned in, stopped the Jeep and switched off the engine.

"This is where I stopped all that time ago. It was a bit warmer then."

She recognised the delaying tactic and his nervousness as he got out. So she followed, her snow boots keeping her feet warm and the tree canopy protecting her from the snow. Apart from the low hisses and groans from the engine as it cooled, there was total silence. Total.

Bess leaned against the bonnet and gazed down the track of virgin snow disappearing into the white wood. It reminded her of the magical forest in *The Lion, the Witch and the Wardrobe*. She smelt the musky, chill air and felt there was more than one mystery in these high hills. If Lucy had come out from behind a tree and bumped into Mr Tumnus under the green lamppost she wouldn't have been surprised.

A distant crack in the forest brought her back to reality and she turned to John with a silent question.

"Bough breaking under the weight of snow," he said. "Come on. Since we're here we'd better go and do it."

He'd just needed a few moments to get his resolve together, she decided, because there was sudden determination in his manner as he drove down the track.

"This is the spot with the view," he said.

But there was no view this day. Anything more than 100 yards away was masked by the snowfall. John switched the transmission from automatic to manual and placed it in first gear so the Jeep could descend the last, steep slope under its own weight, before pulling up beside a large vehicle, buried in snow.

"Jesus!" said John.

"What?"

"Charlotte's police cruiser."

Bess looked again at the vehicle.

"How can you tell? It's covered in snow. It's probably ....."

"It is covered in snow but look at the shape of that contraption on the roof." Bess looked again. "I realise you've led a sheltered life, lass, but can you think what it might be?"

The penny dropped.

"Flashing light array?"

He smiled grimly.

"And there's no second vehicle for Lizzie, unless she's put it in the barn."

"That's what I'd do in this weather if I wasn't going out. Wouldn't you? Besides, if Lizzie isn't here, why's Charlotte visiting?"

He didn't answer, simply stared through the windscreen at the front door of the snow-covered cabin, which remained obstinately closed. She sensed the reticence had completely gone. In fact, he seemed calm and thoughtful, as he glanced round at the barn and back at the house. Give him a problem to think through and he was back on track.

"She's waiting for us to get out," he said. "It's what I'd do."

They slipped into their anoraks as they stepped out of the vehicle and Bess put the furry hood up. She followed her uncle as he crunched through the snow, the bobble bouncing on his ski hat. He stopped at the foot of the stairs and waited. After a few moments the door opened and a woman with dark, flowing hair stepped onto the porch. She was wearing a denim shirt and well-worn jeans, and from her right hand hung a shotgun. Bess thought she looked magnificent; like one of those fictional warrior women of mythology. She placed legs apart and raised the weapon.

"State ya business!"

Bess watched John smile.

"I thought the years might have mellowed you," he said.

Bess watched the mouth open slightly at the British accent and she thought there was recognition in the dark eyes. John reached up and removed the hat and identification was immediate.

"John!"

Bess watched her uncle continue to smile.

"Hello, Charlotte. We were passing and thought we'd drop in."

She seemed in shock and just stood there, lips parted. After a while John looked at the sky and said, "I'll bet it's a lot warmer inside," and she suddenly jumped back into reality.

"I'm sorry. Of course. Come on in. I'd be obliged if you'd leave your boots on the porch," and she held the door for them as they entered, eyes all over Bess.

There was no problem adjusting to the light as there'd been for John because the room was well lit in several places. It was just as he'd described it, with rugs over a wood floor and a whole wall taken up with books. A wood-burning stove seemed to be the source of heat. In fact it was so warm in the room Bess immediately shrugged out of her anorak, as John was apologising.

"I'm really sorry for just turning up like this."

"That's my fault," said Bess.

John seemed to remember me.

"Oh, I'm sorry, Charlotte, this is Bess, my favourite niece."

Bess stepped forward and they shook hands awkwardly.

"Actually, I'm his only niece."

They all stood back after that, still feeling awkward, and Bess watched John and Charlotte look at each other, as if remembering their parting nearly 16 years earlier. But there seemed to be no hostility and she knew instinctively that she'd been right about this women. Simply from John's writing she'd thought he'd got her wrong. He was correct about one thing, though. Bess knew she was over 40 but you'd never have guessed it. She was wearing no make-up at all but she was quite stunning.

"Wow," said John, "it's warm in here," and he shrugged out of his jacket. Bess watched as Charlotte took in the muscles on his arms in the short-sleeved shirt, then her face seemed to harden a little.

"I guess you're here to see Mom."

John opened his mouth to reply but nothing came out and Bess could see his dilemma. Charlotte seemed to as well.

"She isn't here." Bess had already accepted it. "Hasn't lived here for quite a spell." She looked up at John. "As a matter of fact, she moved out soon after your visit, as I recall. She now lives in a cabin in Montana, much like this one." Bess noticed that John's description of her was spot on. Charlotte didn't use her hands to assist articulation. Her face didn't change much either. "She seems to spend most of her time, though, on Curacao, just off the coast of Venezuela. She has a friend there. A male friend."

John nodded.

"That's good," he said. "Is she happy?"

Charlotte examined him for a few seconds.

"Seems to be. She visits now and again, to make sure I'm looking after the place."

John smiled and, eventually, so did she.

"I'm forgettin' my Southern hospitality and you've chosen a hell of a day to visit. Can I offer you some refreshment?"

John looked round at Bess.

"I think we'd both like coffee," he said.

"Comin' up."

John turned towards Bess and raised an eyebrow, then followed Charlotte into the brightness of the kitchen. Bess followed but stood outside the door. She could see and hear but wasn't part of the conversation. John was touching a uniformed jacket that lay over the back of a chair.

"Somehow I knew you'd make Captain," he said.

She switched on the coffee maker and turned towards him, leaning back against the sink with her hands behind her resting on the low rim. It had the effect of thrusting her breasts forward, as, Bess knew, was intended.

"So did I."

It was said with no ironic smile and no humility. It was simply a statement of fact. John grinned and gave a little laugh.

"I see modesty is still your strong suit."

Charlotte continued to look straight into his eyes, almost challenging him.

"You once told me you were gonna teach me modesty."

He smiled broadly at that and so did she. Then he became serious.

"Listen, I'm sorry I left you in the ABC."

She shook her head.

"In your position I'd have done the same." She shrugged. "I was young, new to the job and took it too seriously." She looked away and back at him. "I wanted to get in touch, to tell you that, but I didn't have ya contact details." She shrugged again and shook her head. "That's not true. I could 'ave got the details but I didn't try hard enough, cos I wasn't sure I had the guts to do it."

It was quite a statement and Bess was a little taken aback. John had definitely read her wrong.

"You've changed," he said.

"You haven't," and they both smiled at each other again, then turned away, slightly embarrassed.

The coffee was bubbling away and Charlotte busied herself with mugs and milk and sugar.

"You know, it's kind of funny," she said. "I knew this weather was comin in. It's been forecast for a quite a spell. Yet I came up here in the cruiser, knowing it couldn't handle the snow, so knowing I'd be stuck." She seemed to smile to herself. "I can still be called out, of course, but it'll have to be real urgent and they'll have to send an SUV to collect me."

"No need for that. We're staying in Blue Ridge. That Jeep handles the snow pretty well."

"Just passing through, huh?"

He gave a small, embarrassed laugh and there was a silence for a while. The coffee had percolated nicely and she poured some into a mug for him.

"Help yourself to milk and sugar." Then she stopped and looked up. "But you don't do you."

He picked up the mug.

"Well remembered," then unexpectedly, "You never married?"

"Sure."

Bess, still listening, felt a stab of disappointment.

"I married the damned job," Charlotte said without a smile. "What about you?"

She looked up at him and Bess saw again that direct, challenging way she had of looking at you.

"No. Not sure why. What do *you* think, lass?"

He inclined his head towards Bess. She'd begun to wonder whether he knew she was there but the conversation was starting to get onto dodgy territory and he was looking for moral support. She walked slowly into the kitchen.

"Why you haven't married? I've often thought about that, as it happens."

"Oh, oh," he said.

She smiled contentedly as she took the proffered mug and added milk. She was going to enjoy this.

"To begin with you have a modernistic approach to it, which is good in its way. For you, marriage is not an end in itself, merely an institutionalised vehicle for being with someone. So, why not just live with them? But, despite the fact that you've had a lot of opportunities to shack up with someone permanently, you've never actually done that either, have you Uncle John, so there's definitely something else going on here."

Charlotte's beautiful face held a puzzled frown.

"You'll have to forgive my niece. She's in her final year at uni and has a particular, incomprehensible way of saying things. I can't think where she gets it from."

"So, let's look at those other factors," continued Bess, picking up the rôle he'd given her. "From the woman's side, Uncle John, women like to be romanced."

"I can do romantic," he protested.

Bess looked at Charlotte, who now seemed to be enjoying the exchange.

"He can't."

"This a criticism?" he asked.

"Merely an observation."

Bess felt confident as to how Charlotte thought about him and that whatever she said wouldn't make any difference.

"But the main reasons are on his side. To begin with, he's too reticent. He never makes the first move and you have to push him from then on. He shows no commitment."

"That's a bit of an old female chestnut, isn't it?" he asked.

She sipped her coffee and looked up at Charlotte.

"This is good. John, how many women have you been out with in, say, the last 10 years?"

He shook his head, struggling.

"Oh, I don't know?"

"8, 10, 15?" she ventured.

"Christ, I haven't kept count!" he protested. "Six?"

"How long do they last? Two, three, four months? Then the relationship just kind of fizzles out. But that's not the main reason," looking back at Charlotte.

John stretched a hand over his forehead.

"Boy, do I wish I'd never asked this question!"

Charlotte was smiling.

"He's too much of a perfectionist. His expectations are way too high."

"Nonsense!"

She spoke directly to Charlotte.

"They are."

John was shaking his head.

"I feel like I'm being dissected."

But he was grinning. Bess thought there was another reason, too but she thought she'd embarrassed him enough.

"You two know each other pretty well, huh?" asked Charlotte.

Bess took her uncle's arm and squeezed it.

"Pretty well," she said.

"Too well," he replied, heavily.

Charlotte nodded and sipped her coffee.

"Would ya'll like some lunch? It won't be much but I can knock up somethin'. I got bread, cheese and tomatoes?"

"We don't want to put you to any trouble," said John.

Charlotte grinned.

"I was right. You haven't changed."

She looked out of the window.

"Snow's stopped, Bess" she said. "The view over the mountains should be spectacular soon. Why don't you take your coffee on to the porch? Lunch'll be a while."

Bess knew Charlotte was trying to get rid of her but she wasn't ready for that yet. She had a few questions for her uncle first.

"Great! John, let's go and see."

So, Bess grabbed their jackets and smiled to herself as she picked up a look between them when they thought she wasn't looking. Grabbing their coffee they stepped outside into the purist air Bess could remember. The clouds hadn't completely passed over but she could see a shaft of sunlight to the north and a patch of startling blue over distant mountains. They sat down on brown wicker chairs, oblivious to the cold, their breath frosting the air. She couldn't get worked up over the view, though. There were too many questions and she had to ask them now, before he started on another topic and before Charlotte came out.

"John?"

"Yeh?"

"I'm going to suggest something and I don't want you to be angry with me."

He peered at her with a kind of amused indignancy.

"When have I ever been angry with you?" He guffawed. "In fact, I'm beginning to think I've been too indulgent. That was heavy in there."

"Only for you. But this is going to be heavier."

He sensed her seriousness then.

"Christ, lass! What is it about you today?"

"I don't know."

"Is this about Charlotte?"

She smiled.

"No. In fact I think that's love at second sight. Hey, great title! Bet it's been used."

He said nothing; just waited.

"I've got to go there, John. It's killing me not knowing. If I'm right, I don't blame you. I simply need to know the truth."

He watched her warily and she knew she'd have to be blunt to get the answers.

"How often do you travel abroad?" she asked.

"About three or four times a year. Why?"

"Where do you go?"

He was frowning.

"You know where I go. I tell you every time. I travel to research my books, largely. Well, I have a good time, too, mind."

He smiled.

"Ever been to Curacao?"

He looked at her intently.

"No. Do you fancy it?"

She looked away momentarily, planning her attack to best gauge his reaction.

"I thought you might know Lizzie's man."

"Why would you think that?"

She let a silence develop but he didn't change his puzzled frown.

"Is he still alive, John?"

"What?!"

"Is he living in Curacao under another name, with Lizzie?"

He seemed shocked and expelled air, as if spitting out a bone.

"I can't believe you're asking me that question." His mouth was open as if completely taken aback. Then he suddenly smiled. "You're not serious. Jesus, lass, you scared me for a ….."

"John, I am serious. I think it's a possibility that your father may still be alive."

He stared at her for a while, then looked at the door as if expecting to see Charlotte.

"You've picked a hell of a time to raise this, lass."

"Look, I'm sorry, I haven't thought it through. It's probably complete nonsense but I've got to go there, don't you understand? I began this journey last spring, in your garden, and it's not finished. In my mind it's not finished!'"

His eyes were angry. She'd never seen that before.

"And you're not going to drop it are you?"

"I can't."

"Jesus!"

"Granddad had the French passport and he had money. He could have escaped Europe and gone on the run anywhere, in the hope that they'd never find him. Grow a beard, let his hair grow. Curacao sounds ideal."

He began moving his head from side to side, as if searching for an answer. Then one seemed to come to him.

"Bess, I identified the body."

"John, I don't think you've quite grasped what I'm saying. If there is a conspiracy, you have to be part of it."

He went very still suddenly and his eyes flickered over her face.

"So," he said eventually, "if it wasn't Dad where did the body come from?"

Bess sipped her coffee and noticed the widening blue sky. That was the one thing she had thought through.

"Do you remember I asked you 'why Venice?' Why did he go all the way to Venice to die? That really bothered me and I didn't know why it didn't bother you. I couldn't think of an answer to either question; until now." John was staring at her intently. "It's because he already had a body in cold storage."

"A body?"

"Baxter." He seemed in shock again. "In *Cold Eating* Granddad said he drowned him, so cause of death would be the same. He had time to plan the whole thing. What if they pulled Baxter's body back into the boat and placed him in a deep freeze, probably under Francesco's supervision. All he had to do, later, was unfreeze the body, switch identification papers and dump Baxter in the water off the Lido. Baxter would have had English dentistry and he would have had a Parachute Regiment tattoo. They were probably about the same size, too. But even if they weren't that wouldn't matter. Of course, the whole plan was dependent on his son making false identification of the body. The Italians probably didn't even do a proper autopsy, they were so keen to get rid of it."

He was silent for a while. Then:

"Jesus, Lass, you're scaring me!" He was shaking his head, then held up both hands. "Hang on a minute; slow down. If you follow that argument then Lizzie knew, too. It means she lied to me and it means she was a bloody good actress."

"No, it doesn't. I'm sure everything that took place here 15 years ago really happened as you said. Charlotte could confirm that I'm sure. Lizzie believed then that Granddad wasn't going to come back for her." Bess took a deep breath and ran a hand through her hair. "But sometime before the fake death he contacted Lizzie and made arrangements with her."

There was a long silence, during which a massive slab of snow slid off the roof and fell into the yard. Bess realised with a start that the clouds had completely blown away and the yard was bathed in sunlight. The snow was so bright she couldn't look at it without shades, so she focused on a rocking chair at the end of the porch.

"I think you and Granddad worked this out on the Ancholme. If I'm right it means you missed out an important part of the story. Or you worked it out later." She shook her head. "It doesn't matter when. The fact is, if I'm right, you haven't told me the whole story and, it appears, Lizzie hasn't told her daughter, either."

She sat back and said nothing for a while, exhausted from the intensity of her narrative.

"Nice theory," he said, smiling now, "but you have an over-active romantic imagination. I've told you this many times, lass."

Bess, noticing that she was now 'lass' again, became aware that her coffee had gone cold in its cup. Looking over, John's had, too.

"Don't patronise me, John. I have got an imagination and I do appreciate that, even if the substance of my theory is correct, you couldn't admit it to me. Although maybe one day you will."

He shook his head and smiled the big smile. She looked up at ridge after ridge of snow-covered mountains disappearing into the distance, sparkling in crystal sunlight. Behind the closed barn door to her right, goats started to bleat, just before the swing door sounded and Charlotte stepped out in a white ski jacket. She'd put her hair back in a pony-tail and added a little make-up. She looked a million dollars. Using his private school manners John automatically stood.

"That's gonna take a while to cook," she said with a smile. "You guys not too cold out here?"

Bess hadn't noticed the cold at all.

"I need to spend a penny," she said, getting up.

Charlotte looked at her vacantly.

"The toilet's down the hall," said John, "on the left," and Charlotte laughed.

"Spend a penny?"

John laughed, too.

Bess paused inside the door, listening unashamedly. There was a long silence before John spoke.

"You know, I've thought about you for over 15 years."

"I know," she said and Bess could imagine her smiling up at him.

"Is this so that I can teach you modesty?" and she laughed.

"You should have come back sooner, you bastard!"

"I know," and he slipped a hand round her waist.

They were silent again and Bess was just about to go when Charlotte said:

"Did you know you can see three states from up here?"

"Really? You ever been to the UK?"

"You asking?"

"Got any vacation time owing?"

Bess wandered slowly into the kitchen, as if drawn to it, and then over to the window, where the view over the mountains was indeed spectacular. She imagined her grandfather standing here, admiring the vista, whilst the love of his life made supper at his back.

"Okay, Granddad," she said aloud, "It had been time and now it's done. What was it you said? The secret to life is to recognise those key moments when they stare you in the face and to make the right choices, or something like that. Well, whether you're alive or dead, he is your legacy and, although I never really knew you, this is mine".